THE WELL OF TEARS

THE DREAM STEWARDS

ROBERTA TRAHAN

47NORTH

Text copyright © 2012 by Roberta Trahan

Published by 47North
P.O. Box 400818
Las Vegas, NV 89140

ISBN-13: 9781612183725
ISBN-10: 1612183727

Dedication

For my husband—the hero of my story and champion of my heart

THE PROPHECY

Even before the seeds of the first civilizations were scattered, sorcerers walked this world. For a time, they trod in the formidable footfall of the gods, serving mortals as the arbiters of faith and fate. And, with their guidance, the societies of humankind flourished. But with prosperity came avarice, and with avarice came ambition. Before long, the world knew tyranny.

Dark and terrible times followed. Chaos descended upon the land, and for a thousand years, her peoples suffered at the hands of tyrants. And yet, somehow, the seeds of salvation survived.

In the province Ystrad Tywi of the Kingdom of Seisyllwg, a handful of those devoted to the old ways found refuge in the abandoned sanctuaries of their ancestors. Hidden deep within the mystical woods of Coedwig Gwyn, nestled at the headlands near the tiny village Pwll, stood one such ancient and sacred place—the all but forgotten temple called Fane Gramarye.

Cloistered within an enchantment that hid the temple from the eyes of mortals, the mages who served the order of the Stewardry at Fane Gramarye endured to fulfill a single sacred vow—to protect the king who would one day unite the peoples of Cymru in a long and lasting peace. An ages-old prophecy foretold that a son descended from a line of noble rulers would rise to rule a new era and that by his hand the ancient beliefs would be resurrected and the sorcerers returned to reverence. And so it was that, for nine generations, the Stewards served in silence, awaiting an omen in the birth of a boy.

In the year 880 AD, it came to pass that a son begotten of Cadell, King of Seisyllwg, was delivered unto the world and anointed by the gods. Upon reaching his manhood, the boy called Hywel would seize his destiny and the ancient prophecy would finally be fulfilled. The Stewards of Fane Gramarye would be called to raise the first sorcerer's council to serve a high king in more than a millennium.

But it was also foreseen that there were those among men of power who would stop at nothing to prevent such an alliance. As the age of peace approached, the grand wizard of the Ninth Order moved to protect the prophecy, secretly naming four sorceresses of uncommon character and ability to the sacred council. The sorceresses were then sent into hiding, scattered to the four corners of the earth so that if one were discovered, the others might survive. For more than twenty years, they lived in exile, until the summons to return arrived.

ONE

Summertide in the White Woods, 905 AD

"It is time." Aslak, long the captain of the castle guard, stood at the door stiff-lipped and sober. He had come clad in riding dress and bearing battle gear, prepared for a long and perilous journey. "It will be dark soon."

Madoc nodded and hauled himself from the flattened seat cushion that had so well served his backside. After all this time, the weave still held against the chafe. If only he had worn so well, Madoc thought as he struggled to tug the heavy indigo velvet mantle of the Ard Druidh over his stooped shoulders. This day he felt the full weight of his robe, and his years.

"Hardly spry," Madoc grumbled. He shuffled across the thunderstone floor to the hornbeam and hazelwood desk in the corner of his chamber. "But then, a gnarled old wizard of one hundred and fifty-three can hardly expect to scurry, can he."

"Such is the tithe of time, Sovereign." Though he managed a weak smile, Aslak's usual drollery was muted, if not altogether absent. Madoc paused to look long on his friend, taking in the full measure of the man upon whom he'd relied so completely these past thirty years.

Aslak, too, was a bit past his prime. Fifty odd years fully lived had coarsened his flaxen good looks and whitened his beard, but Aslak scarcely seemed bowed by his age. The raw vigor and steel of his youth were still fully evidenced by his barreled chest, strong shoulders, and long, straight spine. Aslak's character and carriage exuded an ease and authority that could only come from a man's full knowledge of his expanse, and his limitations. If anything, Aslak was more imposing in his middle years than he ever had been as a younger man.

"Yes, for some of us." Madoc flashed a wry grin. "And a high a price we pay for it, too. Thin skin and even thinner blood, and the complaining of old bones when they are bid to bend." He chuckled at Aslak. "Just you wait."

Madoc waved away the discussion and began to rifle through the mess on his desk. "Enough of my grievance. Time is too short now to be wasted on wallowing."

"My men are waiting in the woods beyond the gate," said Aslak. "Unseen and unheard, just as you asked. There'll be no advantage lost on our account, I promise you."

"Ah. Here we are." Madoc separated four neatly rolled scrolls from the rest of his writings and set them aside. He pointed toward the divan against the wall next to the hearth. "Hand me that bag, would you?"

Aslak retrieved the leather haversack from the divan and set it on the corner of the desk. "Good man." Madoc pulled the bag close. "We'll have you on your way in no time."

Madoc caught a glimpse of Aslak's expression and regretted his rush to hasten Aslak's departure. He let the sack slouch back onto the desk and reached for the silver flagon on the table instead.

"On second thought," he said, "time is not so short we haven't the time for a proper farewell." Madoc turned two silver cups open end up. "Sit with me."

Aslak sidled a single step toward the divan and hesitated. "Much as I am tempted to partake of your graciousness, Sovereign, the sun is soon to set. We'll require what little light is left to make our way through the woods before dark."

"Sit, man." Madoc decanted the wine and offered a cup to his friend. "I insist."

Aslak reluctantly accepted the drink and Madoc walked round the desk to settle again in his own chair. "We'll drink to my health," he chortled, sipping at the sweet-smelling mellow liqueur.

"'Tis a bittersweet drink, one of parting," Aslak said softly.

Madoc heaved a weary sigh. "So it is, Aslak, though this is not a final farewell. We shall meet again, old friend. If not in this life, then in the next." Madoc gulped the last of his wine and held out his cup. "Pour, will you?"

Madoc watched Aslak rise to refill both cups and then return to his rigid post on the divan. "Wine is a blessed potion," he observed. "It dulls a man's aches and eases his pains. Looks as though you're in need of a goodly bit tonight."

"The spirits are sometimes more easily swallowed than the demands of duty," Aslak confessed.

"The Cad Nawdd is no easy calling," Madoc agreed. "I know well the burden of the pledge."

But then, so he should. It was he who had imposed it. Service in the castle guard of Fane Gramarye required a man to foreswear his worldly obligations in favor of lifelong loyalty to the Stewardry. Aslak had ceded his birthright to the high seat of some faraway northern settlement to join their ranks. This was no small sacrifice, but Madoc held that the greater the cost the deeper the vow and, naturally, the more prized the honor. Even the children Aslak had fathered had chosen his calling. Both his sons served the guard, and with distinction.

"I suppose one could say I've done well, Aslak, if I were to be judged by the love you've shown me." Of all the captains Madoc had appointed in his time as sovereign of the Stewardry at Fane Gramarye, none had more pride, or heart, than Aslak of Norvik. Tears of pride welled in his old eyes. "Very well, indeed."

"No man could be more honored than I." Emotion choked Aslak's strong baritone to a coarse whisper. "I have had the command of the finest soldiers, and all in the most sacred service. I've no regret."

Madoc chuckled. "Well, there's time enough yet. No man who has really lived dies without regret. Your lack of it seems to me evidence enough that you've many more good years ahead of you."

"If you say so, so it must be." Aslak grinned, and the deep furrows in his brow softened. It seemed the wine had begun to work its magic on Aslak's harried nerves.

Madoc leaned forward. "Well then. I suppose it is time we spoke of the business at hand."

Aslak upended his cup and squared his shoulders. "All I require are your instructions, Sovereign."

"You'll need more than that. I'd say luck, at the very least, and the blessing of the Ancients. I'm afraid we've many a hard fight ahead of us." Madoc regarded his friend soberly. "In the end, the fate of the Stewardry is tied to Hywel. Our numbers dwindle as the clans turn away from the faith of their forefathers. It has been nearly two decades since the last mage born foundling was brought to the Fane. The Stewardry bloodlines are dying, Aslak. The temple halls echo with emptiness. Even as the signs come to me, I worry our time is already past. We are little more than a whisper in a windstorm. The people cry out for peace and prosperity, yet still they fight amongst themselves and ravage their own lands. They have forgotten how to shepherd their own destinies. If only I was certain the world will accept the wisdom the Stewards can offer."

"The Ancients have sanctioned our cause, Sovereign. They have given us the prophecy, and a king who is promised to resurrect the old ways." Aslak's gaze was steady and intent. "There is still hope."

Madoc laughed. "And so you remind me of the very essence of faith, Aslak. Something apparently even I can forget."

Aslak shrugged. "We are each such a small piece in the enormous design of infinity that a man can easily convince himself of his insignificance."

"Ah," Madoc countered. "But lest you forget, the wondrous untold truth of this universe is that we are infinite in our influence. Every one of us. Mankind has forgotten how closely he is tied to this earth, how much what he does affects his own prosperity, his destiny." Madoc suddenly realized he was waving his cup as he spoke and set it down on the side table to spare the wine. "And yet—" He sighed, folding his hands into his lap. "In this, I am powerless. Our success depends upon you, now." Madoc beckoned Aslak closer.

"Events are unfolding just as they were foretold. Hywel is on the verge of his ascension," Madoc said quietly. "Though he is young, he has already begun to consolidate his power. Hywel's marriage has brought the kingdom of Dyfed under his control, and now his father's death has given him claim to Seisyllwg. He must still bring the other territories to heel and fend off his brothers and their ambitions, but there is no doubt Hywel is the king of the prophecy."

"You have seen this?" Aslak asked. Though a practical man by nature, he was ever fascinated by evidence of the surreal. The mystical and magical held great sway over him.

Madoc nodded. "The Ancients have visited the future upon me in my dreams, or at least this much of it. He will need our magic to survive his enemies. By now I suspect you have guessed your part in this."

"I've some idea." Aslak smiled. His eyes shone with keen interest. Aslak was never happier than when charged with a trust or a challenge.

"It is time to summon the council," said Madoc. "The Mistresses of the Realms must return. You're the only man alive I can trust to bring them home."

Madoc rose and returned to his desk. He carefully tucked the four scrolls into the haversack. "Herein you will find my letters to each of my chosen. The scrolls bear my seal. If they no longer recognize the standard of the Stewardry, or you, they will surely recognize that."

"But will I know them?" said Aslak. "It's been a long time. Even sorceresses of the Stewardry must change in twenty years."

"So they do." Madoc winked. "They gain beauty with time, and allure. No doubt all four of them will have been altered by the world, but there will still be something of the girl in the woman. If nothing else, you will know them each by their talisman."

"Yes, the amulet. I remember," said Aslak.

"Be certain you see it, Aslak. Examine each talisman closely no matter how sure you are of the woman who wears it. The talisman is the only true sign of allegiance to the Stewardry, and to me."

"My arrival will no doubt come as a shock," Aslak said. "I expect they have gone on to live full and purposeful lives. They may have husbands, children. They might not want to return."

Madoc's impatience prompted a scowl. "The sisterhood is a blood vow, not a request. It is written that only the daughters may serve the Circle. The council cannot be complete without all four bloodlines, and we need the strength of unity more now than ever. If that alone does not persuade them, you must find something that will."

"Madoc." Concern dug deeper harrows into Aslak's already worried brow. "There's something else. What haven't you told me?"

Madoc sagged under the weight of his fatal misstep. His old friend was the only soul Madoc could bear to tell. He had learned more than a thing or two about regret.

"The trouble with tradition is that it narrows a man's field of vision," he said. "You see, Aslak, no woman has ever sat in the seat of the Ard Druidh. 'Tis true the guardians of the realms have always been mothers and daughters of the guild, but since the beginning the sovereign has sprung from the spear side. In my haste to carry custom into the next generation, I fear I may have initiated a dissident into the line of my ancestors." Madoc shook his head helplessly. "It seems I have been my own undoing."

Aslak flew to his feet, eyes stark and wide with the shock of it all. "What has happened?"

"The Ancients have been kind." Madoc offered a faded smile. "They have shown me my fate." He chuckled. "Or at least my arrogance."

"I do not understand." Aslak's expression begged for an explanation Madoc was not prepared to give. And then the light of recognition flickered in Aslak's eyes as he pieced together Madoc's cryptic hints. "Machreth?"

"You must make haste, my friend." Madoc stepped from behind the desk and handed the bag to Aslak. "Our only hope is in the strength of the Circle. And then," he tried to smile. "If the gods of the Ancients are willing, my legacy may outlive me, after all."

Aslak slung the sack over one shoulder and offered Madoc the other as they left the room. Madoc guided Aslak in silence along the upper corridor of the east annex, past the docent's quarters, to the very end of the hall where a small recess gave access to the service stairs. Adjacent to the recess, hung beneath the glass-paned transom high on the exterior wall, was an ancient tapestry depicting an offering at the altar of a long-forgotten god. Madoc smiled to himself as reached behind the edge of the tapestry and depressed a lever cleverly fashioned to match the surrounding stones. Almost silently, an equally camouflaged door swung inward to reveal a second set of steps that led to the tunnels running beneath the castle.

"My forefathers were cunning," Madoc said, pointing at the stairs. "Our people have fallen in and out of favor more times than anyone can remember, and a quick escape is always a good defense."

Aslak lighted a torch with the dwindling flame of an oil lamp still burning on the wall to help guide their descent. The smell of smoldering tallow was overpowering given the poorly ventilated channels below. Madoc paused halfway to the bottom, hoping to catch his wind.

"Good grace, but these stairs are steep," he gasped. "I'd forgotten how many there are."

"We can rest a bit," Aslak offered.

"No." His old lungs were hard pressed, but the longer they lingered the less chance Aslak stood of an unobserved departure. He nodded toward the wrought iron gate at the bottom of the stairs. "Keep on."

They navigated the underground passageway at Madoc's direction. He alone knew the route through the labyrinth of catacombs. There was only one true path to the cavern, and from there, only one true path beyond the veil.

"Through there, Aslak." Madoc pointed through a narrow opening just ahead. "It widens on the other side. Bear right at every turn, then up a steep rise, and out."

"I remember." Aslak stepped ahead and turned to face him. "It goes against my grain to leave you here. There are others I would send in my stead."

"No, no." Madoc waved off the idea. "I trust only you to see this through."

Aslak nodded but was reluctant still. "I have given Emrys command of the Cad Nawdd in my absence. He is capable, and trustworthy. You can rely on him."

"No captain should ever be forced to leave behind his regiment, and his master." Madoc offered Aslak his hand. "It is an unbearable sacrifice, but a necessary one."

Aslak's grasp on Madoc's arm was warm and unyielding. It pained Madoc to see the conflict in his friend's eyes, but it was time to set him on his way, and quickly. "Now hurry, man. 'Tis the only tribute I ask."

At last, his friend released the handclasp and turned away. Madoc waited, watching until Aslak was swallowed by the shadows and the echo of his footfalls had faded. The passage would take him to where his men waited deep in the heart of Coedwig Gwyn. From there they would make their way unhindered, for now.

Thankfully, Aslak never looked back, and Madoc had no need to hide his watery eyes. He made the difficult and solitary journey back through the maze, his footsteps echoing in the empty corridor.

As he climbed the cursed stairs to his rooms, one aching step at a time, Madoc chuckled a bit to himself. Dreary and dismal though his prospects might be, it wasn't all done. Not just yet. His dreams would bring him news of Aslak's travels, and the gods would keep the wolves at bay a while longer. He was ready. When the end came, Madoc would face his fate from his chair, arse firmly planted in its well-worn seat.

TWO

Autumn in Norvik, 905 AD

The shrill peal of the herring gull echoed over the pounding waves and then faded on the winds. Alwen's gaze followed its tail feathers eastward, toward the edge of the earth, and found the day near to dawning. She had spent most of the night on the cold Northland beach, waiting.

In answer to her silent beckon, the gull banked right and returned, traveling parallel to the coastline. Alwen launched her thoughts and released her soul to the bird, joining her mind with the gull's in such a way that the two beings coexisted within the one. She would have called it sharing or borrowing, as Alwen only chose the creatures, animal or human, who accepted her freely. She preferred the birds. No creatures were freer than the winged ones.

The herring gull hungered, insisting they glide low over the shoals in search of fish. Together they traveled south from where she stood, to a small, shallow inlet on the channel side of the tiny Frisian isle. Not the quay on the northeastern tip, where the village fishing boats were moored. A landing there would have been noticed.

Alwen nudged her host slightly inland, expecting to come upon the ferry still moored and strangers camped on the bank. She had discovered them making the channel crossing during her spirit-faring the previous morn. Instead, through the gull's eyes, she spied the riders already on the road. They must have risen before dawn. The messenger would reach the village before long.

She released the bird and returned her consciousness to her own being, grounding herself once again in rock and sand. Even before she had seen the travelers approaching, Alwen had felt the call: an echo of distant, ancient voices pulling her toward a life she had left long ago. Remembrances she had held in sacred keeping for more than twenty years had begun to surface.

But it was not the memories which made her anxious. The summoning was at hand.

In deep, even respiration, Alwen drew in the dawn and slowly exhaled the residue of unrest. Thick, damp mist salted her lips and sated her lungs, though even the sea's soothing vapors could not bring the calm. Destiny hung on the horizon, looming ever larger like the rising sun. Her days on this tiny isle were nearly done.

"Where did the wings take you this time?" Rhys hauled himself up to balance on a surf-and-sand-scrubbed boulder and grinned down at her from his perch.

"Hither and yon." She offered a halfhearted nod to her son, not quite ready to be interrupted. Rhys liked to come upon her earlier than expected, always hoping to find her entranced, with her psyche soaring along with some unsuspecting carrier on what he imagined to be a grand adventure. And it was. The spirit-sending was the magical art that Alwen most treasured, and the one her son most envied. She regretted that she had no way to share it with him.

"I see." Rhys eyed her suspiciously as he held out his hand and waited for her to take half the pebbles he held in his palm.

Alwen couldn't help a smile as she accepted the stones. As a small boy, Rhys had called them wishing rocks. Even now he sought her out nearly every morning to help him cast his secret desires into the water, as far out to sea as either of them could throw.

"Nothing unusual, then?" Rhys began to throw the stones into the waves.

Alwen noted the familiar lure in his tone but did not respond. Instead, she attempted to distract him. Focusing intently on the next stone as Rhys released it, Alwen caused it to hang in mid-flight.

"Remember the dancing stones?" With just the slight bobbing of her chin, Alwen directed the rock in wanton hops and skips, as if it were waltzing on the water.

Rhys groaned aloud with the agony only a grown man can experience at the hands of his mother. "I remember."

She laughed, releasing the stone so that it plopped into the surf and sank. "Well, you used to find it amusing."

She regarded her son with deep affection, watching the stretch of his arm and the proud jut to his jaw. Though his build was lean and lithe like hers, Rhys had inherited neither her fair hair and light eyes nor her sorcery. Rather, the son was so much like the father there were times it nearly took her breath away. At nineteen, Rhys was the very semblance of his sire in much younger days. He had the same thick, dark hair that shaded intelligent green eyes and the same engaging grin.

For several long minutes they traded tosses in silence, until Rhys could no longer contain his curiosity. "You're keeping something from me, or me from it," he prodded, gaze trained on the horizon in an unsuccessful attempt to feign casual interest.

A sudden gust sent a shiver through her bones, and Alwen shrank deeper into the folds of her cape. Wild, snow-white locks escaped her cowl at the insistent tugging of the brisk North Sea breeze, whipping wet and cold against her cheeks. She chucked the last of her stones in one pitch and tucked her hair back inside the hood.

"We have visitors."

"Visitors?" Rhys teetered on his heels as he turned to look. "Where?"

"You should be able to see them by now." Alwen turned to point out three horsemen making their way north through the flats on the one narrow byway that transected the island. From their vantage point on the jetty at the northern tip of the island, they could see the entire length of the coastal road. "Change marches toward us."

"Is that a flag?" His gaze followed hers, traveling the waterline beyond the outermost edge of the village. Rhys nodded slightly as the herald's colors drew nearer. "A messenger."

"Yes," she said. "They came ashore last night, just before sunset."

"Last night?" Rhys sounded shocked, even insulted. He dropped the last of the pebbles and brushed the sand from his hands. "Why didn't you tell me?"

"There are some things I keep to myself, Rhys." She sounded more abrupt than she had intended. In truth, she was reluctant to admit that she had wanted to be alone with the news, at least for a little while. Her children knew little of her past, except that she owed a duty she would one day be called to serve.

"Well, naturally, there would be." Rhys adjusted his tone to reflect proper deference for his mother, but his deeply furrowed brow revealed a bit of resentment. "Do you know the colors?"

Alwen nodded absently, not acknowledging his words so much as dismissing him. She was distracted by the deep indigo standard of the Stewards Guild. The sight of it evoked an old but familiar heart song. "I know them well."

"You are nervous," Rhys observed. "You're fisting your hands so hard I'd guess the nails are digging into your palms."

"So I am." She relaxed the absent minded clench and clasped her hands together beneath the cuffs of her cloak. Rhys was observant and knew her better than most, but Alwen had been trained to quash telling signs. Obviously, she would need to redouble her discipline. "I suppose I find this all a bit unnerving."

"Unnerving?" Rhys laughed full out. "That is an outrageous understatement, even for you."

"If you say so." Alwen couldn't help but smile. He was right, after all, and not about to let her get away with pretense. Candor was a trait she particularly favored, especially in Rhys.

"Very mysterious." Rhys rebalanced himself on the boulder and turned to face the open ocean. "This is what you have waited for, is it not?"

"We will know soon enough."

"The realm of possibility is endless." Rhys smiled to himself as he stared into the water's infinite depths. "I can think of no greater adventure than the unknown."

"Nor greater peril," she warned. "The realm of loss is also endless."

"Hah," he scoffed. "The greater the peril, the more prized the purse. Half the fun is in the risk, and in the end, it's all just a matter of what you're willing to wager."

Rhys fell suddenly silent, as if sobered by the deeper meaning in his own words. Nothing stirred but the surf. Alwen watched as he gradually surrendered to the sea, lulled by the languid suck and rush of the water washing over the scaur and the distant, haunting caw of the herring gulls.

It wouldn't take a spirit-faring to know what he was feeling. Alwen could sense the yearning that afflicted her son. His instincts stirred to the call of the sea, as did all of the island people. But that was understandable. She had come to feel rooted here as well.

Norvik was a tranquil, unassuming place. A Varangian name for a Frisian settlement, but that was fitting. This was the birthplace of the great Norse warrior, Aslak, legendary captain of the castle guard at Fane Gramarye. Aslak's family lands were as close as Alwen could ever have come to finding content on any foreign soil. Rhys, however, was completely at peace on these shores.

"You are happy here," she said.

He snuffled his sleeve as he swiped the brine and wind-blown curls from his brow, as if to savor the scent of the sea on his shirt linen. "I suppose I am. It's a quiet life, maybe too quiet, and I don't like the cold. Especially now, with winter edging in on the wind."

"Speaking of understatement," she taunted. "It will be hard for you to leave."

Rhys shrugged. "Norvik has been home to me all of my life. And Eirlys, too."

Home, he said, as if the land and the village were all that he worried to leave. Alwen understood the word for what he really meant, even if Rhys had not yet fully realized it. For Rhys and his sister, home was also family, and family included Bledig.

"Your father will find us on the road."

"No sign of him?" Rhys could not keep the disappointment from his voice.

"With the dead season looming, the birds prefer to keep close to shore. I can only go where they care to take me," she said. "Bledig and his men are yet beyond my sight."

Rhys nodded, resigned to truths yet unspoken. "We'll be leaving without him, then."

"Yes." It saddened her to say it, but Alwen was relieved that Rhys had drawn the conclusion on his own. If only Eirlys would be as accepting. "Worse yet, I fear I must foul your sister's wedding plans."

Rhys turned his head to grin at her. "Change marches toward us, isn't that what you said?"

"So I did. But it doesn't necessarily follow that the two of you should suffer for it."

"Doesn't it?" He was only half teasing.

Alwen understood his frustration. Rhys had spent time enough in his father's charge, in travel and training, and in the earning of his manhood. Bledig was the clan leader of one of the nomadic tribes of the Obotrites, renowned for their tracking skills and ruthless, cunning tactics in trading. It was assumed that Rhys would one day take his place at his father's side, as second man to the chieftain. It was an honor he respected, but Rhys longed to find his own adventures. On that account, he had her compassion in greater measure than he would ever know.

"Rhys," she said gently, "you are your own man. You are entitled to choose the path you want."

"What I want," he said, sighing, "is to know what I want."

Alwen laughed softly. "You have no idea how lucky you are to be plagued by such a delicious dilemma. For you, everything is an adventure into the unknown."

Rhys shook his head at her. "You have the oddest sense of humor."

"Your future is not yet fixed. Until you set your own course you stand at the center of an enormous turnstile. No matter which way you turn, no matter which direction you look, there is yet another path to take. As you say, the possibilities are endless."

"Well, I guess those endless possibilities of mine will have to wait a bit longer." Rhys slid off the rocks as if to ground himself. "We must first greet your destiny."

THREE

By the time Alwen and Rhys reached the village commons, the three riders had already gathered in there. The newcomers were men of military bearing, still astride and fixed in formal posture, seemingly unaware of the growing throng surrounding them. She scanned them for familiar faces, settling her gaze on the burly warrior at the head of the line. The leader pushed his horse through the crowd and dismounted before her.

"Alwen of Pwll." He smiled.

She searched this stranger's face for something she could recognize. He was even taller than she'd thought, towering a full head and shoulders above her. Though his features were camouflaged by beard grizzle and road dust, his voice was familiar. As were his thoughtful gray eyes. She knew him, somehow.

"I doubt you'll find the man you remember in this old face." He smiled wide. "The years have been far kinder to you, Alwen."

"Aslak," she whispered. It came to her suddenly, his name, skipping over her thoughts and straight to her lips.

"To be sure," he said. "You may believe your heart, if not your eyes. It's been a long, long time."

Alwen shook her head in disbelief. "But I do know you."

Aslak leaned toward her to whisper. "If there is a more private place to talk, there is other business."

"Of course," she said, immediately regretting her offer. The only privacy that she could claim was her living quarters, which were not entirely appropriate and probably not at all private by this hour. Those of the townsfolk not already gaping agog around her would likely be waiting to purchase the healing tonics and other remedies she sold at her door.

"The beach," Rhys suggested.

"Yes," she readily agreed, grateful for his intervention, especially considering she had forgotten him altogether. "Allow me to present my son." She turned to acknowledge him. "Rhys, son of Bledig Rhi."

Rhys offered his hand to Aslak. "I would like to say I've heard only the best of you, but I've heard next to nothing at all. You're the stuff of legend around here, to be sure, but my mother rarely speaks of her past."

"Frankly, I'm relieved." Aslak laughed and returned the handclasp. "If that's the case, I've only the tall tales to live up to."

"Shall we, then?" Alwen was anxious to hear what news Aslak had brought her. She beckoned toward the beach and then paused, interrupted again by afterthought. "Forgive me, Aslak. This is your home, after all. Surely you would rather first greet your kin."

"You are kind to offer, but Fane Gramarye is my home. It's been nearly a lifetime since I last visited these parts, and even longer since I last lived here. Whatever kin I've got left won't miss me any the more for waiting another hour or two. And my men could use a spell at ease." Aslak gestured to the riders, still astride and fully alert. "We've come a fair distance in short order."

He frowned as he peered at the faces around her. "What's become of Fergus MacDonagh? Surely he should be here."

"For pity's sake," Alwen exclaimed. "I must beg your forgiveness again, Aslak, and your patience. Poor Fergus is yet unaware of your arrival."

Aslak's left eyebrow cocked, as if with disapproval, though he nodded. "I see."

"I saw your boats come ashore yesterday and elected to keep the knowledge to myself. And since his cottage sits some ways outside the village proper, he can't possibly know you've come."

Alwen felt frustration welling. Fergus was responsible for her safety, charged with her care by Aslak himself. His attendance would naturally be expected in his commander's presence, no matter how many years he'd been on his own. There was no avoiding the appearance that Fergus was derelict in his duty, when truly the indiscretion was hers.

She looked askance at Rhys. "Find Fergus and send him along. Be quick."

"I'd rather you sent him to the alehouse instead." Aslak's smile was warm. "He can keep these rogues of mine in line. I'm sure it's the first place they'll go once they've stabled their horses. Fresh meat and ale, and the company of these town folk, will be welcome after so many days on the road. I'll go and find him there once I've spoken with you."

"Very well, then," she agreed, and gestured toward the trailhead.

Rhys sped off to fetch Fergus, and Alwen led Aslak back across the commons and down the path to the water's edge. It was a short walk back to the beach, but long enough for her anticipation to grow. With every step she took her heartbeat quickened, stroke after stroke, pace after pace, until Alwen thought her chest would burst.

"It is pleasant along the shore," she confided. "I find it a soothing place."

Aslak's expression softened, as if in remembrance. "So it is."

"Shall we stroll, or shall we sit?" Alwen waved her hand at a pair of flat-topped boulders tucked in the curve of an embankment, just far enough from the water's edge to afford them some buffer from the wind. "Perhaps these stones will do."

"As good as any," Aslak agreed, bowing slightly in deference to her.

"I long ago lost my taste for courtly conduct, Aslak." Alwen set herself primly on the edge of the other rock and waited for him to sit. "And apparently my aptitude. You'll forgive me if I forget my manners."

Aslak settled his bulk across from her. "There's no call for ceremony with me, nor the nerves, neither. If anything, it is I who should be fretting over first impressions."

"You flatter me." Alwen managed a smile, but the suspense had begun to take hold of her. She was eager to get to the point. "Well then, Aslak. What news?"

For the first time, his face took on the gravity of the occasion. "I must ask you to indulge me a moment more. There is one thing I must do before we begin."

"Anything," she offered. "Anything at all."

"I daresay I would know you anywhere." He smiled. "You are the same flawless, fair-haired girl of twenty that I remember. There is no doubt in my mind that you are Alwen of Pwll, High Sorceress of the Stewardry, and guardian of the realms. No doubt at all. All the same, I am required to examine that amulet of yours."

Alwen's fingers instinctively reached for the silver and lapis pendant at her throat. She hesitated a moment, but only because she had never removed it. From the moment it had been placed round her neck, it had been more than a symbol of her rule over the spiritual realm. It was the lifeline to her past. "Of course."

She unfastened the clasp on the chain and handed it to Aslak. He cradled the amulet in his hand and then tumbled the silver casing in his palm, as if feeling for balance and bulk. Turning the pendant face up, Aslak held the stone into the stray sunlight that filtered through the clouds. Apparently satisfied that the gem was true, he flipped the casing over and drew the metal close to his eye.

The sovereign's mark, she thought. Aslak was looking for the tiny visage of a bearded wizard encircled by a wreath of oak leaves hidden in the scrollwork on the back of the amulet. "It is there."

Her words stopped him midpeer and a smile curled the corners of his mouth. "Indeed."

Aslak lowered the pendant and turned his eyes toward her. "That you know the mark is there is enough for me, Alwen of Pwll. It is such a closely guarded secret that I did not know of it myself until Madoc charged me with recovering you."

Alwen retrieved the amulet and fastened it again round her neck. "Madoc meant that it should serve as proof against forgery, but I know every facet of this pendant," she explained. "Every crevice and curve. In the beginning I spent hours searching for secret magic in the stone, or some hidden message in the design."

"And what did you find?"

Alwen found comfort in Aslak's warm smile and his confident bearing. The more time she spent in his company, the more she recalled of his kindly nature, and the more he reminded her of another gentle giant. "I am still searching."

Aslak pulled a small parchment scroll from a hidden pouch beneath his tunic and held it out to her. "Perhaps this will help."

Alwen could only nod as she accepted the parchment. Sealing wax roughed against her palm and she turned the scroll to see the imprint, knowing without looking what she would find.

"It bears Madoc's seal," she whispered. The sound of his name spoken aloud after so many years kept safe in silence almost frightened her.

"Aye. It does," said Aslak. "I hope it gives you some assurance that I am who I say I am."

Alwen felt herself smile. "I am fully assured, Aslak. Am I to read this now?"

"Madoc's words to you are a private matter, though what I have come to say might offer some insight."

She raised the scroll. "I assume this is the summoning."

"It is," said Aslak. "Hywel, son of Cadell, has arrived at the eve of his ascension, as it was foretold. The time has come for you and the other guardians to return to Cymru to safeguard his succession and secure his reign. With the four of you as his divine council, Hywel will unite the three kingdoms and, one day, bring a true and lasting peace. I expect anything else you need to know is on that parchment."

The enormity of the calling she was about to face rendered her speechless. Finding the words to express what she felt was like trying to pluck the clouds from the air.

"I hope you can forgive my befuddled haze, Aslak. You'd think I would be more prepared."

"How else should I expect to find you after all these years?" Aslak offered her a look filled with compassion. "Madoc never intended that your time in hiding should be a time of suffering. Naturally you would seek to thrive, to grow wise in the world and its ways. All the better for serving the king and the Stewardry, when the time came. By the looks of things, I'd say you've done well."

"Yes," Alwen spoke with pride, thinking of her children and their father. "It has been a lifetime. Twenty years exiled, hiding my true self. But Norvik is an unassuming place, a welcome place for one like me. Though it has not been easy, Aslak." She flashed a sly smile. "I am made of magic, after all."

Aslak's unrestrained grin pleased her. "So you are, Mistress."

"What of the others?" she asked abruptly, turning the conversation back to the business at hand. Alwen could scarcely recall them now. They were four in all, sister sorceresses who were not really sisters at all. Bred of the same ilk but not of the same seed, and each of them possessed of a unique elemental magic—a distinct arc in a universal circle which could only be complete when they were rejoined. Just like her, the others had all been sent into hiding to await the call. "Who of them has returned?"

"None, yet. I have come for you first, at Madoc's behest."

"I see." Alwen could not imagine why Madoc would make such a request, but she understood that there was significance in it. It was then that Alwen sensed in Aslak the suppressed desire to speak some secret thought. She'd been too preoccupied with her own thoughts to notice before. "What is it, Aslak?"

Aslak's smile straightened, as did his posture. One eyebrow arched, as if he had been caught unaware and worry wriggled into her mind. When Aslak did not answer readily, Alwen entered his thoughts.

While she had not yet fully mastered the manipulation of minds, she did possess the power to force her way in. This, however, was a violation that Alwen felt should only be used in the most necessary circumstances, and only then when all else had failed. Rather, she would encourage his disclosure by assuaging his conflicting emotions. A less intrusive use of her skills, most akin to an intimate empathy, the kind of connection one might have with a lover or a child she had borne. After several long minutes and a difficult inner struggle, she felt Aslak relent.

"I will speak on this if for no other reason than for you to be forewarned." Aslak adopted a more sober attitude as he faced her, and the casual familiarity between them was replaced with deference due her rank. Alwen recognized these as signs of respect for her power, though the display was not as appealing as she had expected it would be.

"The young king in waiting is plagued by his enemies and his crown will be threatened from the day he accepts it. Though Madoc prepares, already there are forces at work against us. No one can require your return, not even Madoc. Only you or one of your bloodline can claim your place on the council, but it must be your choice. You are free to accept or deny your claim to the guardianship and send me on my way, but know that you are needed, Alwen."

"Refuse?" Alwen scoffed. "I would no more deny my calling than my own existence."

But therein, she realized, lay an unacknowledged irony. One that Aslak had already considered. Returning to the life she had left behind required she leave behind the life she had come to love. Aslak wondered whether she had reconciled herself.

"Rest assured, Aslak, I am ready," she avowed, with the certainty of a long-held conviction. "When do we go?"

FOUR

Alwen poured a cupful of aleberry from the small pot she kept warming in the coals and settled herself onto the chair beside the rock-rimmed fire pit dug into the center of the two-room house she shared with her daughter. Rhys had taken to quartering with Fergus, as much to escape her mothering as for the freedom it afforded him. Alwen was grateful to find solitude, however little it might last. She sipped absently at the spiced wine, meditating on the glowing alder embers in the hearth.

It had been a full day and even more was promised on the morrow. These were the last hours she would spend in Norvik. Aslak was prepared to leave at dawn and there was much yet to do. But for a moment, or maybe two, Alwen decided to sit in the stillness that fell with dusk, hoping to quell the many voices in her head. And perhaps, for just a little while, she could abdicate her thoughts and defer her responsibilities.

The aleberry was not much of a healing brew this night. Two full cups later, Alwen found herself still feeling plagued by restless thoughts. Apparently she had rendered herself temporarily immune to the aleberry's numbing magic. The more she tried to quiet her mind, the more agitated she became.

Alwen sighed and lifted her feet onto a squatty three-legged stool, only to be distracted by the rustle of parchment against cloth. Madoc's letter was yet to be read, and a better time would never come. Lifting the skirt folds of her woolen apron dress, Alwen pulled the vellum roll from a lambskin pouch sewn into the hem of her linen underskirt.

The single sheet took on the weight of rock in her hands. Great words awaited her, the sovereign's words. With a snap of her fingers, Alwen brought the embers in the hearth to flame. The fire brightened the room, but it was still too dim for reading.

"Alight."

A single word, and the wicks of two oil lamps mounted on the wall beside her began to burn. In the privacy of her hut she could risk this little bit of magic. Soon she would be free to spin spells without worry. Alwen was tired of hiding.

With bated breath, Alwen slit the seal with the nail of her forefinger and settled back into the chair. As she uncurled the scroll, a swarm of emotion whelmed her. The paper smelled of ink dust and pipe smoke, of tallow and sweet tea. The familiar scents tickled her senses and long-dormant memories flared. Visions of home came alive and tears of longing filled her eyes. Reminiscence appeared in her mind's eye so crystal and purely preserved it was as though it had all occurred only moments ago.

She saw Madoc, just as he had been on that last, long-ago night, gnarled and white capped by his years and yet still imperious as he paced the floor of his chambers. His voice rang in her mind with the clarity of presence rather than past. So real were his touch on her cheek and his whisper in her ear that she nearly reached into the fire as Madoc extended his arms toward her.

The fate of our world rests in your hands.

So the letter began. Madoc's message, inked in his distinctive hand, somehow made the summoning far more real. Alwen's hands trembled so roughly that she could hardly hold the page steady enough to read. Her mouth had gone too dry for even the aleberry to wet it, although she emptied her cup again in the vain attempt.

The rest of the message was simple, succinct—and commanding. Hywel was soon to gain control of all the great kingdoms of the land. Once he was seated as high king, the pledge of the prophecy would come to pass. It was foretold that Hywel's would be a lasting legacy, more eternal than the lineage he would produce. Before his death he would set forth a codicil that would decree the first abiding law of his land. Through this law, true peace would come. But first he would have to survive a reign threatened at every turn. A Stewards council would be sent to sustain him, to guide him through treachery and see him safely to his destiny. Madoc had discovered that Hywel's enemies were gathering strength and resources, and Alwen was to return with haste.

These were the words she had awaited all these years in Norvik. Though they were merely ink lines on paper, she could feel Madoc's sentience through them. His feelings of urgency underscored her own, and anxiety was suddenly a sensation so strong it was palatable.

Familiar voices outside her door interrupted her thoughts, signaling an end to her privacy. Alwen quickly folded the parchment back into the hem of her skirt, refilled her cup from the pot in the hearth, and then sat back to wait. Soon enough, Eirlys slipped inside and quietly latched the door, unaware at first that she was watched.

"I'd begun to wonder if I should expect you to come in at all," Alwen said softly from the shadows.

Her daughter's flushed cheeks betrayed a tryst and wicked delight shone in her smile. Eirlys of the impish face and elfin grin whose iridescent eyes, violet blue like her mother's, sparkled with mischief no matter what her mood. Her silken, coal-black curls and milky skin mirrored her brother's, though Eirlys was more magical than he. She burned with the blood of the faerie folk, inherited on their father's side. Bledig's mother had been a tangie, a shape-shifting river spirit who had taken mortal form to seduce him, and then found herself so beguiled by the nomadic raider she had remained mortal to stay with him. After giving birth to a halfling son, she could no longer hold human form and had returned to the river from whence she had come. Bledig had followed his father's path, but he was affected by his faerie legacy in subtle ways that manifested in Eirlys most of all. While Bledig and Rhys considered themselves more mortal than mystical, Eirlys embraced her magical heritage.

"I was helping Odwain prepare for the journey, that's all."

"Hmm." Alwen would let her daughter keep her secrets. It was not so long ago that she had felt her own heart so full of anticipation, swelled with intimate yearnings yet to be realized. "And you, daughter, have you prepared?"

Eirlys flopped onto the woven-rag hearthrug at Alwen's feet and laid her head against her mother's knee. A blissful sigh escaped her lips as she gazed dreamily into the fire. "What's to prepare? My bag is packed."

"Things as you know them will change." Alwen stroked her daughter's unruly locks. "A new life, a new home, new allegiances."

Eirlys shrugged. "As long as I have Odwain with me, I am content."

"Odwain is blooded to the Crwn Cawr," Alwen cautioned. Odwain had come to Norvik as his uncle's ward, and like him lived in service to Alwen as her protector in exile. "He owes an oath to the Stewardry, as does Fergus."

"I know this." Eirlys was impatient with her mother's subtlety. "Where you go, Fergus will follow, and where Fergus goes, Odwain will go. And I will follow Odwain."

"Yes, but Odwain's first duty will be to the order, Eirlys, not to you."

Eirlys raised her head to frown at Alwen. Though her rationale often appeared more like a flurry of random thought, she had come to the only natural conclusion, self-serving though it was. "Well of course, Mother. I'm not an idiot. The wedding will have to wait, at least until Poppa arrives."

And, just as quickly as she arrived at one assumption Eirlys was off to the next, usually leaving whoever happened to be listening completely confounded. It was but another piece of her natural charm. "And Poppa will follow you anywhere, from one end of the earth to the other, and twice around the moon."

Alwen's lips curled in an involuntary smile. "Once around the moon, perhaps. Twice for you though, of that I am sure. But, he *is* overdue, Eirlys."

Alwen stopped short of stating the obvious, hoping her daughter would come to this on her own as well.

"Poppa will come. How else could he give Odwain his consent? You will leave word, won't you?"

"I already have," Alwen assured her.

Eirlys smiled, thinking again of weddings, and then peered sideways through long, dark lashes. "Is it wonderful? To be with Poppa, I mean."

Such a question, but this was Eirlys. She was absolutely unabashed in her innocence and yet so eager to embrace the life ahead of her that it made a mother's heart ache with joy—and fear. So young, this girl child, and yet she was so grown. A woman now at seventeen, Alwen realized, with a woman's needs.

"Your father rescued me," she said. "He spared me a life of utter loneliness and made me feel safe. He honored me with his compassion and his devotion, and he offered me his heart. He accepted me as I was, without question and without expectation, and that was more than I could have ever hoped. Because of your father I have known what it is to love, and what it is to be loved. And, to answer your question, yes. It is wonderful to be with him. Absolutely wonderful."

"Poppa is a very handsome man."

Eirlys's sly grin made Alwen laugh. "Bledig is more than handsome, little girl. He is irresistible."

She sobered. "But he is also gentle, and giving, and respectful. He is never brutish or rough or unkind, though he is just enough of a rogue to keep things interesting. Don't you ever allow anything less, Eirlys, not from Odwain or any other man."

"Odwain will be good to me, I know it."

"I am sure he will." She smiled at her daughter. "And if by some happenstance he were not, he would have Bledig to answer to. That ought to be enough to keep any young buck in line."

Eirlys giggled. "Poor Odwain. What have I got him into?"

"Oh, my dear," Alwen whispered as tears filled her eyes. "The most amazing and unendingly glorious journey of his life."

Eirlys fell quiet, for good this time, soon drifting to sleep curled on the knotted rag rug near the hearth. Alwen covered her with a woolen shawl and tried again to relax as the heat of the hearth warmed her feet, just as her child's contentment warmed her heart.

The late hour and earnest confessions had sent her mind wandering in dangerous territory. Bledig's excursions kept him away for months at a time, and she missed him. The longing was insufferable, more so now than ever.

For a moment she indulged herself, invoking his memory. Images of her lover snapped to life like flames igniting and danced wildly through her mind—his raucous laugh, the salt of his skin on her lips, the scent of his musk. She looked again into his smoldering green eyes and felt his hands on her face. Bledig Rhi, the wild and roguish Wolf King—and the most fiercely noble man she had ever known.

He was also the only man who could have possibly possessed the confidence, courage, and understanding it required to be her mate. What other would have welcomed her as she was when they met, a sorceress in hiding and in need of his protection, and then continued to accept her, such as she was deigned to become, knowing one day what her destiny would demand of them both? She was blessed—of this she had always been sure.

Alwen loosed a sigh and swallowed the last of the aleberry in her cup. Too much thought on Bledig would only do more harm than good. With luck and enough wine, she might yet find sleep. The morning sun was soon to rise, and with it a new horizon.

FIVE

After a western crossing over the North Sea that brought them ashore in Northumbria, Aslak led the caravan of eight men and two women south, along the less traveled byways through the Briton countries, avoiding the cities and trading routes in favor of a quiet although lengthier journey. Alwen knew he worried about kidnappers or worse, those who would consider a sorceress an abomination. For nearly nine weeks, it was his daily routine to send a scout ahead, leading the rest of the contingent himself, with Alwen between him and Fergus. The soldiers rode in a loose but defensive formation behind them. Rhys and Odwain had melted in with the Cad Nawdd, enjoying the camaraderie of the other men. Eirlys rode with her mother, except when Odwain sought her company.

Most days, the sky dawned clear but there blew a constant crisp breeze, hinting at the coming frost. Autumn had begun to strip the trees of their verdant splendor, daubing the rowan, alder, and oak leaves copper and bronze. Hemlock stands, ever green, stood in defiant contrast against the gilded backdrop. Yet, even in the fade of fall, the dense forests and fertile lowlands had a familiar look and feel. The landscape seemed to speak to Alwen's soul, in a distant whisper she still had to strain to hear.

Once they passed the tiny border towns into the Powys provinces and neared the northern hinterlands of Seisyllwg, Alwen began to feel impatient.

"It's been a long journey." Fergus noticed her fidgeting. "We're all of us road weary."

Alwen managed a smile. "Apparently I am not as well suited to travel as I was in my younger days."

"You're suffering the call of the motherland to all her wayward sons and daughters," Aslak interjected. "No native child can resist it. It is inborn, like instinct."

"Yes," she acknowledged, glad to have an explanation for what she was feeling. For days Alwen had experienced an excruciating sensitivity to everything—the bone-jarring trod of the horses, the screech of the woodland creatures, even what little sunlight that penetrated the trees. "Every mile it grows stronger. If I were to judge the distance by my discomforts, I'd say we must be close."

Aslak reined his mount alongside. "Then, perhaps you know this road?"

"It is familiar." Alwen glanced to either side of the well-worn track, first at the barren farmland and withered orchards to her left, then the deep, untamed overgrowth to her right. "I have traveled this way before, though I remember it unspoiled."

"Twenty years of border skirmishes has left ugly scars, on the land as well as the people," he explained. "Cymru remains a nation divided by conflict, but the Ancients willing, not for long."

"Up ahead, beyond that bend." Alwen suddenly envisioned a cluster of small stone and sod huts. "There is a sleepy place, a town."

Aslak smiled wide. "That would be Pwll. Never was much more than a huddle of crafts folk and merchants, an inn and an alehouse or two."

The village had stood nearly as long as the Fane, though the townspeople lived unaware that magical folk often walked among them. Madoc had called it hiding in plain sight.

"The temple is near." Alwen was beginning to feel oriented.

"Not far, about a day's ride into the forest." Aslak pointed into the brush. "We'll leave the road here."

He led them onto a narrow path that took them parallel to the byway, under the cover of shrubs and brush. Thankfully the horses were able to pick their way through the scrub and vines. They hadn't traveled much more than a few hundred feet into the woods when Alwen sensed an intruding presence ahead.

"Aslak."

Heeding her warning, Aslak pulled up and signaled the halt to the rest of his men. He watched the trees, anticipating. "Where?"

As if in answer, the spit and image of Aslak, though younger and beardless, emerged from the woods not more than ten yards ahead. "About time. We've been waiting here for two days."

Aslak grinned at his son. "You've youth on your side, Thorvald, and not as many miles to travel. "You found Cerrigwen?"

"Yes." Thorvald scowled, as if he were counseling himself that it would be best to stop short of speaking his full mind. "She is an impatient woman. If she'd had your knowledge of the secret trail, she'd have ordered us to go on without you. It's good you're here."

Aslak's grin grew wider. "Where's your camp?"

Thorvald motioned into the thicket. "There's a good-sized clearing through here. We've made camp along the stream. It will go easier if you walk the horses."

Some distance beyond the trail, the woods opened to a narrow strip of barren ground edged by river rock and a rush of water. A small tent stood near the bank, and horses milled in the reeds and scrub. Several young men sprawled around a fire pit entertaining an even younger auburn-haired woman, while an elder warrior stood guard.

"We'll spend the night," Aslak advised as they dismounted. "Better to cross the veil in the morning, when we have more light."

Fergus took the reins from her hands. "We'll pitch canvas for you and Eirlys. The rest of us can manage with blankets and a good fire. It'll make for an earlier start in the morning if there is less camp to break."

Alwen felt a sudden swoon. She had all but forgotten the quickening of breath and blood that revealed one Steward to another. "Cerrigwen is here."

"Once I've had my speak with her, I'll send her to you if you like," Aslak offered.

"Be forewarned," Thorvald advised. "She has a...well, a strong personality." He gestured toward the campfire. "And that's Finn MacDonagh there, keeping watch over her daughter, Ffion."

"Hah!" Fergus let loose a rare display of delight. "The entire MacDonagh clan in one place! Thought I'd never see the day."

Finn was Odwain's father, Fergus's elder brother. Finn and his first son, Pedr, had been Cerrigwen's escorts all these years.

"No doubt there will be plenty of celebrating round the fire tonight," said Aslak. "But let's see to the horses and camp first."

Fergus wandered away, barking orders right and left. Alwen thought she had never known him to be happier. While some of the men unburdened the animals and raised her tent, she lingered near the tree line, observing introductions and long-awaited reunions around the fire. Eirlys was quick to make friends with Cerrigwen's daughter, while Rhys joined Odwain's family circle. In the midst of the merriment, Alwen noticed Aslak slip into the first tent, near the stream.

She imagined the encounter, Aslak examining Cerrigwen's amulet, as he had her own, verifying her place in the Circle. Moss agate, Alwen remembered, the stone of nature and healing. This was Cerrigwen's realm.

Alwen began to anticipate the end of an interminable oneness. Bledig and her children were family, the one true gift exile had given her. But much as she loved them, even needed them, they could not replace the magical kinship she had lost. Alwen had learned to live without her own kind, but she had never overcome her yearning for belonging, for sisterhood.

As if she had heard the thought, Cerrigwen swept through the tent flap, draped in the indigo velvet mantle of the Stewards Guild and elegant brocaded cloth skirts more suited to a woman of substance than a sorceress in hiding. An imprudent display, Alwen thought. Her own robe was packed away, awaiting the appropriate place and time.

"So here you are." The words fell dull and cold from Cerrigwen's lips as she approached. "And in the personal escort of the great Aslak himself, no less, while I, it appears, warrant only his son."

"Thorvald is of the Cad Nawdd, blooded to the service of the Stewardry. I would say he is a credit to his father, and to you."

"I suppose I should feel honored." Cerrigwen shrugged. "But it is hardly a great triumph that the son should manage to stumble along in his father's footfall."

Cerrigwen stared hard at Alwen, as if she were leaving time for Alwen to be properly impressed. She appeared nearly untouched by age, though aside from the unspoiled skin and the honey-colored tresses that curled over her shoulders and billowed about the cowl of her cloak, few hints of the sanguine youth remained. Alwen recalled a friendlier girl than the austere woman that stood before her now. Not at all the person Alwen had imagined.

Alwen stepped forward, uncertain, considering whether a handclasp or embrace would be welcome. They had been childhood friends, after all. Cerrigwen's stance, however, indicated that an approach of any kind would be unwise. "You have spoken with Aslak?"

"Aslak has adjudged me to be who I say I am." Cerrigwen cocked her head pointedly at Alwen. "If that is what you mean."

"It gives me gladness to see you, Sister." Alwen used the familiar address, one sorceress of the order to another, in an attempt to breach the distance between them. "At long last."

"Hmm." Cerrigwen tipped her chin in response to Alwen's greeting, though she remained both wary and distant. Her amber eyes narrowed. "You've hardly changed. I would have known you, even without that amulet hanging from your neck. You have the same sanctimonious bearing, the same superior airs."

Alwen smiled at the slight. Though unexpected, the insult offered Alwen at least some shallow insight into Cerrigwen's character. She behaved as if she felt threatened. Strange, Alwen thought. Even more disconcerting, however, was a turbulent emotional undercurrent that Alwen could sense but not completely perceive, despite her best efforts to penetrate the surface of Cerrigwen's mind. "You misjudge me, Sister."

Cerrigwen shook back her hair with a casual toss of her head and leveled a sidelong look at Alwen. "We shall see."

She turned to leave and then paused, glancing back with what might have passed for admiration in her smile. "I have felt you prodding my mind, Alwen. To no avail, I'm afraid. I am immune to your gift."

"Forgive me." Alwen feigned regret and quickly withdrew her probing thoughts, surprised a bit. It had been twenty years since she had last tried to sense the psyche of one of her own. Perhaps the skill suffered from the lack of use. Then again, perhaps Cerrigwen had in fact developed the power to resist. "It was an impulsive intrusion."

"Gifts are given to be used, and you are wise to use them to your best advantage," Cerrigwen acknowledged. "But you would be advised not to waste your talents on me."

Cerrigwen's skirts rustled in concert with the breeze as she departed, leaving surprise and disappointment in her wake. Alwen regretted the lost opportunity, wishing she had been more successful in her attempt to detect Cerrigwen's deeper motives. Certainly her sister sorceress was not to be underestimated.

"Well, that was short." Fergus had left the revelry to find her. "And not particularly sweet, I'd say, given the look on your face. Do I dare come any farther?"

Alwen had to smile at the burly, red-bearded old Scotsman. All these years inseparable and the man still showed her absolute reverence. Fergus MacDonagh was a credit to his calling, a true defender of the oath, and a true friend. "Of course. Come ahead."

"She troubles you, aye?"

Alwen sighed. "Time has the power to alter many things, Fergus, even the course of one's character."

"So it does," Fergus nodded. "From what little Finn will say, I gather the years have not been as kind to her as they have to you."

"Is that so?" Alwen had not considered Cerrigwen's life in exile. She wondered now where Cerrigwen had been, how she had survived her years outside the protection of the Fane. "All the same, she is more complicated than she appears."

"Well," Fergus chuckled, "so are you. Any witch is a formidable mistress in her own right, but give her rank and command and she is a damned indomitable force."

Alwen narrowed her eyes at him in jest. "Do you mock me, Fergus?"

"Mock you?" He tried hard to pull a look of injury as he straightened and folded his arms over his chest, but his eyes belied the tease. "I revere you."

"As well you should." She smiled. "Go back to the merriment, Fergus. Please. I'm poor company just now."

"All right, then. I'll leave you to your thoughts. Your tent is ready, whenever you are." Fergus gave her a wink as he made to leave. "Trust your instincts, Alwen. I always do."

SIX

A lwen awoke with a start, responding to a discordant energy that had encroached upon her dreamless sleep. It would not be ignored. And so it was that she arose just before dawn to witness a terse exchange between Aslak and Cerrigwen.

Aslak was taking the full brunt of Cerrigwen's considerable wrath while Thorvald and Ffion stood in obvious discomfort at the edge of the conversation. Rather than approach them, Alwen chose to observe through her tent flap. Though at first she could catch only bits and pieces, soon enough she overheard more than she would have liked.

"Thorvald is captain of this expedition, Cerrigwen," Aslak asserted. "If I did not have faith in his judgment, I would not have given him the commission."

Cerrigwen pulled herself tall and straight. "The soldiers of the Cad Nawdd serve the Stewardry, and those of the guard selected to the Crwn Cawr serve the Mistresses of the Realms. Is that not so?"

Aslak remained composed, despite the displeasure Alwen could easily sense in him. "Yes, it is."

She thumped him in the chest with her extended forefinger. "Then there need be no further discussion. I have given Thorvald my instructions, and it is *my* judgment that shall stand. Ffion will accompany him as my emissary, a gesture of goodwill from the guild. It is not only fitting, it is prudent."

"It is unsafe, Cerrigwen," Aslak insisted. "Surely you do not mean to put your daughter in harm's way."

Alwen watched as the girl stepped forward. Cerrigwen's chin lifted in what looked like genuine admiration, but Alwen easily sensed a stronger, truer underlying feeling of self-assuaging pride.

"I am well trained," Ffion asserted. "And well traveled. I will be no burden, curry no threat. If anything, my presence will be a help, not a hindrance."

The girl presented far more confidence than she actually felt, another truth Alwen could easily sense. It was equally clear, however, that Ffion would do anything in her power to please her mother. No matter what it cost her.

Aslak held his ground in silence for several long moments before finally agreeing. He had no choice, really, but Alwen appreciated his intent to be clear that he acquiesced unwillingly.

"It will be a hard ride, to outrun the winter, and a difficult winter to weather so far north. Make sure she has the proper clothing." Aslak gave his son a curt nod. "We'll start to watch for you once the first signs of spring show. Shouldn't be much longer than a few fortnights beyond that."

Without further exchange, Thorvald led his small contingent of three soldiers and the formidable Ffion away from the campsite. Their journey would take them northeast, past the lands of the Saxons and deep into the Norse kingdoms. Precisely where, Aslak would not say. For safety's sake, none but he and his son knew the exact destination. If all went well, Thorvald would return with his older brother and the youngest of the four women named to the Stewards council.

Alwen emerged from the tent just as Fergus lumbered up, agitated and short of breath, tugging her horse by the reins. "Would ye believe? That woman has insisted her daughter accompany Thorvald on his quest to find Branwen. And Aslak agreed!"

"To be fair, Aslak could hardly refuse her." Alwen pulled the bed rugs from her tent while Fergus began to take down the canvas. "He can refuse none of us any request, though I can not begin to guess how her interests are served by sending her own emissary."

"Nor can I," said Aslak, reaching out to take the furs from her as he joined the conversation. "But she'll be safe enough in Thorvald's charge."

"He strikes me as a remarkable man," Alwen offered, sensing the worried father in him. She also felt Aslak's strong memories of a woman who had stolen his heart and been lost long ago. His love for her still lingered. "He carries his mother's influence in many ways, but he is also every bit the warrior and leader his father is."

"Aye, though I am hardly to credit. He has taken to this life as though he was born for it rather than to it, but it is never easy sending him off."

"One of the many pains of parenthood," she commiserated.

"You have fine children yourself." Aslak smiled over her head as he took the last of the rugs from her and then rolled them into bundles. "Take *your* daughter, for instance. Small wonder that Odwain is so taken with her."

Alwen glanced around to see Eirlys already astride. "I hadn't the chance to meet Cerrigwen's child."

"Ffion is lovely, and certainly seems a capable lass," said Fergus. He had finished lashing the canvas behind her saddle and waited to help her mount.

Aslak knelt to gather the rolls, lowering his voice to avoid being overheard. "Though she does have her mother's airs. If

Ffion has even half of Cerrigwen's demanding nature, Thorvald will have aged years by the time I see him next."

Alwen noted Aslak's veiled observations with a smile of understanding, imagining poor Thorvald's plight. He'd already had the dubious pleasure of shepherding mother and daughter for several long weeks. "Cerrigwen is not an easy woman."

"Be that as it may." Aslak pulled his impressive frame to a stand, arms loaded with fur. "My first concern is to get you both safely home."

Aslak's tone plainly implied that he felt it was not his place to make judgments, putting an end to the intimate moment. Alwen still wanted to hear what else he knew or thought, but decided not to pry.

As he passed, Aslak spoke so softly that Alwen nearly missed his words. "I am glad enough, though, that she'll soon be Madoc's to manage."

* * *

A few hundred yards out of the clearing, Aslak pulled up and pointed into the shadows. "There is a path here. It leads straight through the heart of Coedwig Gwyn."

The fabled White Woods shrouded Fane Gramarye. Alwen had no memory of the forest aside from a wild ride in the dark twenty years before. She nudged her mare closer to what should be the trailhead. "Where, Aslak?"

The scramble of spurred hooves overrode his answer as Cerrigwen inserted herself between them. Fergus grumbled loud enough for his annoyance to be heard, but pulled back to allow her horse room.

"There." Cerrigwen waved wildly at the trees. "The temple is this way."

Alwen's heart skipped a beat. How had Cerrigwen known, when she had not? Forcing logic to rule, Alwen reasoned that it was due to Cerrigwen's affinity to the land. As Mistress of the Natural Realm, her bond with earthly things was far stronger. Or perhaps it was only that Cerrigwen's memory was stronger. Then again, perhaps it was something else.

Aslak turned his horse full round. For a fleeting moment, his face belied the same concern as he leveled a curious and somewhat suspicious gaze at Cerrigwen.

"Keep close," he warned. "The oak trees are so dense it can be hard to see the trail even as you are upon it." Aslak tipped his chin at Fergus. "Watch the rear."

Aslak led them into the copse. The trail, if there actually was one, was overgrown with thistle and furze. Very little light filtered through the mass of leafless limbs overhead, and yet Aslak knew exactly where to go.

Their progress was slow. It took hours to ride but a few miles. Deep into the day, they encountered a hazy fog. The farther they rode, the thicker the fog became, and soon it muffled them so snugly that Alwen could scarcely see the hindquarters of the horse in front of her. *Blind faith or fool's folly*, she thought, placing her trust in the animal's experience and sure hooves.

"Keep pressing forward," Aslak called. "We're almost inside."

A moment later, Alwen noticed a change in the fog. It tingled on her skin as it thickened, and the scents of the forest gave way to a sweet fragrance that Alwen instantly recognized. They were breaching the veil. Fane Gramarye was hidden by an impenetrable spell, a shroud of enchanted mist that enveloped the castle and shielded its existence. The fragrance she sensed was an intoxicant, a bewitchment created to disorient intruders and keep them from stumbling too far into the Stewards' realm. There was an opening, but the secret to seeing your way through was closely guarded and revealed only to a trusted few. Aslak knew the passage, but neither she nor Cerrigwen had been given the knowledge.

And what of Cerrigwen? Alwen wondered again. She was as aloof as she was assertive—traits that Alwen had not seen in her younger days. Was her behavior evidence of something more than a roughened temperament? Certainly hardship and isolation could be to blame, but wouldn't she then be all the more welcoming of rescue? Alwen tried again to reach beyond Cerrigwen's defenses, but to no avail. The answers she wanted were expertly hidden. For now, Alwen would observe and, as Fergus had reminded, pay heed to her instincts.

There was also the matter of Alwen's magic. She was beginning to experience unexpected surprises, burgeoning skills she had never had before. She had first noticed it earlier, with Aslak, when she had sensed his lost love. Alwen had come very near to seeing the countenance of the woman, as Aslak remembered her. Until that moment, Alwen had been limited to the empathy that allowed her to feel another's emotions. Now it seemed she had developed a kind of envisioning. Curious, she decided to experiment.

Alwen focused her thoughts on Fane Gramarye. The image of the temple gates formed in her mind immediately, just a few moments before the mist thinned and peeled away to reveal the thunderstone battlements and iron stiles at the postern. Alwen's breath caught in her throat. The great metal monstrosity was a rusty, rarely used relic from bygone days and such a welcome sight her eyes filled with tears.

Cerrigwen charged ahead, commanding the guardsman who waited to allow them passage. "What are you waiting for?"

Finn MacDonagh spurred his mount, making a valiant attempt to rein in his Mistress. "Perhaps you should allow Aslak to announce you, Cerrigwen."

Cerrigwen ignored him, staring down the sentry, who properly waited for Aslak's nod before throwing the gates wide. Asserting herself with even more boldness, Cerrigwen entered first and proceeded with unimpeachable confidence down the cobbled road lined with evergreen hedges.

"Audacious," Fergus mumbled, urging Alwen to take an equal position alongside Cerrigwen.

"It's no matter," Alwen assured him. "She is eager, as am I. Let her have her way, for now."

Fergus relented, though not happily. Alwen was content to ride at Cerrigwen's right flank, preferring to take in her old surroundings as they passed the guardsman's barracks and the stables, the forge, the feedlot and livestock pens, and then the living quarters. The apprentices were assigned to two rooming halls, segregated by gender. Novices, she recalled, were quartered in a dormitory near the temple, under the care of prefects selected from the apprentice class. The acolytes, accomplished apprentices who served the docents such as she and Cerrigwen, were roomed in the temple itself, on service porches on the lower floor.

"Aslak," she wondered. "These lodges look deserted."

"The Stewards are dwindling, Alwen. There haven't been novices for years and these old outbuildings have fallen out of use. The apprentices have the dormitory now."

Just then, the cobbles ended at the temple courtyard, where the entire order had assembled. Mere dozens awaited them, not the hundreds Alwen had expected. Excitement dulled as foreboding trilled along her spine. "So few?"

Aslak gave a halfhearted shrug. "Such is the tithe of time. In the years you've been gone, we've lost many to the new religion. We've not had a mage child born in the temple in nearly twenty years. And, there've been no new foundlings."

"But how can that be?" Alwen was incredulous. It was true that times had brought change, but surely not extinction. In the beginning, Fane Gramarye had been the training grounds of the mageborn. The clans had proudly sent any youth who showed the signs to the Stewardry. When invaders had supplanted the old ways and driven the Ancients into the sea, the people feared persecution, and their mageborn were abandoned. As had at least two sovereigns before him, Madoc had rescued as many as he could find. Alwen herself had been one such foundling, as had the other Mistresses of the Realms.

Aslak shook his head. "Madoc says the bloodlines are dying."

Alwen shared his deep sadness. The mighty Stewardry had dwindled to but a shadow of its former glory. She made it a point to acknowledge the somber faces that lined the courtyard, who greeted her smiles with reverent stares. The silence was heavy with the weight of desperate expectations, and failing hope.

"Well, here we are." Aslak dismounted at the temple steps and waited for Alwen and Cerrigwen to do the same.

Alwen looked to Cerrigwen for some indication that she was also affected by the mood of the place, but Cerrigwen displayed concern only for herself. She smoothed her fine skirts and turned her imperious airs on Aslak.

"Is there no one to take my bags?"

Aslak gestured up the stone steps toward the open doors of the vestibule that gave entry to the Stewardry. "Glain will assist you."

A delicate wisp of a girl wearing an acolyte's white robe stepped forward at Aslak's beckon.

"Thank you, Aslak." Alwen laid a hand on his arm, half in gratitude and half in empathy. "It is good to be home."

He returned her kindness with a smile of genuine caring. "Fergus and I will see that everyone gets settled."

Everyone, of course, meaning Rhys and Eirlys—a thoughtful gesture that Alwen found touching, and reassuring. With that important trust in capable hands, Alwen felt free to indulge in whatever awaited her.

She could have easily made her way through the corridors blind. Alwen's mind began remapping the temple, piecing together memories and new impressions until the soul of the keep overtook her. Every few feet some sight or sound brought her to a pause—the comforting fragrance of incense and tallow, the ancient arras and faded tapestries that decorated the walls, a familiar sculpture. Even the hewn stone walls invited her touch. Alwen felt as if the temple itself were welcoming her back.

"We've prepared your rooms." Glain ushered them past the assembly hall to the main stairs.

Cerrigwen bristled and pulled to an abrupt stop at the foot of the steps. "You've entered my private space?"

Glain's eyes grew wide with worry. "Only to air out the rooms and refresh the linens. I'm certain you'll find everything just as you left it."

"No doubt, Glain," Alwen interjected, redirecting Cerrigwen's focus. "How wonderful our rooms have been preserved all this time. I never expected such courtesy, and have every confidence you've taken great care."

Cerrigwen narrowed her eyes at Alwen. "We shall see."

"An apprentice has been assigned to attend to your comforts, Mistress." Glain, though ever dutiful, was quick as a whip. She appealed to Cerrigwen's sense of entitlement. "But if there is anything lacking or something special you need, I will see to it myself."

This seemed to satisfy Cerrigwen, though it did not stem the tide of demand. "I expect warm water for bathing, at the very least, and someone to put up my things."

Cerrigwen continued to tick off her requirements, step by step, until they'd nearly reached the second-floor landing.

"We've had no new pledges to the Stewardry in a very long while, but the apprentices still use the spell rooms for practice," Glain explained as they continued up the stairs. "The acolytes have use of the scriptorium for research, though there haven't been directed studies for some time now, since the last of the elders succumbed this past spring."

Alwen remembered the unending rows of books and scrolls, centuries of innovation and knowledge. She had spent many, many days in those dusty stacks. "What happened to them?"

"The one remaining docent, other than Machreth, suffered a mysterious illness that lasted for weeks and ended in his death. We lost three others some years before, in the defection."

"Defection?" Cerrigwen's interest was piqued at last.

Glain was unhappy to speak of it, but she shared what she knew. "There were those in the order who lost faith. These halls are empty now, save the two of you."

"You mean they just…left?" Alwen could not believe what she was hearing. Besides Madoc's rooms, the third floor housed the private residential quarters of the docents—the leaders and teachers of the guild. In the days of Alwen's youth, the rooms on this floor had been full. The docents had numbered eight—four men and four women. She and Cerrigwen had barely made this highest rank before they had gone into hiding.

"Yes, I'm afraid it's quite true." Glain paused at the top of the steps. "I have the quarters nearest Madoc's, to see to his needs. And then there is Machreth, of course."

"His rooms are on this floor?" Cerrigwen asked.

"At the far end." Glain pointed down the hall to her left with one hand and gestured to her right with the other. "Masters in the west annex, and Mistresses in the east."

They had arrived before the entrance to Madoc's chambers—a recess on the third floor where the annexes joined the main hall. Here dwelled the grand mage, high priest, sovereign of the Ninth Order—who had sent Alwen and the others out into the world to fend for themselves, protecting them until they were needed. Instinctively, Alwen stepped forward and pressed her palms against the massive oak door. She trailed her hands over the planks, feeling the knots and pits in the grain that gave the wood its character. Even through the door, she could sense him. Alwen closed her eyes and opened herself to the warmth and feeling of well-being that greeted her.

"Alwen, for pity's sake," Cerrigwen interrupted. "Must you be so sentimental?"

Alwen smiled to herself, eyes still closed. "I keep telling myself that it is only a matter of time until you rediscover the kindness and grace I know you possess, Cerrigwen."

Umbrage ignited, but it was little more than a flash. Cerrigwen regained her defenses quickly, but not quickly enough. Whether she knew it or not, Cerrigwen had revealed the tiniest weakness. Perhaps she could be read, after all.

Alwen opened her eyes and gestured for Glain to continue, engaging Cerrigwen's glare with a benign but unflinching gaze. "I suppose I can wait a bit longer."

Cerrigwen held the exchange long enough to let it be known she was not one to yield, but she did not completely ignore the point. "The summoning was long in coming."

"So it was," Alwen agreed, acknowledging Cerrigwen's half-hearted attempt at conciliation. "But we are here, now."

Cerrigwen gave a curt nod and strode after Glain. By the time they reached her quarters, first door on the right, she had completely regained whatever self-possession may have slipped from her grasp. "When will Madoc receive us?"

"He intends to receive you each, privately, in his chambers," Glain answered. "For now, settle in, make yourselves comfortable. I will come for you in due course."

"You are the eldest, Alwen. I expect you will be first." Cerrigwen paused in her doorway, her tone thick with sarcasm. "Privilege is bestowed upon age."

Glain flashed a look of apology toward Alwen. "Madoc has asked to see Cerrigwen first."

"He has, has he?" Cerrigwen unfurled a triumphant smile. She squared her shoulders as she withdrew into her rooms and flung the door closed behind her.

Another unguarded moment, and even more revealing than the last. Finally Alwen caught a full measure of the only real emotion Cerrigwen had experienced since they had met.

Pride.

SEVEN

lwen's was the very last apartment, at the very end of the hall. It was a simple, tidy place. The sitting room was furnished with a plainly upholstered divan and two slat-backed oak armchairs facing the hearth. A small dressing table that also served as a desk stood under the shuttered double transom on the far wall, overlooking the gardens. The stone walls were bare except for the heavy draperies hung over the sash to stave off the cold, but the room was warm. Someone had left a fire burning.

"We've given your daughter the rooms next to yours." Glain supervised from the doorway as a parade of attendants silently entered the room carrying plates of bread and cheese, a tea tray, and a bucket of warm water for the basin on the table. "Your son will billet in the guardhouse, with Aslak's garrison."

Alwen smiled at the thought of Rhys bunking in the barracks. She would have guessed he'd prefer the creature comforts of the Fane, but then he was his father's son. Bledig would never have been happy confined by stone bulwarks.

"Thank you, Glain." Alwen tossed her heavy riding cloak over the back of the divan and took a moment to really look at the girl. Young woman, rather, Alwen now noticed, a bit older than Eirlys.

She was a wistful beauty with full lips and straight ginger-brown hair that framed an angular, aristocratic face. Thick brown lashes veiled intelligent gray eyes that offset a proud nose. She presented herself as docile and dutiful, but Alwen sensed the makings of a spitfire.

"Have I time to wash?"

"Of course." Glain glanced down the hall and excused herself. "I'll see to Cerrigwen, and then come for you."

Alwen rinsed her hands and face and nibbled at the bread, standing at the window. Autumn had razed the gardens, and the grounds were littered with the withered remains. The only color left was the evergreen of the bittersweet hedges that ringed the yard and the clear, ice-blue shards of sky peeking through gray clouds. She had missed this place.

"Pardon, Mistress." Alwen turned to greet another young attendant who had arrived carrying her bags. "You'll need your robe."

Before Alwen could answer, Eirlys scampered through the door and wrested the satchels from the attendant's grip. She lugged them to the bed and upended them on the crimson velvet coverlet.

"I have my own rooms, you know, just next door," she announced, rummaging through her mother's things until she found a gray flannel bundle tied securely with a leather thong. "Here we are."

Eirlys lifted the indigo velvet mantle with gentle, reverent hands. She had always been enchanted with it. When she was small, Eirlys would ask to be allowed to remove the robe from its hiding place, to run her fingers over the weft and ask about her mother's mysterious past and what wonders the future held. Alwen remembered those sentimental occasions with fondness and gratitude, especially for the pride that had shone in her daughter's eyes. The same pride she saw now, as Eirlys held out the cloak.

"I've never seen it on you, but of course it will be wonderful." Eirlys laid the robe aside with deliberate care. "What else have you to wear, beneath it?" She frowned with disappointment as she sorted through the rest of her mother's belongings. "Surely this isn't all you have with you."

"The robe is enough all on its own." Alwen smoothed the skirts of the plain gray woolen apron dress she wore. "This will do."

"I suppose. But at least let's do up your hair," Eirlys insisted.

"Too much fuss, Eirlys." Alwen was not one to be overly attentive to appearances. "You are the one with the dramatic flair. Simple serves me best."

"Don't be silly." Eirlys crossed her arms across her chest imperiously. "This is no ordinary day, and you are no ordinary woman."

Alwen paused. "I suppose the occasion warrants a bit of fuss. A very *small* bit."

Eirlys tugged her mother to the divan and ordered her to sit, gleeful to be indulged. "This place is grand, but so somber. Such a small number for so many rooms, but then, I suppose it wasn't always like this. Still, it seems to me there is a lot of worry here. The attendant who showed me to my rooms told me there is a discontent in the ranks."

Alwen was disturbed by this news. "In what way?"

"They're not all discontent, only some. Those that think Madoc should wait, and those that think he should not, whatever that means. There are many here near my age, all pledged to your cause, and all of them with duties to perform."

"They are readying themselves for what is to come," Alwen explained, thinking on the underlying issues of the guild. There had always been differing opinions on the interpretation of the prophecy. Madoc held true to the original decree that the king could not be seated until the Circle of Sages had been joined. However, there had always been those who felt that this was too literal and that dire times demanded action. Madoc required strict adherence to the order of events as he saw them, but how and when to bring the king to power had been the cause of heated debate for generations.

"But what, exactly, is to come?" Eirlys prodded as she carefully plaited Alwen's fair tresses from the nape of her neck to her waist and then tied off the twist with a leather thong.

"And what am I to do about it? Has Madoc duties for me as well?"

"You know the prophecy, Eirlys. The Stewardry has begun to prepare for the arrival of the one king, the ruler ordained by the Ancients to restore order to the world and bring the old ways back into the light." Alwen was not so sure how to answer the rest. "Now that you ask, I confess I hadn't thought how you might serve. We've never seriously discussed what place you might take in the order. Do you mean to say you have interest in such a life?"

Eirlys grinned. "My only interest is in becoming Odwain's wife, but if I am to be here with him, I might as well find some way to be useful, don't you think?"

"Well yes, of course." Alwen felt a swell of pride. "I shall speak to Madoc about it. There must be some place in the Stewardry for a girl with faerie blood burning in her veins."

"There," Eirlys announced, stepping back to admire her handiwork. "All done."

When Alwen stood to inspect her reflection in the looking glass angled on the mantle, she saw the beauty in herself she rarely acknowledged. Eirlys had added an unexpected air of sophistication to what Alwen normally considered a plain appearance. Perhaps it was the soft light and familiar surroundings, but Alwen thought she looked as different as she felt.

"Wait." Eirlys skittered across the room to snatch something else from the pile of clothing on the bed. "Wear these."

Eirlys had chosen a pair of camlet slippers, souvenirs from Bledig's travels to the east. They were a delicate fashioning of bluish-gray goat hair, embellished with a gold thread design that complemented the indigo velvet and the Steward's insignia. Alwen approved, of both the style and the sentiment.

"A lovely thought," she smiled at her daughter as she pulled off her riding boots and slid her feet into the shoes. "Most appropriate."

Eirlys was pleased, as much with herself as with her mother, and not afraid for it to be known. "As you say, I have a flair for such things. You look wonderful."

Eirlys lifted the Steward's mantle from the bed. "And now, the cloak."

Alwen trailed her fingers over the thick velvety weave, almost hesitant to take it. "It has been more than twenty years since I last wore this."

"About time, then, don't you think?" Eirlys held the robe out to her mother. "After all, this is who you are."

The words gave Alwen pause. After so many years in obscurity, she had lost sight of part of herself. She was a high sorceress of the Stewardry, a guardian of the realms, a member of the first Stewards council assembled in a thousand years. The cloak's deep indigo color signified her rank and seniority as second only to Madoc and his heir apparent. "So it is."

She allowed Eirlys to sling the cloak over her shoulders and then fasten the silver chain that anchored it. Alwen's skin trilled under the weight and great import of the mantle. She felt taller, stronger. It seemed as though, in taking it onto her body, she had donned an entirely new identity. Indeed, she supposed that she had.

A sudden clang resounded through the halls, and moments later, a slightly pale and harried Glain arrived. "Whenever you are ready, Mistress."

Alwen smiled at her, hoping to encourage the girl to relax a bit. "Cerrigwen has finished her visit?"

Glain swallowed hard and nodded. "Indeed."

"Was that her chamber door?" Eirlys did not even try to hide her amusement. "She is a high-minded one."

"Eirlys," Alwen reproached.

Her daughter merely rolled her eyes. "Come now, Mother. Truth be told."

Alwen thought to caution her daughter about her manners, but Glain interceded. "Madoc is ready."

"And so am I."

Alwen shot Eirlys a warning look and followed Glain into the hall. Meaning to forge a more casual acquaintance with the girl, Alwen attempted to walk alongside her rather than behind her. As soon as Alwen stepped up, Glain hopped ahead, trying to maintain the requisite formal distance. After several tries, Alwen grabbed her arm. "Please, Glain. A moment."

The girl stopped, wide-eyed and unsure of herself. "Yes, Mistress?"

"It would honor me greatly," Alwen said kindly, "if you would not honor me so greatly."

The corners of Glain's lips curved upward, however brief the twitch. She squelched the smile before it escaped, but bemusement still twinkled in the girl's eyes. Even if Glain could not yet bring herself to behave with familiarity, Alwen had made her point.

"You won't need me to find your way." Glain gestured ahead, toward Madoc's chambers. "But I'll escort you. It *is* customary."

"Well, if you must." The long walk down the hallway suddenly seemed too brief. "Lead on."

Alwen proceeded with careful steps, aware that her emotions were beginning to get the better of her. The energy it took to tamp the anticipation and exhilaration rendered her light-headed and wobbly. By the time she reached the doorway to Madoc's rooms, her mind was awhirl and her knees were weak. She was about to stand in the presence of the Ard Druidh, the highest power in all the earthly realms, and the divinely anointed sovereign of the Stewardry. Alwen could barely breathe.

Just before she crossed the threshold to announce their arrival, Glain turned toward Alwen with the warmest of smiles. "Take a deep breath, Mistress, and then let it out. You'll be fine."

EIGHT

Madoc stood in the center of the room, regal in his golden-trimmed, indigo velvet mantle. His appearance had hardly changed. Whatever worries she had carried with her across the threshold melted away in his presence. Alwen felt as though she had stepped into the very source of benevolence and wisdom. These were the lost comforts of her youth.

"Welcome home, my child." Madoc spread his arms wide.

Alwen thought her feet would fail her, or perhaps her sensibilities might, and either way she would be mortified. Madoc smiled kindly on her and waited with patience as she hesitantly brought herself before him, but Alwen could not bring herself to speak.

She beheld his well-worn face and gentle, wizened eyes and remembered all that he had been to her. Anguish and relief rippled through her, and Alwen ached from the rush of emotion. It was as if she had been living only half a life all these years, and now, finally, she was whole again. Her exile had finally ended. And it was almost too much to bear.

Madoc reached out to touch her cheek and she began to tremble. "Alwen, dear girl."

He laid his hand on her shoulder to offer his comfort and give her time to overcome the moment. Restraint was more difficult to manage than she expected. Tears threatened to pour from some deep well of abandoned feelings she hadn't known existed within her. Until that moment, Alwen had never allowed herself to acknowledge how homesick she had been.

After what were more likely minutes than the eons she thought them to be, Madoc gripped her by both arms and squeezed. "Come now, child."

Alwen was finally able to recover her senses, though she was more than a bit embarrassed. She cleared the emotion from her throat and began to apologize, but Madoc shushed her with a slight shake of his head and a wink.

"This has been a long time coming." He squeezed her shoulders before releasing her, and though he had removed his hands, their warmth remained.

"I am overwhelmed," she admitted, hoping she could look at Madoc now without worry of further disgrace. "It can't be helped."

Madoc smiled. "Nor should it be. You've a right to that little bit of honesty, and more."

He took her hands in his and regarded her closely. "I am very pleased. You, Alwen, are a woman of substance."

Alwen wondered what she could possibly have displayed that would impress him. As she puzzled over Madoc's meaning, Alwen began to feel love and pride welling within him. In the same instant that she felt his emotions, she realized she had sensed them because he had wanted her to.

"Yes." Madoc nodded to himself as he peered at her. He was sensing her as well, but with more depth. "Formidable, I would say, in character and conscience, and every other way that matters. And you have done well for yourself by way of a fine family. Children," he smiled. "A boy, and a girl, eh? And their father? Ah, yes. The Wolf King." Madoc shook his head. "He is late."

"All of this at a glance?" She laughed, astonished. "Such a penetrating intuition is remarkable."

"Well, I am the sovereign, after all. I have great skills upon which I rely, masterful instincts, you know." He chuckled. "And, of course, the scrying stone."

"Crystal gazing," she remembered.

Madoc walked to his chair and gestured toward a second chair placed facing him. "Sit for a moment."

He settled into his seat and waited for her to join him. "Aslak sends his regards, and his apologies. Had I given him the time I am sure he'd have made a proper farewell, but I've tasked him with yet another urgent journey."

"Oh?" Even as she queried, his thought came to her. "Tanwen, of course."

"He'll be some weeks in search of her. In the meanwhile, Finn and Fergus will lend their experience to Emrys and the rest of the guard." Madoc nodded. "Now then."

Alwen understood that the pleasantries had been dispensed with and that serious business was at hand. As was his nature, Madoc wasted no time in coming to the point.

"The king of our prophecy has reached the eve of his ascent," he began. "And, as our ancestors foretold, a Stewards council will guide him. It is the greatest honor ever bestowed upon our kind. You and Cerrigwen, Branwen and Tanwen, were selected to become the first such council convened in a thousand years."

Madoc paused, peering at her intently as though to gauge her readiness for what he would say next. Alwen sat forward, hands clasped in her lap.

Madoc took on the air of the pontiff and began to expound. "In the time of the Ancients, the Stewards held tether on the whims and ways of the world through the guidance we offered to great leaders. We guided the fates of man from the shadows, until the people were strong enough to steer their own course. Then, for a time, we served openly, alongside our mortal brothers. The Stewards had the ears of the kings and chieftains of every known tribe. But those were days when men had tolerance and love for each other and respect for things greater than themselves.

"When men were wont to listen to wiser voices, there was reason and rhythm in the forces of this place. As it is, we live in times when most men will follow rather than lead, even when it comes to ruling their own hearts. Mankind is the only beast on this earth that will forsake his instincts in favor of a false promise."

Madoc's hands waved all as he spoke. To Alwen, it seemed his voice had the power to move the air and the earth, if he so wished. She recalled these teachings from her early training, but now the tenets had a new depth to their meaning.

"There are invisible strands of light and life coursing through all living things that bind us to one another," he continued. "They make us all accountable for the good and evil that befalls our fellows. But, the push and pull that evens the tension in the threads is a delicate balance to hold. When the weave is pulled too taut, order becomes oppression. Freedom of will is subjugated, and life itself is choked into submission. Then again," he shrugged. "If the threads are loosened too much, the netting unravels and we are all thrown awry."

"The absence of all order is no better than tyranny," Alwen said quietly.

"Exactly." Madoc appeared quite pleased with her response. "Precious few among men accept this truth, and fewer will live abiding it. What the people of the world fail to accept is the power in their own existence. They fail to notice the subtleties in their own control. This, my dear, is why you are here. Through you and your sisters, our magic will have its place in this world again. And so, here we are."

Madoc tossed both hands in gesture to the sky. "We have waited nine generations for our time to come again, and finally

ROBERTA TRAHAN

we have arrived. When Hywel gains control of the remaining unaligned kingdoms he will have the power, and with the council, he will have the wisdom. But, his rule will not come without peril. He will need the protection we have pledged to him."

Alwen still wondered what role she was expected to play in all of this. "Explain to me, Sovereign, just what this council is. And how am I to serve it?"

Madoc smiled as though he had been waiting for her to ask. "A Stewards council is the Circle of Sages—a combination of four unique vessels of strength and vision, four individual voices that combine to offer a balanced perspective of the world Hywel will inherit."

"Yes." This she had already acknowledged. "But how?"

"Therein lies your quandary, Mistress." Madoc smiled. "That is something you must discover for yourself. For now it will have to be enough for you to trust that when the time comes, you will know what to do and how it will be done."

Alwen was not so certain. "For now it will have to be enough to trust in your good judgment, Sovereign. You must see things in me that I do not see in myself."

"Yes," he said. Madoc had relaxed against the back of his great chair with his arms draped over the arms. "I see a great deal that you do not, at least not yet."

His gaze grew stern and piercing, commanding her eyes to meet his. "Each arc in the Circle of Sages is equal in span and strength, but every circle must begin and end somewhere—a point of convergence, if you will. And, so it is that I have proclaimed that this circle will begin and end with *you*."

Madoc could only mean that she was to lead the council. This was unexpected. "You flatter me, Sovereign. But are you certain it is me you want?"

"Humility is an admirable trait, in small doses. In too great a measure, it is a hindrance." Madoc sat forward to take her hand.

"True strength comes from embracing everything that makes you who you are. You are destined to lead but to seize that destiny you must muster true strength. You must not shy from your place in the circle."

Alwen took comfort in his firm grasp. Despite her misgivings, she found herself eager to prove his confidence in her was well founded. These were the very aspirations she had returned to embrace.

"I must tell you, though, that I have already spoken with Cerrigwen. She is intolerant of disappointment, or at least unaccustomed to it. It may take her some time to accept that the destiny she imagined for herself is to be yours."

"I have found her to be somewhat…" Alwen searched for the most appropriate word, but settled for the most diplomatic. "Difficult."

Madoc patted the back of her hand. "I expect that will only get worse before it gets better, but she'll come around. Cerrigwen is proud, no doubt about that. She is also decisive and determined—qualities that will serve her well, in time."

There was still one question to be answered. "Why me?"

He was surprised by her bewilderment. "Forgive me, Alwen. I have forgotten how little you know of yourself."

Madoc reached for the chain around her neck and pulled the amulet free from the bodice of her dress. "This should not be hidden, not anymore. You should display it proudly. The amulet is far more than just a token of your identity. It is a source of immense power. But then," he smiled as he sat back in his chair, "I would guess that you have already discovered that."

Alwen had long sensed there were deeper truths to her talisman, mysteries that she yearned to understand. "I…suspected."

Again, Madoc nodded. "Any witch or wizard can be taught to wield magic. We are, by our very nature, gifted with such powers. Some rare few among us are born with a singular kinship to the gods, a bond with the unseen forces that arises sparingly in any one generation. You and your sister sorceresses were selected for the council because you possess such kinship. Each of you has a unique strength to bring to the Circle. Cerrigwen, for instance, has uncanny influence over the earthly realm. Her affinity to the organic elements of this world allows her to call upon its resources in profound ways."

Alwen remembered. "She has dominion over all things that spring from the soil."

"Yes," he confirmed. "She is a natural healer of ills, among other things. And then there are the other two. Branwen has the celestial eyes of the oracle, and Tanwen the keys to the divine art of alchemy. The earth, the air, the fire of the forge, and so forth."

Madoc paused, squinting at her as if he were looking for something deep inside. "Your sorcery, Alwen, is rooted in the spirit, in the sentient soul of all beings. Your power is manifested in the waters, from which all life is fed. You are an extraordinary judge of character. A keen advantage to a man who can ill afford to trust the wrong person, don't you think?"

Alwen nodded, thinking of Cerrigwen.

"There you have it. Through the four of you, Hywel will have the power of all of the elements behind him. Now then." Madoc folded his hands in his lap. "You have been too long away from us. Your skills lack daily use, but we'll fix all that soon enough. Perhaps you are already noticing a change. The Fane is a bastion of its own power, you know, and that amulet you wear is a conduit."

This explained so many things. "I believe I have felt it."

"It will get stronger. You will learn to control it, and in time even command it. You must, lest it destroy you."

Madoc straightened abruptly and stood. Alwen rose respectfully in turn, albeit reluctantly. There was still so much more she wanted to know, but she held her tongue. He was finished with her for now.

"This is but the first of many chats to come," he said. "Take time to reacquaint yourself with your home and your training, but prepare. In the months ahead there will be many challenges."

"I am ready."

"Of course you are," Madoc said plainly. He accompanied her to the door. "If you were not, you would not be here."

NINE

Madoc straightened in his chair as Machreth strode into the room and prepared to address his second. It seemed Machreth took longer and longer to respond to a summons. "I expected you long before this."

"I've been occupied with a group of acolytes who have shown a remarkable affinity for the finer aspects of spellcasting." Machreth presented himself to Madoc with half a flourish and a perfunctory nod. "I hope I have not kept you waiting too long, Sovereign."

Madoc smiled at the empty courtesy and then studied his handsome colleague more closely. Too handsome, Madoc thought. Those tawny good looks of his had a blinding effect, particularly on women, who often found him irresistible. Machreth struck quite an impressive figure in his proctor's robe. He wore the trappings of his title with pride. The black camlet cloak with gold embroidery and indigo insignia added dignity to his stature and afforded him nobility his humble birth did not, and he did possess an arrogant charm. Machreth, high sorcerer of the Ninth Order and chosen heir to Madoc's throne, was a formidable man.

Machreth hesitated and Madoc sensed him gathering his thoughts and calculating the risks in voicing them. He was as cautious with his actions as he was in their analysis, careful and deliberate in all things at all times—and ever wary. "So our protégés have returned. Indeed, they have grown strong and sure while they have been away. Remarkable, even."

"As it should be." Madoc assessed Machreth's every move, every turn of phrase. The younger man had earned his rank through dedication to his vocation, hard work, and more than a little talent. Machreth was not a man to be trifled with.

"You put great faith in these women, Sovereign, and in the prophecy."

"In my experience, there is profit in faith," Madoc said calmly. "And in patience."

"Perhaps." Machreth began to prowl the room, hands clutched at his back as he paced. "Hywel has long since come of age, and he has more than proved his worth in both battle and benevolence."

"Yes," Madoc said slowly. He was still waiting for Machreth to get to his point. "So he has."

"And yet you still have not endorsed his reign." Machreth glanced sidelong as he passed. "If Hywel is the chosen king, if true peace will only ever come at his hand, what advantage could there possibly be in waiting any longer? Surely your wise guidance is enough to sustain him."

"My duty, as is yours, is to sustain the Stewardry," Madoc said firmly. "The council, when the time comes, will sustain the king."

"I still say there is no reason to wait. Present this Circle of Sages of yours to Hywel later—as a coronation gift, if you wish. The Stewards council will only add to his strength. In the meantime, let us take our rightful place in the light."

"The dictates of the Ancients are quite clear, Machreth. We will wait until all of the members of the council have been found and returned. Only then will we consecrate Hywel and reveal ourselves again to the world. Only then will we be strong enough."

"So you will insist, then, on holding us hostage against the promise of a thousand-year-old myth?" Machreth's frustration was showing.

"All legends sprout from seeds of fact. Perhaps it follows that the grander the tale, the more potent the truth from which it has sprung." Madoc frowned. "But the prophecy is not a myth. It is a promise."

"On that I have only your word," Machreth countered. "Though I grant you it has been a most powerful yoke. You and your predecessors have indentured the membership for centuries in the name of this prophecy, in the name of a truth that is revealed only unto you."

"And so we come back to faith, Machreth," Madoc counseled. "And patience."

"Faith can be a blinding virtue," Machreth argued. His gaze remained fixed and intent upon Madoc. "And patience a shallow well whose stores are quickly drained. Shall we speak to the point, Sovereign?"

"By all means."

"Hywel's success depends upon power *we* grant him." Machreth stopped directly before Madoc. "He is but a means to an end. We are the true rulers of this world."

"By *we* you mean *you*—hmm, Machreth?" Madoc shook his head in disbelief and disappointment. "You would put yourself in his place?"

"I would put us above him," Machreth insisted. "It is where we belong. I say we no longer need to whisper our wisdom in the ears of kings. We should raise our own voices."

"Blasphemy," Madoc spat.

"I am not alone," Machreth warned. "Some of the acolytes are as restless and weary as I, eager for the waiting to end. You have grown impotent, plying the ghosts of your ancestors with quiet words of faith and praise, and the order grows old and impotent with you. The time has come to lead the charge, Madoc. If you will not take us boldly toward the greatness to which we are entitled, I will."

So there it was, the threat of insurrection. But it was not the sting of Machreth's words or the depth of his disdain that troubled Madoc now. It was the ambition and resentment burning deep behind the resolve in his dark, cunning eyes.

"You put me in mind of a half-starved scavenger anticipating the last gasp of a wounded beast." Madoc smiled wryly. "And a bit too eagerly, I might add."

Machreth was losing his grip on his composure. "You've hung on beyond your time. Your days are waning, Madoc."

Madoc tensed, alerted to the danger in Machreth's undertone by the prickling of instinct and gooseflesh. "Take care you don't swoop too soon, Machreth. I still have plenty of fight left in me."

Machreth's eyes had narrowed and his jaw was set. "All in good time."

Madoc watched as Machreth strode from the room, disappointed beyond imagining. Though he had been expecting Machreth to reveal himself, the loss of his loyalty still struck hard and sharp. The sad truth was that Madoc had held out hope for a better end, despite all evidence to the contrary. Now there could be no denying that Machreth's heart was turning away from him. Madoc would have to act quickly.

Very soon seditious forces would be at work within the guild, if they were not already. Machreth was trusted and respected by the novitiate. His voice would be enough to raise unrest among the ranks, no matter what Madoc said to counter him. Machreth would have to be routed, somehow, but in the interim, Madoc would have to prepare. There was far more at stake than the prophecy now. The Stewardry itself was at risk.

Madoc pulled his weary frame from the throne and shuffled heavyhearted to his desk. He sensed the skein of his life threads thinning. It seemed at times that he could feel his very soul unraveling. With a baleful sigh, he slid onto the bench and searched the disordered desktop for paper and quill.

There was much to do. Another successor would have to be named in Machreth's place. Indeed, there was a true heir, one whom Madoc now wished he had acknowledged much sooner. But before this new beneficiary could be named, he had to ensure he would still have a legacy left to bequeath.

And then the circle was yet incomplete. Madoc would have to trust in Aslak's sure heart and great skill to see that the other two sisters were brought safely back. Without the Circle of Sages, Madoc held little hope the prophecy could be fulfilled. Still, it would be weeks before Aslak returned. Until then, Madoc would be vulnerable, but he was not really alone.

Alwen was a natural leader. While she had not come to fully appreciate the traits in herself, she had already proved her ability to make difficult decisions. He knew that she had sacrificed her word to her mate to honor Madoc's summons. Yes, she was wise and strong, and of the two he had encountered thus far, she would best weather whatever storms lay ahead. So long as he left her properly prepared, the prophecy would be safe at her hands. And if it came to it, he could trust Alwen to see his rightful heir safely onto his seat when the time came. In that there was a bit of comfort.

By the time he had finished transcribing his thoughts, the day was fading. As was his vigor, he admitted, but there was too much to do yet to sleep. Madoc carefully separated the four sheets of vellum, rolled them one by one, and then sealed each scroll with melted wax embedded with his signet. He slid the papers onto a small, hidden ledge beneath the desktop just as an acolyte arrived to light the oil lamps in his rooms.

"When you've finished there," he said, "send Glain to me."

* * *

Alwen would have preferred to assert her presence within the membership more quietly, but Madoc insisted. Cerrigwen, on the other hand, was so delighted by the order of a formal presentation the day following their arrival that she had taken on the organization of the entire event.

Several apprentices were conscripted to Cerrigwen's service and assigned preparations for what Alwen considered an unnecessarily lavish celebration. But Madoc himself encouraged the excess, requesting an array of delicacies and indulgences be added to the already sumptuous table fare. In a matter of hours, revelry had overtaken the temple. The return of the first two sorceresses named to the Circle of Sages heralded the beginning of a new era, and even Alwen could concede, reason enough to be festive.

"You are seated at Madoc's left." Glain ushered her into the great hall and gestured toward the sovereign's table, stationed in front of and centered along the grand dais. From where he sat, Madoc could survey the entire company of guests. "Across from Machreth."

Alwen took her place beside Madoc's empty chair and smiled to the others already seated. Cerrigwen offered a nod in welcome from her perch at Machreth's right. Also seated around Madoc's table were Glain and the three others who had reached the rank of acolyte, and Emrys, the interim captain of the castle guard.

No sooner had Alwen settled did a hush descend. Madoc had arrived. As he entered the room, the entire assembly stood in his honor, and a cheer erupted from the crowd. Madoc waved as he crossed the hall to his table, clearly pleased with the revelry that greeted him. As Madoc sat, so did his guests, and the merriment resumed.

"A rare occasion," Emrys observed. "The entire order rejoices. Even those assigned to serve and the soldiers standing watch do so with happy hearts."

"As well they should." Cerrigwen tilted her head in such a fashion that her sidelong glance in Machreth's direction was only half-veiled by her lashes. A flirtatious gesture, some might think. "Is this not the advent of our glory?"

"The first step on a long march," Madoc cautioned, reaching for the platter of game meats. "But it is a start."

"All in testament to your great faith, Sovereign." Machreth picked at the figs and roast boar on his plate with one hand while swirling the contents of his wine goblet with the other.

The shade of mockery in Machreth's tone was unmistakable, at least to Alwen's ear. If Madoc noticed, he ignored it. Alwen took flat bread and soft cheese as it was passed, taking note that a kind of nervous tension had taken root round the table.

"Hear, hear." Ynyr, the eldest of the acolytes though still a youngish man with flaxen locks and a chiseled chin, could not let Machreth's comment stand unanswered. He stood and raised his goblet high, his toast ringing loud enough for all to hear. "To glory!" he cheered. "To Madoc!"

A deafening echo answered Ynyr's call, and every Steward and soldier stood in Madoc's honor. Alwen noticed that Cerrigwen was among the last to rise, waiting for Machreth to do so before following suit. It seemed to Alwen the two shared the familiarity of old friends, perhaps from the days before exile. Whatever it was, the closest thing to warmth she had seen Cerrigwen display thus far had been toward Machreth.

For several long moments the cheer resounded, until Madoc took to his feet and quieted the crowd. He gestured for the audience to return to their seats and then took advantage of the heady atmosphere to speak his piece.

"Brothers and sisters of the guild, Stewards of the prophecy, these are the days of days we have awaited. After nine incarnations of our order, our perseverance is rewarded, our faith redeemed. The time of our resurrection is dawning. The journey has just begun, and the true trials yet to be faced, but tonight we rejoice. The first of the guardians of the Circle of Sages have returned. All hail Alwen and Cerrigwen, Mistresses of the Realms."

Alwen and Cerrigwen rose again, this time to receive their own accolades. While Alwen was eager to be released from the moment, Cerrigwen basked in it. In some ways, Alwen admired her sister sorceress. Cerrigwen was naturally regal, visibly confident, and seemingly far more comfortable bearing the burden of expectation. Again, Alwen questioned how it was that Madoc considered her the best choice to lead the Circle.

Finally, Madoc concluded his declaration. "Take your fill, Stewards, and may the echoes of your revelry send up such a raucous thunder it awakens the Ancients."

"Wine," Madoc bellowed as he returned to his plate. "More wine at my table."

As Alwen glanced around the room to find her children and other familiar faces, she could not help but feel the joy. Neither could she help but notice that the crowd numbered only dozens around a score of tables—a devastating wane from the hundreds of voices that had filled this hall in her youth.

"Yes, more wine." Cerrigwen held out her cup as the pitcher was passed. "And another toast, to Machreth, second only to Madoc. His leadership and loyalty also keep us strong."

Alwen's was not the only surprise; she felt a collective lull, as if everyone had skipped a breath. All eyes turned toward Madoc, who was implacable.

"Of course," he said, lifting his cup high. "To Machreth."

Alwen responded in kind, and the others followed suit. Cerrigwen's tribute could have been innocent. Perhaps Madoc had not shared his concerns about Machreth with Cerrigwen. Perhaps she was merely paying homage to his title, which would be proper at such an event.

Machreth bowed his head as he raised his drink in return. "I am honored, though you credit me too much. I serve my oath, as do you all."

"You are modest." Cerrigwen reached out to pat Machreth's forearm and then cast a knowing glace around the table, which she eventually settled on Alwen. "As Madoc's burdens have been great in our absence, so have Machreth's. However few remain, that the membership has survived at all is due in no small part to his devotion and inspiration."

"Inspiration, eh?" Madoc raised his cup. "High praise, Machreth, to be lauded a beacon of light in dark times."

The look that passed between them then could never be mistaken for anything but the challenge that Alwen knew it to be. The conversation had taken a dangerous turn. She glanced at the others to see if anyone else had sensed the troubled waters stirring beneath the surface, but other than Cerrigwen, who was raptly attentive to Machreth, they were more occupied with the food than the discussion.

"I am humbled, Sovereign, by Cerrigwen's kind words. If they are deserved in even the smallest measure, I am redeemed."

Madoc smiled, as if what was unfolding were a grand drama playing out for his amusement. "Are you in need of redemption, Machreth?"

Machreth returned the smile with his own sly, half-turned lip curl, completely unperturbed by Madoc's remark. "Aren't we all, in some way?"

And in that statement, Alwen witnessed another challenge issued. In the baited silence that followed, Madoc and Machreth held each other in a pointed and unyielding eye-lock so unabashed that the rest of the guests began to show discomfort. Ynyr openly glared at Machreth while Nerys pandered to Cerrigwen; Glain turned still as stone and Ariane stared at her plate. Emrys looked at Alwen, who in turn looked to Madoc.

Oddly, it was Cerrigwen who was flustered into interceding. "Never have we depended more on our leadership than we do now. We take heart in your guidance, Sovereign, and comfort in your constancy in these dark hours. But in the echo of your wisdom, Machreth's voice is raised in reminder of our pride and our honor, of the legacy stolen from us. These are important words, as well, Sovereign."

Alwen was aghast. Had Cerrigwen meant to avoid disgracing either man by praising them both, or had she meant to argue for Machreth against Madoc? Alwen had the distinct impression that alliances were being declared.

"When the one king is crowned and we are renewed in the eyes of the peoples, the mageborn will come to us again and the order shall be reborn." Emrys offered a diplomatic attempt to draw a stalemate. "That is the promise of the prophecy, the end we all desire, is it not?"

"Indeed." Machreth answered without breaking his eye-lock with Madoc. "That *is* the promise, unless we have withered into extinction before it can come to pass."

"Our number may be small, but there is life enough left in these halls to withstand whatever is to come." Alwen could not remain quiet any longer. If Cerrigwen's voice would be heard on this, so would hers. "Courage and devotion and conscience, as well."

"Hah!" Madoc blinked and sat back in his chair, waving a handful of fatty pork in her direction. "What say you to that, Machreth?"

The dark and measured gaze Machreth leveled upon Alwen gave her a chill. Whatever she may have thought of him before this night, she knew now beyond any doubt that Machreth was so dangerous that even Madoc might be no match for him. She could feel power seething from him, as if it strained at the confines of his bone and sinew.

He nodded slightly, as if to say he saw her for exactly who she was. "I would say there are those among us who have the heart and gut to hold their ground to the very end, no matter where they stand."

TEN

Glain clawed her way through the nightmare and awoke gasping for breath. Darkness greeted her bleary eyes as she stifled the shuddering sob in her throat. Her lungs were tamped with fear, and the harder she fought for air, the more panicked she became. Glain leapt from her bed and scuttled on bare feet across the room to fumble about her writing desk for the candle ends.

"If the dream be a vision, I would rather be blind," she whispered to the dark. Her hands shook as she willed the wicks to light. "If this omen be mine, I would rather forget it."

She would not forget. She could not. Glain knew the difference between a dream and a vision. Signs of things to come had been visited upon her in her sleep nearly all of her twenty-one years, giving her the ability to alter the minor fates should she choose. What had come to her this night was something more potent than a mere glimpse of some possible turn of events. This was an unavoidable, hideous horror. Too hideous to believe had she not known the revelations for the holy epistle they were. Glain had been given a warning from the gods.

"Blasted thing," she muttered helplessly at the lifeless wax. Just as she despaired, the wick sparked and the tallow smoldered. The small, defiant flame brought tears of gratitude to her eyes.

A shiver rattled her teeth. The nightdress was thin cover against the cold night air. Glain pressed the wax stem into a brass holder on the table and padded over the floor stones back to her bedclothes, trembling now from the draft. Wrapped in wool and goose down, she curled on the end of her cot and concentrated on the candle flame to help calm her nerves.

Some called her blessed to behold the specter of truths to come, and she supposed this was true. But what blessing could this haunting be? And if this was blessed, then what unbearable affliction must be a curse? Glain moaned aloud. If only she could wipe the images from her mind.

She did not fully grasp the vision beyond the unspeakable horror of armored giants with red eyes storming the castle gates astride vicious bull-like creatures with jaws that could crush a horse. She had seen their legions standing over the slaughtered remains of the Cad Nawdd, led to this gruesome victory by a man she knew, but whose face she could not see. Whatever it was, Glain knew the message was not intended for her alone. Nor could it wait on the morrow. Madoc needed to know now.

Glain searched the floor with her toes for her slippers and then reluctantly squirmed free of the blankets. The white finely woven wool of the acolyte's robe was warm enough to help her brave the cold halls. But still she shivered.

Glain slipped from her tiny room and crept carefully through the acolytes' quarters. Only the most senior of her rank—she and the three others who served the docent's floor—were afforded the privilege of a private chamber. This was to allow them to come and go as they were bidden, no matter the hour. The rest of the attendants shared a common apportioned porch lined with cots. If she were cautious, and quiet, no one would ever know she had gone.

The long, high-ceilinged corridors were well lit by oil lamps mounted in iron sconces. She made her way quickly down the passage from the annex through the castle foyer and skidded to a stop just outside the assembly hall. Voices.

Glain had expected everyone else to be asleep, but a meeting of strong minds and opinions over a pitcher of ale could stretch long into the night. Wagering that the men she heard in the hall were surely too ale sodden to notice the scurries of one small chamber attendant, Glain dashed past the open doorway, holding her breath all the way to the end of the corridor. As she reached the darkened annex that led to the service steps, Glain offered silent thanks for having avoided any witness to her mission.

"Oh!" Glain stumbled into the proctor's grasp as he stepped from the shadows at the foot of the stairs.

Machreth steadied her and then roughly set her back from him. "What business have you in these halls, at this hour?"

Glain was so startled she did not immediately notice the robed figure behind him. The tall, slender form shrank into the shadows and quickly disappeared up the stairs. A woman, she realized, but whom? Glain's sense of foreboding tingled but before she could see who Machreth's consort was, he distracted her.

"I asked what you are doing here," he snapped. "Have you nothing to say for yourself?"

His umbrage unnerved her, though she was tempted to ask the same of him. Surely he had no more business than she, skulking through the halls in the dead of night. A wizard of Machreth's rank using the back stairs was beyond odd. It was suspect. He was her superior, however, and not to be openly questioned by the likes of her.

"Well?"

Glain was dumbstruck. She was unable to pluck a single plausible excuse from her disheveled thoughts. She had not been summoned. Her primary duty was to Alwen, who had long since retired. Machreth would know that. If only she could only offer some explanation, he might well give her leave to pass. But Glain could think of no recourse other than to beg his pardon and return to her bed. "I—"

"There you are."

Machreth scowled over her head. "And what is *your* business here?"

Glain had never been so relieved. Some other subversive soul had rescued her from the brunt of Machreth's burning scrutiny. She mustered her wits and turned to see who owned the kindly voice of her deliverance, only to find herself staring into compassionate eyes and a devastatingly handsome face. Why ever, she wondered, would Alwen's son Rhys be looking for her?

"My friend and I are lacking a table maid to fill the ale pots." He shrugged apologetically. "This one will do, if you've no further use for her."

Unnerved by Rhys's steady gaze, Glain looked away. It wasn't the first time she had noticed him since he'd arrived, nor was it the first time she had noticed him noticing her, but she had never encountered him quite so closely before. Caught between Machreth's icy scowl and Rhys's infectious smile, Glain began to feel decidedly faint hearted.

Hospitality was one of the few customs even Machreth would not dare deny, no matter how unreasonable the request. Rhys was Alwen's son, after all, and due some special favor on that account. But it was unusually late. After several uncomfortable moments, Machreth narrowed his glare and cocked one stern eyebrow in warning to her, then bowed his head slightly to Rhys.

"Of course." Machreth was courteous, but hesitant. Suspicious, she feared. "Glain will lend you her service."

"Very good, then." Rhys gestured toward the assembly hall with a quick tilt of his head and a sly wink.

Glain was not so befuddled that she missed the opportunity to flee when it was offered. She slipped past Rhys to the corridor entrance, glad to have him between her and Machreth. He was a real champion, even if he did not know it. Because of Rhys she'd soon be on her way, once she saw to the ale pots.

"Step lively, and don't look back," Rhys mumbled. He took her elbow and hastened her round the corner. "He's still watching."

Glain was perplexed when he stopped midway to the assembly hall. "My Lord?"

"Hush, now." He glanced back to satisfy himself that Machreth had not followed. "Wait a minute or two and he'll go on about his own business. Then you'll be free to go about yours."

"But the ale pots." She was bewildered.

"Oh, that," Rhys grinned. "I made that bit up. I saw you sneak past the doorway and my curiosity got the better of me. When I caught up to you, you were already in the clutches of our sinister friend there. Seemed to me you needed a way out of a difficult situation."

Glain couldn't help the small smile that tugged at her lips. His dashing manner and cavalier humor were very appealing, and he still had her arm. "Indeed I did. Thank you."

"I am pleased to have been of service." He released her and offered a slight bow, but made no move to leave. "Now, just where are you off to in the middle of the night? Or shouldn't I ask?"

"For your own sake, you should not," she confessed. "I might actually tell you, and then you would be my conspirator. You've already aided and abetted my escape. That alone could be considered treasonous."

"As serious as all that, is it?" His mischievous grin mellowed to a soft, inviting smile that made her stomach quiver. "Well then. I won't keep you from your mysterious task. But when next we meet, please call me Rhys."

Her heart fluttered to think there could, or would, be a next meeting. "As you wish, My Lord."

He chuckled at her insistence on the formal address. Glain felt her cheeks burn with chagrin, but she couldn't quite bring herself to abandon decorum. It was as much her nature as her training, though Glain was not naive. Familiarity led to intimacy, sometimes too quickly. She was fully aware of the power of seduction and experienced enough to know when to yield—and when to resist.

Still, he had not moved and neither had she. It was as if they each were waiting for the other to speak, or act. Glain felt herself nearly enchanted in his presence, lured by the wild spirit in his eyes. That bold realization alone should have been enough to shame her into withdrawing, but she remained. It was the awkward silence that finally broke the spell.

"I must go." Glain spoke with far more conviction than she felt.

Rhys nodded slowly, still holding her with his gaze. "Good night, then, Glain."

He offered another polite bow and then went back to his friends. As soon as he'd left her sight, duty returned to mind with a sickening lurch in the pit of her stomach. She had lost precious time on distraction.

Glain scampered back down the corridor, berating herself for the dalliance. In all fairness, though, she could not fault herself. None of the young men of the order had so instantly and so strongly captured her interest as Rhys. Surely no woman should be condemned for succumbing to his charms.

As Glain turned at the juncture and started up the service steps, she suddenly remembered Machreth's clandestine companion. Foreboding unsettled her instincts anew. Glain hurried her step toward Madoc's chambers, more certain than ever that her nightmares were visions of horrors all too soon to unfold. What she would reveal to him would break his heart, but the truth could not be ignored.

ELEVEN

"For the first few days it was all too apparent how much exile had eroded my abilities." Alwen watched while Glain and the less experienced acolytes she had been training finished their lessons and tidied the spell room. She had discovered that teaching the more sophisticated spells like the concealment they had just learned was good practice for her, as well. "I felt more like a novice than a docent."

"It never showed," said Glain.

"You make it all look so effortless." Ariane, whose days were spent attempting to refine a handful of skills she should have long ago mastered, was still focusing intently on a pair of candlewicks. She was trying with all her might to extinguish the flames with her thoughts. "Cerrigwen says I am hopeless."

"You must breathe, Ariane. Close your eyes," Glain reminded her. "Now, *wish* it so. Imagine the flame already snuffed."

As she had familiarized herself with her new rank and responsibilities as both docent and proctor, Alwen had taken the opportunity over the last fortnight to witness the inner workings of the Stewardry. In particular, she had taken note of Glain's devotion to others, especially the tall, awkward young woman struggling before them. Ariane was plain in appearance and missing her fair share of natural grace. She had plenty of raw talent but lacked confidence. She simply needed someone to believe in her.

"Oh puddles," Ariane sighed. "I give up."

In the instant she let go of her breath, the candlewicks blinked out.

"Ariane." Glain laughed. "See what you've done?"

Ariane opened one eye, and then two. "I don't believe it."

"Huzzah for Ariane." Nerys was everything Ariane was not—clever, fair of face, and self-possessed. She had moved quickly through her studies and achieved the rank of acolyte well ahead of her peers. Nerys had also spent too much time in Cerrigwen's company and had adopted her hypercritical point of view. "She's finally actually earned the robe she wears."

"Better late than never," Ariane beamed, undaunted by her classmate's disdain.

The three founding disciplines upon which all magic was based were sorcery by spell, by gesture, and by thought. Mastery took years of practice and ascending levels of difficulty, but basic command of these three skills was expected by the end of a novice's first year. In the end, Ariane had been awarded the acolyte's robe on her many other merits, not the least of which were her years of unwavering dedication.

"You and I may both wear the white robe, Ariane, but we are hardly equals," Nerys complained.

Glain drew herself to her full bearing. As Madoc's trusted attendant, she stood above the other acolytes. "The same can be said of you and me."

"I simply make the point that favor should be earned through accomplishment, not granted out of pity."

"There are many ways to earn favor, Nerys," Glain bristled, "and just as many ways to lose it."

Nerys rolled her eyes. "It's late. Are we finished, then?"

Rivalry was to be expected, but so was respect for power and authority. Nerys needed to be reminded to offer it, and Glain needed to work harder at commanding it.

"Almost," Alwen said, considering an object lesson. "Perhaps you'd like to learn a new spell."

"A casting?" Nerys was only slightly intrigued. "Or an invocation?"

The distinctions between the two were often difficult to distinguish, but very important. A casting was the use of one's individual energy and power to affect something or someone outside oneself. An invocation was a summoning of an external force to work on behalf of the sorcerer who called it.

"Neither." Alwen thought a minute. "Both."

"How do you mean?" Ariane was uncharacteristically curious.

"You'll see." Alwen looked at Glain. "We'll need a twig or a feather, some sort of indicator."

Glain retrieved a raven's feather from the cupboard above the work table and placed it on the floor. "Will this do?"

"Perfect." Alwen stood over the feather. "This is called a finding. It is used to retrieve a thing lost or hidden."

"How mysterious," said Ariane. "Is it difficult?"

"It is easier when you know what you're looking for," Glain explained, "and can envision a particular object clearly."

"You know this spell?" Alwen was surprised.

Glain's smile belied a hint of mischief. "I've been known to misplace the keys to Madoc's private scriptorium, on occasion."

"Well then, let's try something a bit different." Alwen gestured around the room. "Let's see if you can find something unknown to you. The temple is riddled with secret places—false panels in closets, hidden drawers in chests, for example. Somewhere in this room there is at least one such keepsafe. And I would expect, after so many lifetimes, there is a lost button or rune stone about. It's simple, really. Follow the feather to find its location, and then call upon the object to reveal itself."

Alwen indicated the bag tied at her waist that held her personal implements. Each Steward carried the tools of their trade in a similar fashion. "Your wand, Glain."

Glain drew an intricately carved and highly polished hornbeam twig from the soft cloth pouch she carried. Every symbol and adornment on a Steward's wand had significance. Even the wood from which it was made had meaning. The wand was an extension of one's essence, and as each individual was entirely unique, so was the wand.

With grace and confidence, Glain stepped forward and extended her wand over the raven's quill. She began a circular flourish, concentrating on the feather, and focusing her mind on the task at hand.

"Open your mind to the possibilities," Alwen whispered. "If you think too hard on details, like color or shape or texture, the spell will work itself to your expectations. If you are envisioning a metal box, for instance, the spell will not find a wooden one."

If Glain had heard her, she gave no sign, but Alwen was aware of an unusual intensity within her. From a deep well of inner strength there rose great power that Alwen realized almost too late was newly drawn. Glain's sense of righteousness, her desire to put Nerys in her place, had given rise to something completely unexpected.

The quill quivered and then spun slowly clockwise, full circle once, twice, thrice, and then halfway around again. It stopped with the tip pointing toward the bookshelves beneath windows on the far wall of the scriptorium. Glain reached out with her free hand and a book, snugly cased, flew from the shelf and landed with a bang on the floor, opened at the center seam.

"A thistle." Ariane was amazed. Just as she bent to retrieve the dried flower from the book, a drawer in the work table next to her slid open, several cabinet doors were thrown open, and three stone bricks above the fireplace mantel popped out. A polished brass urn crashed to the floor, spewing its contents, and a rug slid sideways to reveal a recessed lock safe.

"The feather," Nerys whispered.

The raven's quill was spinning wild, rotating left then right, indicating randomly in every direction. Glain stood entranced, lost in the spell and apparently unaware of the chaos she had invoked. Alwen was growing concerned that Glain had unleashed forces she was not equipped to control.

"Glain," she cautioned, just as one of the massive thunderstone floor tiles shifted beneath their feet. "Stop!"

Alwen's stern command broke through Glain's concentration, interrupting the bind between the sorceress and the spell. The commotion stilled, and a stunned silence settled on the room.

"Great gods!" Ariane's mouth fell open. "What was that?"

"All right, ladies," Alwen said, watching Glain make a gradual return to herself. "That will be enough for tonight."

Nerys was already halfway to the door, visibly shaken. Ariane hesitated a moment, awestruck, but also curious. A terse nod sent Ariane on her way, and Alwen turned her attention to Glain.

"Well," she said kindly, taking Glain by the shoulders. "Such mighty magic from such a tiny witch."

Glain looked up, pale and apologetic. "I guess I made a mess of things."

"We'll worry about that later." Alwen ushered Glain toward the door. "What happened?"

Glain sighed. "I've worked that spell many times before, but never like this."

"Perhaps you were trying too hard?" Alwen prodded. She already knew why it had all gone awry but she wanted to be sure that Glain knew as well.

Glain stopped in the hallway outside the scriptorium and faced Alwen with her hands laced in a contrite knot in front of her. "I was trying to prove a point."

"A display of power can be very effective," Alwen counseled. "At the right time, in the right place, and for the right reason."

"I was angry."

A difficult admission for Glain, no doubt, but Alwen was relieved to hear it. "Yes, you were," she said. "Anger is a potent fuel. And quite dangerous when misused."

"Nerys vexes me," Glain frowned. "I wish she cared more for others and less for herself. I wish she had a better sense of her place." Glain shook her head. "I wish I trusted her more."

"Well-meant wishes." Alwen was reminded of her own challenges with Cerrigwen and felt great empathy for Glain. "Sometimes that is all we can do. That, and provide an admirable example."

Glain nodded, clearly humbled. "I can do better."

"You have great talent, and wisdom beyond your years. Have faith in your insight, but temper your judgments with that compassion you've wished on Nerys. Now, get some rest." Alwen smiled. "Tomorrow is a new beginning."

Alwen watched Glain disappear down the stairs and returned to her rooms. So late was the hour that the temple had slipped into the dead silence of deep slumber, and she was eager to follow. She hung her robe on the bedpost and sat on the edge of the bed to tug off her boots and free her feet from the stranglehold of woolen hose.

One day ended so near to the dawning of the next these past two weeks that she had scarcely noted the passage of time. Alwen was exhausted. Her mind was so overwhelmed and overworked that her brain felt bruised.

Glain had raised the question of loyalties, something that concerned Alwen more and more. Daily discussions with Madoc on matters of the Stewardry had made her more mindful of the risks they all faced. And, like it or not, underlying the oath every Steward owed the order were individual alliances and ambitions. How these inner power struggles would influence events was impossible to tell. This was a time for unity, and Alwen was beginning to wonder how strong the ties that held their world together really were. Nights like these she missed Norvik, and Bledig.

A soft rap preceded the creaking of the outer chamber door. "Pardon, Mistress," Glain whispered from the hall. "Are you still awake?"

Alwen padded barefoot across the darkened sitting room to the doorway. "What is it?"

Rhys stepped around Glain. "I know it's late, but I didn't know when else to come."

"Of course." Alwen beckoned him in. Glain excused herself, closing the door as she left. "There isn't much of a fire, but I think the aleberry will still be warm."

Rhys made straight for the hearth and busied himself stoking a blaze while Alwen crossed the room to retrieve two silver cups from the desk under the window. Her son seemed changed to her. It struck her then that it had been days since she'd seen him, even longer since they'd exchanged more than a passing greeting.

"Sit with me." Alwen sat on one end of the divan, leaving ample room for Rhys. She was glad he'd come, no matter what had brought him. "Bring the pot. We'll drink while we chat."

Rather than join her on the sofa, Rhys settled instead on the hearth stone, across from her. Alwen handed over the cups and waited while he plucked the aleberry pot from the coals and poured. "Are you well? You must be worn from your training. Fergus can be a task master."

Rhys nodded as he studied his cup, his brow drawn in pensive lines and his jaw taut with determination. Alwen noted an air of command and self-assuredness about him that reminded her of Bledig. The reflection brought an instant sadness. She missed him.

"The Cad Nawdd is a disciplined regiment." She continued with what should pass as casual conversation. "More reliant upon structure than the ranks you're accustomed to."

Rhys emptied his cup in one full swallow. "It is unlike what I've known," he said as he poured another draught. His tone was cavalier, as if the complete rearrangement of his life had been a minor inconvenience. "I feel useful."

Alwen heard the truth underlying the words. He was not as comfortable or as confident as he professed, but he did impress her as a man more self-possessed. She recalled their conversation in Norvik months before and her philosophizing on the endless opportunities and inescapable consequences of change. While this new life had brought Alwen more fulfillment than she had ever imagined, she had worried that the same might not be true for her son. However, it was clear that Rhys had, at the very least, come to some greater understanding of himself. How she admired this son of hers.

"I had not realized until this very moment how much I have missed your company."

Rhys stretched his legs out before him and reclined on his free arm. "Oh, I'd say you've missed a great deal more than my comings and goings."

Alwen squinted sidelong at him. "How do you mean?"

He smirked at her over the rim of his cup, one eyebrow arched, and made her wait while he sipped. "Take Eirlys, for instance."

"Yes?" she asked. "What of her?"

"Do you know where she is?"

"Asleep in her bed," Alwen answered, suddenly not at all sure. It was a rare day anymore that she and her daughter met in waking hours. Eirlys took very little interest in the order or the training of Stewards, preferring to spend her days wandering the compound, discovering the magic of her surroundings in her own way.

"She should be." Rhys had a wicked gleam in his eye, the look of a boy about to spill his sister's secrets. "She and Odwain have taken to late-night trysts, when they think no one is watching."

Alwen blew a sigh of exasperation and Rhys's delighted expression fizzled into contrition. "And just how long has this been going on?"

"It's innocent, really." Rhys straightened his posture and his attitude as he attempted to explain. "Nothing for you to fuss over, at least not as yet. To be fair, I cannot bring myself to fault them for it. Fergus keeps all of the guardsmen at drill from sunup 'til dusk, and he holds a taut rein after hours."

Alwen took a moment to examine her son and his earnestness, realizing at last that the change she had noted in his demeanor was maturity. Rhys had come to her on family business, acting as the head of his house. Over the years, it had been Alwen who had taken the role in Bledig's absences, but much had changed since their arrival at the temple. It appeared that Rhys, of his own volition, had taken up where she had left off.

"I suppose we can hardly begrudge them a few stolen moments," she conceded, making a mental note to consult Madoc's scrying stone at regular intervals on her daughter's whereabouts. "It seems you have things well in hand. I trust you'd have come to me sooner had you any reason to be concerned."

"Yes," he said. "I would. I will."

Despite his assurances she sensed there was more. *What now,* she wondered.

"Eirlys has all but given up on her wedding plans," he hedged. "But I suppose that cannot be helped."

What Rhys meant but would not say was that Eirlys had given up on her father. Alwen sent her feathered friends as far as they would go on her daily spirit-farings, hoping to catch a glimpse of Bledig's approach. So far, in vain. Even Madoc's scrying stone had failed her.

"Eirlys has waited long enough," she decided. "I will speak to Finn, and then to Fergus. We may not be able to manage an Obotrite ritual, but the Stewardry has its own traditions."

Rhys picked up the pot and bent forward to pour for her. "But have you the time to see to a wedding? There are, after all, more important things."

"Not to Eirlys," Alwen smiled. "I'll see to it straightaway. High sorceress and Mistress of the Realms I may be, but I am mother too."

"You mustn't worry overmuch about mothering." Rhys was quick to assure her. "We are well provided for here, and your first duty is to Madoc now."

Rhys, it seemed, had come under the influence of the Cad Nawdd in more than just soldiering ways. "I can well enough see to my own needs."

He winked at her over the rim of his cup. "And Odwain is more than willing to see to any need Eirlys may have."

Alwen's eyes popped wide at the bawdy thoughts behind his flip remark. "Barracks talk, Rhys? In *my* chambers?"

Dismay and regret washed across her son's face. Rhys glanced at his toes. "I didn't mean that as it sounded."

"Ah, but you did," Alwen chided.

"Forgive me, Mistress." The formal address sounded stilted, coming from Rhys, though a grin widened his mouth. "I had forgot to whom I was speaking."

"Finish your drink," she smiled. Alwen surprised herself with her imperious attitude. Position and authority had put her in the habit of expecting certain protocol, but this was not a tactic she wished to employ in private conversation with her son.

"As I said, everything is different." Rhys saluted her with his cup. "Especially you."

Alwen settled deeper into the cushions on the divan, beginning to enjoy the familiarity between them. "I am the same person I have always been."

Rhys stared at her, as if assessing her anew. "You are changed. Just how many titles do you carry now?"

"I've lost count," she smiled. "Does it matter, really?"

"Not so much to me. But I have seen how the others revere you. *That* is truly impressive." Rhys emptied the last of the ale-berry into their glasses and stretched himself lengthwise at her feet. "Still, it has not been easy for you."

Such a profound observation, she marveled, and yet so entirely inadequate. Rhys could not possibly understand the depth and breadth of the simple truth he had uttered, though he offered it with such empathy that Alwen's heart ached in response. It had not been easy, but to say as much would be to show weakness in a time when a strong example was so needed. However, to deny it only gave the burden more weight and she was growing weary of the load. Alwen upended her cup and decided to give voice to her most secret desire. "I so wish your father was here."

TWELVE

"He underestimates you."

"He does not know me." Cerrigwen was still resistant. "Madoc will come to recognize my strengths. I will have my reward."

"Then it is *you* who underestimates *him*," Machreth warned. "Your time has passed, Cerrigwen. He has already dismissed you."

"He has dismissed you, as well," she countered.

"Yes." Machreth smiled grimly. "That was to be expected. From the moment I first questioned his plans my time was measured. He keeps me close, though, in hopes I may yet be controlled. But you he still trusts."

"And this trust is something you wish to exploit," she challenged. Her eyes gleamed with suspicion, and something else he couldn't yet discern.

"Of course." Machreth circled her and slid his hands around her waist from behind. Cerrigwen tensed and trembled at his touch. From disgust as much as desire, he suspected. "To our mutual advantage."

"I can well imagine how you may benefit from my help," she said. "But how do you propose it will benefit me?"

Cerrigwen was not yet convinced of his potential, of his power. He grabbed her roughly by one wrist and wrenched her around to face him. "Take care that you do not underestimate *me*," he snarled. "Or you will find yourself buried in the ruins of this place alongside Madoc and the rest of his sheep."

Her eyes snapped wide with surprise as she recoiled from the force of his grip. Machreth saw uncertainty, but not the fear he expected. "I am more dangerous than you could ever imagine, Cerrigwen. Either you are with me, or against me. The choice is yours."

He waited, watching the conflict in her eyes. It was always the same. She resisted and he persisted, but that was all part of the game.

He began to circle the room, hands clasped at his back, to give her time to consider him carefully. "I offer you the only chance you have at true power. I offer you the Stewardry, Cerrigwen, to rule at my side. Take it, or not. It makes little difference to me.

"And if not you..." He shrugged. "Then someone else will happen along, eventually. I have waited this long for a worthy consort. I can wait longer, if I must. Pity, though. You *are* of an exceptional breed."

Machreth stopped directly in front of her and lifted her chin with his forefinger until her gaze met his. He almost smiled. There it was—a glimmer of panic in her eyes. Nothing distressed Cerrigwen more than being overlooked or forgotten.

He gentled his expression and his tone. "Do not misunderstand my frustration, Cerrigwen. It is you that I want, but there is no time to trifle with insecurities. I can no longer abide your wavering. I cannot afford the distraction. If I cannot rely upon you, then I must find someone who is truly devoted, truly ready for the greatness I can bestow. I must be prepared to seize opportunity."

Her lips trembled, but her eyes had brightened. "What opportunity?"

Machreth rewarded her with his smile and slid his hands around her waist. "Madoc may be stubborn and set in his ways, but he is no fool. He sees the end of his days, to be sure. Already he takes measures to protect his legacy. Sooner or later, he must reveal his secrets."

"Yes." Her breathing became ragged as he turned her in his arms and pulled her against him. Soon her spine would buckle and her hips would sway. She would be ripe, and pliant. "But he will not reveal them to me."

"No. Not directly." He lifted the long tresses from her shoulders and gently nipped the tender flesh at the nape of her neck. Cerrigwen moaned with the agony of need. How easily she was seduced. It was such an obvious guile, or at least, it should have been. She was just too desperate to care.

"But if you are very vigilant, you will see when and to whom he does. No one suspects you. Your lurking will not be noticed, and once you have what I must know, we will take what is ours."

"You ask me to betray him, Machreth." She pulled away from him, but only slightly, an admirable attempt to show him she was still in control. Her allegiance did not come easily. "You ask too much."

"Yes," he admitted. "I ask a great deal. But you must understand. He leads us to ruin. We are saving him from himself as much as we are saving ourselves."

"But this is treason," she whispered.

"So it is." Machreth stepped back and held out his hand. "You will have everything you have ever wanted, Cerrigwen. I swear I will see to it, if you will only let me."

Machreth smiled as ambition and lust and greed stripped her of the few remaining shreds of her loyalty to Madoc. Cerrigwen took his hand and Machreth led her to his bed. Her allegiance was to him now.

* * *

First light crept over the horizon and reached earthward with its shimmering tendrils. Alwen stood in quiet reverence at the open window as the subtle glow encroached on the night and then overwhelmed the blackness in a sudden rush. The sky came alive with color.

A flutter of feathers tempted her as a hawk's cry echoed against the stillness. Alwen had no more reason to expect to find Bledig on the road to Pwll today than any day before, but she could not deny herself the pleasure of a spirit-faring. The hawk did not seem to mind her intrusion, nor did he object when she gently prodded him on a course that would carry them both along the byway. He took a meandering route, flittering through the open grounds of the temple before skimming the trees of the White Woods as he vaulted over the tiny town of Pwll. Growing impatient, Alwen urged the bird to abandon his leisurely loop around the outskirts and fly directly northeast along the main road.

No more than two furlongs beyond the last of the village farms, a small band of riders entered the hawk's field of view. As the hawk approached, the horsemen took on familiar form. Alwen felt her soul smile and instantly wished her wandering mind back within her own form.

Her consciousness returned to her body, only to collide with the physical sensations her emotions had unleashed. Alwen gripped the dressing table with both hands to steady her wobbly legs. It was suddenly hard to draw air. Several slow, deep breaths brought her rampant heartbeat under control. An unsteady step toward the divan brought Alwen face-to-face with the looking glass above the hearth. There she met the reflection of a woman overcome, with eager eyes and cheeks flushed with anticipation.

Alwen forced herself to take a few moments' pause, reminding herself of her station. This was not so free a place as Norvik, nor was she so free a woman. Her public comportment must project a dignified, even royal profile no matter how flustered she felt.

"Find your head," she commanded herself.

Alwen concentrated on slowing her impetuous urges, focusing on the image in the mirror until the stately Mistress returned. Once confident of her composure, Alwen called for Glain.

"Mistress?" The girl had become a welcome companion and confidante, but she still insisted on formality.

"We have visitors."

"Yes, indeed. Madoc has already sent an escort to guide them through the veil."

"I should have known." She was reminded that he was as fond of his scrying stone as she was of her morning sojourns. Alwen smoothed her hair and straightened her skirts. "Am I presentable?"

Glain regarded her briefly with a critical eye. "You are, as always."

"Bring me my cloak, would you?"

Glain helped her on with her the robe and fastened the chain. "Shall I announce you?"

"That won't be necessary."

Sensing that the riders were near, she brushed past a most astonished Glain and threw open the door. Lively steps delivered her to the temple vestibule just as a Cad Nawdd escort ushered the dozen or so Obotrite warriors into the castle commons. A crowd of acolytes had already gathered to see these swarthy men from a far-off land. They were unkempt and unrefined, not at all like the uniformed soldiers of the castle guard. But at this moment Alwen could not imagine any men more appealing than these, especially their chieftain.

Bledig Rhi stood out among his tribesmen, not because he rode at the head of their ranks, but because he truly led them. He was tall and broad, but it wasn't his size or his handsome looks that drew the respect and admiration of his men. Bledig carried his character as though it were a standard emblazoned with the colors of courage and honor and command.

Fergus stepped forward to greet Bledig as he and his men were presented. "What brings you all this way, you old mongrel?"

"I've come for my boy, and my women!" Bledig vaulted from his horse and landed solid on the ground. "I'd say I was glad to see you, MacDonagh, but you'd call me a liar."

Something between a sneer and a smile crossed Fergus's face as he offered Bledig his hand. "You're as insufferable as ever, but nonetheless welcome. Your men as well."

Bledig chuckled at Fergus as he held the handclasp, offering at least the appearance of admiration. An odd sort of rivalry stood between them, each man possessive of his own role in Alwen's life, all the while knowing there was no choice but to accept the other. They had come to terms after so many years, and there couldn't help but be a hint of affection between the insults. At the very least, Bledig and Fergus had come to respect one another.

Alwen swiped her dewy palms on her skirts as she waited to be acknowledged. Her heart raced, doubling and then redoubling its wild pounding. Finally, Bledig let loose of Fergus's grip and turned his irresistible charm and disarming smile in search of her.

"Alwen!"

Steady. She centered herself, mindful that the eyes of the crowd were on her, as well. "You are overdue, Wolf King."

Bledig swung toward the sound of her voice. His eyes riveted upon her with such unbridled ardor that Alwen's heart nearly folded in on itself. Longing and relief flooded her eyes with tears that threatened to undo her fragile calm, but she required herself to retain the decorum the novitiate would expect.

"I am." He offered her an abject nod, but his gaze never left her. "Better late than lost, though, don't you agree?"

"I do." Alwen fought the wild impulse to run to him. Such a noble beast was her barbarian king. Even haggard and weather beaten, Bledig was still the most handsome man she had ever seen. "Though I caution you against such an inconsiderate delay in the future."

"You do, do you?" Bledig couldn't contain the grin tugging at his lips any more than she could maintain her air of authority. "Don't I always come?"

"Yes." She allowed the smile to surface. "Eventually."

Bledig started toward her then, with swift and determined strides. His closeness set her skin afire. He was a comfort far too long denied her.

Just as he arrived at the first step, and just short of her reach, a wild-haired faerie child flew through the crowd and straight into her father's arms. "Poppa!"

Bledig howled with delight, swallowing Eirlys in his big, brawny hug. His eyes glistened with joy and fatherly pride so heartfelt that Alwen could barely stand to open her senses to his emotions. Her own feelings were already more than she could bear. As glad as she was for her daughter's happiness, Alwen was anxious to have him to herself.

At long last, Bledig kissed Eirlys on the top of her head and set her aside. He bounded up the steps, and before Alwen could react, she found herself in his arms. His touch sent waves of sensation shivering through her. What was left of her composure melted in a blaze of desire, and Alwen succumbed to his embrace, digging her fingers deep into the taut muscle beneath the shirt cloth and fur cape on his back.

Bledig pulled Alwen closer, cinching one arm tightly about her waist while the fingers of his other hand gripped the hair at the nape of her neck. The heat of his breath against her ear made her knees weak. "I expected you to wait."

"I know," Alwen sighed with regret. "It could not be helped."

A low, frustrated growl rumbled in his throat as he relaxed his hold on her and pulled away to look into her eyes. "I have been too long without the sweet scent of you on my bedclothes, Alwen."

She felt herself smiling at the intimation in his words and the thought of his skin against hers. "It is always too long, Bledig, whether it be a day or a year."

He nodded, tracing his fingertips along her jaw and across her lips before taking her chin between his forefinger and thumb.

Alwen gazed at his well-seasoned face, revisiting the fine lines around his dark green eyes and noticing there was now more salt than pepper in his beard. His tousled ebon mane was a bit grayer at the temples, but he was none the worse for wear. Whatever it was that had held him up, he was safe, and that was all that mattered. Alwen slid her hands around his neck, reassured enough to confess her fears. "You worried me."

Bledig sighed in reply to her quiet admission and bent to kiss her. "It could not be helped."

Her lips parted, inviting Bledig to reclaim her mouth just as he would reclaim the rest of her once they were alone. The sinew beneath his skin quivered as their tongues entwined, his body anticipating the more intimate coupling to follow. Alwen found his arousal so intoxicating that she no longer cared who witnessed their passion. She sacrificed restraint to the power of the kiss, a willing captive to Bledig's unrelenting hold. His mere presence instantly quelled the strain of time and distance and uncertainty, once again grounding her with the security of knowing she was loved.

"Unhand my mother, you scoundrel."

Bledig broke the kiss to glance over her head at his son and flashed a grin. Alwen caught the pride that shone in his eyes and turned in his arms to watch the playful banter. "And who are you to call me out, boy?"

"I am the son of Bledig Rhi," Rhys boasted. "Surely you've heard of him."

Bledig chuckled. "That old goat?"

"He's more than a match for the likes of you," Rhys answered. "And that's his woman you've got hold of."

"Your mother answers to no man, lad." Bledig squeezed her arms. "And your father will be the first to admit it, though he'll defend to the death his claim to *be* the first." He released her and stepped forward to seize Rhys. "Come here."

Such a great affection and respect held father and son together that it filled her heart near to bursting just to witness her men embrace. Rhys needed his father as much as Eirlys, and from the looks of things, Bledig was in need of being needed. He was devoted to his family, and he was the only person outside the Stewardry that Alwen had ever relied upon. It did her good to see that, though duty and distance could separate them, neither had the power to alter the bonds between them.

Bledig clapped his son hard on the back and finally let him go. Rhys had sense enough to know he had worn out his welcome for the time being and wisely stepped aside.

"Your well-mannered estate looks to have been overrun by thugs," said Bledig, referring to his men. He surveyed the courtyard and outbuildings, taking note of the unfamiliar surroundings as he took Alwen's hand. "They are a raw bunch for such a refined people."

"You and your riders are a welcome sight." Alwen threaded her fingers through his and led him toward the temple vestibule. "I am so grateful you've come."

Bledig chuckled. "Would you like to show me just how grateful?"

Alwen felt herself blush. After all these years, he could still catch her off-kilter. "You are a rogue, Bledig."

He stopped short and turned to face her, his expression sobering as he assessed her more closely. Alwen tried to guess Bledig's thoughts, sensing unease in him. Rhys had called her changed, and so she was. In these many weeks since leaving Norvik, Alwen had fashioned herself into a sturdier version, stronger and more self-sustaining. Alwen wondered what he would see in her now.

"The robe is regal," Bledig said, fingering the cowl. "It suits you."

"Do you think me regal, then?" she teased. She had not considered how Bledig might receive her newness. "Or is it just that the color complements my eyes?"

"Both." He took her hands in his and looked directly into her eyes, as if he expected to glean some deeper sense of who she had become. "You must have a tale or two to tell."

"I do," she admitted, "though that can wait."

"Ah, but the question is"—he smiled down at her—"can you?"

Alwen was relieved to see his casual cheer had returned. "I've already waited far too long. Come."

THIRTEEN

"So," Bledig marveled, glancing about at the architecture and ancient appointments along the castle halls. "This grand monstrosity is your home?"

"It is." Alwen led him through the halls and up the stairs, pausing at the entrance to her rooms.

"I see." Bledig scanned the colorful arched ceilings artfully adorned with centuries-old frescoes depicting the history of the Stewardry. Finally, he brought his curious gaze to rest on the massive carved oak door that guarded her chambers. "And this is where you sleep?"

"It is." Alwen smiled at his less than subtle query.

"Well then." He reached around her to yank the latch and shove open the door. "I believe you offered me your gratitude."

"Stay yourself, barbarian." Alwen held her ground at the threshold, returning his frustrated scowl with a coy smile. "These are the private chambers of a high sorceress and Mistress of the Realms, no less. I've not yet granted you entry."

As he recognized the game, Bledig's annoyance quickly melted into amusement. He cupped her chin in his palm and peered at her with playful suspicion. "Of course, tribute is expected."

"Yes," she taunted. "And the tithe is high. Have you the means?"

Bledig grinned. "Name your price, Mistress."

"I'll settle for another kiss."

"Is that all?"

Alwen stretched onto her toes to tease his lips with hers. For several heartbeats, she savored his taste, suspending the moment so anticipation could work its own magic. The familiar scent of his maleness mingled with the heat of his breath was dizzying.

"No," she whispered.

Bledig responded like a hungry beast unleashed. Seizing her with an embrace that lifted her feet from the floor, he gave her the kiss she asked for—fierce and devouring.

"Bledig," she murmured against his teeth. If the sound of her voice pierced the haze of his passion, it only served to inspire him. His arms cinched tighter.

"Bledig," Alwen urged. "Let me breathe."

His grasp relaxed just enough for her to regain her feet and let her lungs expand. "How long do you intend to keep me waiting in this hall?"

Alwen slid her hand under his shirt and coiled her fingers into the fur on his chest. The thick sinew of Bledig's arousal quivered against her belly, insisting. She hadn't the strength to hold him off any longer, no matter how delicious the seduction. It had been far too long.

"The kiss will do." Alwen stepped back and gestured into her rooms with exaggerated ceremony. "You may enter."

Bledig's grin made her blush. "Indeed."

"Again, you presume." Alwen closed the door before crossing to the curtained alcove where she slept. She released the chain clasp of her cloak and let it slide from her shoulders. "I have only yet permitted you past the door."

Bledig cast an appraising glance around her quarters, familiarizing himself with the surroundings, particularly the bed, before turning his complete attention to her. "Well, woman, what are you waiting for?"

Alwen couldn't help but be unnerved by his brashness, but it was this self-assuredness that so aroused her. That, among other things. Under the burn of his gaze, she unhooked the gilt belt that cinched the waist of the simple beige silk gown she wore beneath her robe and then unlaced the ribbon that anchored the sheer fabric in loose gathers about her shoulders and bosom.

Bledig pulled off his boots and loosed the fur cape he wore, taking in every movement as she undressed and all the while stripping the layers of shirt cloth and leggings from his own body.

She had almost forgotten how good it was to be Bledig's woman. In Bledig's bed, he was master. This appealed to her more than ever, especially in this place where the fate of the entire world turned on the decisions she made. Alwen had not realized how much she had been suffering under the weight of responsibility until now. But here, in the privacy of her chambers, she could cast off duty and majesty and allow Bledig to tend to her just as he always had—by taking command of her body and her needs. In fact, he would demand it.

As if he had heard her, Bledig took control of the moment. He strode across the sitting room to her bedside, pausing briefly to admire Alwen's entire form before reaching for her. In a single well-practiced swoop, Bledig snared her at the waist with warm, firm hands and drew her against him. Alwen gave herself over to the dizzying effects of his touch, allowing each wonderful sensation to swallow her whole.

Bledig brought her with him as he backed onto the bed, pulling her on top of him to better reach the rest of her and still have her mouth. His hands began to rove in an unhurried retracing of fondly remembered travels. Captive to his tongue and completely enthralled by his touch, Alwen lay prone and pliant against his torso as his palms pressed firmly into her flesh and stroked the length of her back from shoulders to hips. She groaned aloud.

"I lie awake nights aching to hear you sigh in want of me," Bledig muttered between gentle nibbles at her lips. His hands slid over the curve of her hind to clasp her buttocks and urge her lower on his frame. "You do want me. Don't you."

He shifted his weight slightly, which brought the tip of his rigid shaft to throb and probe against her. Every muscle in her body quivered, waiting.

"Say it," Bledig rasped. "I want to hear you say you want me."

His knees bent and he pressed himself into her just enough to make her squirm toward him, and then caught her hips to keep her from satisfying herself. The sensation forced Alwen to gasp.

"Tell me," he demanded.

Alwen wilted onto him and buried her face in his neck. "I want you, Bledig," she sighed in desperation.

With agonizing and deliberate ease, Bledig entered her firmly but slowly, pushing deeply until he could go no farther. Alwen cried out as sparks of sensation flared and rippled through her like a comet's tail flaming the sky. He withdrew and then plunged inside of her again, harder this time. She clung to him and bucked wildly against his thrusts. Incited by her writhing, Bledig's rhythm surged and quickened in response to hers while he held her securely against him.

Alwen felt vaulted outside of herself. An intense heat began to smolder in her loins, burgeoning and receding until it finally erupted in an enormous fiery flash. Overwhelmed, Alwen collapsed against his chest, sobbing.

Bledig seized hold of her hips and dug fiercely into the flesh, heaving into her with his own urgency, stronger and faster until he tensed in anticipation. She felt his body shudder as he erupted with a deep groan of release. His satisfaction gratified her, though her tears still drenched the wiry curls on his chest.

His want appeased, Bledig was suddenly aware of her trembling. "Well now," he murmured, "what's this?"

Every ounce of self-control had abandoned her, leaving Alwen powerless to force the tears to subside. Bledig wrapped his arms around her in answer to her cascade of emotion, his fingers combing gently through her hair as he tried to soothe her.

"It's all right, Alwen. It's been too long, that's all," he said. "Cry or laugh or fight your way to me, if you have to, but come to me. I will always be waiting."

Bledig reached across her to tug the bedclothes over them both and then returned to coddling her. He nuzzled her neck and sighed quietly against her ear. "I love you, woman. I hope you know that by now."

She knew. She always had, but the words, spoken so earnestly and with such conviction, gave her heart reassurance she hadn't realized she'd lacked. Alwen could not yet find the voice to say she loved him, too. Instead, she nestled even more deeply into his embrace and gave him the one thing he coveted even more—her absolute reliance upon his comfort.

"So," Bledig said softly as she nestled contentedly in his brawny arms. "If there's tales to tell, I'm more inclined to listen now."

Alwen smiled to herself and rested her cheek against his shoulder. What a powerful force love was. It amazed her still, even after twenty years. In a matter of moments, it was as if the months they'd spent apart had never been. But in truth, there was much to share. Where to begin?

Before she could collect her thoughts, Eirlys burst through the door that linked the antechamber to Alwen's rooms and stood frozen in place just inside, staring wide-eyed at her parents. The blank, befuddled gawk quickly turned to giggling.

"Oh!" she said. "Oh, my."

"Whatever it is, it had better be good and you had better be quick about making it known," Bledig barked at her.

"You do realize, don't you," she lectured, crossing her arms over her chest, "that it is still daylight outside."

"And what of it?" he growled.

Eirlys laughed at him. "You are shameless, both of you."

Bledig sighed thickly, scratching impatiently at his nose. Eirlys was sorely wearing on his nerves. "Now say what it is you came to say."

For all her cheek, Eirlys was quick to know when she'd reached the bounds of tolerance, especially with her father. "Well," she offered, "there's to be a feast in your honor. That's all."

Bledig, for all his bluster, was quick to know what mattered most to those he loved. He never missed it, ever. It was a truly amazing talent, but then, Bledig had his own sort of magic. Of sprite and spriggan and wicked though it often was, Alwen smiled to herself.

He raised himself up on one elbow to look at his daughter. "Am I to understand, then, that you will have a hand in this meal?"

Eirlys beamed with pride. The girl had a way with palatable delights, a gift of her faerie folk. She was an extraordinary cook, and her father had an extraordinarily appreciative appetite. "Yes, I do," she announced. "Both hands, even."

Bledig grinned at her. "Well then, I'll look forward to it. I don't think I've had a meal worth mentioning since the last one you made for me, and that's been so long I can hardly recall."

Eirlys peered curiously at them both. "Are you going to stay in here all day?"

Bledig flopped back to the bed and growled in exasperation. "By all the gods, girl. Will you just get out?"

"All right then," she sassed. Eirlys turned as she pulled the door shut, unable to resist herself. "But just imagine the tongue wagging when you finally show yourselves."

Alwen had to smile. "It makes her happy to please you."

Bledig nodded and then suddenly he frowned, as if he'd been reminded of some terrible thought. "Now, what is it you wanted to say?"

Many things quickly came to mind, but the news she most needed to give him gave her pause. Alwen wondered a minute how best to deliver it.

"Well?" he prodded, turning onto his side to face her. "Out with it."

"Odwain will be asking to speak with you."

Bledig's frown deepened. "And what would Odwain be wanting of me?"

Alwen smiled at his befuddlement, hoping to ease the blow with a gentle tone. "I'm afraid he intends to marry your daughter."

"*My* daughter? You can't be serious."

"Odwain is quite serious."

"Ha!" Bledig snorted. "He stands about as good a chance as horseshit sliding uphill."

"Now, Bledig. If you're half the man I know you to be, you'll let the boy prove himself to you. Besides," she teased, "Rhys has already approved."

"Passing muster with Rhys comes nowhere near earning my favor," he grumbled. "We shall see."

"Please, Bledig. As if you would refuse that girl anything."

He grinned a bit sheepishly. "True enough, but I won't give in as easily on this as you might think. Odwain will still have to show me his mettle. But," he said, softened by fatherly affection, "if Eirlys wants him, he must have more merit than I've credited him."

"He loves her," Alwen said. "I am glad to see both Eirlys and Rhys happy here. It was a lot to ask, uprooting them from their homes. This is a new land, a new life. They tell me it isn't so, but I'm sure it has not been easy for either of them."

"Love demands sacrifice, Alwen. It's the price we pay for the privilege and any man or woman worth a damn will pay it with pride and pleasure."

"A lovely sentiment, Bledig, but I wonder if you will still feel so generous once you fully understand what I've got you into."

"Perhaps you should do me the favor of allowing me to determine my own mind on the matter."

"The ways of the Stewardry are mysterious, even deadly," she counseled. "There are things you will be hard pressed to understand."

"Come now," he scoffed. "Surely you cannot think me so green, Alwen. Have you forgotten my mother's faerie blood?"

"Of course not." He had no idea who she had become or what she faced. "But this is not your world."

Bledig was still for some time, staring intently at her. Alwen waited. She had not meant to offend him, but she did not like that he took her cautions so lightly. It seemed the best strategy to just keep silent and let the tension pass.

"So tell me, Alwen. What use will I be to you here?"

An unexpected statement, coming from Bledig. In all the years she'd known him, Alwen had never seen Bledig Rhi tentative about anything, least of all her need of him. The thought that he might question his worth to her hurt her heart. "I have yet to know what my destiny holds, but I do know I cannot face it alone."

"Perhaps you will find your destiny does not include me."

"Bledig, my love," she said, tracing his nose with her fingertip. "There can be no destiny for me without you."

"Welcome words." He looked more closely at her, still sobered by some nagging thought. "But we shall see."

She smiled into his pensive green eyes, thinking how much she loved this man. "Shall we, then?"

"Shall we what?"

Alwen nestled against him. "Stay in here all day."

FOURTEEN

"**O**f all the hell-fired hog swill," Fergus blustered, clutching a muck rake in each hand as he balanced on one foot to examine the other.

Rhys and Odwain were both startled around by the bark. Fergus's highland brogue happened in and out of his speech, especially when he was irked. And irked he was.

Fergus had plodded right through a pile of manure, and Rhys stifled the giant guffaw rising in his throat. The stable hands had taken the horses to water and feed, but the giant Frisian steeds had left behind the remnants of an earlier meal. "Looks like the grounds are as fouled as your mood, Fergus."

Fergus glared at Rhys as he scraped his boot clean with the teeth of one rake, muttering in the strange language used by the native folk in these parts. "I'll be deviled and damned before I'll ever understand your father's appeal, Rhys. He and his ruffians show themselves whenever they please, and everyone cheers and applauds. Good thing I haven't to worry about making them fit for the Cad Nawdd. I doubt even I could make honest soldiers of his thieves."

Rhys's eyebrows shot up in indignation. Fergus often forgot himself. "Remember who it is to whom you speak, Fergus. They are my people, as well. And am I not worthy of the Cad Nawdd?"

He winced. "I'm a hairy-assed, witless old bastard, Rhys, and I beg you to just put me out of my misery here and now."

"Maybe later," Rhys smiled, reaching for the rakes. "After we take care of this mess."

"Where is Bledig, anyway?" Fergus grumbled.

Odwain nodded toward the temple.

Fergus's eyes narrowed, but he held his tongue. "I'll be off then, to see what ruckus those barbarians are up to in the guard-house."

Poor Fergus. Since he'd been old enough to notice these things, Rhys suspected that Fergus's affection for his mother was deeper than any of them would want to admit.

Rhys noticed that Odwain's gaze had traveled across the courtyard to the herb patch just outside the temple kitchen, where Eirlys was harvesting sprigs and leaves. The barest hint of a smile came to Odwain's lips, and the blue of his eyes seemed to soften and deepen, as if they were somehow enriched by the view. Rhys felt both moved and annoyed. With love in full flourish all around him, he couldn't help but notice how much his own life was lacking. It was pitiful.

"She spends a great part of every day alone in the garden or the wilds, in some sort of kinship with the things that live there, whatever they are. Flora or fauna or fey," Odwain mused. "Is it true that Eirlys sees the pixie people?"

"Haven't you ever asked her?" said Rhys, a bit surprised.

"I was never quite sure I should." Odwain half turned and shrugged at Rhys without really taking his eyes from Eirlys. "Sometimes it seems that she speaks to herself."

Rhys grinned at the thought. "Well, I suppose it would look that way, but she is never really alone. My father has blood ties to this land, from his mother. She was kin to the faerie folk, and Bledig says the fey have claimed Eirlys as their own, in my grandmother's name. They have promised him never to take her unwilling from the mortal world, but she passes freely between the here and the there, as she wishes."

"Bledig speaks to the faeries?" Odwain frowned.

Rhys shrugged. "So he says."

"And you believe this?"

"I wouldn't underestimate my father, Odwain," Rhys warned. "Or my sister, for that matter."

Odwain's expression stiffened. "I would never."

Rhys regretted his snipe. Odwain hadn't deserved it, but Rhys couldn't seem to help feeling irritable. "It would seem, my friend, that Eirlys prefers the mortal world to the magical one. And," he added, "it would seem that is because of you."

Odwain very nearly smiled. Whenever a smile did grace his sober countenance, it generally had something to do with Eirlys. "Whatever the reason, I am grateful."

Again, Rhys felt a pang of empathy and envy. What must it be like to hold someone in your heart so dearly? And how much more amazing it would be, he imagined, to know with such certainty that someone adored you so in return.

"I am grateful as well. Eirlys is an extraordinary girl who requires an extraordinary man." He turned to face Odwain with sincerity. "And I am relieved indeed that she has found one."

Odwain nodded, as though lost for words, or prevented from speaking by emotion. Rhys hated the awkward silence that followed these sorts of moments, though he had meant what he said. It had needed saying, but now that it was said, neither one of them knew what to do with it.

"Isn't it all so exciting!"

Eirlys nearly skipped into the stockyard, swinging a harvest basket. It was a contagious affliction, his sister's effervescence, but a more appealing ailment Rhys could not imagine.

Certainly Odwain was badly infected. The look he gave Eirlys held such sentiment and reverence it was excruciating to watch. "What have you got there, pet?"

"Mm." She smiled. "Savor and spice and all sorts of delights. We'll feast tonight, in honor of Poppa."

"It makes my mouth water just to think of it," said Rhys. His sister had the most amazing gift of culinary creation. "Bledig will be elated."

"He will, indeed." Eirlys was proud of her talent and the effect it had on people, especially their father. She hadn't had much opportunity for fussing about a cook fire in recent months, and this occasion pleased her.

"When will you speak to him, Odwain?" she asked.

Odwain blanched. "When I have the chance."

"You mean when you've found the courage." Rhys watched with amusement as his friend's teeth set in a nervous grind, thoroughly enjoying Odwain's distress. "I am glad I'll never have to stand in your shoes."

"What do you suppose he'll make of me?" he asked.

"He already knows you, Odwain. I'm sure he's made you out to be exactly whom you are. For all his gruff and bluster and blow, my father is an unnaturally good judge of a man. The biggest mistake you could make now would be to attempt to impress him."

"Well, what the devil am I supposed to do, then?" Odwain was flustered. "What do you mean, don't impress him?"

"I think what I said, you idiot, is don't *try* to impress him," Rhys chuckled. "He'll see through it right away and then he'll be insulted, and that is the last thing you want. Trust me. Just be yourself."

Odwain eyed Rhys. "What happens when he's insulted?"

Rhys shrugged. "I've seen men skinned alive for less."

"You jest!" Odwain exclaimed.

"No, Odwain." About this, Rhys was quite serious. "I do not."

"You might want to get started at the cask now." Eirlys giggled. "By supper, the ale will have you so well sodden Poppa might take pity on you."

Rhys laughed. The truth was that both he and Eirlys knew full well that, while he might have trouble accepting the whole idea, Bledig would find no fault with Odwain. Still, it was good fun watching Odwain wrestling his nerves. "Well, at least you won't remember anything if he doesn't."

Odwain rolled his eyes. "I think I'll manage without getting soused, thank you, though a draught or two beforehand isn't a bad idea. I'll take Rhys with me to keep me out of trouble."

"Rhys will get you in to trouble, not keep you out of it," Eirlys warned. "Besides, I want you to stay with me."

"Odwain and I have work to do yet."

She wrinkled her nose as though she'd only just noticed the stench of horse sweat and dung. "Leave it to the stable boys."

"Sorry, lass, but Fergus has put this task to us," Odwain counseled. "We want his good graces, too, you know, along with my own father's blessing."

"I suppose so." The pixie pout disappeared and a sweet smile took its place. "I'll leave you then, for now. "

Odwain stepped close to Eirlys and took both her hands. Rhys had the distinct feeling he was in the way and about to witness something he didn't think he particularly wanted to see. While he was busy examining his reactions, Odwain leaned in and kissed her.

Not a little peck, either. Oh no, hardly a passing greeting, this, but a more leisurely stay. And an enjoyable one, he noted. There was nothing innocent at all in their kiss. Rhys felt the need to say something stern, though he couldn't begin to think what. He wasn't even entirely sure why he was bothered, except perhaps it seemed the right thing to be. He should be bothered, he supposed, concerned for his sister's honor.

Unable to stand it any longer, Rhys cleared his throat. Brotherly duty would demand no less, he figured. He waited, fully expecting Odwain to respond with haste. Odwain did not, though through no fault of his. Rhys was almost shocked when he realized how eagerly his sister offered herself. Torn between amusement and angst, Rhys groaned aloud. And then, finally, they parted.

"I'll have to hope my father will make up his mind quick about this wedding," Rhys groused. "Else there will be nothing saved for the wedding night by the looks of this!"

Eirlys flashed her impish grin and all but ignored him as she flounced away. Odwain was hardly contrite, though he averted his eyes as he reached to take one of the muck rakes and turned to work. More out of his own frustration than irritation with Odwain, Rhys smacked him on the back of the head.

"Bloody hell!" Odwain whirled around and snarled at him like a wildcat ready to strike.

"You had that coming." Rhys grinned as he stepped back, just in case. "What sort of brother would I be if I didn't at least pretend to defend my sister's maidenhood?" He studied Odwain skeptically. "There is still maidenhood to defend, isn't there?"

Odwain narrowed his eyes and heaved a sigh of exasperation. "You can't really expect me to answer that."

Rhys shrugged at his friend's indignation, though he was nonetheless relieved by its inference. "It's a fair enough question given that bawdy kiss, though I'll assume that insulted scowl of yours means Eirlys remains chaste."

Odwain's expression turned pained. "Between you and your father, I'll be a lucky man to live long enough to relish my own wedding night. And don't think I can't see how much you're enjoying this."

Suddenly Rhys regretted his taunts. He hadn't really meant to challenge Odwain's character. He would be honored to call this man brother. "Let's finish this," he offered, gesturing toward the mess. "Then we'll go looking for that ale cask."

FIFTEEN

"Be alert," Machreth instructed, admiring the dark green sateen dress Cerrigwen had chosen as he draped her robe over her shoulders. The color complemented her honey-brown hair and green eyes. "Allegiances will make themselves apparent."

She frowned. "Yours, or Madoc's?"

"One never really knows, do they, Cerrigwen?" Machreth warned, offering her his arm as they left her chambers. "Enjoy the food and the wine, but not overmuch."

Cerrigwen sniffed. "Do you worry I'll have too much drink and reveal you?"

"If you reveal me, you reveal yourself, and you are far too cunning for that. I worry more that too much wine might tempt you to vent your true feelings for Alwen. You must at least pretend to befriend her, if for no other reason than to keep whatever trust Madoc is willing to place in you."

"You insult me, Machreth. You can't possibly think me so stupid."

"Stupid, no, but envious, that you are." He ushered her down the stairs. "Jealousy must not be allowed to overrule your reason, Cerrigwen."

"Now." At the bottom of the steps, Machreth separated her hand from his arm and straightened the cuffs of his black camlet robe. "We should not arrive together, lest we give Madoc any more reason to suspect."

Her breath caught for a moment while she considered—and then reconsidered—her reply. "As you wish."

Cerrigwen tossed her hair, lifted her chin and cut smartly in front of him, sweeping ahead toward the doorway of the great hall. Machreth appreciated her sense of dignity, particularly when it could be manipulated to serve his desires.

By the time he made his own grand entrance, Cerrigwen had situated herself. Machreth was pleased. Madoc headed the table with Alwen at his left, directly across from Machreth's chair, to his right. Next to Alwen sat her Wolf King, with Cerrigwen seated at his left. Perfect.

Once Machreth had taken his seat, Glain made formal introductions, presenting the newcomers to Madoc one by one. The Obotrite captain, Domagoj, who never strayed far from the chieftain's side, was also a guest at Madoc's table. The rest of the barbarian horde, which numbered only seven in all, was being hosted at the lesser tables, where their fearsome oddity made them the objects of the awed curiosity of his apprentices. This was annoying, but of no real consequence to him. It was Alwen who concerned Machreth most. She possessed power she did not yet understand, and that, coupled with her righteous devotion, could move worlds. Machreth could not allow her to threaten the relationship he had begun to forge with the sons of Cadell, and the king-to-be, nor his plans to supplant Madoc's vision of the prophecy with his own.

Machreth spent the meal dabbling in polite conversation while covertly observing, waiting for proof of a vulnerability he could exploit. Alwen smiled with rare abandon this evening, doting on her barbarian king and obviously more confident than ever. Still, Alwen presented herself with all the decorum one would expect in Madoc's presence. She was too committed to the old wizard to allow the warlord to interfere. It would take more than Bledig's presence to distract her. If anything, he seemed to bolster her.

For her part, Cerrigwen played the role of the contented disciple well, keeping her resentments secreted beneath warm exchanges and inviting gestures. Even Madoc appeared to find Cerrigwen engaging, a relief considering how close she had come to insolence at the last affair. Tonight, she was better prepared and focused on the task she had been given. Machreth's last worries over Cerrigwen's discretion were allayed, for now.

"Perhaps the Wolf King would regale us with tales of his travels," Cerrigwen prompted, resting her hand on the barbarian's arm and affecting a coy tilt to her chin and a fawning smile. "I understand your people to be successful traders."

Well played, Machreth thought, noting the slight flush to Alwen's cheeks over the rim of his wine cup. Enough of a rift already existed between the two sorceresses that any overture Cerrigwen made would be met with suspicion, especially if it were focused on Alwen's family.

"Traders?" Bledig chuckled. "A nicer name for it than I'm accustomed to hearing, but yes, Obotrite horsemen have been known to travel great distances collecting wares for trade, to provide for our families and the tribe. We're only just a few weeks returned from Ausoria. The journey there and back is long, the better of two seasons, but the most exotic riches find their way to the ports there."

"You must be a very wealthy man," said Machreth.

Bledig paused to glance briefly at Machreth before helping himself to more meat and bread. "It is my honor to lead, but every householder in the tribe takes an equal share. Most years we are fortunate enough to have more than we need."

"Risky business, the transport of fine goods over such long distances," Madoc interjected. "You and your men must encounter a fair number of thieves and miscreants on your excursions."

"No match for *you*, I'm sure," Cerrigwen nearly cooed. "I can't imagine any raiding party daring enough to take on the likes of your warriors."

Bledig shrugged, appearing more interested in his food than the conversation. "Oh, they dare, though none have ever lived to regret it."

Whether it was his casual tone or the nonchalance of his phrasing, Machreth regarded Bledig with keener interest. The Wolf King was a pragmatic beast who considered killing a practical solution to threat. He was unfettered by moral compunction, and yet it was evident he held true to his own code of honor. This was a far more complex man than Machreth had initially assessed.

Cerrigwen redoubled her efforts to engage him directly, but once again, he conferred his attention on his plate. "And where do you and your people call home? Are you also from the North?"

The captain, Domagoj, answered while Bledig drank his wine. "The Obotrite confederate inhabits many of the Slavic republics, though we have no true kingdom of our own."

"The Wolf Tribe is kin to the Drevani, though we are more than three generations removed from our native Wendlands." Bledig tipped his cup to Alwen. "We have made the Frisian islets our home these past twenty years."

"We are fortunate, Bledig Rhi, that you and your fine brethren have come all this way in aid of our cause," Madoc said. "I bid you most welcome here, as long as you will stay."

Bledig then raised his cup to Madoc and offered him a grin. "I thank you for your hospitality, Sire, but I must confess I have come all this way for Alwen, and for her alone. That your cause is also hers is where your luck lies."

"He makes light in sport, Sovereign, but you may count on his support as if it were mine." Alwen spoke with pride and passion. "You have my word."

"So be it, then." A broad grin broke across Bledig's face. "It seems we are conscripted to your service."

The glance of solidarity that passed between Alwen and Bledig told Machreth all he needed to know. Their bond was strong, but only as strong as their belief in one another. Alwen had revealed herself in the courtyard when Bledig and his horsemen had arrived. She needed him. If Machreth could not openly thwart Alwen, he could, perhaps, undermine her with doubt. For this, he would need Cerrigwen's help.

Machreth set his gaze on Cerrigwen and waited for her to notice and acknowledge him. It took some time, as she had become the center of several conversations. She was quite beautiful, especially when she smiled. Once he had her attention, Machreth nodded toward the door and excused himself from the festivities. Several minutes later, Cerrigwen followed him into the hall. The affected pleasantry was replaced by her natural bitterness and cynicism.

"She is stronger than ever now," Cerrigwen hissed. "With the barbarian king and his men at her call? Even the Cad Nawdd is under her control. Madoc adores her, and Fergus would never betray her."

"True," Machreth acknowledged. "She is lifted by the strength of others. But one's greatest strengths can also be our greatest weaknesses."

"How so?" Cerrigwen was frustrated."

"Woman to man, mother to child, friend to friend," he mused. "Even the tightest of bonds can be broken, or at least strained."

"You are devious, Machreth."

"So I've been told." He smiled. "But then, so are you."

SIXTEEN

"There are many days and many ways a man might be asked to eat mutton," Bledig said with a belch. "But that, well…" He scuttled sideways across the ground to lean against a nearby birch tree, stretching out his legs to ease the strain on his gut. The fresh air and clear skies outside the barracks was a welcome respite to the formality of the temple. "That was the sort of meal that would send a man glad to his grave."

He sucked greedily from the wineskin and offered it to Rhys. "I've missed that girl's cooking almost as much as I've missed your mother's…Ah, well, never you mind about that."

Bledig peered at his son over the flames of the small campfire near the tents that housed his men, surprised by Rhys's silence and rueful excuse for a smile. He'd expected a wink or a jeer. "What bothers you, boy?"

Rhys shrugged as he swilled from the skin. "Nothing much worth mentioning."

"Nothing much, you say, with your nose stuck in the bag," Bledig chided. "I'd say you're feeling the weight of the world tonight."

Rhys looked up finally. "It shows, does it?"

"Only to a man who knows what it looks like."

"In the blink of an eye, I found myself conscripted into the service of a grand campaign to save the world. I never imagined myself on such a journey." Rhys stared hard at Bledig, his conflicted loyalties showing in his eyes. "But given the choice to go another way now, I don't think I would."

"Your mother's calling is an uncommon thing. She belongs to a destiny that is grander and greater than any one of us, than all of us." Bledig eyed his son. "I'd wager that you have found the adventure intriguing."

"On many counts," Rhys admitted. "And I have come to believe what she stands for is a cause worth serving. It is a duty I have taken to heart."

"So." Bledig nodded. "You've taken the damned blood oath."

Rhys looked askance at his father. "Are you disappointed?"

"Disappointed?" Bledig frowned. He was, some, but not about to let Rhys know it. Every man envisioned his son as his legacy. "You're old enough to choose your path. Besides, a man can owe more than one allegiance in his lifetime. You have blood ties to two proud clans, Rhys. You will never dishonor one by serving the other, so long as you never deny either. I suppose I am proof enough of that," he conceded. "Your mother needs you now. She serves a prophecy that affects us all."

"She needs *us* now," Rhys pointed out.

"So she does." Bledig grinned and reached for the wine. "Woman is a gentle, gracious mistress, as long as she gets what she wants. It's a cruel trick nature plays on men, my boy. Her favor is so sweet an elixir a man will do anything for the promise of another sip."

"So that's what keeps you tied to my mother all these years?" Rhys joked.

"I confess." Bledig gave a sly nod and a wink. "She has me spellbound."

Rhys rolled his eyes. "I've heard many a man claim enchantment as the culprit when he's fallen for a woman's wiles."

Rhys didn't know the half of his mother's allure. Bledig had wanted her the moment he saw her. She'd roused a part of him that lay so deep and dormant he hadn't quite recognized it at first. Her delicate, wistful beauty had stirred his mother's pixie blood and rattled him clear to the core. Elf shot, he was. His entire being had been struck to a dead stop by the unfathomable depth of spirit in Alwen's eyes.

"Well," Bledig said soberly, "whatever charms she may avail upon my desires, she has my heart. I love your mother, boy. Let there never be mistake about that."

"Have you regrets?" Rhys asked.

Bledig gave pause. It was an honest question, and one that deserved an honest answer. "I would say that from time to time I've found myself tried beyond my tolerance, but the truth is that loving your mother is easy. It's everything else that's a damned difficult struggle. Sooner or later every man must decide for himself what price he's willing to pay for love. I admit that some days it's harder than others to come up with the purse, but no, I have no regrets."

Rhys smiled. "Such sentiment from a barbarian."

"Ha," Bledig snorted. "Keep it to yourself, else you'll ruin me."

"Your reputation for bloodlust and butchery will be safe with me, but I'd be a lucky man to find a woman who moves me as much as my mother does you."

"A lucky man, indeed." Bledig did in fact think himself very fortunate. "Love is a treasure, a rare and elusive jewel. Not every man will find one so bright and precious as she, but luck has a way of finding a man just about the time he's given up looking for it. If it hasn't found you yet, I'd say it's about to, as lovelorn and woebegone as you show yourself to me now."

"It's not really as bad as all that. I haven't given up." Rhys stared thoughtfully into the fire. "I've only just begun to look."

"Good." Bledig was pleased that Rhys still felt hopeful. A man should feel useful and potent, and a cause would give him that.

But more than anything, he should have passion about something, or someone.

"Well then." Bledig loosened a small camlet cloth pouch that hung from his belt and unknotted the drawstring. When he upended the bag over his open palm, a small ring made of two twining golden vines tumbled onto his palm and Bledig held it out to Rhys. "I say it's about time you had this."

Rhys gingerly lifted the ring and held it up to the firelight. "This looks like a joining band."

"It could be. It was my mother's. I've held on to it in remembrance of her, but I expect you'll put it to better use. Though rituals and joining bands don't make a marriage, mind you."

"It isn't the ceremonial vow that matters, but rather the one you make in your heart," Rhys grinned as he carefully placed the ring back into its sack and tucked it into his boot. "Isn't that what you say?"

"Wise words, my boy, well worth heeding," Bledig counseled. "It might take more time than you'd like, but you'll find a worthy woman. Now tell me something more of Odwain. Something I can't see for myself."

"Well," Rhys began slowly, "I have to say I find Odwain more like you than I would have ever guessed, at least where Eirlys is concerned."

"How is that?" Suddenly this young man was more interesting.

"When Aslak arrived with the call to duty, I believe Odwain was ready to forsake his uncle and his father for her."

"Not an easy thing, to stand against your family."

"No," Rhys said. "But I believe he would, if it came to that. As you say, every man must decide what price he's willing to pay for love. And for Eirlys, Odwain would pay dearly."

Bledig was impressed. Odwain was a man of grit, praise be. No doubt about that, though he had seemed overly grim and dour when Eirlys had presented him at supper.

"Would you also say that he has as much kindness in his nature as he does courage?"

"I would."

Bledig sighed, as much with relief as with reluctance. It seemed there'd be no finding fault with his daughter's suitor. He hadn't really hoped to disapprove, but acceptance hadn't a much better feel to it.

"All right, then. Unless you can give me some reason otherwise, I suppose I'll give the boy my consent provided he has the stones to seek it."

"That's it?" Rhys was appalled. "That's all the test you'll put him to?"

"What else would you have me do, Rhys?" Bledig laughed. "Dare the man to take her from me? Hell, I'd say he's already done that."

"Bledig." Fergus appeared from nowhere, grim and wraith-like in the white light of the fire. "You'd better come. Now."

Bledig dragged to his feet, surprised by Fergus's grave tone. "Trouble, eh?"

"Just come along," he said curtly, turning back toward the barracks at a brisk clip.

Rhys stumbled up alongside, a bit too well oiled by the wine. "What is it, Fergus?"

Though Fergus offered nothing else but his worried scowl, it was all clear enough to Bledig long before they reached the stable yard. In front of the barracks buildings that housed the temple guards were his tribesmen, skulking and pacing like a wolf pack spoiling for the kill. Behind them hovered the men of the Cad Nawdd, though none of them seemed to be involved.

Bledig wanted time to assess the situation before intruding and led Fergus and Rhys along the tree line behind the barracks to avoid being seen. His were trusty men, but ruled by a feral code. He could smell the menace on them. His own hackles quivered to the scent of threat and Bledig tensed. Any one of them might spring on instinct and strike with merciless intent at the slightest provocation, even at their chieftain. Especially when they'd been drinking.

"Domagoj." Bledig's lieutenant stepped from the shadows near the buildings where he'd been watching and waiting for the Wolf King. "What is this?"

"That Bretland helldog has taken Sobol down over an insult," he said. "And now he asks your leave to kill him." Domagoj grinned. "He has the heart of a volchok."

"Volchok, is it?" Bledig nodded approvingly. Already Odwain had earned the respect of the cagey Domagoj. *Wolf cub* was a proud title and an unusual bequest to someone not born to the tribe. It was especially rare tribute from Bledig's suspicious friend. Domagoj was slow to the praise of any man. "What say the others?"

Domagoj shrugged. "He is a foreigner, and Sobol is family, but it's what you say that matters. Once you hear the offense, I can guess what you'll decide."

Bledig was curious, but apprehensive. He would not have been called to intervene in the dispute unless it was particularly foul. "All right then. Let's settle this."

He approached the ring of bystanders and shouldered his way into the center of the crowd, with Rhys and Domagoj at his heels. Fergus stood with the others, who had stepped back a bit in deference and respect. Bledig nearly laughed aloud, so surprised was he at the sight that greeted him.

Sobol, a large and lumbering lad some years elder and far more experienced than Bledig had adjudged Odwain to be, lay flat on his back with Odwain's heel jammed against his larynx. From the looks of it, Sobol had been fighting to breathe for quite some time. Odwain, on the other hand, appeared none the worse for wear save the strain of malevolence on his face. He'd rested his sword tip on Sobol's breastbone, with both hands clenched firmly around the hilt.

"Well, Sobol," Bledig said, "I must say I'm disappointed to find you at the lethal end of this boy's pig sticker. Whatever the devil you've done, it must be serious."

Sobol struggled to rise, but Odwain shifted his weight, pinning him hard and fast to the ground. "It began as a point of honor," Odwain answered. "And it shall end at the point of my blade."

"Sobol has taken exception to Odwain's claim on your daughter," Domagoj explained. "And Odwain has taken exception to Sobol's exception. It might have all ended with a good brawl if Sobol hadn't tried to drag the girl off by her hair." Domagoj shrugged at Bledig. "She *is* a beauty."

"She is *my* daughter," Bledig snarled. "If I'd seen him lay hands on her, he'd be dead already." He glanced around for Eirlys. "Where is she?"

"Gone to her mother." Domogoj snorted at Sobol with disgust. "So. Do we let the volchok here have his justice?"

Bledig glared at Sobol, considering his own revenge. But, this was not his fight. He turned his eyes to look long into Odwain's, peering hard at what lay inside this subtle man. Odwain met his gaze with a dark, quiet stare. Within the young warrior, Bledig saw a sleepy beast—slow to rage but ruthless when roused, and coldheartedly brutal when it came down to the kill. Despite the gesture of respect in leaving judgment to Bledig, Sobol's fate was fixed. One way or another, Odwain would have his blood. And Bledig approved.

He gave Odwain a slight nod and turned his back on Sobol. None among his men objected. When it came to Bledig's family, especially his daughter, there would be no leniency, and they all knew it. Sobol's bold affront infuriated him, as much for the lack of respect it revealed as for the assault on Eirlys.

Bledig paused long enough to hear Sobol's muffled groan as Odwain's boot crushed his windpipe. Retribution then staked its claim with a startling snap and crack as Sobol's ribcage splintered and caved beneath the force of Odwain's blade. Bledig strode away, satisfied that honor and authority had been served.

"Sobol was a fool," Rhys said quietly. "Had it not been Odwain's vengeance, it would have been yours, or mine."

"Yes. Sure and quick." Bledig stopped short and turned to Rhys. "Give him time to settle down and then bring him to me."

"Odwain puts himself to the test," Rhys grinned. "I like him better and better."

Bledig began to feel well and truly satisfied with his daughter's man. Hard to see, though, how Odwain and Fergus could be cut from the same cloth.

Just beyond the ring, Fergus glowered in his path. "Barbarian justice?"

Bledig grunted. "Odwain might have spared him, Mac-Donagh, but only to suffer him sniffing after his woman again some other day. It would come to this eventually." He shoved past Fergus. "Perhaps I should have saved myself the same trouble when I had the chance."

"I could say the same of you, Wolf King."

Bledig stopped short and turned to face Fergus with cold regard. His affection for Alwen was such a poorly kept secret that Bledig never could escape the nagging suspicion that Fergus was ever waiting for his chance. "Tell me, then, old man, what keeps you from gutting me?"

Fergus glared at him. "I wish I knew."

"So instead you dog my heels and sleep in my shadow. To keep me honest and true, for her sake?" Bledig laughed dryly. "Or is it to be sure she never hears how savage a civilized man can be?"

Fergus stepped up to him. "To hell with you."

Bledig nodded and edged closer. Close enough to see the hatred on Fergus's face. "Yes, MacDonagh. To hell with us both."

Fergus had no quick quip in reply to that. To be fair, the whole business shamed Bledig as well, though he had garnered the better part of the deal. Duty had its price, and Fergus was forced to barter Alwen's chastity away in return for Bledig's silence and protection. When Bledig and his cohorts had come upon the strangers camped in the Frisian wilds, his first thoughts had been mercenary. His second thought had been carnal, and Fergus had quickly realized which option was the lesser evil. MacDonagh had spilled all his secrets, and Bledig had been intrigued. In the end, he'd agreed to provide escort to Norvik and to keep quiet about what he knew in exchange for the woman, or at least one night with her. As things had turned out, she had wanted him. But had she not, he'd have taken her anyway, and this was Bledig's disgrace.

It was a desperate gamble that, in the end, had favored them all. And by the grace of all the gods everywhere, Alwen had never asked what bargain Fergus and Bledig had struck. While on every other matter they stood at loggerheads, on this they had pledged a truce. Her dignity need never be tarnished by the knowledge of the baseness between men.

Bledig knew, though, that the lasting trouble between the two of them was the unspoken truth Fergus held in his heart. He'd wanted Alwen for himself.

"Rhys has gone to fetch Odwain back to my camp. You can join us, if you like," Bledig offered. It was time to talk of weddings. "Bring your brother along."

Fergus seemed befuddled at first, not sure what to make of the invitation. It occurred to Bledig then that Fergus had no knowledge of Odwain's intentions. "Come now, MacDonagh. I'll furnish the wine. It's high time we made peace."

"Well," Fergus hedged, "I suppose there's no sense in letting good wine go to waste."

While Fergus went off in search of his brother, Bledig returned to camp. He found it just where he'd left it, though it was quieter now without Rhys. Bledig lowered himself to sit beside the neglected coals and poked at the smoldering embers with a birch twig to stir the life back into the fire.

Bledig searched the ground for the abandoned wineskin, more than relieved to find it still bloated. He popped the cork and squeezed the spirits into his mouth. It was the burn of good, strong drink that stung his eyes, of course. Not the loneliness he felt.

It wasn't as though he hadn't expected this. Still, he'd held on to the illusion that Alwen had been content with him all these years. *A wild daydream that was*, he chuckled to himself. More so today than ever before, he'd say, what with the fire of a cause alive in her eyes. As much as it pleased him to see her so full of purpose and intent, it also nearly broke his heart. Eirlys was every bit as grown as Rhys and just as ready to make her own way, and Alwen had finally been called to face her fate. In the end, Bledig knew they would all leave him. It was all in the whim of the winds and the tug of the tides. Nature had its own plan. But had Bledig any command at all over the circle of life, he'd keep them all close, forever.

"Here's your 'volchok,'" Rhys announced. He flopped to the ground while a stern and far too gloomy Odwain stood stiffly in the shadows.

Bledig waved him forward. "Sit and drink with me. With us."

He waited awhile for the boy to wrestle his emotions, knowing well the bittersweet struggle between revenge and remorse in the aftermath. The slaughter of a foresworn enemy in the rage of battle or killing in the heat of a desperate fight in defense of life and liberty had some nobility in it, a justification in honor and duty. Taking life in a conscious, calculated, and cold-blooded moment, however prudent or practical, tested a man's conscience in uncomfortable ways.

"Odwain," Bledig said kindly, "you're a smart man. Smart enough to know that if it hadn't been Sobol, it would have been some other rogue among my tribesmen who would have challenged you for Eirlys. She is the chieftain's daughter. This was to be expected, and now it's done with. So, drink to his memory if it eases your mind, and then let's talk about your wedding."

With the weariness that could only come of a heavy heart, Odwain consented to sit. A full wineskin had the power to heal most ills, and they would see him well cured before the night was out. Bledig offered the first draught to Odwain.

Odwain raised the skin in silent salute and then guzzled. When at last he'd swallowed enough to hold him and had passed the wine to Rhys, he spoke. "I should speak with my father and Fergus first."

"You've told them nothing of your wedding plans?" Bledig smiled. "Now, that's a conversation I won't want to miss."

"What wedding?" Fergus stepped out of the shadows and between Odwain and Rhys, with Odwain's father and brother close behind.

Odwain's pained expression returned. "Mine."

"Sit." Bledig waved the MacDonagh men into the circle. "Wherever you like."

Finn nodded in acceptance and settled to Odwain's left, while Pedr perched on a nearby stump. The elder MacDonagh was a sober man, much like his younger son. Quiet, too.

"Odwain's wedding?" Fergus turned his demands on Finn. "Why have I heard nothing of this?"

"You're hearing it now," Finn said calmly. "As am I."

Rhys flung the wine bag at Fergus. "Sit down, Fergus."

Fergus caught the bag but rather than sit he began to pace, grumbling obscenities in Odwain's direction. "You make questionable alliances, nephew. It's one thing to woo the barbarian's daughter, and quite another to wed her."

"I don't understand you, Fergus. You would lay down your life for Alwen and her children, yet you damn Bledig as though he was the very source of evil." Odwain frowned hard at his uncle. "I admire him. I admire his character."

"Ha!" Fergus spat and sputtered in his fury. "Character? Is that what you call Bledig's arrogance? It's nothing more than the conceit of his rank. A king, he calls himself. King of rogues and thieves, I say, savages who would strike at each other as quickly as they would any enemy. You admire his judgment because it fell in your favor, this time. Barbarian justice," he snarled. "Next time it might just be your innards on the stick."

"I see no real distinction between this barbarian justice and any noble code I know." Finn's quiet tone held an air of authority. "If, in the end, honor is served."

"Bledig's law is severe, but it *is* just," Odwain attested. "Though I take no pride in Sobol's death."

Bledig was thoroughly enjoying the exchange, barbs and jabs at his expense notwithstanding. He was used to such slights from Fergus. It was Odwain's show of bravado that was truly remarkable.

"You can't have thought this through." Fergus looked toward Finn, expecting his brother's support. It was not forthcoming.

"So that's it, is it? Odwain was enraged. "You think me so reckless as to risk everything on an impulse?"

"Don't you put words in my mouth." Fergus cast his gaze downward. "That's not what I meant. Eirlys is a fine girl and will make you a fine wife, one day. But there'll be time enough for her when Hywel rests comfortably on his throne. It's your priorities I question most, Odwain. You've forgotten who you are and what that means."

"I have forgotten nothing," Odwain said. "But my word to her means at least as much as my oath to the Stewardry, maybe more. I *will* honor them both."

Fergus sighed and flopped to the ground alongside Finn. "You are your own man, Odwain, and clearly you know your own mind. Addled as it is." He snorted. "Even as a small boy you were always too quick to question your elders. Too damned smart for your own good then, and now."

"Come now, MacDonagh," Bledig goaded. "Don't be so hard on the boy. Surely you can appreciate what agonies a man will suffer for the love of a woman. Or are you too old now to remember?"

"I remember a thing or two," Fergus mumbled. "If your own father does not object, Odwain, neither can I."

"No," Finn said simply, taking the wineskin from Fergus. "You cannot."

"Is it agreed, then?" Rhys asked. "There will be a wedding?"

"It is agreed." Finn raised the bag in salute.

It seemed the fight had left Fergus. "At least one of the Mac-Donagh men should find some luck in love."

For a moment, Bledig almost felt sorry for Fergus. Though the old goat was a burr to his very soul, Bledig hadn't the coldness of heart that could give rise to a callus. He couldn't actually muster compassion for the man, but Bledig did understand that his devotion had cost him.

"So be it." Bledig rose to fetch a fresh wine bag. "Tomorrow we make plans. But tonight, we drink."

"First, we drink to Sobol," said Odwain.

"And then I think we'll drink to you, Volchok," Bledig said, feeling great warmth and admiration for this quiet young man. "You are one of us now. You belong to the tribe of the Wolf King."

SEVENTEEN

Odwain rolled back on his heels to contemplate his life as well as his scraggly, stubble-bearded countenance. He grimaced at the bedraggled reflection that greeted him in the swollen stream behind the barracks houses and raked his hands through wet hair in an attempt to groom his wayward chestnut locks. Vague hauntings of the events following the feast and an overabundance of wine had made it impossible to sleep, and the hard night showed. A haggard figure of a man he would make were he to present himself to Eirlys now, not that she would mind. She loved him in spite of himself.

He scarcely dared to believe his good fortune. Part of him had shared his uncle's concern, that he would never be able to serve both his duty to the Stewardry and his duty to his own heart. Some part of him still worried. There was no knowing what Hywel's reign would demand of him, nor was there any knowing what marriage would require. He'd have to hope he could rise to any challenge. Surely a man could love his king as well as his wife and somehow manage not to fail either of them.

"Here you are." Eirlys knelt in the reeds behind him and wrapped her arms around his neck. Odwain braced to support her weight as she leaned against his back, guiltily enjoying the warmth of her pressed against him.

"I wondered if I might catch you trying to drown yourself, once you realized what you'd got yourself into," she whispered near his ear. Her breath smelled of mint leaves and honey cakes. "But you'll not escape me now, love."

Odwain gazed into her reflection as it shimmered just behind his on the surface water, bewitched as he always was by the thick, coal-black curls coiling about her cheeks and the supple, pink lips that turned up at the corners in a coy, come-hither smile that seemed to say she knew what he was thinking.

Sometimes he wondered if she knew how much she tempted him, but Eirlys was so artless and unabashed in her affection it had to be in innocence. She trusted him so completely that he lived in constant fear of failing her, especially in moments like these. The sooner they wed, the better. He couldn't hold off forever.

"Why ever would I want escape?" he said.

Eirlys rested her chin on his shoulder, quiet and content and absently stroking the hair on his chest. The caresses sent tiny convulsions shivering down his spine that ended in a merciless, fiery eruption of sensation in his groin. Odwain grabbed her hands to spare himself the torture, blissful agony that it was, and her fingers interlaced with his to fashion a sort of lover's knot. He could stand to let her stay there this way, as long as she wanted, even with her hair tickling his neck. "What will you do today, pet?"

"Make ready to marry you, I think, lest you've some other idea in mind of how I'd better be spending my time," she murmured.

"Ah, lass," he sighed, "what I have in mind will have to wait a bit."

He felt the gentle brush of her lips on his ear and nearly groaned aloud. "Can you abide the wait?" she teased.

Odwain turned to hold her close. Suddenly he couldn't bear for even the air to stand between them. "I don't know," he whispered recklessly. "Can you?"

He felt her breath catch in her breast and the quickening of her heartbeat—or was it his? All he knew was that he was completely lost in the kaleidoscope of violet light and faerie magic that were her eyes. Her lips parted slightly as if she were to speak, and then Eirlys answered him with a kiss.

One of longing, he knew, longing every bit as deep and undeniable as his. Odwain silently cursed himself even as he greedily accepted her passion. Eirlys was willing. She had made that known long ago. All he'd ever needed to do was to ask, but he hadn't. He couldn't. He wouldn't. Oh, bloody hell. He just had.

It took Herculean strength to force his lips from hers. "No, Eirlys. Not yet. Not here."

Her eyes pooled with frustrated tears, and Odwain thought his heart was going to crush itself to dust. He couldn't breathe. *Merciful heavens*, he begged in desperate thought, *don't let her cry*. If there was anything that he was certain he could not survive, it was her weeping.

She gave a tiny sigh and nodded. Odwain was so relieved he almost offered her his thanks. But when she blinked, her lashes swept a single teardrop from her eye and sent it sliding down her cheek. He was horrified. This had to be more than any man alive could bear. All he could think to do was kiss her, but that would only befuddle things. He was doomed. He just knew it.

Eirlys laid her head against his chest, and Odwain decided he was safe for the moment. He gathered her into his arms and held her while they both reclaimed their senses. The last thing he wanted was to give her cause for regret. While she might have readily made love to him in the reeds along the riverbank, seduced just as he was by the quiet intimacy of the early morning, he wanted it to be something more than just an impetuous act of passion. At least, the first time.

"You are going to have to save me from myself," he said softly. "You had better go now."

Eirlys gifted him with her smile and let him pull her to her feet. "I suppose the sooner I leave, the sooner you'll recover."

He grinned at her. "I'll find you later."

Odwain took her hand and pressed his lips against her palm, suckling the sweet smell of her skin, like rosewater and buttermilk and honeysuckle nectar on a warm spring breeze. *Get the girl gone*, he chided himself, *before things get out of hand again.*

She untied a small bundle hanging from her waist chain and shoved it into his hands. Honey cakes. The smell made his mouth water. He watched her leave, thinking that she reminded him of a butterfly dancing on sunlight, gracing everything that she touched. Him, most of all.

* * *

If one could actually hear joy, Eirlys was sure that she did. To her ears, the universe seemed made up of melodies that hummed in a natural harmony, a glorious chorus that tuned itself to the ever-changing rhythms of life. Ever and always amidst the constant thrumming sang the many small and sonant voices of the fey.

"Fare ye well."

Eirlys smiled at the familiar whispers from the meadow beyond the garden gate. "And the same to you, wee friend."

They all had names, or so she expected, though she hadn't asked. She thought becoming too friendly might make them more difficult to resist. Not that the faerie folk were baddies, really, but they could be troublesome. No matter what task Eirlys had set for herself, they did their best to keep her from it. It was sure and certain, though, that wherever she went, she never went alone. In the Frisian isles where she was born, the gnomes had been her childhood companions. Here, in her mother's homeland, she had encountered several new faerie tribes. The pixies, who were mischievous and fun-loving, were her favorites.

The faerie kinship was a gift from her father's mother, and Eirlys cherished it. It was because of her father's ancestry that the invisible draping that separated one world and the next was parted for her, as it once had been for him. Eirlys could roam hither and thither on a whimsy or a wish and always go home again. And all on account of a bargain her father had struck.

Her father had petitioned for her human half—just as his father had done for him. All of the Wolf Kings—Bledig and his father and even his father before him—had such ferocious reputations that even the fey feared their wrath. Bledig had traded his own welcome in the faerie realm for her right to choose her own path. On pain of any manner of horrible tortures, her faerie cousins had honored the pact and never claimed her, though by right they could. She belonged to them as much as she belonged to anyone.

Thus, Eirlys had been granted the benevolence of both worlds, magical and mortal. Not that it amounted to much that she could see beyond the lively company of the magical people and the secrets they shared. She was privy to the vast pixie larder and trove of culinary tricks, and a welcome guest in their secret herb gardens. Eirlys hadn't any formal magic, not like her mother, but she did have certain sensitivities. Sometimes she thought she could hear the winds change or feel the seasons turn. For certain, however, the grounds that surrounded her mother's home had a soul that spoke to her.

"*Come a-courtin'*," came the spriggan call. He presented himself, dapper in his elfin way, bedecked in a rich brown tunic and matching hose. This happy-go-lucky ragamuffin she'd seen before. He had a terribly lecherous smirk.

"Not today, little man," she answered firmly. "Besides, I'm to be married."

"*Pish. So fair of face and ebon hair, and of the faerie faith ye be. 'Tis a pixie pairing ye should pine for, no mere mortal man for ye.*"

Eirlys giggled. *Randy little rascal*, she thought. Flattery would hardly turn her head, but she might be tempted to walk the meadow and orchard behind the castle a bit. Though it wasn't as balmy a day as she'd hoped for, it was pleasant in a fall-come-winter sort of way. It was warm enough to leave off her cloak in favor of woolen dress sleeves as long as she kept moving. The sun burned bright behind a shade of high, hazy clouds.

She decided to let the sprite lead her along the trail that skirted the castle boundaries. It led to a small orchard where the proper grounds would meet the forest, were it not for the tall stone wall that surrounded the keep and all the outbuildings. She had been warned to stay clear of the forest. The White Woods were bewitched, though she hadn't needed to be told to know it. Eirlys had sensed the potent magic in the oak and rowan and witchen trees just beyond the wall almost the minute they'd arrived at Fane Gramarye. It intrigued her, in a perverse sort of way, and she had risked going too near once or twice before just to satisfy her curiosity. She had never dared to pass through any of the gates and actually enter the woods, not that she could loose the chains that held them closed. But the forest sorely tempted her. It actually seemed to call her name.

The overgrowth along the wall where she entered the orchard was unexpectedly thick, and Eirlys noticed breaks in the rockwork where the forest wilds had begun to encroach. Some decay would be natural over the years, but she had not seen these gaps on her previous trips down this trail.

More curious than that, though, was the aura of the place. It had changed. Eirlys noted a distinct lack of noise. The birds had stopped singing, she realized, and then grasped the real truth. The birds were *gone*. This, she knew, was altogether odd. Even in the dead of winter one would hear the raven's caw or the hoot of an owl.

Perhaps some sort of rot or disease had infected the orchard, made it unfit. Curiosity turned to concern, and Eirlys decided to look closer. Her investigation took her down a less traveled path through the fruit trees, but Eirlys considered herself safe enough so long as she stayed on the castle side of the wall. She knew the grounds well, and she had her faerie friends for company.

The farther she wandered into the orchard, the uglier it became. It looked to her as if the trees were dying. She could, after all, hear and feel the withering. But what could be the cause?

A sudden, unfamiliar fall of shade and shadow gave her pause. Eirlys glanced around and realized that she had somehow lost herself. She did not recognize this small clearing. Her heart leapt and began to flutter in fright.

"How can that be?" she wondered aloud. Eirlys had traipsed every inch of the grounds, including the thickets. But this place didn't look like the orchard she knew. It was dense and dark, like the forest. Eirlys shuddered.

She hadn't crossed into the forest, though. At least she thought she hadn't. She desperately hoped she hadn't. It was said the trees of the White Woods moved about to create an ever-changing maze that always and forever led a wanderer back to where he began. Whatever the truth of that, Eirlys knew, if only by instinct, that she was standing somewhere that she had never been.

She turned to find the trail, but it was gone. No passage or even a cut through the brush. Eirlys couldn't make sense of it. She had felt the packed earth beneath her feet at every step, yet here she was in the middle of a copse with no path in or out. She couldn't say for certain—in fact, it was silly to think it—but it was almost as if the undergrowth had suddenly sprung up around her.

Eirlys felt her throat close in, and she fought to catch her breath. Not once had she ever been lost. A keen sense of place and space was as common a trait to her as was the nose on her face. What was she to do?

Just as she began to panic, Eirlys felt a tug at her skirt and nearly laughed aloud with relief. She was not alone. The fey would lead her back. "Thank goo—"

She froze. A subtle rustle caught her ear, and a scratching sound. And then a creaking. Or a groan.

Eirlys gasped and jumped back as the vines reached out to grab her. Her skin began to crawl. Unless she'd altogether lost her mind, the woods really were growing round her, right before her eyes.

The tugging at her hem was more insistent, but Eirlys shook free. Something was moving about in the brush, and she wanted to know what. Eirlys pushed aside a stand of spindly brush. She peered into the dusky shadows, wondering were it man or beast she had happened upon. Sudden recognition struck her. She sensed what they were before she actually saw them, but if it hadn't been for her faerie blood, she'd never have seen them at all.

On the edge of the veil between mortal ways and magic, evil was hard at work. Dark, twisted goblin creatures called the devilkin were weaving a spell—a thicket of thistle as tall as a house and so dense she couldn't see light through it.

Eirlys stifled the shriek rising in her throat and staggered backward, stumbling over tree roots and rocks in her fright. She turned and bolted blindly through the forest. At best guess, she was heading westward, back the way she had come.

Not more than a furlong farther, she ran headlong into the black briar she was frantic to escape. She turned again and fled south along the hedge, looking for a thinning or weak patch. The faster she ran the faster it seemed to grow, taller and thicker until she could hardly see the sun.

Sheer terror drove her to scale the thistle. Thorns tore at her skirts and shredded her hands as she hauled herself frantically up and over the top of the hedge. She hit the ground belly first, so hard it knocked the breath from her. Her hands burned and she hurt all over. Eirlys pushed herself to her knees, gasping and gagging for air until she finally caught enough wind to scream.

The shrill sound startled a flock of hedge hens to flight. They burst from the brush nearby and scared Eirlys nearly to tears. She flew to her feet, glanced frantically about to get her bearings, and set off at a dead run for the Fane.

She heard footfalls pounding behind her, and fear spurred her to take the last several yards across the open in bounds. Not far now to the road, and home. Her lungs burned but her terror carried her, all the way through the waist-high wild grass and over the mulch in the herb patch. Just a few more strides and—

The road rushed up before her eyes. A dull, jarring thud reverberated through her wrists to her elbows and shoulders. It rattled her teeth and settled to a ringing echo in her head. Her knees and palms tingled, numb and hot at the same time.

"Uh," she groaned, stunned by the fall. Eirlys carefully pulled the toe of her left shoe free of the root knot that had caught it and staggered to her feet. Before she could manage to gather her wits and her balance, she heard the sounds of a frenzied pursuit gaining on her rapidly. Eirlys turned to look just as the chase overtook her.

EIGHTEEN

"**B**lazes, Eirlys!" Rhys pulled his horse up short just ahead of her and slid from its back. "What are you doing? Didn't you hear me calling you?"

He stopped in his tracks as he turned toward her, eyes widening as his gaze took in her face, and then the rest of her. Rhys reached for her wrists and lifted her hands to examine them. "What happened to you?"

"I fell. I think. Once. Or maybe twice." She wasn't entirely sure, but she was surprised to hear the calm, even tone in her voice. Certainly she didn't feel calm, not a bit. If anything, she felt horror-stricken. And sore to the bone. "What are you doing out here?"

"Why, I..." Rhys stuttered blankly. "You've been gone for hours, Eirlys. Odwain got worried when you didn't come back by midday. And then I saw you making a mad dash from the woods and naturally thought there was something the matter. Foolish of me, I suppose."

Ignoring his sarcasm, Eirlys brushed past him and started toward the garden. "I must speak to Mother, Rhys. Right away."

"She'll be in the spell rooms, I suppose, with the acolytes." He walked his horse alongside, peering carefully at her. "But I think you may need some tending. You look as though you've taken a hellcat by the tail. What happened?" he insisted.

"My hands hurt," she mumbled.

"Of course they do. The skin is split to bits!"

"Oh," she said. She glanced at her palms and was surprised, though that was silly. She remembered now. "I had to climb the thorns to get out."

"Get out of what?" Rhys was agitated. He took her arm and stopped. "Tell me what happened. This instant."

"There is devilkin in the woods, Rhys. I saw them. Just now. Building a briar patch or a thistle hedge or something. It's unnatural." She felt uncomfortably warm. And dizzy, too. "It grows by feet and yards, right before your very eyes."

"You need to sit down." Rhys offered his arm for her to lean on. "Soon, I think."

Eirlys agreed. "After I find Mother."

"All right then. We'll have her take a good look at you, too. Your color is wrong, Eirlys." He squinted at her face. "You don't look at all well."

"I'll be fine, Rhys. Really."

Eirlys smiled bravely for her brother, but she was more than a little grateful for his strong shoulder. She was still winded and her legs felt wobbly.

By the time they'd made it halfway across the grounds, Odwain was already on his way to greet them. As he drew near enough to see her clearly, the look of relief fell from his face.

Eirlys smiled at his worried eyes and grim expression. "It's not so bad as it looks, Odwain, I don't think, but then, I don't know how bad it looks. Is it awful? You look so solemn. I must be a frightful sight."

Odwain mustered part of a smile as he reached for her hands. "You're mussed up some, I guess, but still every bit the beauty."

He pulled her closer, and Eirlys nearly fell into his arms. "What's happened to you, pet?"

"Someone's set the goblins to work in the woods," she explained. "My mother will know what to do."

Eirlys noticed the not-so-subtle exchange of worried glances between her brother and her beloved and began to worry a bit for herself. If the scratches on her face were only half as unsightly as the wounds to her hands, she could well imagine the horrible disfigurement.

Rhys tipped his head toward the temple. "Inside, I think. That's where we were headed."

With Odwain on one arm and Rhys on the other, she felt strong enough to make it the rest of the way through the garden. By the time they reached the gate that led into the cobbled courtyard, though, she was truly spent.

Eirlys glanced across the courtyard. Bledig had seen the commotion and was well on his way, with Cerrigwen at his side. Eirlys remembered Cerrigwen's fawning over her father at the feast and bristled a bit, wondering. *What reason could Cerrigwen possibly have to be in Bledig's company?*

"You should wait here," Rhys insisted. "Sit on the steps, maybe. I'll go see if I can find Mother."

Just then, Odwain let loose of her and stepped aside. Which was wise. Over his shoulder, she saw her mother burst through the temple door and swoop down the stairs.

"Eirlys!" Alwen exclaimed. "I had a feeling you needed me. And just look at you."

Eirlys had rarely seen her mother so flustered. She almost thought the whole scene comical, but it wasn't, not really. Everyone was worrying over her, only it wasn't her they should be troubled about. "Mother, wait. I have something to tell you."

Alwen cupped her daughter's chin in her palm and tilted Eirlys's head to examine her face, while the others all hovered around. Her mother gently smoothed the wild curls from her eyes. "How did you get these scratches?"

"Take a look at her hands," Rhys suggested.

Alwen's eyebrows arched in alarm as Eirlys offered her scathed and scraped palms. "Some of these cuts are very deep, Eirlys. We'll need to tend to them right away." "I'm all right." Eirlys tried to pry her hands loose from her mother's fretful grasp. "Really, I am. Don't worry so."

"I'll judge that for myself," Alwen said tersely. "You're a mess and your dress is torn. Come inside. We'll clean you up and then we'll see."

Eirlys huffed in frustration. "Will you just listen?"

"Let the girl speak, Alwen." Bledig had arrived, with Cerrigwen close on his heels. "If she says she's fine, she's fine. Looks like a few cuts and a bruise or two to me. Nothing to make such a fuss over."

Her mother's eyes narrowed angrily, and Bledig stared back for several long moments. Alwen's disapproval was obvious, though Eirlys wondered whether her mother was more perturbed by his opinion, or by his very public contradiction. Or perhaps, Cerrigwen's close proximity.

"Very well, then." Alwen released Eirlys and crossed her arms over her chest, looking insulted and intrigued all at the same time. "I am listening. What is it, Eirlys?"

"Devilkin." Now that she was allowed to speak and be heard, she could barely sputter. "Dozens of them. In the woods."

"What the devil is a devilkin?" Bledig asked.

"The servants of evil." Alwen's tone was cold. Her violet eyes darkened, but her expression never changed. "Spawned to craft the magic of a black curse."

"They were spinning thorny vines and weaving a wall of them. I swear it was growing taller by the minute and spreading faster than I could outrun it." Eirlys looked down at her hands. The redness was worse now. "Finally I had to climb it to escape it."

"What sort of spell might this be?" Odwain wondered.

"Some foul deed, no doubt," said Rhys. He'd begun to pace, obviously anxious to be about the business of rectifying the situation rather than standing around talking about it. He was quick to action, especially when there was trouble. Her brother was brave, but sometimes too brazen.

Alwen nodded as her brow creased in troubled thought. She turned her stern gaze on Cerrigwen. "You have dominion over the natural realm. What do you say?"

"I would need to see it to know for certain," Cerrigwen offered. "But a thicket of thorns is a common spell of defense. It is meant to keep invaders out."

"Or," Bledig said gravely, "to keep us in."

"Well, whatever the bloody hell it is I say we hack it down," Rhys demanded. "And damn quick, before it overtakes us."

"The sooner the better," Cerrigwen advised. "A spell isn't set until it is finished."

"That may be, Cerrigwen, but we do not yet know what we are up against," Alwen countered. "One cannot battle black magic blindly."

"If it is black magic." Cerrigwen was very calm.

"Then let's take a look at it," Rhys challenged. "Eirlys can show us where to go."

Eirlys felt sick. She didn't want to go, but she would if she had to. All she wanted to do just now was sit down.

"No. She will not." Eirlys felt Odwain beside her and leaned into him as his arm cinched tightly about her waist. "I won't allow it."

Everyone fell silent and turned to look at Odwain. The authority and finality in his tone had taken them all by surprise. Even Eirlys.

A faint smile played about her father's lips, but his voice was stern. "Strong words, boy."

"She's already fought it off once and survived." Odwain was defiant and very determined. "I am not sending her back out there."

"Odwain and I can scout it out on horseback, see where it is and how far it's grown," Rhys offered. "Then we'll have at least some idea of what's out there."

"We'll all go," Bledig decided. "Find Fergus and we'll all ride out to see this devil's hedge or goblin vine or whatever it is. Let's deal with it now and be done." He looked hard at Odwain. "Volchok here will keep an eye on Eirlys."

"I should stay and tend to her wounds." Cerrigwen stepped forward slightly. "And someone should give Madoc the news."

Her mother glanced so sharply at Cerrigwen that it gave Eirlys a twinge. She could see suspicion, maybe even accusation in her mother's eyes. "I'd rather you were with us, Cerrigwen. We may need your skills. There are any number of attendants for Odwain to call upon." Alwen beckoned at the girl waiting and watching from the doorway. "And we can send Glain to Madoc."

Alwen and Cerrigwen exchanged a begrudging glare. They held each other at bay in a silent battle of wills that threatened to go on forever or end very badly. It was an uncomfortable standoff for everyone.

Finally, Bledig intervened. "Cerrigwen should stay, in case Odwain needs her. You've said it yourself. She is a gifted healer, and I want my daughter well cared for. We won't be gone long."

Alwen stiffened. "As you wish."

"We had better go now, then, while we've the light and dry ground." Rhys was impatient, ready to ride. "It's going to rain."

Rhys left to find Fergus and gather the horses, clearly relieved to have a task to attend to. Alwen stepped forward to stroke her cheek. Her fingertips were cool, soothing. For a moment, Eirlys was overcome by the gentle touch. She wanted her mother to stay.

It was a childish wish, but there were some comforts one never outgrew.

"Everything you'll require is in my rooms, or within Glain's means," she instructed Odwain. "Put her to bed and keep a close watch for fever."

"I'm fine, Mother," Eirlys insisted as she sank to sit on the steps. "Just tired, that's all."

Alwen smiled, although she didn't look at all convinced. "I'm sure. But it doesn't hurt to be cautious."

"All right then," Bledig chided. "Enough fussing." He winked at Eirlys and took Alwen's arm. "Leave the girl be and let's go."

NINETEEN

The deeper they pushed into the forest, the greater her dread. Alwen felt the thickening of the air. It seemed to close in as if it meant to swallow them up. And though there were still hours of daylight left, the dense gray clouds that had darkened the sky mimicked the eerie gloom of dusk.

"It's a good thing we brought torches," Rhys said. "Do you know where you're going?"

Alwen had taken the lead from the minute they'd left the temple commons. Rhys rode close behind with Bledig and Fergus. "Yes."

"The woods are changed," Rhys said. "I can't see it, but I feel it."

"Mind the trail," Fergus warned. "I swear it comes and goes as it pleases."

Alwen pulled to a halt, listening to the stillness. A distant rustle reached her ears. Something was moving through the brush. Bledig nudged his mount ahead a few paces and stopped again, cocking his head to the breeze.

"Alwen," he whispered. She turned in her saddle to look, and Bledig tipped his torch toward the bracken to his right. "Through there."

"Whoa, now!" Rhys cried out as his horse reared without warning and spilt him hard on the ground. He scrambled to his knees to grab the reins before the animal bolted, and then froze "The ground is moving."

"It's not the ground," Fergus warned, as his mount skittered and cried. He struggled to control the horse and keep hold of his torch. "It's the vines, Rhys. Watch yourself, all of you. There are creepers all around us!"

"Bloody hell!" Rhys jumped to his feet and made quick for his mount.

"Hush!" Alwen whispered, gesturing with her eyes toward the thicket around them. "We are watched."

"Aye," Fergus answered in a low voice. "That would be the devilkin lurking about, now, wouldn't it? I'd venture to say they've been right there with us, all along."

"What do they want?" Rhys reined the horse full circle, uncertain where to turn his back. "What are they waiting for?"

"Waiting for their chance, that's what." Fergus gave a wry chuckle. "The hands and eyes of evil, some call 'em."

"Pay them no heed." Alwen took a moment to get her bearings. "If they had any real power they'd have shown it by now."

Agreeing with Bledig's instincts, Alwen spurred her horse off the trail and into the trees. The thicket was soon so tangled they had to kick and hack at the brush from horseback to break through. They trudged through the blackness for long, silent minutes until they finally reached what at first seemed to be a new copse. Instead, Alwen found herself before an enormous wall of thorns.

Razor-sharp toothlike spindles protruded from tar-colored vines that grew as thick as tree limbs. The growth was too dense for any light at all to penetrate, and Alwen was stunned at the sheer height and breadth of it—she could not tell where the forest ended and the hedge began. It was as if the vines had overtaken the trees, weaving them into the grotesque tapestry.

Rhys followed Fergus and his father into the clearing and dismounted, gaping at the tangled mesh of twining twig and thorn. "Wicked, this is," he breathed.

"It writhes like a vipers nest," Bledig said quietly, still astride.

"It looks far more deadly than that to me," Rhys said. "The whole mess moves under its own might. It's almost as if it means to grow right over us."

"Yes," Bledig answered simply. "I think that is exactly what it means to do."

Fergus pulled up alongside Alwen. "What now?"

Without warning, the skies erupted in a thunderous explosion. Hail burst from the sky. What little daylight remained was completely eclipsed, and the pelting ice snuffed the torches. Instantly it was dark as the dead of night.

"Of all the hell-fired hog swill." Fergus jumped from his mount and stood next to Rhys. "I've seen plenty of magic in my days but never the likes of this. That's black magic, all right. The blackest there is. Sure as I'm standing here."

"Quiet." Alwen slid from her saddle and stepped toward the towering hedge. "We're all well enough aware of what confronts us. Give me peace long enough to think of some way to dispel it."

Alwen marveled even as she trembled beneath the threatening mass, wondering what evil she faced. She was mesmerized by the wicked genius that had conceived it, fully aware that the awe she felt was a dangerous lure. The mysterious was the most devious of all terrors. Its true horrors were concealed behind a beguiling veil that confused the senses and clouded the instincts. The temptation to stand and stare was strong, despite the certain and deadly peril. In all her days, Alwen had never been called upon to face such a thing. And though she would not let it show, she was afraid.

It had a spirit essence, this thing, as if it had breath in its bulk and feeling in the dark prickly flesh that covered its limbs. She recognized the smell of evil, a sickly sweetness in the black sap that oozed through gnarled veins to feed the spell. And its eyes were on her. Her skin burned in the fierce gaze of the sinister sentinels lurking just beyond the limits of her vision. The devilkin skulked closer, sensing that their time was short.

Alwen retreated a step and felt the steamy breath of Bledig's horse against her rain-dampened back. "They will strike soon," she warned. "They will try to stop us."

"They already have," Rhys muttered from the shadows. "Tried to stop us, I mean."

"Hush now," Fergus hissed. "Let her work."

As if I know what to do, Alwen thought. She felt small and meek in the shadow of this spell. Would that she could work some ready-made magic against it, but Alwen could not even manage to call a salient thought to her head, let alone send words of power spewing from her lips.

She wondered dimly about Cerrigwen. Not that Alwen wanted or needed her help. No, she had wanted Cerrigwen present to keep her close and well watched—and away from her child. Almost certainly, she had some hand in this grotesque creation, though the only proof Alwen had was Cerrigwen's obvious resentment of her. She had already considered that this was some sort of perverse challenge, another not-so-subtle defiance of her authority. At best, what confronted her here was a manifestation of Cerrigwen's arrogance and conceit. At worst, it was a blatant attack—an attempt to remove whatever threat Alwen posed to her ambitions, by any means necessary.

But there was but another more hideous possibility, one that Alwen was horrified even to entertain. This was high sorcery that Alwen suspected even Cerrigwen could not have wrought on her own. She must have had help. And if that was so, there was far greater danger ahead than the atrocity that confronted them now.

"Bloody hell!" Fergus sputtered. "Look out!"

Alwen recoiled but not in time to avoid the gnarled, claw-like twig that reached out from the dark to snare her wrist. Horror shivered through her bones and stilled her blood as the vine snaked up and around her arm toward her shoulder. She was all but petrified.

"Don't try to pull your way free," Rhys warned. "The harder you heave, the harder it may heave back."

Alwen tested it with a little tug to be sure. The backlash was instant and cruel. She gasped as the vine cinched tighter, and her fingers tingled. Bledig slid from his horse and started toward her, prepared to cut her loose.

"No," she cried. "Wait."

"Wait for what?" he snapped. "For the bloody thing to swallow you whole?"

She didn't spend her breath to answer, to proclaim this challenge hers to face. He would know. Though he would not stand the wait with ease, he would stand it—unless and until she bid him otherwise.

Alwen forced herself to confront the blackened briar and the brutal hatred that had made it. She would have to save herself. If only she knew how.

Almost as if it had heard her thoughts, the vine began to retract. Alwen felt herself being dragged toward the hedge ahead of her and dug her heels into the forest floor. It was too strong, and her resistance only seemed to make it stronger. Panic stripped her of what little breath she might have had to cry for help. She wracked her mind, prepared to grasp at the wildest thought. But none obliged.

Then instinct spoke to her, piercing the veil of terror that clouded her thoughts. Some quiet whisper from far away convinced her to be still, to let her arm go lax against the pull. A thing not so easy to do as it was to think. She was rigid with fear. With focus, though, her hand and wrist slackened and, quick as you please, slipped loose of the bind. She was free.

"Step away from it, Alwen," Bledig insisted. "Quick. And watch for thorns."

Bledig could be still, it seemed, but not silent. She swooped to catch the wretched thing as it skulked away and yanked off a piece to examine more closely. "These vines have no thorns."

Fergus waved the torch overhead. "But that briar hedgerow does."

"Yes." Alwen looked up and swallowed hard, imagining herself impaled on the deadly bed of barbs. "It surely does."

Bledig was grim faced. "Eirlys climbed right over the top of that spiny fence. It's a blessing she survived it."

Eirlys. Alwen recalled the sight of her daughter's bloodied face. Her child had nearly met her death. Rage swelled, tapping strength she had never before called upon, summoning strength from the depths of her being. Whoever had unleashed this wickedness upon her loved ones would know what it meant to have her wrath. Let them all bear witness, then, to what real power was.

Alwen lifted her face to the mist and turned her eyes inward to visit the secret places within herself, searching for the mystical forces through which she commanded her realm. She felt the rain on her skin and knew it for what it really was. It was not simply the whim of nature. It was a blessing from the gods, and it belonged to her. Alwen reached toward the sky as her spirit roused to the wisdom of her inner voices.

Whispers echoed through her mind. From the primeval instinct that steeped her soul came the distant murmurs of the Ancients. She heard the cant of elders, past generations of the magical bloodline of which she was born, a sacred chorus sung in the tongue of the spirits.

Alwen repeated the foreign sounds as they were given to her. As she spoke, the words took shape to form a single thought, and Alwen quickly recognized its meaning. Water knew no more pristine a form than as it fell freely from the sky. No better cure for pestilence could there ever be than the purification of a purge.

With understanding came assurance, and soon the spell drew strength from her conviction. Upon the issuance of a thought, the mist transformed into a pelting, wind-driven rain. The cool tingle of the droplets that whipped against her face gave rise to a secret revel. Alwen felt full and fierce. She was powerful. She sensed her magic working within the water and opened her eyes to behold what she had wrought.

In answer to her beckon, the sudden cloudburst swelled into a fearsome storm. The sky exploded with a deafening bang, and water fell from the clouds in streams. And then, at Alwen's silent urging, the deluge converged into a single whirling funnel of water bearing down upon the thorny hedge. The devilkin sent up a furious, deafening shriek as they first attempted to withstand the attack, and then fled deeper into the forest to avoid destruction. Unleashed, the vines lashed out like whiptails, even as the consecrated rains pummeled the spiny wall and drenched the soil in which it had rooted.

Alwen sensed the wickedness waning as the briar weakened and began to collapse beneath its own soggy weight. Grim satisfaction curled the corners of her mouth into a wry smile as she watched the twisted, blackened hedge begin to shrivel. The cursed trailing vine quickly dissolved with a foul-smelling vaporous hiss in the thunderous wake of one final lightning strike.

Alwen stood rooted to the ground while the rains abated, shaken by the magnitude of her handiwork. She had thwarted one of her own. No greater victory could ever be realized, except perhaps at the hands of a grand mage like Madoc.

Bittersweet and short-lived was the thrill, though, for in the very instant of owning the triumph, her exultation was drowned by waves of sorrow. She sagged beneath the burden of understanding what she had done. Never, at least not to her knowing, had any Steward turned her powers against another's. This was no proud moment.

No consolation came from knowing that Cerrigwen had broken the covenant first. Alwen had triumphed over this betrayal, but there was no glory to be claimed, not in any name. What rivalry there was between them should have never come to this.

"It's damned cold out here," Bledig muttered behind her.

She was nearly numb to the elements, unaware of the chill until he wrapped his wolf-skin cape about her shoulders. The wet wool pressing against her skin under the weight of the fur sent a violent shudder through her. Bledig braced her with his grip but stopped short of drawing her to him. Alwen was surprised by his restraint, but still embittered and far too exhausted to encourage his affection or his warmth. The cape was comfort enough.

As her senses slowly surfaced and reawakened to the world and those around her, Alwen saw apprehension and expectation in their captive stares.

Fergus let out a low, whistling exhale. "How ever did you do that?"

Alwen considered an answer, but nothing she could say would explain what they had witnessed. It was a thing that defied description, and she hadn't the will or the wherewithal to try. Besides, what words would she use to define who and what she had become? Instead, Alwen blankly accepted the reins as Bledig handed them to her and dragged herself astride the mare. More than anything, she wanted to go home.

"We're finished here." Alwen turned her horse toward the temple, vaguely aware of a faint burning in the skin above her breast, beneath the silver amulet she wore. "It is time to get out of the rain."

TWENTY

"We should get you inside."

"Odwain, you are worse than my mother." Eirlys sighed. "Just a minute more. I haven't the strength to move."

He shifted uneasily on his feet. "All the more reason to get you upstairs and into bed," he insisted.

Before she could argue, a fiery flash parted the clouds. Hail fell from the sky so hard and so fast it ricocheted off the ground like stone pellets launched from an enormous astral catapult. They stung when they hit.

Over the deafening, drumming roar, a rolling rumble peaked in a thunderous crescendo that shook the earth. "Odwain!"

He snatched her hand and yanked her up the steps before she could blink. Odwain flung her into the vestibule and shut the heavy doors hard behind them. "Bloody hell!" he sputtered.

Eirlys giggled through a shudder. Water dripped from his nose. "You're all wet."

"So are you." Odwain took her arms and pulled her against him. When she shuddered, he wrapped his arms about her and squeezed. "And cold. You're shivering."

Eirlys rested her forehead against his chin. "I suppose I'd best let you help me upstairs."

"Well, my pet." He scooped her up into his arms and began to carry her through the halls. "I don't see that you have a choice."

"This is silly," she protested. "For goodness' sake, Odwain."

"Silly or not, you will suffer it," he insisted, taking the first of three flights of stairs to her mother's rooms in swift, determined strides. "If only for my sake."

Eirlys gave in without further fuss. Odwain was quite firm and in truth, she didn't really mind. Eirlys found his gallantry thrilling. Besides, it was an awfully long way and though she would never admit it aloud, she would not have made it even as far as the first step on her own.

Odwain left her on the divan while he tended the fire. Her mother's attendant had followed them in with a bowl of fresh water and a plate of bread and cheese. She set the bowl and plate on the desk under the window and pulled several rolls of cloth and a small leather bag from a pocket at her waist. Eirlys recognized the Steward's medicine pouch. The herbs or salve or whatever it held were consecrated, blessed against all sorts of evils and ills.

"Use this to treat your wounds," said Glain. "It will ward off fever."

"Or worse." Eirlys tried to smile but couldn't tell if she had succeeded or not.

"You really shouldn't make light of this," Glain chided. "Every precaution must be taken."

Eirlys nodded. It was true enough. Even she knew what sort of afflictions could come from a curse. Glain laid the pouch and bandages on the table next to the bowl and quietly excused herself while Odwain finished at the hearth.

She watched him wrestle off his boots and wet tunic, and then toss them in a heap in front of the blaze. He turned to frown at her. "We should get you out of those wet clothes."

"Bring me that bowl first." Eirlys wanted relief from the fire in her hands more than anything. "And the pouch, too."

Odwain obliged without question and set the bowl and pouch on her lap. Eirlys began to bathe her hands. The burn was harsh, even soaked in the cool water. Some thistles stung, like nettles on the skin. She tried to ignore it. It would pass soon.

"Let me see." Odwain squatted before her and gently lifted one of her hands from the water to look at the palm. "What should we do about this?"

"I expect there is some sort of balm in that bag to salve the wounds," she said. "Then just wrap them up, I guess."

He looked up at her with a tender smile. "I'll make it quick, and then you can rest."

Eirlys nodded as her eyes flooded with tired tears. She sat quietly while he cleaned the gashes on her hands and applied the salve, feeling a little better just for his company and gentle tending. It was easy to let him care for her. He bound the wounds with the strips of cloth and then wiped the dirt from her face with the hem of his shirt.

"There," he said. "All finished." Odwain took the bowl from her lap and put it back on the table along with the medicine bag. He offered her a piece of the bread. "Will you eat something?"

She shook her head. "You eat. I'll take some tea, though. My mother keeps a pot in the hearth."

Odwain arched an eyebrow at her. "That is not tea she keeps in that pot."

"Then call it tonic." Eirlys shrugged. "Good for the ills and the chills."

She watched Odwain fumble about for a cup, more in love with him now than ever she'd been. Eirlys had fancied many things about marriage but she hadn't imagined how sweet it would be to have the man she adored see so eagerly to her comforts. But by the time he'd poured the aleberry and offered her the cup, she wasn't at all sure she could drink it.

"Can you hold it?" he asked. "It's not too hot."

"It's just right, Odwain." She would manage. After all, he'd gone to the trouble. "Thank you."

The warm cup was unexpectedly soothing to her hands, and the spicy steam appealed to her nose. A sip or two later, her topsy-turvy insides had settled a bit. Eirlys thought she might even eat the bread.

"Here." As if he'd heard her thoughts, Odwain broke a small piece from the loaf. "Try this."

The salty dough made her mouth water and sat even better on her stomach than the aleberry. "I hadn't realized I was so hungry."

Odwain nodded toward the window. The sky had darkened with dusk as well as the rain clouds. "It is later than you think, and you've had a difficult day."

"Hair-raising, more like," she admitted.

He frowned and tilted his head as if to examine her face. "You should lie down."

"I'm fine." Her voice faded with doubt. She was cold, and it had been an awful ordeal, after all. "But maybe you're right."

"Of course I am right." Odwain led her to the bedside and threw back the coverlet. "Can you get yourself undressed?"

Eirlys clambered onto the mattress trying to avoid the use of her hands, though the burning had eased. She pulled herself to her knees and managed to scuttle around to face him. "I'll need your help with the belt clasp," she heard herself answer. "But I can do the rest."

Odwain held her steady with one hand and deftly removed her waist chain with the other. He stood close to be certain she didn't topple over while she tugged the heavy dress over her head and then stepped several paces back. He even went so far as to turn and face the other room. As if it were some scandal to see her stripped to her underclothes.

"I think your chivalry charming, Odwain," she said. Eirlys dug her way into the bed slip and swaddled herself in the sheeting and blankets. "But you needn't go to such extremes anymore, I don't think. It's not as though I am altogether naked, and we *are* to be married, after all."

"Ah, but we are not married yet." He peeked over his shoulder to be certain she was covered before turning to grin at her. "I know it amuses you, pet, but I rely on my manners to keep me from giving in to my less noble nature."

He reached across her for her dress and kissed her forehead as he passed. "I'll hang this to dry, and you get some sleep."

She watched Odwain spread her wet clothes on the hearth along with his, huddled with her knees curled to her chest. Her skin still felt cold and clammy in spite of the woolen bed rugs. How nice it would be, she thought, to have Odwain's warmth around her.

Once he had finished arranging the clothing, Odwain stuffed another log into the fire and settled himself on the divan. Eirlys was disappointed. This was taking propriety to ridiculous lengths. "Will you sit here, with me?"

He gazed at her over the back of the sofa. "That can't possibly be a good idea, Eirlys."

"Please, Odwain."

She was not above a good whine, if necessary, but it seemed she must have looked pitiful enough. After a proper show of reluctance, Odwain finally walked to the side of the bed and knelt to look at her. He smoothed the damp curls from her eyes and cupped her chin in his palm. "Are you all right, pet?"

"I can't seem to get warm," she chattered.

"Very well, then," Odwain relented. He pulled himself up and perched awkwardly on the edge of the mattress, edging just enough onto the bed to hold her. "But only until you fall asleep."

* * *

Odwain's valiant attempts to hold to his scruples were tested as soon as she nestled herself in his arms and laid her head on his chest. Odwain reasoned that aid through comfort was a noble motive and a defensible argument to even the sternest critic. Even Bledig could forgive something so sublime, so sweet as this— couldn't he?

"Odwain," she whispered, lifting her face to his, her lips so close he could already taste them. "Come closer."

When Eirlys lifted the bedclothes and beckoned him under, Odwain could not resist. His fingers felt the warmth of her skin before he realized that all that separated them were a layer or two of underclothing.

A knock on the door shocked him to his feet, just before Glain let herself in. He was certain she could see his guilty conscience plain as the nose on his face. "Is there something else? Eirlys should sleep. Undisturbed. For a bit."

"Madoc has sent a salve for her wounds." She handed the small jar to him with what looked to him like a knowing smile. "The sooner it is applied, the more it will help."

Odwain nodded, afraid to speak again for fear of what nonsense might escape.

"There's a bell on the desk. I'll be near enough to hear it, if you need me." Glain gave a nod and let herself out, leaving Odwain much relieved.

Odwain returned to the bed and Eirlys's outstretched arms, with Madoc's salve in hand. "Let's put this to use first."

She allowed him to unbind her hands and apply the medicine, but no sooner had he retied the bandages did she pull him under the covers again. Eirlys offered her mouth as she clung to him, and Odwain took her kisses, reasoning that this would comfort her. He allowed his hands to trace the hollow of her back and the curve of her hips, slowly and deliberately, allowing himself to enjoy the nearness of her flesh. Eirlys writhed at the slightest touch, arching into his caresses and moaning against his mouth. It was wonderful. And horrible. What if the others returned to find him with Eirlys, in her mother's bed no less?

But she was willing, and he was only human. No one could deny that she was his and Odwain could not withstand the constraints of decency a minute more. Still, Eirlys was virgin.

This was a far more unnerving worry: an unspoiled girl and a test of skill he'd never tried. Innocence was entrusted, not taken. First love was sacred. Its consummation required reverence and patience. He could not imagine greater proof of the character of a man than gentleness in the throes of raging passion, and Odwain was afraid that he would fail her.

"Eirlys." Odwain pulled his lips from hers. He wanted to see her eyes. "Look at me."

She gazed up at him so openly his heart ached. He held her face in his hands and let her loveliness amaze him all over again. "Are you sure that this is what you want?" he asked. "I must know you're certain."

"Don't worry so Odwain," she said. "I love you. That is all you need to know."

Eirlys was so confident in him, and assured of him in ways he was not assured of in himself. It occurred to him then that the very trust she gave to him, he owed her in return. Odwain put uncertainty aside and placed his faith in the love they had for each other. And in the life ahead they would build together.

He released her only long enough to undress. Her gazing upon him as he revealed himself both unnerved and excited him. Odwain wondered what she expected, of him and of lovemaking. It couldn't help but be uncomfortable for her, but he would be careful.

Odwain stretched out alongside her and drew her closer. Eirlys molded her body to his, as if it were the most natural thing to do, and he struggled to control the wild urges her breasts pressed against his chest inspired. Eirlys slid her leg over his hip and pulled him toward her. Patience, he reminded himself.

He nuzzled the scratches on her cheek and swallowed hard. "That briar patch put up a nasty fight."

Eirlys gave a soft moaning sigh in answer. He moved to kiss her mouth but was greeted with trembling lips and weepy, desperate eyes. His heart raced with panic.

"What is it, pet?" he whispered.

"Don't tease," she pleaded. "Please."

Odwain was lost. He raised himself over her and let her wrap her legs around him. His erection straining against the folds of her burrow made her groan. Eirlys arched and lifted her hips to give him entrance, but he waited.

"I don't mean to tease, only to be cautious."

He reached between her legs expecting to find her ready for him, but prepared to coax her if need be. His fingers stoked gently through moist curls until they found her opening. She was wet and swollen, squirming impatiently against his hand as he slid one finger and then two inside. Odwain encountered the natural resistance there and felt a moment's regret. He didn't want to hurt her, but the many other pleasures he could give her would be better enjoyed once this was done.

Eirlys would not be denied any longer. Her need was insistent, as was his. Odwain pressed himself slowly but firmly into her. Her eyes widened in surprise when he entered, and she gasped as he felt her maidenhead give way in a subtle rupture. Eirlys clutched at him and shuddered. He felt awful.

"I'm sorry, pet." He waited, holding her and searching her face, afraid to move until he knew she wanted him to.

Eirlys answered him with a kiss and a whisper. "Come, Odwain. No more waiting, or wanting."

He needed no more enticement than her arms and legs around him and the soft moans that escaped her lips as he moved inside of her. Eirlys was warmer and more sensual than in his wildest imaginings. Another day he'd show her rapture, but neither his heart nor his manhood could contain his ecstasy much longer. His body screamed for release and Eirlys obliged, meeting his thrusts with her own until he succumbed in a splendid rush of relief.

Odwain withdrew with care and held Eirlys snugly to him, offering a silent promise to never let her go. She burrowed deeper into his embrace and drifted fast asleep. Not comfortable, exactly, but at least she was at ease. Though still wracked with worry, Odwain was deliriously happy just to hold her.

He had never before had the chance to take in her more subtle nature. She was beautiful, breathtakingly so, especially at peace. Eirlys seemed almost fragile in stillness, more delicate and refined in repose than her wakeful spirit ever revealed.

Her breathing slowed until it was nearly as languid as the rest of her. Odwain enjoyed the weight of her body against his. The warmth of her skin and the blankets worked like a sedative on his senses and soon he began to relax. His head sagged against the pillows, and the blissful haze closed in.

TWENTY-ONE

His eyes snapped open to darkness. Some moments had passed, maybe more, maybe hours. Odwain realized he must have succumbed to exhaustion, but he was fully awake now. Eirlys, though, was still asleep in his arms. The rain had stopped, and Odwain wondered about the hour. Was it evening already? He couldn't tell.

Odwain groaned softly to himself. The last thing he wanted to do was to move. He risked disturbing Eirlys, and that would deprive her of much needed rest. It would also deprive Odwain of his own guilty pleasure. An awful dilemma, but the fire was dying and the room growing colder by the minute.

Odwain held his breath as he lifted her shoulders and eased himself out from under, ever so slowly shifting his weight toward the edge of the bed. Once he was free, Odwain gently lowered Eirlys back to the pillows and slid off. He stifled a yelp as his bare feet met the cold stone floor and nearly bolted across the room to the hearth. He hunted on hands and knees in the dusk for his tunic and yanked it on to quell the shivers. The chill was fierce.

Odwain had the fire stoked and blazing in no time. He stood with his back to the blaze to warm himself, and watch over his woman. It made him smile to see that she had curled into the space he'd left. Odwain was tempted to crawl back into bed beside her until he remembered her wounded hands and her mother's warning to watch for fever. It would be best to wake her now, just to be sure. At the very least, the dressings would have to be changed.

Odwain sat on the edge of the bed and brushed the curls from her face, tracing her nose and lips with his fingertips. Her skin was warm to the touch, but she was not perspiring. As far as he could tell, Eirlys had no fever. This, to his great relief, was a decidedly good sign.

He bent and kissed her softly on the mouth. "Eirlys," he whispered. "Awake, pet."

She didn't stir save to draw breath, and Odwain felt dread settle in the pit of his stomach. He gave her shoulder a good shake. "Wake up now, girl. You are scaring me."

Still no sign or sound, and Odwain felt his heart drop into his toes. He shook her roughly and shouted. "Eirlys!"

Her eyelids fluttered open and closed again, and a soft sigh slipped past her lips.

"Eirlys?" He stroked her cheek, and she seemed to come round again. She gazed back at him glassy-eyed and vapid for a moment before slipping back into a dead sleep. Odwain's instincts flared. Something was terribly wrong.

He pulled one of her hands from the blankets and stripped the bandage off. The cuts on her palm were raw and seeping but there was neither pus nor foul smell. Odwain was befuddled. He wrapped the cloth loosely round her hand and looked at her closely again. Why wouldn't she wake?

Whatever was wrong, he needed help. Odwain covered Eirlys snugly, found his boots, and made for the door.

"Glain!"

His shout fell dead in the empty hallway. Where was that blasted attendant now? He couldn't just leave Eirlys alone.

Odwain had no idea what to do. Thankfully, his practical nature soon overcame his panic and Odwain began to reason clearly as he walked the long hall toward the stairs. Somewhere on the main floor were the acolytes' quarters. He would find Glain there.

Odwain's quick clip lurched into an anxious lope, spurred by the cold sweat of fear beading along his spine. Desperation drove him until he was racing at a breakneck pace, leaping down the steps two and three at a time. As he stumbled to a stop at the bottom of the staircase, Odwain realized he had no idea which way to go. He had very little knowledge of the temple beyond the main corridors, and there was no one about to ask. To his right, he figured, past the assembly hall and through the kitchens.

"Were you looking for me?"

The voice chilled his blood. Cerrigwen was the last person he had hoped to find. Although she was by all rights due his respect and consideration, he was uneasy in her presence. "I have come to find Glain."

She emerged from a small, shadowy aperture on the far side of the hall, some passageway Odwain had never noticed before. "Is the girl ill?"

Odwain hesitated, bound by loyalty and respect for Alwen's feelings. He knew she wanted Cerrigwen nowhere near her daughter, but what choice did he have? He would do anything for Eirlys, including defy her mother. "She will not wake."

Cerrigwen frowned a moment and then brushed past him on her way to the stairs. "Show me."

Odwain followed her back in to Alwen's rooms. Eirlys was just as he'd left her.

"You've tended to her wounds, I assume." Cerrigwen swept across the room, her skirts rustling beneath her robe. She was imposing, if not a little intimidating.

"Yes," Odwain said quietly. "The cuts were cleaned and salved. She has no fever, and no infection that I could see."

"Well," she said, "if you didn't find any blight, it's doubtful I will. But bring some light and let's have a look. Dark magic can work in unexpected ways, some too subtle to see or sense right away."

Odwain searched the room for a candle and finally found one on the windowsill. He rooted about the desk for a tinderbox, to no avail. "A moment," he stalled. "I'll use a touchwood from the fire."

"For pity sake, Odwain." Cerrigwen snapped her fingers and the wick alit on its own.

Odwain nearly dropped the candlestick in shock. Magic had never become so commonplace to him that it didn't still startle the spit out of him, even after all these weeks surrounded by sorcerers. He set the candle on the bed stand and hovered awkwardly nearby, uncertain what to do. He was sick with worry and feeling helpless.

"Don't stand there like some timid little stable boy." Cerrigwen unhooked the chain clasp on her cloak and tossed the robe over the end of the bed. She nodded toward the far side. "Sit with her."

"What do you suppose could be ailing her?" Odwain rounded the foot of the bed and sat gingerly next to Eirlys. He took her free hand in his lap and toyed gently with her fingertips. "She will wake, won't she?"

"Only time will tell that." Cerrigwen sat beside Eirlys and began to remove the loose bind on Eirlys's hand to examine her wounds. "No sleeping sickness I know comes on without cause. It stands to reason, then, that if the vines and thorns were cursed, then so would Eirlys be."

She peeled the cloth carefully away from the skin and lifted the palm to look more closely. Cerrigwen sighed and slowly shook her head. "It is worse than I feared."

"What?" Odwain demanded. "What is it?"

Cerrigwen held out Eirlys's hand to him. "See for yourself."

Odwain's breath left him. He snatched her other hand from the blankets and tore the bandage from it. It was the same. Just beneath the torn skin on her palms, deathly black tendrils curled outward from the open wounds like a noxious cling-weed overtaking an unsuspecting spring flower. Ever so slowly, something evil was creeping through her veins.

"She is poisoned, but not by any earthly venom. This is surely a wicked curse, and yet she still breathes. By rights, she should already be dead." Cerrigwen studied Eirlys for several moments. "This salve on her wounds, what is it?"

"I don't know what it is. Glain brought it." Odwain found the small jar and handed it to Cerrigwen. "From Madoc."

Cerrigwen nodded knowingly as she daubed a bit of the ointment on her palm and then placed her hand over the open wound on Eirlys's palm. She closed her eyes and murmured a quiet chant while Odwain waited, daring not to move or speak. He could only beg the unseen powers to aid Cerrigwen in whatever it was she was doing, and hope with all his heart that Eirlys would rouse.

After moments that seemed more like hours, Cerrigwen laid Eirlys's hand back on the bed and reached for her robe as she stood. "I have done all I can do."

Odwain was stung by the finality of Cerrigwen's words. "There must be *something* more you can do."

"She is very strong." Cerrigwen softened. "Eirlys has held it off so far and that is nothing short of miraculous. She has some natural resistance. Perhaps her own magic is at work. But there is nothing to do now but see her through it, whatever the end."

Odwain's blood ran cold. "Surely there must be some cure."

"If there is, I do not have it. It may be that her mother or Madoc has knowledge I do not."

Odwain was startled to his feet when the door burst open. Alwen rushed in with Bledig and Rhys at her heels. Without a word, she shoved past Cerrigwen to get to Eirlys.

Alwen glared at Odwain as she reached for her daughter's hand. "You summoned Cerrigwen?"

Odwain nearly flinched. "What else could I do? Eirlys would not wake," he explained.

What he thought might have been reproach flickering on her face quickly faded. "It's all right, Odwain," she said gently. "Let's have a look."

"Cerrigwen says the thorns were tainted."

"She would know," Alwen muttered, but not so quietly that she could not be heard.

"What is wrong with my daughter?" Bledig demanded. He had taken a protective stance at the foot of the bed, but would venture no nearer. Odwain thought that Bledig looked frightened, which unnerved him completely.

Alwen straightened slowly and turned to Bledig. Odwain's heart sunk as he caught the look of devastation that she gave him. Alwen was reluctant to speak. Odwain could see it in her face. He could see her desperately searching for the words, and he understood her pain. No one wanted to give Bledig bad news. But she did not get the chance.

"The girl is unconscious," Cerrigwen said bluntly. "It is an unnatural sleep. Induced by a spell worked though the venom in the thorns, I would guess."

"When will she wake?"

"As I told the boy, there is no way to tell. Nothing more can be done. Either she will wake, or she will not."

Bledig frowned, but nodded understanding. He seemed oddly calm and collected. "So, we must wait. She seems at peace, at least."

Odwain was confused by Bledig's reaction. He was not a man to rail against reason, but he was too composed. Bledig was a man of passionate moods. Great gods in heaven, Odwain suddenly realized—Bledig was resigned. He had taken Cerrigwen's prognosis completely to heart and was willing to leave it all up to fate. Odwain would not accept hopelessness or helplessness any longer. Nor would he hand either to Bledig without first exhausting every effort.

"She is fighting it on her own," Odwain protested. "And Alwen has yet to see Madoc. There must be some way he can help."

Odwain looked to Alwen for support, and what he saw made him want to swallow his tongue. She offered him what was meant to be a reassuring smile, but Alwen was clearly afraid. "I will ask him."

Alwen sighed and gently stroked Eirlys's cheek. Her hand trembled and Odwain felt tears burn in his eyes. This could not be happening.

"There must be something I can do," Rhys whispered in misery.

"Sit here awhile," Odwain suggested. He managed a weak smile for his friend. "Perhaps you can keep me from losing my mind."

Alwen laid a hand of encouragement on her son's arm. "The two of you will be good company for her." She gestured with her eyes at Bledig. "And for him. I'll send Glain with water and gruel. See if you can get Eirlys to take something to drink, at least."

She then turned on Cerrigwen with what Odwain could only describe as utter loathing and a deep, angry thirst for vengeance. "I want to speak with you," Alwen said tersely. "Outside."

* * *

"This is not my doing."

Cerrigwen stood calmly in the middle of the corridor with her hands clasped loosely in the front folds of her robe. Her voice and posture belied no remorse, no regret. She had the coolness of confidence, but Alwen would not be convinced of her innocence.

"It is," Alwen accused. Indeed, she did feel it. Time and practice had heightened her senses enough to begin to penetrate Cerrigwen's formidable defenses. Though what she saw she could not yet define, Alwen had the distinct impression of malevolence. "Somehow. I can feel it."

Cerrigwen narrowed her eyes, but she remained completely unruffled by Alwen's condemnation. "You are mistaken."

It occurred to Alwen then that while Cerrigwen was surely possessed of some evil intent, perhaps there was something even uglier inside than her ill will toward Alwen.

Alwen stepped closer. "What are you hiding, Cerrigwen?"

"Oh, so many things." Cerrigwen's smile twitched and twisted with every flicker of the lamplight. She paused as if to listen to a faraway voice.

"It seems you have discovered how to sense what I feel," she said. "But what my moods reveal tells you nothing that matters. You still do not hear my thoughts, hmm? How you must be suffering to know."

Alwen did wonder, but she would not be baited. This was little more than a distraction, a vain attempt to rile Alwen's temper so that she would not persist. Instead, she went back to the point. "You were kind once, and reverent."

"Reverence? Is that what you expect?" Cerrigwen laughed. "Your conceit is exceeded only by your ignorance, Alwen. Whatever authority you claim is limited even within the walls of the Stewardry, and it is virtually worthless beyond them, no matter what Madoc has told you. You may well surpass me in years and rank, and certainly you outstrip me in piety. But there is no council here, not yet. There is only you and I, and *you* do not rule *me*."

Alwen straightened to her full height, at least a hand span above Cerrigwen. "I have no yen to govern you or anyone else, but I do intend to see that the covenants of the order are maintained. Perhaps you have forgotten your vows, but I remember."

"What do you remember? The distant echoes of some dark night so long ago it has faded into a figment of your imagination? Memories are illusions, Alwen. They resemble whatever truth you choose to mold them into."

She cocked her head and raised her chin to cast a mocking look at Alwen. The movement caused the moss agate pendant to slide aside and reveal a circular blaze beneath. Alwen's hand instinctively rose to her own chest, remembering the burning sensation she had felt in the forest. The mark was proof of something. At the very least, Cerrigwen knew more about the black magic worked in the woods than she was willing to reveal.

"And what is your truth, Cerrigwen?" Alwen demanded, more convinced than ever of Cerrigwen's treachery. "Do you even know? Is there anything or anyone you care for more than yourself?"

Cerrigwen's eyes widened, revealing ominous depths and bitter strength in their fierce glare. She sauntered closer. So close that Alwen could nearly smell the venom in her words. "What I know is that I have a destiny beyond the one Madoc would allow me. There is a hierarchy far greater than your precious council, Alwen. You will see. In the end, *you* will rule *nothing*."

Alwen considered Cerrigwen carefully. Envy was an ugly, soul-sucking disease and Cerrigwen was ravaged with it, along with many other blights. "That may well be, my sister. But I will trust my fate to Madoc, no matter what the end."

"A prudent plan. No less than I would expect of you." Cerrigwen folded her arms over her chest. "And no more, either. True greatness requires sacrifice. Risk. I do not believe you possess the courage, Alwen. There is a thin veil between caution and cowardice, and I see fear in you." Cerrigwen's smile returned, creeping wide across her face.

Indignation sparked within Alwen like a flash fire. Cerrigwen was clever, but Alwen still refused to trip the snare. She squared herself to Cerrigwen and met her rigid pose with equal bravado, nose to nose and spit to spit.

"The only truth that matters here is where your loyalty lies. But know this." Alwen spoke boldly, with threat and forbidding she meant with every ounce of her soul. "Whether you concede to my authority or not, you *will* concede to Madoc's. I will demand it, Cerrigwen, one way or another. It will be both my duty, and my pleasure."

Alwen paused to be sure that Cerrigwen heard the promise in her words. "And if it is you who has brought this pox on my daughter, I shall not hesitate to destroy you."

Cerrigwen blanched, ever so slightly. "This was not my doing. Even if it were within my power, it is not within my heart. I am a mother, as well, Alwen. I could never bring harm to your child."

"Alwen." Bledig had entered the hall without her knowing it. "What the devil is this? We can hear you all the way inside."

"Pardon, Mistress." Glain appeared from the shadows. "Madoc is asking for you."

"Wait." Alwen was frustrated by the intrusions. She was not satisfied that enough had been said. Cerrigwen, however, seized the opportunity for escape.

"Perhaps this is a discussion best left for another time," Cerrigwen said. "You shouldn't keep Madoc waiting."

"Go," Bledig urged. "He may be able to help. I'll sit with Eirlys."

Before she could answer one way or another, Cerrigwen slipped into the shadows, and Bledig reached for the door handle. Alwen watched him disappear behind her chamber door, desperately torn. Her loyalties were at odds for the first time in her life. Every feminine instinct Alwen had cried out to follow him, to stay with her family and look after her child. But she could not. The sorceress in her knew that there were other deadly threats afoot.

So this was it, she thought. So many times she'd wondered. True sacrifice was the surrender of one sacred thing in favor of keeping another. No matter how prudent or cautious one was, in the end something precious was lost. Whether the claim was in the name of family or duty or honor or truth, it exacted a terrible price. To her dismay, she did not feel the pride or pleasure that Bledig had claimed when he spoke of the sacrifices he had made for her and their children. For Alwen, sacrifice brought grief and guilt, and an unbearable sense of uncertainty.

TWENTY-TWO

"**B**ring the stool from the corner." Madoc waved her forward without looking up from his meal. "There is food enough for two, and I've already poured your wine."

She dragged out the three-footed hassock and settled on the opposite side of his desk—a platter piled with meat and bread, a berry bowl and a wine pitcher between them. Sure enough, he'd already doled out the drink, and Alwen instinctively reached first for the cup.

Madoc cocked an eyebrow. "Still fond of the aleberry, I see."

Alwen shrugged a bit sheepishly as she sipped. "The recipe was one of the few comforts of home that I could take with me."

"You must eat, restore your strength," he counseled. "You'll need every ounce you can muster these next days."

To appease him, Alwen forced herself to nibble. She found it more appealing than she expected, and helped herself to more.

"Your daughter," Madoc said, "I understand that she does not fare well."

Alwen swallowed hard. The words nearly strangled her. "No, she does not."

Madoc shook his head and sighed. "It grieves me no end that the child has come to harm."

Her breath caught in her throat. "Is there nothing you can do?"

"I will look in on her when we've finished here," he said gently. "I sent the best healing magic I know with Glain in the form of a consecrated salve. It is not a cure, but it will aid the girl in her fight."

Alwen stifled the sob that threatened to escape her trembling lips and nodded understanding. Eirlys would live or die on her own.

"From time to time, despite my best efforts, I still find many things fall beyond my control." Madoc lifted the wine pitcher and topped her glass. "It is then I am often reminded that mine is not the only wisdom, nor is it always the best. Sometimes we are given no choice but to have faith in something or someone other than ourselves."

He paused, as if to give her a moment to think on his advice. Alwen presumed his intent was a gentle prodding in a direction he knew she would resist. "Cerrigwen has tended Eirlys, but to no avail."

Madoc nodded. "So tell me of this wall of thorns. Did you find it?"

"We did." Alwen felt the sting of the raw skin beneath her amulet. The burn evoked a vivid vision of the magic she had unleashed and made her wonder more about the mark she had seen on Cerrigwen's breast. "It is vanquished."

"Good." He swallowed the last of his food with a healthy dose from his own cup, then looked hard at her. "I'm afraid this will not be the last of such attacks against us. The Ancients foretold all of this. The nearer the new king's ascension draws, the more horrific the attempts to defeat him will become. Hywel is an indomitable man, forthright and exacting, and intolerant of inequity.

He also believes that sharing power dilutes its strength. For those who seek to retain their own influence over the ways of the world, Hywel is a threat that must be destroyed."

"The devilkin's hedge is Cerrigwen's doing," Alwen asserted. "She denies it, but I am certain she is to blame."

"Cerrigwen?" Madoc's eyes widened, but he did not seem surprised. "What makes you suspect her?"

"I feel it. I can sense the treachery in her."

"I see," he said. He seemed pleased, which Alwen thought odd. "Suppose she did possess the skill. What reason would she have to set such a wretched spell against the Stewardry?"

"Not against the Stewardry," Alwen asserted. "Against me."

"Hmm. Well," he nodded. "Whatever the truth in that, I can tell you that she did not manage it all on her own. If Cerrigwen is working dark spells, it is with Machreth's guidance and on his behalf. And that concerns me far more than any petty jealousies between the two of you."

"Machreth?" Alwen had not considered the possibility that Machreth wished to harm her as well. If Cerrigwen had indeed acted on Machreth's authority or even at his bidding, the implications were staggering. The two of them in consort against Madoc was an immeasurable threat. The events of the day were worsening by the moment. "Has he openly defied you?"

"It's only a matter of time now until he does."

Alwen was stunned. "This is unheard of."

"So it is, or was. Even the thought of treason would have been an unfathomable sin. To set one Steward against another was impossible. Our codes were that strong. But things are different now, as you've already discovered."

Alwen nodded, remembering the hollow victory in the woods. "It is not a triumph I am proud to claim."

"You did what you must. No doubt you will be called to far more distasteful duties. Even as we sit here, Machreth plots. Very soon, he will strike and try to take my seat. But I will be ready for him, Alwen." He shook a crooked finger at her. "And so must you."

Madoc brushed the crumbs from his beard and pushed the platter away. He laced his gnarled fingers together and rested his hands on the table, staring with intense concern into Alwen's face. The deep blue of his eyes glinted black in the flickering light, darkened more by his grave thoughts than the shadows.

"Much as it pains me to keep you from your child, circumstances have conspired to require it. There are pressing matters that we must discuss. Things that dare not wait. Will you stay, or do you prefer to go? The choice is yours."

A piece of her heart leapt at the chance to return to her chambers. If only there was a way to be in both places at once. Though the mother in her cried out to be with her child, the sorceress in her had already answered the call.

She set down her cup and clasped her hands in her lap, resigned to her destiny. "Eirlys is well attended, and Glain will come for me if I am needed."

"Be certain now, Alwen," he insisted. "Once you begin this path there will be no turning back."

Alwen understood. She had warned Rhys herself. Possibility was a deceptive lure. Sometimes it was more attractive when viewed from a distance. When opportunity actually arrived it rarely appeared as one had hoped, but Alwen had learned to expect the unexpected.

What I want is to know what I want. Her son's words were both revealing and perceptive. For him, at the onset of his own life's journey, it was as she had said—a delicious dilemma. For her, it was more complicated. The prophecy was the purpose for which she had been born, and Alwen accepted this role. The fate of the world rested with the Stewardry, and for now, the fate of the Stewardry depended upon her. As did the safety of her family, she reasoned. Perhaps she could serve both duties at once.

Perhaps what Madoc had to offer would help her ferret out the truth behind the curse that afflicted Eirlys and allow her to bring vengeance to bear upon those responsible.

"I have made my choice," Alwen affirmed. "I am prepared to serve it."

"Knowing full well that there will be unforeseen costs," he pressed her. "That there will be consequences."

"Yes, Madoc." Alwen was committed. "Knowing full well."

"Very well then," he said. "But don't lose sight of that cup. You may soon find yourself badly in want of its remedies."

He leaned heavily against the chair back and leveled a sorrowful look at her. "With Machreth and Cerrigwen in league against us, I find I must impart to you knowledge you are not truly prepared to receive. But, someone must hear my secrets before I die."

Despite the chilling shudder that wracked her, Alwen held her poise. She wiped her damp palms on her skirt and reached for the drink. The cup shook in her hands, but she managed to empty its entire mind-numbing contents into her mouth and swallow her heart back into her chest. "Confidences will be spoken between us tonight, Alwen, sacred trusts that cannot pass beyond you. What I am about to share with you is for your knowledge alone. You may not tell anyone."

She felt buoyed enough by the wine to speak with some conviction. "You have my unwavering loyalty, Madoc. Let there be no question."

"There is no question," he answered firmly. "If there were, you would not be sitting before me now. Though I have disavowed Machreth, I have not yet declared a new heir. Should it happen that I do not live to see to the succession myself, the duty will fall to you. You must be prepared to stand in my stead until the new Ard Druidh ascends."

"Have you another ascendant in mind?"

"Yes," he admitted. "A blood heir. But that is a name I will not yet speak. For all our sakes, most especially hers."

Hers. Madoc intended to seat a woman in his place. This, too, was unheard of. Good grace. She could only hope she possessed what he would require of her.

Madoc had begun to drum his fingers lightly on the tabletop. He stared beyond her for a minute or two, as though considering how best to express his next thoughts. At long last, he cleared his throat.

"No woman has ever before held the seat of the Ard Druidh, not even as proxy, and with good reason. The secrets of the Stewardry safeguard the lives of entire populations, of entire generations. Their unwitting revelation could unmake the world. But perhaps even more perilous is the danger having care of these secrets poses to the poor soul who is indentured to do so."

Despite his concerns, it did not seem so unbearable to her. She had the training, the skill, and the desire. "I am ready."

"So you say now," he challenged. "But I must be sure you can bear the full weight of what you are about to undertake. As my proxy, times may come that you find yourself called upon to make difficult choices, Alwen. The most difficult choices you can imagine. You must be prepared to put the Stewardry before all else— before yourself, before even your family. Few women of true heart could find the will to make such sacrifices. But if ever there was such a woman," he said slowly, "I have to hope it is you."

Madoc left his words hanging in the silence, and Alwen was grateful for his deliberate pause. The deeper truths had very nearly slipped past her—and with them, the dire consequence. As far as she could see, though, the odds were with them both.

"This pledge is not so simple a task as you might have thought," he said finally. "But I have no doubts, if you are willing." Madoc sat straight. "So what say you, Alwen of Pwll, high sorceress of the Stewardry and guardian of the realms? Do you accept? Will you sit my throne and hold it in safekeeping, until the rightful sovereign comes forward? I must have your answer now."

"Yes, Madoc." The clear, calm voice that Alwen heard could not have been hers. The voice of her mind was still conflicted, confused, and uncertain. But it was she who had spoken. "I accept."

Somehow, in that moment, Alwen understood the full depth of her own strength, the full measure of her ability, just as plainly as she knew the full weight of her decision. This was the destiny she had waited for her entire life, and she would respond with every ounce of her soul, with every strength and skill at her hand.

"So be it." Madoc nodded with satisfaction. It was the answer he had been expecting, the answer he had already known she would give. He shoved back his chair and pulled to a stand. "Come with me."

Madoc led her down the east annex corridor, past her rooms, and all the way to the farthest end, to a doorway hidden in a recess behind the service stairs. He pointed to a torch leaning in the corner. "We'll need the light."

Alwen lit the torch with the flame from the oil lamp on the wall and followed Madoc's beckon to descend the dark, curving stone steps that led deep below. "How far do we go?"

"All the way to the bottom," he huffed. "Three flights to the castle main, and then two more."

It seemed they were descending into the very bowels of the earth. The air was stale and thick with dust. Alwen wondered how Madoc could withstand it. She was barely able to breathe it herself.

She took the stairs slowly, with Madoc's hand on her shoulder to brace him. When her foot finally felt the earthen floor, she whispered her thanks to the gods. Alwen held the torch out in front of her. "Now where?"

"That way." Madoc took the torch and pointed into the black mouth of yet another corridor. "I will lead from here. Watch your footing, and make careful note of the trail I take. Commit every turn, every passage to memory, Alwen, or you will never find your way through the labyrinth again."

Alwen followed him through an unending series of winding, writhing conduits that seemed to lead nowhere, and everywhere. Memory niggled at the edges of her mind. Alwen recalled the dank, musty air of a secret subterranean escape, and a powerful fear of the dark. She had been through this maze before, once, but so long ago the path was no longer known to her. So she took heed of Madoc's instruction, memorizing every break in the stone or crack in the walls that might mark the course.

"There is only one way in," he puffed. "And one way back. And then, there is the way out." His chuckle choked to a hacking cough that nearly dropped him to his knees.

"Sovereign?" Alwen took his elbow.

Madoc waved her off. "I'm all right, Alwen. Old, maybe, but not altogether feeble."

He pointed to an opening just to his left. "This one. This leads under the grounds and lets out in the forest on the other side of the veil. Guard its location well, Alwen. It is a most convenient means of escape," he warned. "But also a point of breach."

"I have been here before."

"So you have," he nodded. "This far, at least."

With that, he moved ahead. A few paces farther, the passage widened. Beyond the widening was a chamber so dark the flame barely pierced the shroud of blackness. But something caught the glimmer of the torchlight.

Madoc reached back for her hand and pulled her through the entrance alongside of him. He stepped forward to light two torches staked opposite each other a half dozen feet in front of them and then slid the one he held into an iron brace on the wall next to the entrance.

The fragile glow flickered and waned, casting shadowy specters on the hand-hewn walls. A faint shimmer attracted her eye. The light reflected eerily on the dark waters of an underground tarn. Madoc moved forward to kneel beside the pool and beckoned that she should join him.

"Yours are the only eyes other than mine to have seen this place," he said quietly. "Come closer, Alwen. Behold, the Well of Tears."

Alwen could not bring herself to move. Her toes curled at the thought. She stood at the altar of the Ancients, glimpsing evidence of the existence of the legacy she served.

"The well is so old its origin has faded beyond memory. It is said that the stream beneath the pool is sourced so deep in the earth it could only have been sprung by the tears of the gods themselves," Madoc explained. "Since the beginning, these waters have been fed with the wisdom of the ages. Herein is stored the knowledge of every Ard Druidh to rule Fane Gramarye for more than nine generations."

"Madoc," she asked quietly, "I do not understand how it is that water can contain a man's essence. How is the knowledge passed?"

"It is not such a difficult thing, in the magical sense, though it surely defies the laws of nature." Madoc trailed his hand in the pool. "As each Ard Druidh reaches the end of his reign, his experience is poured into the well through a ritual shedding of tears. Thus, the waters are salted with the memories and insights of a lifetime. Some good and some bad, but all of it useful." He turned to smile at her. "It is the most valuable legacy we can bestow upon the generations to come. What better gift than the lessons already learned?"

Madoc then held out his hands to her. "Come. Sit."

He waited for her to find the courage to take her place beside him. Alwen was afraid to even disturb the dirt on the floor of such a sacred place, but she did as she was bid. With great care and reverence, she crept three steps forward, took his hands, and knelt gingerly at the water's edge.

"Here." Madoc held her hands out over the pool and turned her palms up. "Cup your hands."

Alwen complied as best she could. Her hands were shaking too hard to hold them in place. She watched in disbelief as Madoc scooped water from the well with his own hands and let it fall into hers.

"There. You see? It's only water," he joked.

It drained in droplets through her fingers, cold and wet, just as water would. And yet, whether it was just wishful thinking or some spiritual sentience, Alwen would have sworn that she felt the forces within it. As her hands slowly emptied, she watched each dribble ripple the placid stillness. She asked herself what amazing truths could lie below.

"When the time comes, you will drink from the well. And as you partake of the well, you will partake of me. What I know, you will know."

"But I am not the Ard Druidh," she answered. "Nor will I ever be."

"This is true, in the strictest sense, but these are unusual circumstances." Madoc looked on her kindly. "I cede you my rights to the well, Alwen, in safekeeping for my heir."

Madoc was placing his confidence in her. "How can it be that I am worthy of this?" she whispered.

"If you are not already," he said, "then you will become so."

"How can you know such a thing?"

"Faith." He gave a faint smile. "I have faith, my dear."

There could be no greater honor than this, and she silently vowed to herself that she would never fail him. Not ever.

When Alwen finally found her voice again, she asked. "How will I know when the time has come?"

"You will know. Until then, you will have my living guidance. And when I have gone, you will rely on the well. But there is one other secret to these waters. Perhaps the greatest magic of all."

Madoc smiled at her with a sort of wistful longing that tugged at her heart. "In the days when the world was young, the Stewards were sent to shepherd the mortal flocks. Upon the Stewards was bestowed the dream-speak, the ancient tongue of the gods through which their wisdom and guidance could be carried between the world of mortals and the realm of the spirit."

He scooped water into the air and let it splash back to the surface. "The language of the dream is a potent tool. Any sorcerer entrusted with this power can navigate the misty fields between the conscious and the unconscious, and plant the seed of thought in the mind of any soul he chooses, while they sleep. The dream-speak can be used to alter the fates of man, which is why the gift is so sparingly given. Imagine such power in the hands of evil."

"It could unmake the world," she said.

Madoc sighed. "Indeed. And to think I nearly gave it to Machreth."

"But you didn't," she offered.

"No," he nodded. "Fortunately for us all, I did not."

Madoc continued his litany. "The secret is revealed to only one man in every generation—the one man who will wield it with wisdom and reverence. Like the knowledge of the elders, the dream-speak is intended for the Ard Druidh alone. But for the first time in our history, someone other than the sovereign will know that the dream-speak exists. You, Alwen, are the first daughter of the Stewardry to share this legacy."

"The more I hear, the more frightened I become, Madoc."

"You should be frightened," he said. "It is an incredible burden, and I confess to taking more than a little relief in sharing the load."

"We are going to lose the light soon," she noticed. The torches were dimming.

Madoc glanced around the cavern. "There is one more thing I will tell you before we leave this place. There is privacy here I cannot count on elsewhere in the temple, even in my own chambers."

He extended a knobby forefinger to tap the amulet on her chest. "This is a sacred thing, an unearthly thing. The talismans belonging to you and your sisters are the channels to the elements. They are keys. Each unlocks its own realm—the spiritual, the natural, the celestial, and the physical. Once all four talismans, all four guardians are together, it will fall to you to join the Circle. But beware false charms, Alwen. Beware false friends. You will know a true guardian only by the amulet, and you will know the true amulet only by my mark."

Alwen's hand instinctively reached for the pendant as she remembered the tiny engraving of a bearded wizard encircled by a wreath of oak leaves. It matched the image on the signet ring Madoc wore on the little finger of his left hand. The ring was his seal, the one true symbol of his power.

She remembered also that last night with Madoc, so long ago, when he had endowed Alwen with the lapis she wore. To Cerrigwen, he had bestowed the moss agate; to Branwen, the moonstone; and to Tanwen, the bloodstone. The shaman, the healer, the oracle, and the sentinel—each of them a balancing force to the others, representatives of the elements that preserved the natural order. And each of them an essential piece in the workings of the universe.

"Yes." Madoc knew her thoughts and nodded approvingly. "The true legacy of the Stewardry rests with you and the others. It is the council that will save us from extinction, but it must be complete. Each of you is formidable on your own, but when the arcs are joined, they forge a ring of immeasurable strength. Somehow Cerrigwen must be brought back to her duty, Alwen. I leave it to you to bring the Circle together. And so it follows that you must also know where to seek the others, should Aslak fail." He struggled to a stand and held out his hand. "But I will tell you while we walk. We must go."

* * *

It was late, nigh on midnight. But had Glain not been hovering anxiously near the tiny dormer window on the second floor landing of the service stairs, just to be close to Alwen's rooms in case she could help, she would never have known. No one would, and that was just the sort of providence that made the hair on her arms stand on end.

Footfalls echoed in the distance. The sound came from above, somewhere beyond the stairway upon which she stood. The service stairs were at the very end of the annex, built against the outer buttress. To most anyone else, it would have seemed as if the echoes came from within the stone itself. Impossible, of course, except in Fane Gramarye. The temple was an architectural conundrum, filled with hidden rooms, caverns, and a secret passageway or two.

Glain was curious, but it was too dark to see from where she stood. Just as she started up the half flight from the landing to the third floor to investigate, a familiar robed shape emerged. The furtive figure scurried past the staircase on her way down the hall. Even in the shadows, Glain knew to whom that mantle belonged, and her curiosity turned to unease. Machreth's consort was lurking about. Her hackles bristled and her protective instincts took hold. Glain had spied a spy.

It took only an instant or two for her to decide to follow, but her quarry was already disappearing into the shadows ahead. Glain scurried along the corridor in pursuit, trying not to gain too quickly nor lag too far behind. Her heart raced, urging her feet to keep pace. The tallow oil in the wall sconces had all but burned out, and she was forced to hunt nearly blind. Glain's thoughts leapt ahead, envisioning the twists and turns her prey might be taking. But by the time she'd reached the juncture where the east annex met the main stairs, there was no one to be seen.

Glain slowed to a stop outside the door to Madoc's rooms and listened for footsteps or the sound of a door closing in the distance. Nothing. She could hear nothing but deep-sleeping stillness and her own haggard breathing.

"Blast it all," she muttered to the silence. She was disheartened at her lack of stealth, but not completely daunted yet. The spy could have gone only one of two ways. The main stairs were too conspicuous. More likely, she'd have taken the clandestine route. Farther along the third-floor hallway, in the west annex, were the docent's quarters and another set of service stairs that eventually let out in the kitchens.

Glain huffed in frustration. It was no use. She'd lost the trail. No knowing now which way to go. The best she could do was to go back to meet Madoc and tell him what little she did know.

And then she heard voices, muffled whispers from below. A tiny, niggling suspicion tugged her toward the main steps. Glain crept down the stairs, hugging the wall so that the shadows might shield her from view. As she drew nearer to the second-floor landing, the niggling suspicion flared into full panic. From where she stood, Glain could see Machreth in close conversation with his consort. As he turned to lead his companion into his chambers, Glain caught one brief but completely unobstructed glimpse of her face.

"Gods of mercy," she whispered, horrified and confused. It was Cerrigwen.

TWENTY-THREE

"It has been three days, Alwen." Bledig meant to prod gently, but frustration sharpened his point. "She can take no food or drink. She barely breathes." He sighed. "If we wait any longer there won't be anything left of her to save."

Alwen paced the floor between her bed and the hearth in stubborn silence, clutching at herself and frowning in deeply troubled thought. Bledig knew her to be angst ridden, just as he was, and he was not without compassion for her pain. But Alwen was no nearer whatever answer she hoped to find, and all the while their daughter languished.

"Alwen, please." Bledig's heart ached every time he looked upon Eirlys. Her stillness put him in mind of the dead.

She shook her head, dismissing him yet again. "I need more time."

"If not tonight, then maybe never." Bledig paused, hoping for reason to surface. She remained silent.

He was determined. "I have decided to speak to Odwain. It will break his heart, but he will see the sense of it. Rhys has already agreed."

"*You* have decided?" She looked daggers at him over the back of the divan.

"Am I not the girl's father?" he said. "If there is any situation in this damnable place where my say is at least equal to yours, it is this. And if you cannot find your way to reason, I will act on my own. For our daughter's sake."

"You won't." She stopped cold as she realized his intent. "You mustn't."

"I must." Bledig was as firm in his tone as he felt in his conviction. He meant to give Eirlys over to the faerie realm this very night. "I will, Alwen. It is what needs to be done."

She gave her head a terse shake. "It has not come to that. Not yet. You will wait until I am sure there is nothing else to be done for her."

"I would wait an eternity if I could, Alwen. But even Madoc admits he has no cure." And it would take eternity, he knew, for her to reconcile her heart to this. "I cannot give you more time, but I can give it to Eirlys."

"But you would have her exist in a world beyond my grasp," she whispered through tears. "A place in which only she can walk. She is lost to me there."

For a moment, Alwen's mournful face shook his resolve. She feared nothing in the world more than failing her children, but Bledig could not allow himself to be dissuaded.

"Eirlys is lost to you anyway," he sighed. "The faerie realm is a happy existence. There she can live without pain or grief."

"But she will live alone," Alwen lamented.

"At least she will *live*."

"You must give me the chance to set it right, while she still clings to the mortal world. You must promise me, Bledig. One more day."

Alwen looked to him so desperately it tore at his heart. Bledig sorrowed for her. Alwen could no longer see anything but her own judgment and was too frightened to recognize it. He could hardly fault her for it, but he had come to realize that he might well be forced to save Eirlys from her mother.

"We do not have one more day," he insisted, still hoping that gentle persuasion would turn her around. "Tonight we have the full moon. Tomorrow will be too late."

Alwen folded her arms across her chest and glared at him, refusing his counsel.

Bledig had had enough. He could no longer restrain his frustration. "Have you completely lost all your senses? How can you allow your own daughter to languish?"

She remained silent, standing rigid before the hearth with her arms wrapped around her middle as if she were trying to hold herself together. Bledig regretted every word he had uttered, every word he was about to say. But he meant them all.

"Alwen, it is my duty to Eirlys to do what is best for her no matter how difficult it may be. I came here hoping you would come to see reason but I will not argue the matter any longer."

Bledig pulled to his full height and most foreboding bearing. "Hear me on this, Alwen. Make your peace with Eirlys before dusk tonight. I will do what I must, with or without your consent."

* * *

Alwen went rigid with the chill of his words. She blinked back tears as Bledig left, pulling the chamber door closed behind him. She began to pace, more determined than ever to help her daughter. The knowledge she needed, however, would not be found within the confines of her rooms.

After asking Glain to sit with Eirlys, Alwen went to the scriptorium to continue her search for a counter curse or a healing spell. She settled onto the bench at the broad wooden work table against the one wall of Madoc's private library that wasn't faced floor to ceiling by towering oak bookshelves. Every shelf in the room was filled, an inestimable collection of sacred works, most of them centuries old. Alwen had begun a methodical investigation, starting with the most familiar reference and working to the arcane.

"Have you found what you seek?"

Alwen had recently begun to hear Madoc's words in her mind a split second before he actually spoke. It was a dizzying reverberation she was slowly learning to anticipate.

"Not yet." Despite the endless hours of poring through the tomes, she was no closer to finding a way to help Eirlys than she had been when she started. "But soon."

"Hmm," Madoc mused. "Perhaps you already have the answer."

Alwen placed her finger between the pages of the book to hold her place and swiveled on the bench to puzzle at him. She sensed he had come to make a point. "What do you mean?"

"I understand Bledig has proposed a solution."

Alwen was surprised that Madoc had an opinion on the matter. "And you agree?"

Madoc lowered himself into the overstuffed armchair beneath the window. "It is sensible, don't you think?"

"There is another way," she insisted. "It's only a matter of time until I find it."

"Time is something you do not have." Madoc offered her words that were both kind and knowing, but she was not so sure she wanted to hear them. "Eventually we all find ourselves faced with a crossroads, forced to choose between what we want and what is right or best. Maybe this is best, Alwen. Even if it is not what you want."

"But it is not for Bledig to say." Alwen expected his agreement on this. "I am her *mother*."

"So you are." Madoc folded his hands in his lap, a gesture that Alwen interpreted as the patient resolve a parent would present to a stubborn child. "But perhaps you recall my counsel a few nights ago. Sometimes we are given no choice but to have faith in something or someone other than ourselves."

"Yes, I remember." Alwen was beside herself. She could not believe what she was hearing. "But you can't mean I should abandon my daughter altogether. That cannot be right, Madoc."

"Neither is it right for others to suffer for your limitations," he counseled. "In the end, isn't that what will happen? Bledig is her father, after all. He has her best interests at heart. For the sake of the child, perhaps you should give this over to him. Beyond this place, he has known the respect owed a chieftain, even a great king. He has had command of an army, and provided for his tribe and his family. Surely after all these years he has earned the right to your trust."

Madoc paused to allow the weight of his words to be felt. Alwen was uncomfortable with his line of reasoning. It rang of a truth she was unwilling to entertain.

"To become who you must be you must let go of who you were. And to do that, you must be willing to entrust some obligations to others." Madoc pulled himself to his feet. "But, I'll leave you to sort this all out for yourself."

With that, Madoc shuffled back across the thunderstone floor and through the scriptorium doors. Alwen was so stunned she had no final words, though every ounce of her wanted to argue. She had full confidence in her own mind. She was Mistress of the Realm, Madoc's appointed proxy, *and* wife and mother. Surely she would find a way to save Eirlys. Alwen returned to the stacks, more determined than ever to prove it.

* * *

"You have done well. The girl's malady has given us just the diversion we need." Machreth pulled Cerrigwen deeper into the shadowed recess underneath the main stairs. "Even Madoc has taken her plight to heart. As we speak, he is in the scriptorium helping to search for a cure."

"No magic of mine caused the girl to fall ill. I wrought the spell just as you gave it to me, Machreth. A binding, you said, to keep Madoc and the others contained when the time came." Cerrigwen looked closely at him. "And yet Eirlys is dying."

Machreth took careful note of the suspicion in her voice. She was not easily duped. If he could have seen her face clearly, would he have glimpsed accusation in her eye? He would have to watch her.

"I am as perplexed as anyone by her reaction to the thorns," he said carefully. "It is regrettable. But fortuitous, nonetheless."

"Your indifference amazes even me," she snapped. "Though there be no love between Alwen and me, I have no quarrel with Eirlys. She is but a child, not so much younger than my own daughter, and an innocent."

"Don't tell me you've suddenly found your conscience." He chuckled. "A bit late for that, I'm afraid."

Her form went rigid, and Machreth resolved to go more cautiously. He could ill afford to lose her loyalty now. "Distasteful as it may be, Cerrigwen, we must take whatever advantage we are offered.

"Now then." He clasped her by both shoulders. "My forces stand ready to strike. I trust you have seen to the rest?"

Machreth waited with bated breath while Cerrigwen considered her response. Her part in this was crucial to his success. She must come to it willingly now, so that he could be sure she would not waver when it mattered most.

His plan was to bring down the veil that shrouded the temple. It had taken him years, but he had finally found a hex that could pierce the magical defense. It would require time to work such a complicated spell. The sentry men on the wall would have to be distracted—so distracted, in fact, that they would abandon their posts. And despite his considerable talent, even Machreth could not be in two places at once. Not this time, at least.

"I have prepared," she said finally. "But before I give you what you want, I will have something from you in return."

"Anything," he cajoled. "Of course."

"An oath, then, Machreth," Cerrigwen demanded. "Sworn from your own lips. Even the likes of you would hesitate to break his vow. In the end your promise is all I will ever have to bind you."

Machreth considered himself an honorable man. His word was his law. Whatever she asked would have to be granted. "Name your wish."

"I will hear you speak the words," Cerrigwen challenged, "for whatever they may be worth. Swear to me that once you have the temple throne, you will give me command of the council. It shall be my voice that whispers your wishes in the ear of the high king."

"I swear it, Cerrigwen. No one but you shall ever lead the council."

Twenty-Four

"I cannot fight what I can neither see nor understand, but the time for vengeance will come, I swear it. For now, this is all I can do for her." Dread thickened the air, and the room grew too quiet. Bledig raked his hands through his hair and leveled his somber gaze on Odwain. It was difficult to meet the pain in the boy's eyes. "A decision had to be made."

Bledig found it hard to look upon Eirlys, but found it even harder to tear his gaze away. Every moment was a precious treasure stolen from the hands of fate. She seemed so small and frail, almost withered. He noticed a pallid hue to her face and a grayish tinge about her mouth. Bledig breathed deep and swallowed the retch of emotion as he rose slowly from the stool by the fire. He wished to see her smile, to hear her chatter and prattle and laugh. And oh, how he missed those dancing eyes.

"What does Alwen say?" Odwain asked quietly from her bedside.

Bledig was reluctant to answer. She would be devastated beyond grief and angered beyond fury, possibly beyond forgiveness. "Alwen still hopes to find a way to counter this. I know it feels wrong to go against her, but if we wait for her to come around it will be too late."

Odwain cast a desperate glance at the footboard. "Rhys?"

"She belongs to you, more than any of us." Rhys spoke from the shadows. "What comes next is for you to decide."

Odwain nodded, though he looked pale and frightened. Bledig laid his hands on Odwain's shoulders, swallowing twice to regain his voice. He wasn't sure he'd have the will to hold his own heart together. But he would fight with his last breath to face this all with dignity and find solace alone with the wineskin later.

Odwain still held her limp hand as he sat in vigil, knowing just as Bledig did that Eirlys would never wake. "She left me before I knew that it was time to say good-bye."

Bledig blew a heavy, tormented sigh and dug his fingers deeper into Odwain's shoulders. Odwain collapsed against him, wracked by silent sobs so deep it felt as though they were shattering him from the inside out. A man's tears were the blood of his soul, and Odwain was bowed before him, mortally wounded.

Bledig pulled him close, knowing no way to comfort Odwain save to hold him up against the weight of his grief. They clung to each other, bonded by sorrow and pain and the love of the same sweet girl. No promise or wise word or offer of affection could salve this hurt nor appease the aching in his heart. It would never heal. What had been taken from Odwain could not be replaced. She would always be mourned. Even time in infinite measure would only allow a man to learn to live with the loss.

If borrowed strength would get him through this, then Bledig vowed to lend what he had left. A burden shared might be easier to shoulder, but it must still be borne the full distance. Bledig was first to find the fortitude to set aside his pain. Perhaps it was his greater years or just the experience of a chieftain and father who lived all his life with the constant obligation of caring for others.

He pulled Odwain to his feet. Forcing him to stand under his own weight might help him find his footing, but Bledig held on a bit, just to bolster him. "Follow your heart, Odwain. It's the best that any man can do."

Odwain released a shaky sigh and nodded. "What must I do?"

"You'll find a faerie ring in the field beyond the garden. That meadow is a thin place, a place where the seen and the unseen walk so closely alongside one another that the veil between them can be pierced. Take her there. Tonight, under the light of the moon."

"And then?" he whispered.

"And then you wait," Bledig said gently. "The fey will come for her."

Bledig bent to leave a last kiss on his daughter's cheek and then beckoned Rhys from the shadows. "Say your good-byes, Rhys, and then we'll leave Odwain to his own."

He'd thought Odwain's pain unbearable, but it paled beside the agony Bledig felt for his son. Rhys had lived nearly all his life with Eirlys. They shared a unique heritage, a unique understanding. Bledig could not begin to imagine what it was for Rhys to be torn from his sister.

Rhys stepped forward, haltingly, as if every pace took all the grit he had. Bledig was struck by the calm on his son's face. The boy had the look of his mother, stoic and constrained. Her strengths just might see Rhys through this, Bledig thought with relief. For the gods only knew how he would survive it himself.

Bledig turned away as Rhys bent to whisper words of parting. He could not bear to watch, nor could he stand to see Odwain's stricken face much longer. The urge to rage and wail was suffocating him.

Finally, Rhys straightened and turned to Odwain. "We'll be waiting for you at the barracks. Take as long as you need."

* * *

Bledig stood with Rhys at the edge of the courtyard, long enough to watch Odwain disappear into the garden with Eirlys in his arms. He was glad for the shadows that camouflaged the tears. It was hard enough just to hide his own anguish, and then he saw Rhys shudder. The boy made no sound, but Bledig did not need to hear the sobs to know his son was weeping.

"Rhys."

Bledig reached out to take his son's shoulders, but Rhys pulled back, trying to turn away. Bledig held hard. He forced Rhys to face him, and waited.

Rhys dropped his head. Bledig understood every one of the reasons why his son would resist comfort. The codes of honor and manhood were unforgiving of weakness. Rhys was fully possessed of manly honor and proud of his emotional fortitude. Still, even the strongest man would have cause in his life to unburden his heart, and Bledig was determined that Rhys should know this. He was also determined that his son should not grieve alone.

Bledig gripped his son's arms and tugged at him, gently but firmly. "Let it go, son," he whispered. "The harder you try to hold it back the worse it will be. Let the grief go, and make room for anger."

Another shudder rippled through Rhys's body as Bledig felt his son struggle against his need. Finally, he fell forward against Bledig's chest and allowed his father to hold him. And then the tears came—both the son's, and the father's.

Bledig clasped Rhys close and held tight. Rhys clung to him, wracked and heaving with agony. It hurt to share his son's sorrow, more than he thought possible. If he could do nothing else, Bledig was grateful for the chance to be a source of strength for Rhys, to be relied upon in dark hours and vulnerable moments. Bledig had also found that offering comfort was often comfort itself.

At last, he could feel the waves of misery in Rhys begin to subside. Bledig loosened his hold and slung one arm around his son's shoulders. "There's a good store of stiff spirits back at the barracks," he suggested. "I'm thinking we might as well get a good start."

Rhys nodded. He glanced up at his father with what Bledig supposed was meant to be a confident smile. All Bledig saw was the tear-streaked face and sad eyes—a lost and half-frightened look he hadn't seen since Rhys was a small boy. Bledig had to choke back a groan. He squeezed Rhys's shoulders a little tighter, and hoped there was enough wine to drown them both.

They held each other up through the courtyard and down the cobbled lane, past the darkened outbuildings and the stables. The barracks were all dark as well, save the captain's house. The quarters Rhys and Bledig shared with Fergus and Odwain were aglow with what could only be a heartily stoked blaze in the hearth.

To Bledig's surprise, Fergus was waiting outside on the steps holding a wineskin in each hand. Behind him, the door to the barracks stood open, a sign of warmth and welcoming. It was the best Fergus could do, and it was enough.

Fergus tipped his head toward the door. "Unless you've an objection, we'll all wait with you for Odwain."

Bledig wondered for a moment whom Fergus meant, until he got a better look through the door. Finn was seated with Domagoj at the long table in the center of the room, and Pedr stood near the fire. Bledig was pleased. It seemed the Cad Nawdd could muster true kinship, after all. "I see the bad news got here ahead of us."

Fergus handed Rhys one of the wineskins as Bledig nudged him through the door. "I had some idea what you were up to."

Bledig stopped before Fergus and returned the old Scotsman's troubled gaze with one of gratitude and respect. "It's good to see the gathering of family and friends," Bledig said. "Odwain will be sorely in need of the comfort."

"So will you, barbarian." Fergus put a hand on Bledig's shoulder and guided him into the room. "Especially when Alwen finds out what you've done."

Bledig's gut clenched at the thought. He lowered himself onto the bench next to Rhys while Fergus pulled a stool up to the table end and sat between Bledig and Finn. He uncorked the wine sack and offered to pour for Bledig.

"For what good it does you," Fergus said, "if it were me in your place I'd have done the same."

Bledig was stunned, and humbled. "I will take heart in that, Fergus. If ever there were a time I found myself grateful for your support, this is it."

"I don't believe it." Domagoj's low chuckle rumbled from the far end of the table as he raised his cup in salute. "Truce between the Wolf Tribe and the Cad Nawdd. An unholy alliance if ever there was one."

Finn leaned forward over his elbows, his hands clasped in front of him. What little Bledig had come to know of the eldest MacDonagh had impressed him. Like his youngest son, Odwain's father was a sober man of commanding presence. He seemed a practical sort, and quiet. So rare was Finn's comment on any matter that whatever opinion he did offer carried real weight among the men of the ranks. He had them all hanging on his every word.

"When it comes to honor, the only measure of a man that matters is that there is something, or someone, for which he will stand and fight. Be we savage or civil, we here around this table are all men of honor. We are kindred," Finn avowed. "If not in blood or by marriage, then we are bonded in heart."

Bledig felt the sting of tears welling again and coughed to keep them at bay. There were important words to be spoken at times such as these, deeply held gratitude and regard that Bledig could not trust himself to voice with any dignity. Instead, he offered his cup to the sky in silent tribute to these true friends and family all around him, and nodded his thanks for their fellowship.

* * *

The temple grounds had taken on the glow of the moon. It seemed dead to him, all of it. The place, the people, his world—it had all ceased to exist. Odwain felt nothing, not the night air or the ground beneath his feet, not the bitter winter cold. Even Eirlys was weightless in his arms, as if she were already gone.

It was the numbness that saved him. It was what allowed him to carry her from the castle against his heart wish. It was what allowed him to lay her out and offer her over to something he did not know or understand. It was the numbness, and faith.

Grim comfort though it was, Bledig's solution had offered him hope, given him something to hold on to. If one day a cure could be found, perhaps Eirlys could return to him. If not, she would at least be safe.

Had he the chance, Odwain would have gladly laid down his own life in place of hers. He would have begged it, would it have done Eirlys any good. Giving her up was the only sacrifice he could make that would matter, and this was a fate far more cruel and brutal than death. Eirlys would live, but in a world beyond him. And he would have to learn to survive without her.

Odwain found the faerie ring, just as Bledig had described it. A faint circle in the middle of the meadow, near the tree line where the orchards met the field. It reminded him of a rounde-lay—the grass was tamped down in a perfect ring as if from danc-ing feet.

He stepped gingerly over the circle's edge, fearing to disturb it. Eirlys was to be placed in the open, but he could not bear to leave her unprotected in the cold. Odwain laid her down, wrapped in the bed covers, and sat beside her to wait.

"Well, pet, here we are." It was odd to hear his voice breaking the silence, but it seemed odder still not to speak. "It won't be long now."

Part of him still hoped for an answer. Odwain wondered whether she could even hear him.

She is never alone. Rhys's words had new meaning now. Odwain was not fully convinced that faeries were real, but he would believe it tonight with all his heart. They *had* to be real.

The whistle of the wind through the trees made his heart race. For a time, he started at the slightest movement or sound, expecting the little people to come scurrying. When after several minutes of anxious anticipation, no miniature men had appeared, Odwain forced himself to relax.

He tried to ignore the cold by distraction, counting the stars between the wafting cloudbanks and watching Eirlys sleep. The shifting moonlight cast an ethereal glow that made her appear untouched. Her peaceful repose was a cruel deception. If he hadn't seen for himself the evil that ravaged her body, Odwain might have succumbed to the illusion of a beautiful dreamer soon to awake. Even though he knew better, his heart still longed for her eyes to open.

Odwain shuddered from the strain of resisting. He'd been fighting tears and holding back rage for days. Every inch of him ached with grief, with longing and sadness. He wanted to sleep. He wanted to curl alongside Eirlys and gather her into an embrace so tight that nothing could force him to release it.

The urge to hold her tormented him until he could withstand it no more. This was the last time he might ever be allowed that joy. It was all he might ever have. Even if Eirlys could not feel his arms about her, could not feel his warmth surrounding her, Odwain would.

He stretched out on his side, as close to Eirlys as he could get, and slid one arm underneath her shoulders to bring her head to rest against his chest. With the other arm wrapped snugly around her, blankets and all, Odwain leaned his head against hers and shut his eyes to the truth.

Soon his breathing was keeping time with hers, in a slow and even rhythm. The warmth of their bodies pressed together began to soothe his soul. In his dreams, Eirlys was as she had ever been, flitting along on gossamer wings and gracing everything that she touched. Him, most of all.

"Odwain."

Her voice seemed so far away. He struggled to focus his thoughts enough to answer. Odwain opened his eyes and sat up, trying to remember where he was. A chill rifled through him, reminding him of the crisp night air and the damp grass beneath him. And there was a mist. There had not been fog before, but now it covered the meadow. It was all around him, eclipsing the moon and the stars and the rest of the world. He could see only a few feet before him.

"Odwain."

Eirlys. He glanced at the ground beside him, but she was gone. His heart leapt to his throat. "Eirlys?" he whispered.

He scrambled to his feet and turned full circle to find her. It was then that Odwain realized that he was not where he expected to be. He was no longer inside the faerie ring, but beside it.

"Here, Odwain. I am here."

His gaze followed the lilt of her voice, hither and yon, and then she appeared in the mist. Eirlys stood directly before him, in the center of the circle. Relief swamped him, knocking him to his knees. "Praise be," he sobbed.

Even through the haze of his tears he could see her smile. She looked to him as she always had, vibrant and happy—and alive. He staggered to his feet and reached for her, only to find himself grasping at the air.

"You cannot reach beyond the veil, my love."

Odwain was desperately confused. He could see her, hear her. How could he not *touch* her? Anguish wracked his body, forcing tears he did not wish to shed. He gaped at her, speechless and yet beseeching.

And still she smiled at him. "Don't fret so, Odwain. Please. I so hate to see you sad."

"Is it really you?" he rasped. "Do you live?"

"I exist," Eirlys nodded. "But not as you know it. Not as you remember me."

Odwain shook his head helplessly, unbelieving. "But you are well?"

"Well enough," she reassured him. "So long as I remain here, with the fey."

At last, Odwain remembered what Bledig had told him. His heart crushed in on itself. Eirlys was now in a world to which he could never gain entry, and from which she might never emerge. She lived, but she was lost to him.

The realization hit him so hard he cried out. Odwain doubled over, gasping for breath. What had he done?

"Odwain." Her words seemed to touch him. He could feel them, somehow, as if they were her hands on his face. "It's not so bad as it seems, really it isn't. I'm not so very far away."

Inexplicable warmth swathed him as the mist began to thicken. Before his eyes, Eirlys began to fade from his view. Odwain panicked, frantic for some way to hold her near.

"You must let me go now, Odwain." He could no longer see her, but he could hear her as clearly as if she were whispering in his ear. "When the moon is full, come to the meadow. Look for me where the veil is thin. I will be waiting."

Odwain could have sworn he felt her lips brush his. He tasted the mint on her breath, and honey cakes. He searched his mind for the words, for the things he most wanted to say while he thought he might still have the chance. But she was gone. There was nothing within his reach but the mist, and his memories.

The aloneness was suffocating, heart singeing. It burned his blood. Odwain wanted to scream from the pain but he could not catch his breath. He dropped to his knees, fists and innards clenched against the agony. And then, from the roots of his soul wrenched the only thought that existed. It howled from his throat with the entire force of his being. "*No!*"

TWENTY-FIVE

Alwen propped her elbows on the table and pressed her palms against her eyes, trying to rub away the burning behind them. The words on the pages had begun to blur several hours and half a dozen volumes ago. She had been so certain that somewhere in the vast stacks of the scriptorium would be a remedy, some lost or forgotten healing spell. She'd thought it only a matter of time.

Time, however, was fast slipping away, completely unhindered by her desperate clutching. It seemed what precious little of it there had been to begin with was all but wasted on a fool's errand. Frustrated, Alwen shoved the piles of paper away and contemplated angrily on the candle flame.

Perhaps she had erred in carrying out her own judgment to the exclusion of any other possibility. Madoc had managed to pierce her stubbornness with his practical advice. It had been needling her ever since and now it was even harder to defend her convictions. Doubt seemed to creep closer with the shadows as the candlelight waned.

No matter how many ways she tried to rationalize her arguments, one glaring flaw in her logic remained. She owned no special power or skill that would save her daughter. Even Madoc had told her that none existed. She just could not believe it to be true. She had lost her way.

Alwen moaned and dropped her head into her hands. Fortunately, Bledig had sense enough to defy her. Alwen had longed for his reliable good sense and his strength—and then dismissed his wisdom. She needed him now, but Bledig would not be coming to her comfort. It was time to admit her helplessness and concede to Bledig's wiser voice before it was too late for confession, too late for forgiveness, too late for Eirlys.

"Gods of mercy," she cried. The moon was already on its rise.

Just as the realization struck her, a stabbing pain slit her psyche. Alwen clutched at herself to stop the sudden tremble in her bones that seemed to root in her stomach and ice her veins as it forced its way through to her skin. The breath in her lungs was too thick to move.

The chair clattered to the floor as Alwen leapt to her feet. Before she could blink, she swooned, grabbing frantically at the edge of the table with both hands to stop the fall as her knees buckled. Alwen dragged herself to a stand and gasped for air.

If she could breathe, she could think. Alwen pulled air into her lungs and focused on the wall for balance. Vertigo threatened to flatten her. She clung to the table until the spinning subsided. Once her stomach settled and her vision cleared, so did her mind.

Alwen then recognized the grief she felt was not her own. It belonged to Bledig, to Rhys, and even Odwain. It had already begun. Just as he had sworn to her, Bledig had taken matters into his own hands.

"Let there yet be time," she begged the silence, hoping she could still offer her blessing and free them all from the agony of acting against her.

Just as she reached the first floor and dashed past the assembly hall, Alwen was struck dead by a bloodcurdling wail. The cry of a desperately wounded soul pierced her mind as if she had been run through with a lance. Alwen stumbled against the wall, struggling to keep her feet as she tried to identify the source of the pain.

Who was more important than *where*, but the force of the emotion was difficult to filter through. This person had to be close to her to reach her so deeply, near in space and in spirit. Alwen calmed herself with slow, even breathing and worked to center her intuition.

She sifted through the impressions, unraveling the tangled weave of sensations that ensnared her until she found a single thread she could trace. Alwen followed the longing. Though it was as tumultuous as any of the other feelings that assailed her, at least it was an ache she could bear. No sooner did she begin to concentrate on the emotion did she have her answer.

It came to her in a searing flash and a single blinding image. The realization flooded her senses with horror and fury and fear. Alwen bolted for the foyer and through the temple doors, racing like hellfire for the meadow.

Before she had even reached the garden gate, she knew that she would find him in the meadow, alone in the dark and crumpled on the ground. Alwen stumbled to her knees beside him and tried to pull him up. He was dead weight in her grip.

"Oh, Odwain," she cried, "what have you done?"

At the sound of her voice, Odwain raised himself and crawled forward to bury his head in her lap. It shattered what was left of her heart. Alwen wrapped her arms around him and held him as he wept. He did not need to answer. Odwain did not need to tell her what she already knew. Eirlys was gone.

She had been so long in coming round to reason that it was too late. Alwen looked to the moon, still bright but low and on the wane, desperate to be wrong, desperate for the chance to say good-bye. And yet, here lay Odwain—broken before her, vulnerable in his despair. Alwen could feel his heart crumbling with the weight of what he had done. She knew what it had cost him, the pain that threatened to tear his soul to pieces. But in that knowing, she also fully understood the vast stores of his courage, the magnitude of his selflessness, the true nobility of his nature. Odwain had forsaken all of the happiness and joy he had ever hoped to have to save the woman he loved.

Alwen was humbled. Her anguish could not compare to his, no matter how righteous her rage or how great the gape the loss of her daughter had torn through her heart. Odwain, by his act of sacrifice, had saved her from having to make one of her own. He bore the burden for them all, and for that, Alwen would be forever in his debt.

Her tears fell unrestrained for Odwain. Of all the wishes a mother could make for her child, to be so well loved was the first—and the best. Alwen ached to ease his suffering. It was unbearable as it was, split between the two of them.

"Dear, sweet boy," she told him, "I would take this pain from you, if only I knew how."

Alwen tried to pull him closer. What good was her sorcery if it could not help him? Her hold was nowhere near comfort enough. It could not quiet his moans nor quell the sobs that wracked his body. Nor did her touch reach the emptiness that was hollowing him.

Would that the knowledge of the elders could aid her, but their wisdom was beyond her still. Alwen shut her eyes tight and silently begged the universe for guidance. She waited for the whispers that had come to her in the White Woods as she faced the black wall of death that had wounded her child. She waited in vain, while Odwain lay dying of a broken heart.

"Will you not speak to me now?" she cried to the heavens. Alwen did not know what greater power she beseeched, but she knew that she was heard. "Is this any less a travesty? Is this one man any less worthy of your charity?"

"Or is it me that you forsake?" she sobbed. "If this be your judgment, if you will not aid me even to help him, then make his penance mine."

But she did know how to take Odwain's torment. The thought was not her own, at least she did not think it was, but the knowledge was hers—and hers alone. The gift with which to ease his suffering was within her command. She could not give him a different truth. She would not, even if she possessed the ability. It was part of who he was now. But she could dilute the reality he was forced to live with, make it less vivid.

It was a way to honor Eirlys as well. Alwen could no longer care for or protect her daughter, but she could look after the man Eirlys loved. Yes. For all their sakes, Alwen would give Odwain the illusion of inner peace until his memories faded.

Just the fragments of the idea as it formed in her head gave rise to a heat in her veins. The same heat she had felt in the forest. Alwen sensed the power of the gemstone at her throat, remembered the faint burn on the skin beneath it. More aware of herself and the magic within her, this time she felt the opening of the floodgate.

This time, the sorcery was not spell driven. Alwen required no incantation for spirit-faring, never had. To join another human psyche with her own came as naturally to her as her heartbeat. Gently, she reached into Odwain's mind.

Alwen closed her eyes to help her focus. She wanted Odwain to dwell on something sweeter, on something hopeful. As she searched his memories, Alwen's thoughts turned to Eirlys and she wondered. Though she did not know how to breach the veil, Alwen could sense it near. And if the opening to the faerie realm were near, so would Eirlys be.

"She is here," Odwain rasped in response to her thoughts. "Somewhere. In the meadow, where the veil is thin."

For a flit, Alwen imagined that she might have the power to find Eirlys despite the barrier. When she opened her eyes it seemed she could see in all directions at once, many perspectives in a single glance. She could see beyond—beyond the world in which she knelt and into the spiritual dominion with which the physical realm coexisted. She could not see Eirlys.

But she could *feel* her. The warmth of her smile, the smell of her hair, the silk of her skin—every bit of Eirlys existed in that meadow. Alwen's emotions became physical sensations that swamped her body and flooded her mind. Tides of grief and bliss collided, intermingled, and a bittersweet euphoria took hold. Oh, by the grace of the gods, Alwen could feel Eirlys as if she were folded within her embrace alongside Odwain.

It was then that Alwen realized what was happening. This was a sprit-faring she could never have imagined, a true melding of sentience without physical form. Eirlys was not with them in body, but she was with them in spirit. In a way Alwen could not describe, she could touch her daughter. And through her, so could Odwain.

Rather than create an illusion of contentment by manipulating his thoughts, she would give him something real. Alwen opened her mind and her heart to his, and allowed Odwain to share what she felt as it came to her. Almost instantly, his trembling subsided and his soul stilled.

"Yes, Odwain," she whispered through her tears. Odwain relaxed in her arms and Alwen let herself revel in the sweetness that was her daughter. "Eirlys is here."

TWENTY-SIX

Glain awoke drenched in the cold sweat of panic, the echo of her screams still ringing in her ears. The vision had never seemed more real, nor more near. She clambered from the bed and rushed to dress, feeling more frantic with each ragged breath. Glain sensed the threat lurking just beyond the shadows, as if nothing more than the thick dark of the night stood between her and the horrors to come.

The Fane was at rest—but not at peace. Something or someone other than Glain skulked the temple passages. Something apart from the deadly pall surrounding Alwen and her ailing child, which was a bodily presence in its own right. No, this was a new haunting. Glain did not need to meet this specter to know how real it was. The harkening of her instincts was enough. She hurried her step. Madoc would know what to do with her foresight, and her fears.

Glain took the service stairs from the kitchens and nearly ran the full length of the annex hall. Low voices wafting from the landing below stopped her short of the main staircase, with the safety of Madoc's chambers across the divide. Glain shrank against the cold stone of the inner wall, camouflaging herself in the shadows under the steps. If she were found out, all hope would be lost.

The rustle of robes ascending the steps announced her worst suspicions. First Machreth appeared, then Cerrigwen. They hesitated, and Glain strained to hear the muffled words whispered before Machreth turned to make his way down the hallway beyond her—toward the hidden passage at the corridor's end. Cerrigwen did not follow. Instead, she watched intently as Machreth disappeared into the dusk at the far end of the hall.

Suddenly Cerrigwen spun about and Glain bit her lip to keep herself from shrieking. Cerrigwen's gaze swept over Glain as she turned, but their eyes did not meet in the shadows. Glain's body trembled from fear and restraint, waiting for Cerrigwen to fully retreat down the stairs.

Glain held her breath so that she could hear to count Cerrigwen's steps. Nearly halfway, she figured, nearly past the second-floor landing and safely out of earshot. So intent was Glain on her surveillance she was startled nearly to death when she felt firm fingers grip her elbow. Madoc's wizened face emerged, wraithlike in the dark.

Madoc cautioned her against a gasp with a shake of his head and a gnarled forefinger to his bearded lips. Dizzied from the shock and shivering in the cold, Glain could not move for fear of fainting. Madoc took her arm and towed her around the corner and through the recessed entry into his rooms. He paused to listen a moment and then carefully pushed the door closed behind them. When at long last the sovereign turned and nodded for her to speak, Glain began to spew.

"Why did you let them pass unchallenged?" she fretted. "What if Machreth has found his way into the labyrinth? Surely had he known you were watching, he would have retreated."

"Perhaps," Madoc said. "But only to rise against me another day. I choose the now over the later. No more waiting," he announced. "I say we let the fates unfold as they will and take destiny as it comes. What little time you would have me glean by skewing his plans will gain us nothing in the end."

He smiled as if he knew her frustration, her yearning to rail against the injustice. "Much as it grieves you to do so, you must mind my wishes in this. Let it comfort you some to know that wherever else he might prevail, Machreth will never have what he covets most. Oh no." Madoc chuckled. "I'll see to that if it's the last deed of my days."

Glain shuddered. That Machreth would in fact be Madoc's end was what she was dreading most, and he knew it.

"It has begun." It was all she could say. All there was to say.

"You needn't waste your words on me." Madoc spoke with tenderness. "I know what monsters you have seen in your dreams."

But what Glain also feared was what she had *not* seen in her dreams. And he knew this as well. Madoc took her hands in his and looked at her, and Glain worried he would see the great sadness in her eyes. But she could not tear her gaze from his face. Glain was unaware of her own weeping until he wiped a tear from her cheek with his thumb.

"A gruesome thing it is to behold the visions, as you have. What will befall us in the next hours is truly unspeakable. But know you this, child. It would have gone all the worse for us had you not had the strength and the good sense to speak of them to me all along.

"Now." He cleared his throat and released her hands. "Now you must find Alwen and bring her here, to me."

"I can't bear to leave you," she whispered. Agony had robbed her of her full voice. "You've no sentry at your door, no guardsman to protect you."

Madoc looked at her long and hard, without further comment, and then turned toward the doorway in order to usher her out. "Speak to no one unless you must," he advised. "Be cautious in your movements and let neither your task nor your intent be discovered. We must assume that Machreth has more than a few allies among us."

Glain waited as Madoc reached for the door pull, feeling both anxious and reluctant. Her palms were damp with tension and worry. "The gates will hold," she muttered, trying to convince herself. "They must."

"For a while." Madoc smiled kindly at her. "But not for long. The veil that hides us from the outside world has already been pierced, and sooner or later Machreth will find his way through the catacombs. My only hope is in completing the rites before he does. You must hurry."

Madoc yanked open the door, only to find Fergus Mac-Donagh preparing to knock. "Bah!" he snorted in surprise. "Well, don't just stand there, man. Come, come."

Madoc invited him in with a brusque wave of his hand. Fergus gave a slight bow to Madoc as he entered and a polite nod to Glain as she passed. He took his post just inside the door, tight-lipped and stern. Glain noted that, despite his ample size and ready stance, Fergus seemed small defense against the enormous loom of this unnatural night. She felt the chill of doom in her bones.

"There you have it, Glain. You see? I have my sentry after all."

"So it would seem." Glain was still hesitant to leave. She wished for one last reassurance that she might yet see Madoc again in this life. But before Glain could voice a word, Madoc wagged a finger to shush her.

"You will find Alwen in the meadow. Go quickly," he said, and closed the door.

* * *

Finn was conflicted as he watched Cerrigwen scurry back up the temple steps. At Cerrigwen's order, he and Pedr were to stand the midnight gate watch, which was an odd request. And from outside the castle walls rather than inside, which was even odder.

"I can't imagine what has her spooked," Pedr grumbled. "There is no safer place than the Fane."

"Hard to tell with that one." Finn shrugged. "Though I daresay there's trouble aplenty to go round tonight."

Pedr nodded and sighed, clearly saddened at the reminder of his brother's grief. "I'd be happier at the barracks, with Odwain." Pedr dismounted at the guardhouse to open the gates. "The general ranks can well enough stand sentry. Why would she demand this of the likes of us?"

"Cerrigwen has her reasons for wanting us here," Finn said. "And none that needs knowing unless she sees fit to tell us."

Pedr huffed. He begrudged Cerrigwen her snooty airs. Finn was tolerant, if only for duty's sake. He would allow that she had been handed a hard lot in life, and the years in exile had not been especially kind to her. Some of that, though, had been of her choosing. Cerrigwen was, by any account, a cold woman who preferred to keep to herself. Even her daughter had hardly touched her heart, which to Finn's thinking was the worst of Cerrigwen's failings. He'd done what he could to make things go easier for the girl, but he held little sway with her mother. In all the many years they'd spent together, Cerrigwen had never warmed to him. Not to him or anyone else, except when it suited some selfish purpose.

"I would still like to know what we're doing out here." Pedr closed and latched the iron stiles behind them and took his ground in front of the entrance, back to the gates and eyes wide and wary on the White Woods. "Can't see the trees for the mist," he muttered.

Finn chuckled. "I'm no happier than you to find myself on the forest side of these walls. The White Woods is an eerie place."

Knowing that the fog was for their protection did not make the billows and shadows any less unsettling. Nothing and nobody ventured through without permission, nor without intent. Nothing and nobody could, not without considerable might—and powerful magic. That was exactly what made the watch from out-side the gate so uncomfortable. And so dangerous.

"Look sharp, lad." Finn paced the tree line on horseback, scanning the bulwarks for sign of the sentries in the watchtowers at the east and west cornices. "Something's amiss."

"That much my own bones are telling me," Pedr acknowl-edged.

Finn turned his horse to face the forest. He trained his fierc-est gaze upon the dark beyond, watching and waiting. If only he knew for what.

* * *

Sudden, gripping panic jolted Alwen to her senses. A wash of fear had spilled into her grief and now compelled her to her feet. They were vulnerable in the open, and she was needed in the Fane.

"Come, Odwain." Alwen tried to push him to his knees. "We must go."

He complied as best he could, unsteady at first but alert to his surroundings. "Aye," he mumbled. "As if we haven't troubles enough already."

Alwen had barely managed to pull him to a stand by the time Glain reached them. The very sight of the girl was unnerving. She had the look of a madwoman, disheveled and wild-eyed, and breathless from running.

"What is it?" Alwen demanded. "What has happened?"

"Machreth has made his move. Very soon now the veil will be breached, and then there will be nothing standing between us and his forces."

Glain's words struck Alwen speechless, but Odwain responded on base instinct. He broke for the barracks, tearing through the courtyard at a dead run. His abandon shook Alwen to action. She took after Glain at a quick clip toward the Fane, only to stop short again at the foot of the steps.

"Madoc awaits you in his rooms," Glain insisted. She was already halfway up. "Why do you wait? There is no time."

"We have no weapons or armaments here, save our wits," Alwen thought aloud. "And those are likely to be in short supply when real trouble hits."

Alwen took a moment to survey the grounds. The yard was barren and the entry wide open. The temple itself had the proper fortifications, but with the exception of the corner towers, the castle's defense posts were unmanned. "There should be soldiers posted here."

"An assault on the walls is just the threat for which the Cad Nawdd has been prepared, for generations now," Glain said. "We can trust the defenses to their training. Come now, Mistress. We must hurry."

Alwen shook her head and beckoned Glain back. "No doubt they are well trained, but they are untried."

Glain was reluctant, but she complied. "What would you have me do?"

"Warn Bledig," Alwen ordered as she brushed past Glain on the steps. "His men have experience the Cad Nawdd lack. And then tell Rhys to send sentries to the temple. Tell him he's to man the guard himself, if he must."

Alwen turned at the top to be sure Glain had heard, but the girl was already gone. She, too, felt the urge to hurry. Alwen took the stairs to the second floor two at a time, barely pausing for breath at the top. Before she could reach for the handle on Madoc's door, it swung open. It was Fergus who greeted her.

"Hurry." Madoc reached around Fergus's bulk and pulled her inside, glancing warily up and down the hall before resecuring the latch.

"We are in need of an escort and Fergus here has obliged us."
Madoc beckoned her farther into the room. "Who better, I ask,
than a man sworn to your protection as well as mine."

"Aye." Alwen nearly smiled with relief.

Madoc turned toward his desk. "Come closer, child, so you
may see."

Alwen followed him to his writing table. Madoc pointed to
the recess beneath it, below and beyond where the legs of his
chair would fit. "Reach under and feel around."

Alwen lowered herself to a squat and craned her neck to see.
"Where?"

"No, no. Not like that," he chided. Anxiety and impatience
tinged his tone. "Crawl under."

Alwen shifted forward onto her knees and poked her head
under the desk. As she stretched her hand into the darkness, her
fingertips brushed against a small ledge deep under the desktop.
She stretched a bit farther and felt parchment. Four scrolls in all.

She sat back on her haunches and looked at Madoc. Alwen
could guess what the papers were, some of the measure and
weight of the secrets they held. "Your last requests?"

"We'll not bring the scrolls out just yet," he said. "It is enough
that you know where they are. When the time comes, Alwen, I
shall need you to honor me. For the time at hand, however, I shall
need you to honor your duty."

Madoc took her arm and helped her to stand and then turned
away. Alwen watched with solemn reverence as he donned his
robes. He dressed in all the formal adornments of his rank, as if
he were preparing to preside over some rite or offer sacrament.
She hoped with all of her heart that this was not his end, but she
could not ignore her instincts. Madoc was making ready.

"One task remains," he explained. "Before I face Machreth,
I must visit the well. And you, my child, must drink the waters."

Madoc glanced toward Fergus, whose brawn was barricading the chamber door. "You and he shall see me safely there, and then Fergus shall see you safely back. Many will be called upon to forfeit their hearts and souls this night." His face furrowed with sorrow as he continued. "Some among us have already been called, I know, but we cannot speak of this now. It is not the time."

Alwen's heart clenched and her eyes swelled with tears. Of course he knew what had become of Eirlys and what that loss had cost her. It was she who had been the last to see.

Alwen lifted her gaze to meet Madoc's. "As you say, Sovereign."

She hoped her voice carried the resolve she intended to convey. Madoc took her elbow and nudged her toward the door.

Fergus checked the hall to be sure they were alone. He took two torches from the sconces outside Madoc's rooms and handed one to Alwen. Madoc paused at the vestibule and reached for a staff that leaned against the wall near the door. Alwen had never seen him use it, though she knew it was more to him than just a walking stick.

While Madoc directed Fergus through the catacombs with furtive gestures and hushed commands, Alwen counted their steps and took careful note of every turn in their path. As Madoc had said, there was only one way in, and one way back. It was now up to her to remember.

TWENTY-SEVEN

"**O**pen the gate and let me pass."
Startled by an unexpected voice in the silence,
Finn yanked the bit too hard. His horse reared and
scuttled sideways before circling around. Cerrigwen was at the
stile, dressed in her fine Steward's cloak and sitting astride the
silver mare she favored.

"What the devil are you up to?" he snapped. Finn realized he
had spoken too harshly, but she had given him a good scare.

"Open the gate," she demanded. "Be quick."

Pedr obeyed out of habit, trained to her tone. He opened
the gate to allow her to pass, glaring through the iron bars at his
father. Finn was still assessing Cerrigwen's unexpected arrival. As
she guided the mare into the open, he glimpsed a knapsack and
bedroll slung across the mare's haunches, hidden for the most
part by the folds of her cape. Cerrigwen was prepared to travel.

Before he could question her, Cerrigwen slid from the saddle
and strode with purposeful steps toward the edge of the woods.
She pulled a small pouch from her dress sleeve and unwound the
thong that held the bundle together. Finn watched, both anxious
and intrigued, as Cerrigwen knelt in the dirt to spread a piece
of parchment on the ground before her. Her body blocked him

from seeing the contents, but whatever it was, she was fully fixed upon it.

Pedr had absently taken the mare's reins and stood a few paces behind her. "What are you doing?" He turned to Finn, knowing Cerrigwen would not answer. "What is she doing?"

"I do what must be done," Cerrigwen murmured, more to herself than to them. "What others fear to do."

"Please, Cerrigwen." Finn dismounted and took a several steps forward, hoping to force her to acknowledge him. "You should not be outside the protection of the Fane."

"My protection is your duty." She was dismissive, not at all troubled. "Why else would you be here?"

"Why else, indeed," he muttered at her back. "You might have told me as much to begin with. And if this was your purpose in posting us at the watch—to see to you while you see to your business—why not just say so?"

Cerrigwen's tone was curt. "See to your work, then, so that I may tend to mine. Soon we will have nothing at all to fear from our enemies."

"What enemies?" Finn was puzzled at first, and then he realized what must have brought her out here. "Is it Machreth?" he sputtered. "What's happened? Have the others been warned?"

"You worry too much."

Finn bristled. "You cannot deliver some dire omen as if it were an afterthought and then expect me to shrug it off with a smile and a nod. I mightn't be privy to the workings of the Ancients, Cerrigwen, but I have wisdom enough to know when things are awry."

"Hush now." She had grown impatient with him. "No more of your distractions."

"Hear me, Cerrigwen," Finn insisted. He trusted his instincts more than he trusted her. "No more of this foolishness. Whatever it is you have to do, you can do it from a safer distance. You belong on the other side of these walls."

Cerrigwen paused long enough to glance at him over her shoulder. She smiled and wagged her head as if to express her disdain for his limited understanding, and then returned to her work. "This is where the veil is thinnest."

She offered the comment as if it should be explanation enough, and then returned to ignoring him. He watched from a safe distance, half-curious and half-afraid, as Cerrigwen pulled a vial of oddities from her wand bag—herbs and such, and what all else he didn't want to know—and tapped out a small mound in each corner of the parchment. Next she pulled out a lock of hair, which she placed in the center. Last she drew her wand and passed it over the parchment, all the while muttering unintelligible words, until suddenly the whole mess disappeared in a flash of flame.

Finn took a step back, swallowing his shock. He had no more understanding of what she had done than influence to prevent it. She was, after all, a high sorceress of the Stewardry and in Madoc's trust. Cerrigwen must have some knowledge he did not, and he had unfailing faith in who she was and what she represented.

Finn glanced at Pedr, still holding the silver mare by the bit. Pedr had begun to fidget, not from fear so much as the urgency a wise man's instinct would naturally stir. Finn felt it, too. Something was seriously amiss.

At long last, she gathered her implements and regained her feet. Finn experienced a great rush of relief and scrambled astride his mount. "Get the gate, Pedr."

"No." Cerrigwen took the silver mare by the reins and led her toward the woods. "This way."

Finn's jaw dropped, but before he could object, the forest groaned. "What the devil was that?"

Pedr nearly leapt into his saddle. "The forest has come alive."

Cerrigwen laughed as she walked right into the trees, laughed as though she thought them both simple and silly. Pedr hemmed and hawed, nudging the horse with his knees even as he pulled back on the bit. The horse, thank the gods, had the sense to stay where it stood.

"It's you that's daft, you bloody witch," Finn snapped. "I'll not follow you in there!"

She half turned and shrugged at him, completely unperturbed by his outburst. "Do as you will, Finn MacDonagh. I had meant that you and the boy should be spared, but it matters no more to me. Come, or stay, but I'll not be waiting while you decide."

As she disappeared into the shadows, Finn weighed the consequences of defying her. He had learned long ago to silence his doubts, quash them in favor of Cerrigwen's wisdom, even when he was sure he was right. Many a time she had shown herself possessed of instinct and foresight he could not comprehend. And well he knew the awesome, unfathomable power she commanded. He'd witnessed it, witnessed her true nature as it had been revealed in her all these years. This was the time of trial they had waited a lifetime to face, and he would not abandon her now just because he was not capable of understanding her motives—even if he suspected they were evil. Only when that suspicion proved true would it be his duty to refuse her. For now, he would watch and wait.

"What now, Da?"

"Follow her in," Finn waved Pedr ahead. "What else?"

* * *

Rhys witnessed the shattering of the predawn stillness from the barracks door, bleary-eyed and thickheaded. He blinked and strained to overcome the lingering effects of his grieving and an ale-induced haze. The soft pink glow of the sun rising through the clouds over the frosty landscape gave Rhys serious pause. Such beauty was an affront to his loss, but he could not help but acknowledge the moment.

Thinking on his woes brought a sudden bone-jarring ripple, deeper and harder to shake than the chill of the morning air. Rhys was alert now, sobered by an instinct that he didn't fully recognize, and a generous dose of anxiety, which he knew quite well. But what could be the cause?

"My Lord."

Rhys jumped and nearly stumbled off the barracks steps at the sound of Glain's voice. He steadied himself and mustered the courtesy to greet her, all the while silently cursing his distraction. "What in blazes are you doing out here at this hour?"

As he spoke, Rhys actually looked at Glain, realizing with some chagrin that he hadn't acknowledged her presence before leveling a reproach. The sight of her nearly sent him off balance all over again. The girl affected him in amazing ways. Even now, in such sad straits, he could not help noticing how the reddish cast to her hair took on a golden gleam in the light of day. He wanted to reach out and brush the wisps from her eyes.

And her eyes, well, they were the light of her, lit by a fiery nature and intelligence that he suspected most people overlooked. Their soft, dappled gray centers had a steely edge to them, he noticed. She looked tired, and distressed.

"I've come looking for you." Her head bobbled side to side in exasperation as she began to speak. "But your mother has sent me to warn you. An insurrection has begun and Emrys has sounded the call to arms. Alwen wants sentries to stand guard at the temple doors and men to prowl the catwalks and parapets. Whoever you can spare, and if there are no men to spare"—she stopped long enough to breathe—"well, then, she says you are to come yourself."

"I see." Rhys stepped down so as not to tower over her, though he still had to look down to see her face. Her rant had amused him and he wanted to smile, but she was clearly unhappy to have been dispatched on the errand.

"Rhys!"

Bledig appeared before them out of nowhere, nearly startling Rhys to death all over again. His father had such a look of storm and thunder in his eyes that Rhys was concerned. "What is it?"

"Finn MacDonagh is nowhere to be found, and Emrys has split the guard into two regiments. Odwain has taken command of half the Cad Nawdd upon himself." Bledig was aggravated. "Odwain has skill and wit and he can handle himself in a skirmish, but he hasn't any more real battle experience than you. Maybe even less. And what does he know about command? Fergus would make a better captain, but he is with Madoc and your mother."

Rhys shared Bledig's lack of confidence. He admired Odwain, even loved him, and would be proud to fight alongside him. He was not, however, prepared to follow him.

"I would have made another choice." Rhys eyed his father.

Bledig almost smiled. "No barbarian chieftain will ever lead the great Cad Nawdd."

"Ah, but let them see you ride in battle. You are far more impressive on horseback."

Bledig turned his grizzled look upon Domagoj, who had arrived astride his own battle-scarred beast and leading Bledig's.

Domagoj greeted Bledig's glower with his familiar jeer. "Though I'd wager if your sword arm were to fail you, that foul and sinister look of yours would be enough to scare the devils back to their den."

Domagoj's poor attempt at humor was enough to lift Bledig's spirits. Or maybe it was having the company of another well-seasoned warrior. Either way, Rhys noticed at least a little softening in the rigid set to his father's jaw.

Bledig took the reins and turned to face the gates. "They will come from the south."

Domagoj nodded knowingly. "From where the trees are thickest, and the gate widest. This 'they' you speak of. Have we any idea who, or what they are?"

"Does it matter?"

Domagoj shrugged. "Not as long as they die when I run them through."

"Odwain is intent on defending the outer walls."

Rhys followed his father's line of sight. What he surveyed from his position lacked martial precision, but Odwain's deployment seemed to mirror that logic. Half of their contingent of two hundred odd men were scattered along the stone ramparts and on the catwalk between the north and south watchtowers. Only twenty or so had been assigned as cavalry, and those few looked lost and alone huddled together facing the gates.

"An Obotrite warrior would rather chase an enemy down than draw him in," Domagoj scowled. "Besides, those walls will not hold. Nor will his men. They are too green. When the mayhem begins they will run."

"No," Bledig countered. "They will die where they stand, Domagoj. Every last one of them."

"A brave death," Domagoj conceded, "but an unnecessary one. Your Volchok would be wiser to mount his defense at the temple. He hasn't enough men to hold all this open ground. What's to save anyway but empty outbuildings and flower gardens?"

Bledig heaved a sigh and Rhys shared his anguish. It was precisely the gardens—or rather, the meadow beyond them—that concerned Odwain so. Eirlys was past harm, but he had not fully accepted that truth. "I've told Odwain as much, but he is rigid. This temple is a holy place to him. He considers the soil itself to be sacred."

Domagoj grunted. "Odwain's holy soil will soon be soaked with the blood of his army."

"It is his command."

"But you have your own ideas." Domagoj was grinning again, expectant.

Bledig waved toward the horsemen of the Cad Nawdd, milling nervously in the courtyard. "Once it begins, they will realize their stand is hopeless. It will fall to you to herd whoever is left back to the castle. As you say, the real fight will be there. Send our warriors to hold the line between the outbuildings and the temple itself."

"A half dozen Obotrite horsemen are worth two dozen of the Cad Nawdd. Nothing shall pass them." Domagoj turned to Rhys. "And where will you be, Wolf Prince?"

Right beside you, Rhys meant to say, but his reply fell short of his lips. He was interrupted by an eerie, distant howl. "What the devil *is* that?"

"The sound of Machreth's legions gnashing their teeth." Bledig threw a terse nod over Rhys's shoulder. "What is that girl doing out here?"

Blazes. Glain. "She waits for me. Mother sent her to bring sentries back to the Fane."

"Well, take her back where she belongs," Bledig growled. He glanced around, reconsidering his options, and then pointed at his horsemen. Bledig's warriors had taken a loose stance between the outbuildings and the gate, behind Odwain's pitiful cavalry. "Take them, too, and make your stand at the keep. And clear the dormitory of stragglers as you go. Best that Madoc's followers are gathered in the temple and under your watch. That way I'll have at least some peace knowing your mother is in good hands."

Rhys took note of Bledig's concern for Alwen. His father hadn't seen Alwen since the sad business with Eirlys. "Do you think she knows? About Eirlys, I mean?"

"She knows." Bledig's worried scowl deepened as the wailing drew nearer, accompanied now by a rumbling not unlike the thunder of charging hooves.

Domagoj was almost unseated when his horse skittered and snorted at the sounds of unseen danger. "Not long now."

"What of the villagers?" Rhys thought of the merchants and crafts folk in the tiny hamlet of Pwll on the other side of the forest.

Bledig threw him an exasperated look, as though he felt both helpless and angry. "Now you wonder."

"It is already too late. Pwll is overrun." Glain's unexpected words unsettled them all. "What comes upon us is an army unlike any you have ever imagined. They tower over the earth, swathed in bloodred mail and armor atop monstrous beasts that trample over everything in their path. They are the Hellion—man and yet not man. Demon warriors in mortal form, but they are not mortal."

Glain glanced at Bledig, and then looked straight at Rhys with terror in her eyes. "I have seen them in my dreams," she whispered. "I'd rather not wait here to see them awake."

The ground beneath them began to shake. The horses jumped and threatened to bolt, but there was nowhere to run. The quaking was all around them, the ground pitching and rolling in violent heaves that grew more violent by the moment. Across the fields, the stone and mortar of the outer walls began to crumble.

"Bledig!" Domagoj wrestled with his panicked mount as he shouted to be heard above the deafening pound of the earth. He had drawn his sword. "It rains hellfire upon us!"

Rhys glanced wildly above at the dawning sky as it darkened and then erupted in flame. It *was* raining hellfire. Flames streaked the heavens with deadly intent, guided by an unseen hand to strike deep into the compound and set the buildings around them ablaze.

Bledig threw himself onto his horse and yanked the heavy blade from the sheath strapped to his saddle. "Don't just stand there gawking, boy," he barked. "If you wait to see what it is, you'll be dead before you know what hit you. Go. Now!"

TWENTY-EIGHT

Alwen had not remembered the passage to the well to be so far. The long tunnels echoed with emptiness, and yet Alwen found herself anticipating Machreth's shadow to darken every turn. No one knew where he was. More than once she mistook the distant scuttle of rats for his feral footfall. Just the thought that somewhere in the darkness Machreth could be stalking them sent her senses a-skitter, and Alwen needed them sharp. She could ill afford to let anxiety interfere with her perception of place and time.

By redoubling her focus on mapping their steps, she was able to hold a steady course and keep a clear head. It occurred to her, as yet another of the cavern creatures scurried across her path, to use the rodent. Perhaps the tiny thing could show her what she was unable to see. A spirit-faring could certainly serve them now, but Alwen had never attempted the sending while distracted by another task. Could she split her concentration between the path she needed to map and the trail the rat would wander?

"Blood and thunder," Fergus muttered. He'd grazed his head on the low-hanging rock formations on the tunnel ceiling. "This place is not built for the likes of me."

"The tunnels close in as you go," Alwen observed. She had not noticed this before. "They are growing smaller, Fergus."

Madoc chuckled. "Or Fergus is growing bigger."

Fergus grinned, and Alwen felt a partial venting of the tension she had been harboring. Madoc's jab was as well timed as it was well intentioned. Alwen felt relaxed enough to try her hand at the spirit sending. Now to wait for a willing collaborator.

Soon enough, a small white mouse darted out from behind a pile of loose rock and scampered down the corridor toward them. Just as it sprinted toward a crevice at the base of the passageway wall, Alwen reached out with her thoughts.

Suddenly she was away with the mouse, her consciousness stowed alongside its tiny mind. It was an odd sensation to be oriented so close to the ground. Alwen, being so accustomed to wings and a slow aerial soar, found the wild jostle almost invigorating. The mouse took a haphazard course, dashing in and out of one hole after another, only occasionally traveling the corridors themselves. Her companion, she sensed, was not comfortable in the open and avoided exposing herself whenever possible. Alwen expected to catch sight of sinister boots, at least, but she saw nothing other than the blur of the barren dirt floor and hand-hewn granite walls. Perhaps Machreth had not made it into the catacombs at all.

"Alwen." Fergus's sharp tone cut into her daze. "Breathe, before you swoon."

Her eyes focused on his concerned face. Fergus had her by both shoulders and was shaking her. With an ethereal thud, Alwen found herself grounded again in her own psyche. It was a sudden and almost brutal shock. "All right, Fergus. Enough."

He released her and stepped back to allow Madoc to move closer. Madoc held Alwen's torch in his hand. "Well?"

"Well." Alwen blinked hard and reached for the light. She felt breathless, as if it were she who had been scurrying. "That was hardly what I had hoped."

"A true spirit-faring is an all-consuming venture," Madoc advised. "But you know that now."

Alwen realized that she had held up their progress with her little sojourn. "I was wrong to think I could be in both places at once, but Machreth is not in the labyrinth, at least not that I could see," she offered. "That's something, I suppose."

Madoc gave only a somber nod in reply and resumed his plodding into the darkness ahead of them. He did not share her relief. Several hundred twisting paces farther, they finally came upon the fork in the tunnel that signaled they had reached the cave. This was the crossroads, Alwen recalled. The tunnel to her left was an escape, a hidden passage that led out of the temple and deep into the White Woods. The opening to her right was the mouth of the cave that contained the Well of Tears.

Madoc entered the cave without hesitation and Fergus followed close behind to light their way. Not that it seemed to matter. Madoc moved as if he did not require sight. Sensing his shepherding was not necessary, Fergus fell back to take a protective stance at the cavern entrance.

Alwen pointed to the iron brace on the wall near the entrance and Fergus seated his flame. "Shall I light the others, Madoc, or do you prefer the dusk?"

Her voice seemed loud in the silence. Alwen hung on tenterhooks, midway between Fergus and the well, clutching the torch she carried so tight her fingers tingled. Anticipation was driving her heart so hard she expected to hear its echo pounding in the chamber. The cave was different, as if the space had taken on a living aura. It had a voice—many voices—whispering from the shadows. In this place, the past and present converged, and Alwen felt the touch of others she could not see or name.

Madoc did not answer. He stepped to the edge of the pool and, with a mighty heave, planted his staff in the loose rock and dirt of the cavern floor. The folds of his robe splayed as he lowered himself to his knees, arms outstretched and palms open, as if he expected the waters to leap into his embrace.

He had begun the rite of succession. Eyes closed to everything but his deepest, innermost sight, Madoc raised his hands in silent beckon to the Ancients whose essence he would soon join with his own. Alwen began to sway in time with the cadence of his incantation, drawn by the call to the spirits.

The waters of the tarn began to swirl with their own rhythm, churning as if moved by hidden currents or an unseen force. And then Madoc began to weep. His tears fell into the pool, and with the tears, he shed bits of himself. Pieces of Madoc's knowledge and wisdom melded with the magic liquids already stored in the spring and caused it to roil and bubble, fermenting the potent mystical potion that begat the dream-speak. From this well would spring the legacy Madoc intended to entrust to her, and Alwen began to tremble.

Froth from the surging waters spilled onto the cavern floor and raised a mist that filled the air, just as Madoc's fervor overpoured the banks of his restraint. Alwen could not escape his emotions. Her natural empathies were enticed by his sorrow, joy, and hope until she felt herself reeling with him. Madoc's quiet chant grew frenzied as his soft weeping turned to shuddering sobs, and then, suddenly, he stopped.

Madoc's eyes opened. He drew his arms down, pushed himself back onto his haunches, and slowly rose to a stand. The waters of the well receded and then quieted completely, as if they had never been brought to life in the first place.

"Why do you still lurk in the shadows, Machreth?" Madoc called out, peering into the dark.

Alwen turned to see and Fergus made half a move to intercede, but Madoc waved him off. He tugged his staff from the ground and shook it at the blackness before him.

"Show yourself!"

Machreth emerged from a darkened corner at the back of the cave as if he had stepped out of the stone itself. He walked from his hiding hole to the far side of the pool and stood with his feet apart and arms folded loosely across his chest. His posture was effective. Alwen found him unnerving.

Machreth spoke. "You sensed me in spite of my celtar."

The celtar was a spell of concealment, and a difficult hex to accomplish. But apparently he had not mastered it well enough to fool Madoc.

"Nothing masks the stench of death and betrayal," Madoc said.

"I think you smell the reek of your own decay."

"I may be well on my way to the next world, but I am not maggot fodder yet." Madoc stepped forward, nearer the water, as if to peer more closely at his former apprentice. "You found your way here sooner than I expected. I had thought the labyrinth too well conceived and the cave too well hidden for anyone to ever stumble upon."

"This was no accidental discovery, Madoc. I did not stumble upon it. Divinity led me to your Well of Tears." Machreth answered with the assertion of a man who truly believed what he said. "I was chosen."

"The Ancients have graced you with their guidance, have they?" Madoc chuckled.

"It is a sign," Machreth bristled. "Proof of my righteousness."

"Is it?" Madoc challenged Machreth's assumption in the same manner he would chastise the most ignorant novice. "Perhaps they merely brought you here to put your righteousness to the test. All men stand with one foot on either side of the mortal abyss, Machreth—on one side, redemption, and on the other, damnation. A man's very destiny hangs in the balance, and which way it swings depends upon where he chooses to throw his weight. A precarious position for even the best of men, don't you think?"

Machreth began to prowl the far edge of the pool in long strides, which brought him in and out of the flickering light. His gaze remained trained upon Madoc. Alwen thought his eyes had the look of a mountain cat stalking its prey.

"Men make their own destiny," said Machreth. His calm, quiet words were a stark contrast to the way he carried himself. "On this we agree. But in the end it is power that tips the hand of fate."

"Power has its influences, yes. Good and bad." Madoc's tone was tolerant, even conversational. "It is a strange brew. An alluring elixir that all men thirst after, but not every man will drink. Nor will all who indulge in it succumb to its darker appeal. You are weak, Machreth. You've been seduced by the worst part of your nature." Madoc wagged his head in disgust. "Worse yet, you've seduced the dark side in others."

"Cerrigwen, you mean." Machreth's thin-lipped smile was unseemly. "I'm afraid you underestimated her thirst."

"I have always known that she shared your ambition," Madoc said. "But I believed that in the end, she would be stronger. I believed she would see beyond her own needs and choose to serve the greater good, rather than succumb to yours."

"Ah, but we share more than ambition and a lust for power," Machreth intimated. "Cerrigwen has served me well, in many ways."

"I see." Madoc spoke with regret, maybe even disgust. "Apparently I have also underestimated your appeal."

"I had only to offer her what she coveted most." Machreth smiled. "What she knew you would never give her. This, you see, was your fatal mistake. You failed to reward Cerrigwen's loyalty with your trust—something else she and I share. I, on the other hand, brought her into my confidence. I offered her my respect. Such little things, really, easy enough to accommodate, and for these small enticements, she came to me with barely a hesitation.

Think of it, Madoc. Cerrigwen betrayed you for little more than the favor of my attention."

"And perhaps an empty promise or two."

Machreth shrugged. "Even now she aids me, in the woods, beyond the veil. She has breached your defenses so that my forces may gain entry. Already they ride upon the Fane."

Madoc stiffened, almost imperceptibly, but Alwen felt his agony. She shared it. The small glimmer of hope that had persisted in spite of her suspicions was snuffed—and with it, any hope of avoiding a civil war. The ranks of the Stewardry would split between two loyalties. Blood would be spilled. Innocents would be trampled, and a way of life destroyed.

"So now we face subjugation at the hands of our own kind." Madoc glowered across the pond.

"It did not have to come to this," Machreth snapped. "This was your doing, old man. You left me no choice."

"You fool." Madoc shook with rage. "You will reveal us to a world that is not ready to accept us. You will expose us to those who would destroy us, and you risk the life of the one king in a thousand years who is sympathetic to our ways. You have doomed us, Machreth. You have doomed everything we are."

"You are wrong, Madoc," Machreth raised his voice as he answered. He paced back and forth with furious strides, still eyeing Madoc. "But you still refuse to see. It is for Hywel's protection that all of this is necessary. Had I allowed you to wait and watch any longer he might not have survived to fulfill your prophecy. Chaos would ravage these lands for another ten generations and the Stewardry would have continued in oblivion forever. But no matter. Nothing you can do will stop what I have set in motion. Your time has passed."

"That may be," Madoc conceded. "But I will not hand you my throne."

Machreth stopped directly opposite Madoc. Alwen sensed a malevolent turn in Machreth's mood. Even Fergus tensed, prepared to intervene at any moment. Madoc was unmoved.

A long-drawn and unbearable silence followed. Alwen was anxious, trying to calculate what was to likely happen next. Through careful observation of Machreth's movements, she believed she could anticipate his behavior. As Alwen stood longer in his presence, she became aware that his emotions were open to her. She had somehow entered his mind, although Machreth did not seem to notice. It was an uncomfortable coexistence. His emotions were raw, conflicting, and hatred permeated his entire being.

Machreth took a step forward and squared his stance. His arms hung stiff and straight at his sides, his voice steeped in anger. "Then I shall take the throne from you."

"I believe you will try." Madoc ground his feet deeper into the sand, as if to brace himself. "You may even succeed. But I promise you this, Machreth, you black lord... You will never have the well."

As he spoke, Madoc spread his arms and raised his palms high. The air in the cavern chilled and dimmed the torchlight to a ghostly glow. Madoc uttered a single sound and a sudden wintry breeze blew through the cavern. Alwen swallowed her breath and felt ice on her tongue. Frost formed on the cavern walls and coursed across the rocky canopy above as icy veins crept across the floor toward the well.

Alwen saw Machreth's face pucker as he, in the same moment as she, realized that in this holiest of places, Madoc's power knew no limits. Madoc would stop at nothing to keep the secrets of the Ancients from Machreth's use. He would invoke all the sorcery he possessed, and Machreth knew it.

Machreth howled in fury. Before she could shout or even think a warning, he threw his own hex. Madoc was distracted, lost in his incantation. He was vulnerable. The torch in Alwen's hands slid from her grasp as she lunged toward the well and the two men.

"Alwen, no!" Fergus snatched her arm as she tried to push forward. "Stay back. There's nothing you can do."

"Let me try," she argued.

Fergus would not release her, though she fought hard against his grasp. Soon Alwen realized that it was no use to struggle. Even had she been able to break Fergus's hold on her, Alwen could never have approached them. The force Madoc and Machreth exuded was repellant, electric. The very air around them quivered with the charge.

It was a terrible spectacle she and Fergus could neither engage nor escape. Before them battled the most powerful Stewards in existence, but the struggle within was fiercer than the fight they could see.

Sorcery by thought was a discipline of the highest order, a tool of true mastery and a weapon against which there was no defense but a stronger mind. Never, even for a moment, did either man loosen his stranglehold. To Alwen, Madoc and Machreth were so intertwined with one another that they seemed conjoined. And then their magics locked.

Madoc had invoked the natural elements all at once and Machreth had countered with the same spell. In so doing, they had unleashed the wrath of the universal dominions upon one another, and the forces of the cosmos converged within the cave in a cataclysmic rush. The frozen ground beneath their feet heaved until it crackled and split. Small fissures opened in the earth.

"Blood and thunder!" Fergus staggered as the cave began to crumble around them.

"Get out, Fergus, while you still can," Alwen ordered. "Warn the others."

His pained scowl bespoke his feelings more strongly than any words. Fergus would never leave her. Alwen knew of no way to stop Machreth, and even had she possessed some knowledge to aid Madoc in his fight, his consciousness was focused too intently on Machreth for her to penetrate his thoughts. It was moments more before Alwen realized that his thoughts could reach her.

The water.

His message rang in her ears, as if he had spoken aloud. The meaning was not as clear, but the impression of the ancient tarn was just as vivid in her mind as it was before her eyes. Whatever Madoc meant for her to know, it had to do with the well.

"Great gods," Alwen said to herself. Madoc's rites had been interrupted. The succession was incomplete. Madoc's knowledge could not be passed unless she drank from the well, and its waters were hardening under his spell.

The earth shuddered again. Fergus caught her elbow as she toppled to her knees. His strong grip was all that kept her from falling flat on her face. Alwen eyed the well, calculating the odds of reaching it without being caught in the war of the wizards.

"I've got to get you out of here," Fergus shouted.

Alwen felt herself being tugged away. Fergus had her by the wrist and was trying to haul her out of the cave. "No, Fergus. Wait!"

"Wait for what?" he barked. "You're going to be buried alive in here! We're all going to be buried in here."

"The well, Fergus." She resisted with all her strength, throwing her weight against his grasp.

Whether he released her intentionally or simply lost his grip, in the next instant, Alwen tumbled free. On hands and knees, she scrambled the dozen or so feet to the pool. Freshly broken sandstone and razor-sharp granite shards raked the skin from her palms and shins while dirt and rock pelted her from overhead.

Fergus tried to follow but stones the size of half a man broke loose and crashed around them, between them. "Watch yourself! The ceiling is buckling."

She heard him, but Alwen dared not look up. A matter of moments might be all she had. She was within reach. With her left hand clamped around a small stone outcropping, Alwen was able to cup her right palm and dip it into the water. She needed only to scoop a single mouthful to finish what Madoc had started. Just as Alwen felt the ice in her grasp, a deafening rumble shook the cave. The earth beneath her pitched and rolled and a dark form plunged over her, into the well.

The splash that followed swamped her and she fell forward, slipping head and shoulders into the well. Alwen thrashed, struggling to pull herself out of the freezing pool with her free hand. The other flailed in the frigid, thickening slush until it struck something solid. Alwen recoiled from the unexpected contact, but her hand was caught. She forced her eyes open to see what gripped her, and for one fleeting instant, Madoc's gaze met hers. He had fallen into the water.

Alwen held on, but she was not strong enough to pull him to the surface. Madoc grew heavier as the water iced, and Alwen grew weaker. Her breath was waning. The need to surface burned her lungs. Alwen's fingers numbed so far beyond feeling she no longer knew if anything at all remained within her grasp. And still she clutched at him, or at least the hope of him. Her vision faded as consciousness ebbed away, and then Alwen felt hands hauling her up by her hair.

Up, until she broke the surface, gagging and gasping for life. More water than air filled her swallows. She had meant to drink, not to drown. The enchanted water would do her little good if she did not survive to use it. Her limbs were sodden, too heavy to lift. Alwen felt herself floating, sinking, and then her head landed hard against an unyielding surface. Rocks tore at the flesh between her shoulder blades and dug into her haunches.

A heaviness compressed her chest and she was unable to move her arms or legs. Alwen struggled to see, only to meet Machreth's malevolent gaze. It was his weight that had her pinned to the cavern floor. Machreth had straddled her waist and was throttling her with his long, sinewy fingers.

Alwen struggled in vain against his chokehold. She had almost no fight left. A moment's panic fueled one last thrash. She kicked hard, but his grip only tightened, and Alwen's thoughts began to blur. Deep mourning and regret for the lives she would not live to save set upon her as the darkness closed in.

TWENTY-NINE

Bledig was unaccustomed to doubt, but he respected its niggling. Instincts were to be trusted in times such as these, even when they encouraged a man to overrule his sense of heroism and abandon a daring plan. As eager as he was to plunge into the fray, Bledig was wise enough to wait until he understood what he was fighting, and how to kill it.

His horse, battle trained and more experienced than most men, moved toward the fighting without urging, at first. As the air grew thicker and blacker with wood smoke, the animal grew more cautious. Bledig goaded the steed but did not dismiss the horse's reluctance. He trusted its instincts as well.

"Where are they?" Bledig called to Domagoj, whose mount had carried him a little farther ahead. "What do you see?"

Domagoj sat stone still in his saddle, listening. He pointed into the dust and smoke ahead, just as a pack of rampaging horsemen burst through the haze in desperate retreat. Bledig could not find Odwain in the throng as they passed. The boy might already be dead, he agonized, or was wounded and waiting for rescue. Bledig spurred his horse.

"Bledig!"

Domagoj sidled alongside and grabbed the bit of Bledig's horse. He turned his mount toward the castle and insisted that Bledig do the same. "I know what you're thinking, but it is too great a risk. You can help the wolf cub best by leading what is left of his men to victory. With you, they may yet survive, and the temple can still be saved."

Domagoj was right. If by some chance Odwain were not yet dead—he soon would be. Bledig knew without seeing that the temple forces were overwhelmed; he could hear the enormity of what Odwain's men had confronted. He could also still hear the clang of clashing metal and the screams of the dying.

Bledig cursed himself and jammed his heels into the horse's hindquarters, charging headlong into the smoldering haze. Garbled epithets wafted over the din as Domagoj hurtled past, racing Bledig for the wall. Bledig was relieved. In battle, he knew no better ally, no better friend. Domagoj had a wild spirit, matched in equal measure by his loyalty.

It was the horses that saved them both from barreling blindly into the unknown. The animals sensed doom long before either Bledig or Domagoj, and skidded to a stop several dozen yards from the gates. Bledig's nostrils flared at the stench of seared flesh. He had never acquired a tolerance for the taste of death, and his tongue was coated with it.

The scene that greeted them was shocking, beyond Bledig's worst expectations. Evidence of a brutal battle, bloody and short-lived, was strewn across the open grounds. Beneath and beside them, the earth was littered with the fallen—brave young men, just like Odwain. Small fires snapped and crackled in clumps of grass, and lifeless limbs lay pierced with flaming arrows.

Bledig gripped the hilt of his blade a bit tighter, anticipating. Billows of smoke thickened and thinned on the wind, all but obscuring any view of the enemy that remained. He could not see this Hellion army Glain spoke of, but he could feel its presence.

"It is too quiet," Bledig whispered.

Domagoj grunted and uttered an old Obotrite ward against evil. "I can hear something still moving ahead."

Bledig nodded and urged his horse through the smoke, toward a low rustle and murmur in the distance. Domagoj rode alongside, wary and alert. The nearer they drew to the gates, the denser the trail of corpses. Bledig's heart grew heavier with every hoof step. It appeared unlikely that any of the men who had faced the fight could have survived.

"Horses," Domagoj whispered. He pulled up and pointed toward hulking shadows shifting in the haze. "I think."

Bledig peered into the smoke, hoping for a clear glimpse. He could see what looked to be the outline of good-sized mounts, but no sign of soldiers. The sounds were more disturbing than what he feared was lurking in the shadows. It was not the whinny and bray of horses. What Bledig heard was the snorts and gurgle of the gorge—the sounds of wild animals feasting on their kill.

The air ahead of them cleared briefly, revealing a monstrosity that defied belief. Domagoj recoiled. "What are they?"

Bledig did not respond, afraid to speak for fear of being discovered before he was ready. The Hellion loitered in the ruins of a large section of the outer wall that had been toppled by their onslaught. And hellish they were. Dozens of them, each standing the size of two men and clad head to foot in the bloodred armor that Glain had described. Only their eyes were visible, sinister orbs glowing from a visor in their headgear, and the random tuft of mangy hair poking from beneath their crimson cowls. Bledig imagined their true appearance to be more hideous and threatening than the beasts they rode.

The creatures Domagoj had mistaken for horses were indeed horselike, but more massive than any breed Bledig had ever seen. They were taller, broader, and furrier than even the enormous Frisian stallions. Their bodies were bowed by hulking shoulders that supported a barreled chest and thick legs. From their great, bulging heads jutted gigantic gnashing jaws, misshapen by the protrusion of daggered teeth that dripped with blood and sinew.

"They're eating the dead!" Domagoj blurted in horror. "Those creatures are feasting on *men!*"

Bledig's heart stopped dead as one of the Hellion marauders turned toward them. The smoke cloud was not camouflage enough to shield them from the piercing glare of Machreth's demons, and they were but two men against an immeasurable force. In the pregnant pause that followed, thunder rumbled in the distance, and Bledig had only one thought.

"Now, Domagoj!"

* * *

It was an unnatural storm, erupting without warning in a calm sky. Thunderheads formed from nothing and banked the horizon with angry black plumes. And then the rains came, in torrents. Icy winds swept the commons and whipped between the outbuildings, battering the walls already weakened by the incessant rumbling deep in the earth. One after another, the heavy stones that bolstered the parapets slid free as the mortar that held them crumbled, teetered precariously over their heads, and then crashed to the ground.

"The world is falling apart around us, Rhys. Bolt the doors!" Glain tugged at his arm, trying to pull him back into the temple foyer. "We mustn't wait any longer. This storm will strike us down as surely as the Hellion legion."

"There is still time."

He pried Glain's fingers from his sleeve and stepped down to the courtyard to get a better view. When Odwain's guardsman had returned, bloodied and beaten, Rhys had recalled every last man to the safety of the temple halls. Whatever defense they could muster stood its best chances with the stone walls between them and the enemy.

The wind-whipped rains were fierce, and though they had quenched the fires and smoke, it was still impossible to see beyond the courtyard. Glain was right, but Rhys was reluctant to give Odwain and the others up for dead. He was determined to wait until the last possible moment before barricading the doors. Rhys could sense riders coming, and they were close.

Glain shrieked as a bulky oak limb splintered from the trunk of a nearby tree and thudded against the cobbled steps at his feet. Too close to Rhys for comfort. He retreated to the protection of the foyer to wait, with Glain hovering behind him.

His mother was still missing somewhere in the bowels of the castle, and for all Rhys knew, his father had been lost to the very embodiment of evil. Rhys could not bear to imagine what had become of Odwain, and the last thing he wanted was Glain's well-intentioned argument.

"Please, Rhys. Listen to reason!"

"Blazes, Glain!" Rhys turned on her. "Go and see to your novitiate, or tend to the wounded."

The shock on her face surprised him, but only until the echo of his words resounded in his ears long enough for him to actually hear it. Glain's shocked look paled to one of embarrassment and hurt.

Rhys was mortified. The right thing would be to apologize, to tell Glain that his outburst had been borne more of concern than annoyance. He should confess that he fretted for her as much as he worried for his family, maybe more. Before he could speak, she disappeared.

Lightning splintered the cobbled road right in front of the temple. The blast sent Rhys stumbling back against the threshold, and then the earth pitched him forward. He landed in a heap at the bottom of the steps. The rain stung as it hit, pricking his face like tiny frozen arrows. No one could last long in this storm, and Rhys began to worry anew. Had his father and the others survived the Hellion, the elements might well finish them off.

Rhys hauled himself to his feet and started back to the shelter of the temple. Just two steps up, he paused, certain he had heard the insistent staccato of hoofbeats over the rainfall and between claps of thunder and falling rock. He turned where he stood, straining to see some evidence of his kinsmen riding toward him through the squall. The heaving of the earth kept changing the horizon, making it as impossible to see as nature's chaotic din made it impossible to hear. But Rhys was absolutely sure. Despite his many protests to the contrary, he was not completely devoid of his mother's talents. There were some things he could sense by way of the spirits, things he knew and never questioned.

As if in answer to his faith, riders suddenly plunged from the deluge. Rhys counted two horses, then another, and one more, all with men astride, riding like the damned fleeing their fate. Domagoj reached the courtyard first and threw himself from the saddle.

"Here!" Domagoj shouted. "Help me with the horses."

Rhys raced toward Domagoj, struggling to keep his feet and see who followed. Bledig's bulky stallion skittered to a halt, and his father slid to the ground no more than a foot in front of him. Rhys had never been so glad in all his life.

Bledig let loose the reins, and Rhys caught the bit just in time to keep the horse from bolting. "Are you all right?" his father roared.

Only the Wolf King could out-bellow the heavens, Rhys thought. He would have laughed with an absurd sort of relief had he not been sobered by the look in his father's eyes. "Yes," he shouted. "Are you?"

Bledig's answer was to shove Rhys out of the way as the last two horses nearly overran them. A man Rhys could not immediately recognize literally fell from his saddle before his steed could skid to a stop. Bledig bent to haul the injured man to his feet.

"Let loose of the horses, Rhys. They'll see to themselves. Help me get this boy inside. Hurry."

Rhys immediately freed the reins and steadied the wounded soldier on the opposite side. He craned to see the man's face. It was not Odwain, though he hadn't really expected it would be. All the same, his heart sank. His neck tensed as the shrill wail of the Hellion rang out. Rhys glanced over the soldier's head at his father for guidance, only to be further unnerved by the grim expression on Bledig's face.

"Make haste, Wolf Prince. I'm getting wet."

Domagoj had reached the steps ahead of them and stood at the top, holding the temple door open against the wind with a wild man's grip and a grin. The fourth man, whom Rhys had all but forgotten, was making his way up the stairs unaided. Rhys immediately recognized Odwain's gait, unsteady and ungainly as it was. Gratitude swelled over his panic, but only for a moment.

Once inside, Rhys ordered the bolts thrown and the guard doubled. He then asked Glain, who had reappeared without beckon and offered her aid, to take Odwain and his man to have their wounds tended. Bledig stood staring vacantly at the doors in deep thought, assessing the situation. Rhys wanted to know what his father had seen, but was actually afraid to ask. Instead, he deferred command of the temple garrison to Bledig and waited to be told.

Domagoj cursed wildly as the next quake of the earth caused a slide of mortar and rubble to spill from high in the walls. He brushed the debris from his hair and glared overhead at the rafters. "It is magic that keeps this place standing," Domagoj muttered. "But even magic can't hold forever."

Bledig nodded and then suddenly turned his gaze on Rhys. "Where is your mother?"

THIRTY

A lwen bolted upright with a greedy, retching suck. Air rushed into her lungs, dense and icy cold. Her body shuddered violently against the clad of wet wool and velvet as it struggled to take its fill of breath and reawaken. Consciousness returned, but the memory of what had happened to her was slower to revive. Alwen's eyes snapped open, and she did not know where she was.

It was dark, deeply dark, and the air was so thick with dust it burned her eyes and clogged her throat. Alwen could not see past her own nose, but she sensed herself entombed. The ground beneath her backside rolled and grumbled, like some great giant turning over in his sleep. The earth's queasy heave gave her stomach a good lurch and sent her blood quivering. The need to flee this dank, cramped place was strong.

Her vision soon began to adjust to the lack of light, and Alwen realized with great relief that the space in which she was trapped was larger than she had thought. The dust seemed to be settling, and she could breathe easier. As the air thinned, a faint glimmer emerged. Alwen's spirits rose a bit in vague but unmistakable hope. Torchlight, on the far side of the vault, suspended near what she believed was a way out. And then, she remembered.

Madoc. He was still in the well. Alwen wrestled her soggy clothing to get onto her knees and turned to look. The surface had crusted over with frost, and what little she could see beneath had turned brackish. Before her eyes, the waters continued to congeal and darken until they finally turned black as pitch. With a final groan and a hiss, the surface froze solid and fogged the cavern with a frigid vapor.

Alwen stared, horrorstruck and unbelieving. This could not be happening. Madoc, Ard Druidh and ninth sovereign of the Stewardry at Fane Gramarye, had fallen victim to his own spell. He was lost, trapped inside the enchanted well.

What was she to do? Alwen's hands clasped at her breast in an unconscious impulse to cleave to something solid, but there was an object already in her clutch. She unclenched her fist, with difficulty, uncoiling the blackened, frostbitten fingers of her right hand one by one until they exposed the circle of gold metal pressed into her palm.

She had Madoc's ring. A single forlorn sob escaped her lips, breaking the awful silence with a haunting echo. The signet was the only symbol of Madoc's reign. Whosoever bore the ring bore his seal—and with it, his power. In the end, it was just as Madoc had intended. He was gone and Alwen was now his proxy, liege of the Stewardry until the true heir ascended.

You will never be beyond the reach of my thoughts.

Alwen remembered the promise of the dream-speak and clung to its comfort. She had swallowed so much of the con-secrated water when she was in the pool that she had nearly drowned. Whether or not the rite of succession was complete had yet to be revealed, but for now, she would believe it was. Alwen could not bear to imagine otherwise.

"What are you waiting for? Get out of this bloody cave before it buries you alive."

Alwen jumped. "Fergus?"

He did not answer. Alwen turned toward the direction of his voice. Silt and rock still sifted from the cavern roof, but the rumbling had stopped. All but the one torch still braced in the wall sconce had been snuffed. Machreth was nowhere to be seen, and Alwen no longer felt his presence.

"Fergus?" He had to be near. She could sense him, even if she could not see him. "Fergus? Are you hurt?"

A dry, hacking cough and a rush of pebbled dirt from a heap near the cavern entrance were sign enough. Alwen crawled through the dusty haze on hands and knees, feeling her way through the rubble toward the sound.

"Here."

His voice was strained and weak. Alwen knew the need to hurry. Soon she could make out his form, splayed at an awkward angle and obscured from chest to thigh by debris. Fergus reached out as she came near.

"I tried to keep him from escaping but got caught in this mess instead."

"Machreth?" Alwen took his hand and tried to see how he was pinned. A first glance was enough to see that Fergus was trapped beneath a giant upheaval of earth and rock that had already crushed more than half of him.

"Aye," he coughed. "I managed to pull him off ye but he escaped into the labyrinth. Lost in the bowels of this place, I hope."

That was one possibility, but Alwen knew of another more likely and far more disturbing outcome. If Machreth had managed to find his way to the well, surely he could also make his way out of the temple through the underground passage that led into the White Woods. Worse, he might be lying in wait to confront her.

"Machreth will be brought to heel soon enough." She tried to pry the rocks from his chest to give Fergus more room to breathe, but she wasn't strong enough. "Let's just worry about getting you loose."

Alwen glanced at his face to offer him a smile of encouragement, but he did not seem to see her. His eyes were wide and fixed
upon the cavern ceiling above her head. Her heart stuttered with
dread.

"Fergus, please wake," Alwen sobbed, clawing at his breast.
"You cannot leave me here."

But he had. Fergus was already departed, traveled beyond
the sound of her voice. No longer could she sense his comforting presence, nor did she feel the anchoring which he had always
given her. All these years, it was Fergus who had tethered her to
her past. He had held her together in ways she had never truly
understood, until now.

In the heartbeat or two that followed, Alwen glimpsed the gaping hole his loss would leave in her soul. The emptiness she felt
was colder than the ice in the cave. His remains deserved greater
respect than this dusty tomb, but she would have to leave him here.

For the first time since she had left home, Alwen was without his protection. A terrifying thought, so far outside the reach
of helping hands. No one would hear her calls, if indeed anyone
was searching for her. Despair set in with the sobering realization
that no one, save Machreth, knew where she was. In this dark and
lonely place, it was his malevolence that threatened her most.

Alwen's body had taken to a constant shiver, which made it
increasingly difficult to think. She was vaguely aware that she had
been exposed to the elements too long. She had no choice but to
move, now, before she was altogether unable.

"I must have the strength," she chattered. The warmth and
safety of the Fane was her only salvation, if she could reach it.

Machreth. Alwen knew how sorely she had underestimated
him. She had witnessed his power, and it was a gargantuan force.
So strong was Machreth's wizardry that even Madoc had failed to
thwart him, and Alwen had the ring, the one thing left of Madoc
that Machreth could take. And he would most certainly try.

Alwen forced herself to her feet and started to drag herself out. It was only then she realized that the earth had stopped its quaking. Alwen placed one foot afore the other in a shaky but dogged trek across the cavern, half-plod and half-clamber. Every third or fourth step seemed to be more effort than her wobbly legs could manage and sent Alwen faltering over her own feet.

At the cavern entrance, she paused, trying to clear her mind and steady herself. Alwen reached for the torch still smoldering in the wall sconce and peered ahead. A surveying glance of the passageways to either side of her was daunting. In some places, the wooden beams that supported the walls had shifted, and the rockwork looked as though it could give way at any moment. The narrow tunnel had been made all the narrower by the caving in of great lengths of wall, though the tunnels were not fully blocked. Treacherous passage all the same, whether the danger was the passageway itself, or what might be lurking within it.

Alwen braced herself with one hand against the nearest sturdy buttress and closed her eyes to concentrate. Pushing through the heavy veils of exhaustion and despair that threatened to overcome her, she combed her thoughts for the vision of the labyrinth she had so carefully committed to memory. Instead of retracing her steps back to the stairwell, she searched the corridors for the mouse she had found earlier. Machreth would easily repel her direct attempt to sense him, but he would not so easily notice the rodent.

Alwen now understood the faint burning at her breast, beneath the silver amulet. It signaled the channeling of the power she had summoned. With nothing more than a wish, Alwen had created a clear path between her earthly form and the spiritual plane she commanded.

It was easier this time, easier than it had ever been, to find and bend the small creature to her will. With only the effort it took to conceive the thought, Alwen joined her mind with the mouse and sent it scurrying at her bidding. This time, she was better able to stay grounded within her body as her mind traveled outside it. She found herself able to fragment her thoughts and sustain consciousness to some degree in both places at once.

Knowing she had very little time before her body succumbed to the cold and stranded her in the depths of this place, Alwen sent the mouse in a new direction with renewed determination. To her relief, nothing but the wreckage of the battle between Madoc and Machreth remained. The damage to the corridors was extensive, but nowhere did the debris completely block the passageways. Such astounding testament to the forces that had constructed the labyrinth gave Alwen pause to acknowledge the omnipotence of the Ancients once again. And then she realized, with surprise, something else had changed.

She had grown beyond simply guiding the mouse. She was overruling its consciousness, taking it over, becoming one with its mind and sharing its knowledge. Now Alwen knew these tunnels—tunnels she had never traveled before—and she knew exactly where she was going.

Only one way in and only one way back—and only one way out. Without actually thinking to do so, Alwen had sent the mouse to trek the escape way, the passage that led to the forest. Anticipation surged as the mouse carried her toward a lightening in the dusky corridor. She had found the opening. Her small companion balked at the open air, preferring the safety of its underground home. Alwen encouraged it to take her as far as the brush that camouflaged the cavern entrance so she could search for a more capable adventurer.

The hawk rested atop a nearby oak tree. Alwen projected her sentience to the bird and encouraged it to take a low swoop over the grove and then turn back toward the castle ramparts. The bird skirted the outer walls, reluctant to enter the grounds. And then Alwen saw why.

The bloodied ground below her nearly shocked her back into herself. Fallen soldiers—or rather, the half-devoured remains of what had once been the brave men of the Cad Nawdd—were strewn in grisly heaps just inside the blockade. Half-eaten, she thought, yet it was not ravens or wolves that had disturbed the corpses. The thought repulsed her. If the usual scavengers had an aversion to the meat, whatever had set upon it had defiled it. She was sickened but forced herself to continue her faring. She needed to know. This was her keep now.

The outer walls had been breached in many places. Whoever or whatever had overrun their defenses had done so effortlessly, and it looked as though the battle had ended almost as quickly as it had begun. Alwen urged the raven to take her in, to the temple courtyard, noting with sorrow the losses that lay below. *So many men.*

The courtyard was empty of life, though it was littered with the evidence of a mighty storm. Entire trees had been uprooted, fences toppled, and building stone had been torn from the foundations of the temple itself. Alwen had only begun to take it all in when her avian carrier took a sudden, sharp turn, as if shying away from something.

Alwen caught a glimpse from the hawk's steeply banking vantage that stopped her heart. Far below, in the meadow where her daughter had entered the faerie realm, a giant herd of vile creatures huddled. Atop the beastly mounts rode even beastlier monsters, all clad in bloodred armor. At the head of the pack, a single man rode tall astride a pure-black stallion. *Machreth.*

In the instant Alwen thought his name, he felt her. She realized her mistake almost as quickly, and fear shocked her heart back to beating, pounding in a furious rhythm that she could not control. She had lost the advantage of surprise. Machreth turned slightly upward toward the bird, smiling at *her*, just as he ordered the charge.

Great gods. Machreth's Hellion army strained to a halting start and then surged toward the temple while Alwen fought against the hawk's desire to flee. She coaxed the bird to circle, from a safer distance, and began to wrack her brain for a way to fight Machreth, to stop him before he reached the defenseless Fane.

But Alwen was not truly present, not in physical form. She had only her consciousness, and the bird. Spirit-faring was a means of witnessing through the eyes of her host, an existential state through which she could experience but not act. Though she knew it could be done, to conjure by pure thought alone was beyond her experience. Alwen had never manifested magic that did not require her body as a conduit.

Alwen had never, but Madoc had, as had generations of Grand Wizards before him. Their knowledge was her knowledge now, imparted by the well waters she had swallowed, hers to draw upon at will. The spell came to her in the blink of an instant, a string of ancient words resounding in her mind, over and over until she began to utter it with her own inner voice. Alwen repeated the words in a steady chant, redoubling her focus and intent with every turn of the phrase. *Chwil awel o wynt.*

It began as the bird circled the Fane. The wind stirred beneath the hawk's wings, turning in tandem with the bird in a widening arc. As Alwen repeated her incantation, the wind began to reel, faster and faster, carrying the raptor to dizzying heights. The gusts swirled round and round Fane Gramarye until they formed a cyclone of impenetrable force. Nothing could approach, not even demonic monsters empowered with Machreth's dark magic. The wind repelled his Hellion army, strewing the beasts about like leaves while Machreth cursed her name.

Safely aloft, at the eye of the whorl, Alwen witnessed the retreat with triumphant satisfaction. Machreth recalled what remained of his unholy legion and slipped into the cover of the White Woods. Her Fane and her family were safe, for now.

Alwen's sorcery had consumed her thought, taken all of her concentration, and sapped the last of her strength. She had forgotten to preserve her own life force and was too far removed from herself to realize that her body was failing her until her senses began to wane. She felt as though she were floating high above the wings of the bird, soaring farther into a distant expanse. Her sight began to blur and her inner voice faded, receding to a far-off echo that she cared not to strain to hear. As her thoughts dimmed to black, an image of perfect comfort permeated her mind. *Bledig.*

THIRTY-ONE

"Come to, woman. Alwen!"

His bark brought her round. Alwen grabbed burly forearms with both hands to stop them from shaking her shoulders and tried to focus on the face before her. She didn't need to see Bledig to know him, but she wanted to be sure he was real and not just a vision she had conjured for herself. His hands felt warm where they gripped her. That was real enough.

"You came for me."

"What a thing to say." Bledig frowned, letting loose of her shoulders to sit beside her. "Of course I came for you. Are you all right?"

Alwen attempted a nod. She was too worn and weak to offer much more. Tears of exhaustion welled in her eyes.

"Well, you're safe now. We were nearly too late. You were soaked to the skin and far too cold."

It was only then Alwen realized that she was in her chambers, in her bed, not in the catacombs. "How did you know where to look?"

Glain spoke from her nervous hover near the foot of the bed. "Madoc told me where to look, should neither of you return."

"She showed us how to get into the tunnels. It took some time, but we found the cavern, and you half buried in it." His fingertips brushed the stray hair from her eyes. "And Fergus, too."

Alwen choked back a gasp and struggled to pull herself to a sit. Fergus was dead, and Madoc drowned. With the return of that knowledge came the rest of her recollection, and a rush of panic. "We need to go back to that cave."

"Hold on now." Bledig tried to discourage her from rising. "You need to rest."

Alwen shook her head and swung her feet over the edge of the bed to see if her legs would bear her weight. "I need to go back to that cave, Bledig. Now."

"Alwen," he said, trying to be kind, "there is nothing you can do for Madoc."

"I need to be sure," she insisted, waiting for the blood to circulate to her toes. "And I need to see what's become of the well."

Alwen forced herself to a stand and reached for the latch on the wardrobe door, seeking something more suitable to wear than her nightdress. "The tunnels must be passable. How else could you have gotten me out?"

"They are passable, at least as far as the cave," Bledig admitted, with reluctance. "But it isn't an easy walk."

"I may be battered and bruised a bit, but I am more or less whole. Hardly on my deathbed," she argued, struggling to turn the latch on the wardrobe door.

"Alwen"—Bledig reached for her right hand—"what happened to you?"

Alwen puzzled a moment, gazing at the mottled gray fingers curled around the brass handle. Memory returned in a rush and stunned her into a backward stagger that landed her again on the edge of her bed. "It must have been the cold."

"Must have been," he said, examining each finger and nail.

As her mind adjusted to the oddity of it all, Alwen noticed Madoc's signet ring encircling the index finger of her afflicted hand. She could not remember placing it there, nor could she actually feel it. Though the fingers behaved as they should in response to her will, they had lost all sensation from the first knuckle to the tip.

"It is fitting, I suppose, that a battle so bitter should leave an ugly reminder." Alwen withdrew her hand from Bledig's grasp. "I need my robe."

Alwen pulled to a stand again, and this time, Bledig steadied her with a strong hand on her elbow. He'd apparently decided there was no point in arguing.

"Your robe will take days to dry, if not weeks." Glain appeared at the foot of the bed and waited for Bledig to make room for her to pass. She yanked open the closet, rummaged about the wardrobe, and pulled out the plain brown woolen cloak Alwen had brought with her from Norvik. "This will have to do."

Alwen allowed Glain to help her with the clothes while she badgered Bledig for details. "Where is Rhys?" she asked.

"Rhys is fine." Bledig hovered, trying not to look as anxious as she knew he felt. "And Odwain will be, in time."

"What about the others?" Alwen stifled a groan as she forced a swollen foot into a slipper. Clearly it would be some time before her body did not protest her every move. "Is the temple still standing?"

"Domagoj and all of our mangy lot survived, but the Cad Nawdd has suffered heavy losses. The men that are left are hardy, though, and resilient. And, yes, this place still stands, more or less, but there's work to be done."

Alwen glanced at Bledig when he paused, painfully aware of his agony. They had both suffered such unspeakable loss, and his pain added weight to her own. She wished she could keep him from speaking his thoughts, but she new there were things that had to be said.

"I am sorry about Fergus, Alwen," Bledig offered, reticent and yet determined. "And the rest of it, as well."

So many regrets underscored his words, and at the heart of it all was Eirlys. Alwen struggled to keep from succumbing to melancholy. So deep was the well of torment within her that the hurt knew no end, but Alwen hadn't the words to respond to his. Not yet. This was not the time to give in to grief; it was a time to rise above it. All she could do was offer a nod of acceptance. Thankfully, Glain interceded.

"If you must be up, at least take some tea," she fussed, helping Alwen to tie the waist strings of her wand bag, which Glain had done her best to salvage. "And you should eat."

"Later." Alwen waited while Glain hung the brown cape over her shoulders and then made her way across the chamber. She threw open the door and gestured for torches. "Let's go."

* * *

The closer they drew to the cavern that entombed the Well of Tears, the more difficult their passage became. The air, which had been dank and stale before the battle, was now so thick with frost and dust it was difficult to breathe. The stamped-earth floor was littered with fallen rock and sections of tree roots the size of large branches.

Alwen stopped at the last fork in the passageway to examine the tunnel through which Machreth had escaped into the forest. Stone and silt had blocked it tight, from floor to ceiling.

"Looks like the roof has caved in," Bledig assessed, holding his torch close to the opening. "It would take months to dig it out, if it's possible at all."

"Well," Alwen said, remembering Madoc's warning against revealing the secret entrance, "at least we won't have to worry about an underground invasion. This way." She directed them through the widening that opened into the cave, though Glain clearly knew where to go.

Bledig forged ahead, kicking a path through the rubble. "It's rough going, but you can get through. Where would the well be?"

"On the far side of the chamber." Alwen clambered over a knee-high boulder and picked her way across the cave with Glain on her heels. "Wait for me."

"Here," he called, shoving a stone slab away from an opening in the ground. "This must be it."

Alwen's heart leapt to her throat. A strange mix of exhilaration and anticipation burbled, though she knew that this was not a rescue. It couldn't be. Still, Alwen felt her senses tingle and the amulet burning, awakening in the presence of the well. Its draw was strong.

"It's completely hardened." Heartbroken, Alwen knelt at the edge of the cistern and spread her hands across the cold, glassy opaqueness.

Bledig planted one of the torches in the dirt near the marble sill, and the glimmer from its flame revealed Madoc's tomb. Alwen was devastated. Though she remembered Madoc's battle with Machreth and trying to save Madoc once he had fallen into the water, she had hoped those memories were delusions. If her frostbitten hand had not been proof enough, there could be no denying the truth now. Madoc was lost in the deep, beneath a layer of thick black ice.

Alwen could feel him near, or at least what she thought was his essence. There were others, too, though the spirits were indistinguishable. Like voices muffled in pillow feathers, she thought, wondering if the water below was liquid or solid. If only she could break the surface. Perhaps the voices would be clearer.

"Alwen?" Bledig's voice seemed so far away.

She had pushed any awareness of Bledig or Glain so far into the recesses of her mind that it was as if they were no longer in the chamber. Closing her eyes, Alwen turned inward, searching for the magic she had discovered deep within herself. She opened her mind to the voices, but heard only one.

Your sorcery is rooted in the spirit, in the sentient soul of all beings. Your power is manifested in the waters, from which all life is fed.

These had been Madoc's words to her. They had come to her in the forest, when she had asked for a way to vanquish the devilkin. The skin of her breast tingled as she again tapped the amulet's mysterious power. Calling upon all of her strength, Alwen focused intently on the well and concentrated her energy on the water.

She envisioned the thaw, ice thinning layer by layer until it was once again liquid, its hold on Madoc's spirit relinquished, and the power of the Well of Tears returned. With the melting of the water came a melting in Alwen's soul. She felt her body relax, a manifestation in herself of the languid state she had cast upon the enchanted tarn. In her mind's eye, she saw the well waters turn from black and foul to clear and pure, and a deep, abiding calm took hold. Alwen opened her eyes.

Nothing had changed. Alwen let loose a cry of anguish and frustration that shook the cavern walls. She had offered everything she had to the conjuring.

Bledig moved to her side and took her by the arm. "We can't stay here, Alwen. It is too cold."

"Not yet, Bledig." She shook free of his grasp and redoubled her focus. "I will try again."

"Alwen." Bledig took her by both arms and yanked her to her feet. "Enough."

"It took unfathomable power to cause this." Glain still stood behind her, near the entrance to the cave. "It will take as much to undo it."

Alwen recognized the logic, but her heart was not ready to hear it. She repositioned herself over the mouth of the tarn and tried to center her thoughts and emotions. The amulet she wore was the source of immense magic, Madoc had said so himself. She could summon more of it, if only she tried harder.

And yet, even as she committed herself to the attempt, Alwen knew she would fail. She knew it as plainly and surely as she knew her own name. Freeing the Well of Tears was beyond her means.

It was then that she was given understanding. Whether it was ancient wisdom that had somehow escaped the frozen waters or some truth buried deep within her ancestral memory, Alwen came to see the true strength of the Stewards council that Madoc had sought to create. The greatest power of all came from the combining of wise minds, pure hearts, and unique gifts. Without the others, she was but one piece of a greater whole. Until the other sisters returned and the Circle of Sages was joined, the prophecy would never come to pass and the well would never be restored. Alone, Alwen would never be enough.

THIRTY-TWO

"Are you certain you got them all?" Alwen sat on the divan in her room and counted the scrolls again. "There should be four."

Glain looked confused, then panicked. "I found only three."

Alwen quickly slit the seals on the rolls that Glain had retrieved from their hiding place under Madoc's desk. A quick glance revealed a decree of proxy naming Alwen as sovereign until his blood heir was recovered, a map of the known world marked with the locations of each of the exiled sorceresses, and a letter addressed to Alwen that contained a list of directives, the joining spell that would consecrate the Stewards council, and other bits of wisdom meant to guide her.

"Madoc's personal testament is missing. It names his one true heir, his only living descendant." Alwen laid the scrolls beside her and pulled the coverlet Bledig had wrapped around her tighter. The cold in the cave had chilled her to the bone. "Is there aleberry in the pot?"

Glain poured a healthy dose of the mulled ale for Alwen and offered the drink to Rhys and Bledig. Alwen took the cup and tried to focus her thoughts.

"Cerrigwen is nowhere to be found. Finn and Pedr have disappeared as well, though this is to be expected," she said. "Finn will follow Cerrigwen to her death, or his."

"The Cad Nawdd is devastated." Rhys spoke with the timbre of a man burdened by loss. It pained her to see him so somber. "Fewer than half our soldiers survived."

"But we've lost none of our membership." Glain perched on the hearth and clasped her hands in her lap. "Not a one."

"Hmm." Alwen sipped the drink. "They may all be alive, but I fear we have lost some of them, nonetheless."

"There must be others who have turned," Bledig said. "Machreth did not accomplish all of this without a following."

"Cerrigwen's is only a piece of a much larger betrayal," Alwen agreed. "Eventually we'll need to find them all out, but first we must secure the Stewardry. And then, the prophecy. Cerrigwen's place in the Circle stands empty now, and it will fall to me to fill it."

"What will you do?" Bledig asked. "Hunt her down and drag her back? What good is she to you if she has turned?"

"I need her amulet." Alwen began to feel a bit more composed. The aleberry dulled the pounding in her head and eased the aches and pains. And as the feeling returned to her limbs, so did her resolve. "Another healer from her bloodline could be trained to take her place, if one can be found, but the amulet cannot be replaced."

"You're sure it couldn't have been Cerrigwen who made off with the scroll?" Bledig paced back and forth in front of the hearth, assessing the options with his usual tactical logic. "Or Machreth?"

"I can't imagine how. Neither she nor he had the opportunity to take it." Glain dragged the slat-backed oak chair from the desk and joined the others in the sitting area near the hearth. "Madoc would have been wary of their every move in his presence, and no one is ever allowed into his rooms in his absence. And, I have the keys."

"Then perhaps it is still here, somewhere in the Fane." Bledig leveled a stern gaze on Glain. "And, you have the keys."

Rhys was quick to come to Glain's defense. "Any one of the attendants in her charge could have made off with Madoc's decree or whatever it was."

"Glain's loyalty is not in question, Rhys." Alwen gathered the three scrolls onto her lap and repositioned herself on the divan cushions to keep her sore muscles from cramping. "We must assume that however the scroll was secreted away, it has ended up in Machreth's hands. He has information that we do not, which puts us at yet another disadvantage."

"But you have Madoc's proxy," Bledig said. "It is binding, is it not?"

"It is, once I claim his seat. But we must also see to the safety and security of this place, and to the prophecy." Alwen pulled the sheet with Madoc's directives from the pile. "There is a man in the village who awaits our messenger. He is our contact with Hywel."

"I will go," Rhys said. "How will I find him, and what am I to tell him when I do?"

Alwen smiled at her son, grateful for his courage and dedication. "According to Madoc's notes, the man is called Aldyn. He keeps the tavern in town. Send word through Aldyn that Madoc is dead, and that the new sovereign seeks an audience with King of Seissyllwg. Wait in Pwll for Hywel to arrive, and then bring him to me."

"And how am I to find Pwll?" Rhys asked. "It's not as though there is a road to follow."

"There is," Glain spoke up. "Just not one you can see."

"I'm afraid the road is clear as day. Cerrigwen all but destroyed the veil," Alwen reminded them. "Which brings me to the next of my concerns, Bledig. Aslak needs to know what has happened here."

Bledig was not as quick to respond as Rhys, but Alwen understood his reluctance. He no longer had Fergus to rely upon for her safety, and so many other things remained unresolved.

"I suppose Odwain can manage the defenses here, such as they are," Bledig decided, tentatively. "Can you repair this veil of yours?"

"It is a spell I've never tried," Alwen explained. "But I'll do what I can. We need its protection, especially while we rebuild our resources."

"I know the spell." Glain had spoken with strength and confidence, but when they all turned to look at her, she retreated. "Well, I don't actually *know* the spell, but I do have it. Madoc left it with me for safekeeping."

Glain pulled a folded parchment from the sleeve of her robe and handed it to Alwen.

Alwen unfolded the paper and glanced at the writing. In his distinctive script, Madoc had detailed an incantation that involved a blood offering. It was very old and very complex. "Have you ever worked this spell?"

Glain shook her head.

"Seen it worked, then?"

"No." Glain looked defeated now, as if she wished she'd never brought it up at all. "I'm not much help."

"That's not true at all, Glain." Alwen set the small parchment aside to study later. "We'll figure it out together."

Next, she separated Madoc's map from the pile and handed it over to Bledig. "This will show you Aslak's route, among others. There is no one else I would ever trust with it, Bledig."

"I'll take Domagoj and leave in the morning." Bledig nodded his understanding as he accepted the map, looking hard at her. "After we've *all* had a good night's rest."

"Rest will have to wait a bit longer." Alwen turned to Glain. "I have decided that you shall take Machreth's place as proctor, as my second."

"What?" Glain leapt to her feet and then dropped back to her seat. "Me?"

"Come now, don't look so surprised." Alwen tried not to be brusque, but she was too exhausted to argue. "It is what Madoc would want, and you know it. When we've finished here, I want you to call the assembly."

Glain's eyes popped wide with fear. "Today?"

"Strong leadership is needed in uncertain times." Bledig offered Glain reassurance, which would please Rhys. "Until you find faith in yourself, you can trust in the faith the rest of us have in you."

"I know it will be awkward, at first," Alwen allowed. "But the sooner we establish our authority, the better. And let there be no question. There are still traitors among us. Until we know who they are, we can trust no one else with what has been shared here tonight."

* * *

As soon as she reached the garden gate, Alwen felt a tugging at her soul. The sun had dipped below the horizon, leaving an amethyst haze in its wake. Soon the moon would rise, and the veil that shielded the otherworld would thin. The closer she came to the meadow and the faerie ring, the more her instincts trilled. *Eirlys.*

A delicate breeze grazed the tall grass, carrying with it the scent of mint leaves and honey cakes. Her heart soared, and Alwen gave quiet thanks for the blessing she had received.

Bledig stood in the shade of an old oak, the guardian tree that stood at the edge of the field. She had known she would find him here.

"What brings you here?" Bledig joined her at the edge of the faerie ring.

"You," she said. "And her."

"Her very essence fills this place," he said, his voice strained with sorrow.

"Yes." Alwen was reluctant to open herself to his emotions, for fear that Bledig's pain added to her own would be more than she could bear. "I wanted to come to you sooner."

"Well"—Bledig folded his arms across his chest and widened his rigid stance, trying not to appear as uncomfortable as he was, but he met her gaze straight on—"you are here now."

Alwen wanted to reach for him, or for him to reach for her, though she knew neither of them would. Not yet. "Tomorrow we will repair the veil."

"Good," he said, still staring into the meadow. "You'll have some defense beyond what a handful of Obotrite warriors and what's left of your soldiers can offer."

"I hope it will be enough."

"It is," he said. "It must be. And if not, you'll find some other way."

Alwen suddenly felt defeated. She had thwarted Machreth, but in so many other things, she had failed. "How is it that you are so certain?"

Bledig turned to look at her with a quizzical frown. "How is it that you are not?"

"Madoc is gone," she reminded him. "As is Fergus. Machreth has been deterred, yes, but not destroyed. The temple is in ruins, the order in chaos, and I am left with more questions than answers."

"Your enemies are at bay, the temple is still standing, the order has survived, and the prophecy has been protected," he countered. "These are not small victories, Alwen."

Alwen sighed. "I do not feel victorious."

Bledig nodded with the knowing of a warrior and a king. "That is the bitter truth of battle," he said. "Victory is rarely triumphant, and it always has a price."

How true this was, Alwen thought, grateful for Bledig's wisdom. How she would miss his counsel, and his comfort. Yet there was one more tithe to be paid. "Before you leave tomorrow, there are other things that should be said."

Bledig waited, expectant, while she steadied her emotions and her voice. Deciding to offer amends was one thing; doing it was another. Alwen was suddenly desperately nervous.

"Madoc once told me that true greatness lies in having the good sense to know when to trust in the wisdom of others. I failed to heed this advice when it would have helped us all the most. If it were not for you, our daughter would be lost." Alwen forced the words past the lump of grief that suddenly congealed in her throat. "And so would I."

Bledig's posture relaxed, as if the weight of worry had been lessened a bit, but he made no move toward her. "You'd have come around eventually."

"I was arrogant," she admitted. "It was you who knew what was best for Eirlys, and I should have accepted your judgment and your help when you offered it. In the end, it was your magic that saved her, not mine."

"Who'd have thought, eh?" Bledig shrugged. A hint of tenderness hid in his voice. "But I wager it will be yours that finds a cure one day."

"Perhaps." She sighed. "In the meantime I intend to find out who called that black curse and bring them to their knees. But at least for now she is safe."

Alwen averted her eyes, suddenly aware that she was talking through tears. "I was wrong, Bledig. I won't expect your forgiveness, but I will hope for it. With all my heart."

There was nothing left to say, nothing else to do, but to wait for whatever response he would give. Her own emotions were so strong they eclipsed his, and she was unable to intuit his intentions or his thoughts. When at long last he took breath to speak, Alwen forced herself to turn her head and look at him. Tears had pooled in his own eyes, and he was not afraid for her to see them. Bledig's raw honesty tore at her heart.

"All we really have in this life is one another," he said. "Faith and trust in ourselves and our purpose is what keeps us strong. At least, it is what I hold on to. Sometimes the bonds of family and friendship are all that hold me up, and too much has already been sacrificed. Whatever has been done or said, it is behind us now."

Bledig paused to clear his throat. "I am not without fault in all of this, too stubborn for my own good, I know, and too proud." A faint smile tugged at the corners of his mouth. "Seems to me we deserve each other. After all, who else would have us?"

Alwen nearly sobbed aloud with relief. "I love you, Wolf King."

"And I love you, Sorceress," he said, finally gathering her into his arms. "I always have and always will. You should know that by now."

THIRTY-THREE

Glain posted herself at the entrance to the great hall, taking count and careful note of each face that entered the room. She had no idea what it was she expected to see in their eyes or on their persons. Treachery must have a telltale sign, she thought, some subtle giveaway that she could detect.

As she watched, anticipation gave way to dread. What if betrayal actually presented itself? What was she to do then? Intuition alone could hardly be considered an indictment. If it were, though, that snob Nerys would be at the top of her list.

"What news, Glain?" Nerys sidled up close and hovered close alongside, feigning a friendly tone in hopes of being taken into her confidence. "Tongues are wagging, you know. All sorts of fantastic tales are being told. They say Madoc is dead."

"Alwen will speak to us all, when she's ready."

"Alwen?" Nerys was beyond curious now. "It is true, then? And where is Cerrigwen? I've looked for her everywhere."

"We'll find out together, inside."

"We?" Nerys smiled Cerrigwen's sly smile. "You mean the rest of us, don't you? Come now, Glain. You already know."

Glain tried hard to ignore her. "Take a seat, Nerys."

Nerys turned cold, just as Glain had known she would, once she realized she would not have her way. Giving an indifferent shrug, Nerys walked away, as quick to dismiss a person as inconsequential as she was to lavish attention on someone whose favor she wanted. Nerys had no true fidelity, not that Glain knew. Friendships to Nerys were temporary conveniences, means to an end. And yet, Nerys was never alone. Moments later, she was surrounded by a half dozen of her peers, male and female alike, all drawn to her vibrant personality and the self-confidence she exuded. Though everyone knew her for what she was, arrogant and self-serving, they flocked to her anyway. It was beyond perplexing.

"Shall I wait for you?"

"Ariane." Glain had gotten lost in her thoughts. "Go on ahead. I must wait for Alwen."

"Is there anything I can do?" Ariane hovered as well, but Glain did not consider her a bother. Awkward and ill at ease perhaps, but Glain understood. Ariane simply wanted to feel included. "You look as though you've the weight of the worlds on your shoulders."

For half a moment, Glain considered how comforting having a confidante would feel. In the last year, as Madoc had taken her into his private service, she had come to know solitude. Glain had been forced to sacrifice the communion of thought and deed that came with close fellowships. Out of necessity, of course, but she missed it.

"I'll be fine, Ariane." Glain ushered her inside, remembering what Alwen had said. "Really."

Once again, Glain assessed the membership. They gathered in huddles, feeding their worries with half-truths and innuendo. Alwen had been right not to wait. The sooner she took control, the sooner some sort of calm could return to their lives.

"Are they all inside?" Rhys had snuck up behind her. "Have you found out the spies?"

"Everyone is here." He stood so close she could feel his breath on her neck. Glain turned round to face him, in order to keep her mind on her duties. "I can't say about spies, yet, but I do have my suspicions."

Rhys nodded, uncharacteristically grim in expression. "Are you ready for all of this, Glain?"

"Of course." She answered with more assurance than she actually felt, not entirely sure what "all of this" was. With shoulders squared and chin held high, she gave him a look that should have shown nothing but grit and determination. Rhys looked on her with kindness, but the twinkle in his eye undermined her bluster.

"Gods help me," she sighed. "I have all the authority and dominion of a dormouse."

"You'll manage."

Rhys flashed a brash grin, right before he kissed her. It took her by such surprise that Glain hadn't the chance to gather wits enough to kiss him back. Oh, but his lips were warm and soft, even at a glancing pass.

"Are we all assembled?" Alwen had arrived with Bledig at her side.

Glain panicked, wondering what they had seen. "We are." Glain stepped aside. "Sixty-two Stewards in all, counting me."

"All right, Glain." Alwen was so regal, even in plain clothes and after all she'd been through. "Now or never."

Alwen led the way with dignity and poise, up the indigo carpet strip that laid an aisle across the room to the dais. A murmur rolled over the hall as she passed clusters of the devoted. Conversations died and everyone's attention turned to follow. The silence was intimidating.

Glain walked close behind, acutely aware of the curious stares. She took her place at Alwen's right side, and rather than meet the eyes of the order, Glain scanned the crowd until she found Rhys. He stood with his father near the doors, watching. It gave her courage to know he was there. She was not so alone, after all.

Alwen turned to face her audience. The quiet deepened as she waited, stretching the moment to give it the weight it deserved. Glain redoubled her grip on her composure, half dreading what was to come.

"Madoc is dead."

Alwen's voice carried over the hush with strength and clarity. Her words hung in the void, as if they had stopped time from moving. No one spoke. No one breathed. No one moved.

"I have claimed the sovereign's seat." Alwen raised her blackened right hand high, brandishing Madoc's signet ring. "By right of the laws of succession, as set down to the order of the Stewardry at Fane Gramarye by the first Ard Druidh, and as proclaimed by Madoc himself."

Alwen allowed an appropriate pause, opportunity for anyone who dared to make an objection. When none was forthcoming, she made her first proclamation. "So be it."

And then came the flood. It was as if every body in the room had taken a breath and let it out all at once in a rush of questions and demands. The hum of many voices pitched toward a roar as emotions heightened.

To Glain's surprise, Alwen did not attempt to dun the din. Rather, she stood quietly while the membership reeled. Glain questioned the wisdom of this. The collective unrest was so unnerving she began to worry that she should have summoned the guard. Thank the gods Rhys and Bledig were there.

"By what decree?" At the rise of her voice the entire order quieted again, and Nerys stepped forward. "I will see your proof."

Blast Nerys, Glain muttered to herself. Such insolence was unheard of. Further proof of betrayal was no longer needed, not as far as Glain was concerned.

ROBERTA TRAHAN

"As you wish."

To Glain's surprise, Alwen complied, turning to her with an outstretched hand. "Madoc's proxy."

"Oh." Glain had forgotten she carried the scroll. "Of course."

Alwen offered the parchment to Nerys. "Take whatever time you need to satisfy yourself, Nerys, but I caution you, I will not suffer a fool's challenge."

Nerys turned her back to Alwen, an obvious affront, and examined the edict in full view of the crowd. Glain was shocked, and all the more resolved in her loathing. When she finished, Nerys addressed the order directly. Yet even further insult. Glain could hardly stand it.

"It is in Madoc's hand," she reassured them. "Or so it appears to be."

Glain looked at Alwen, expecting some show of anger or offense. Surely she would not allow this spectacle to continue. But she did. Alwen sat patient and calm, as if all were but a minor annoyance.

Nerys turned again to Alwen and approached the steps to the dais, stopping just short. "You have his ring," Nerys pointed out. "And the decree. But what of Madoc's staff? It is also an instrument of his power."

"Buried with him," Alwen answered flatly.

"And Cerrigwen?" Nerys demanded. "Should she not be standing here, with you?"

"Cerrigwen has betrayed us." Alwen spoke as if it were an everyday matter. "She has abandoned her vows, and the temple. As has Machreth."

Nerys paled, quite visibly, but remained composed. "Well then"—she briefly bowed her head in a belated show of respect—"we are your servants, Sovereign."

Alwen allowed the silence to settle again in the wake of Nerys's capitulation, creating a dramatic tension that only intensified

Glain's agony. She understood that the honor about to be handed to her was rightfully hers. Terrified as the whole idea made her, Madoc would have wanted this, and Glain felt bound to serve him in whatever way she could. But it would be difficult, to say the least. While Nerys or any other member of their order would never have seriously challenged Alwen, the same would not be true for her.

"It is customary for the sovereign to name her second," Alwen continued. "And so I name Glain to take Machreth's place as proctor to the order."

Glain would have sworn her heart stopped beating while she waited for some sign of acceptance, or more likely, objection. She had never felt more alone than she did in this moment. This was impossible. What had possessed Alwen to give her such a role? Glain had never had any real test of command, no experience to speak to her abilities that warranted the title of second. Could she still refuse? The thought brought a hint of relief, and Glain began to give it serious consideration as she looked over the audience in search of a nod of approval or some sign of dissent. Glain found evidence of neither in the sea of somber faces, which only served to unsettle her more.

She looked to Rhys then, for his encouragement. He did not fail her, nodding in response to her pleading glance. A slight movement drew Glain's gaze toward the center of the room. Ariane had raised her hand just a bit, to offer a wave of reassurance. But Ariane's support would not be enough on its own. For the first time in her life, Glain began to consider the value in strategic alliances.

"Look to Glain for direction in the days to come, and to each other for comfort, and strength."

Alwen's voice startled Glain's heart back to beating. It was too late to withdraw. But knowing she was committed brought her to a place of resolve, and Glain began to feel right with herself. Good thing, too, as there was no turning back.

"This is the time of trial we have waited generations to meet," Alwen continued. "The purpose to which we owe our lives. We must work together to rebuild our home and our defenses, and to prepare for the battles that must yet be won. Our king will sit his throne and we will rule at his side. The prophecy will prevail."

Alwen's steady calm and air of authority quelled the anxiety in the room. Glain was impressed and made a quiet vow to strive toward Alwen's grand example. Madoc would expect no less of her, and there was nothing she would not do for his sake.

Feeling a swell of confidence, Glain finally looked at Nerys, who stood a mere three steps below her. Glain was not afraid to see Nerys' disdain; she expected as much. What she did not expect, as Nerys calmly returned her glare, was the glint of unmasked loathing in her eyes and the malevolent smile on her lips.

* * *

Glain entered the room silently, but Alwen sensed her presence. "What is it, Glain?"

"I came to see if there was anything else you needed." Glain made a quick sweep of the rooms, clearing away the remnants of the day. She tried to be discreet, pulling the draperies closed to shut out the night air, and the view.

"Thank you." Alwen began to pace in a loose circle that skirted Madoc's throne. "I don't expect I'll need you again tonight."

"If you're certain," Glain insisted, loitering near the door.

Alwen bit her tongue, stopping herself just shy of a very curt dismissal. It was near the last hour of a long and trying day, and Glain's hovering was trying her patience. As she paused to reconsider her words, her attention turned toward a niggling thought that had entered her mind the moment Glain had entered the room. "Something troubles you."

"I've been weighing whether or not to say anything at all," Glain ventured. "It may well be nothing more than my own prejudice and pettiness."

Glain's hesitation told more of what was in her heart than any words. Alwen ceased her pacing to focus on this young woman who had been so close to Madoc and was now so close to her.

"Whatever it is," Alwen counseled, "I'd rather you let me decide whether it warrants real worry or not."

"Nerys," Glain blurted.

Alwen had suspected as much. "I know you find her difficult to deal with."

"It is more than that," Glain protested. "I am convinced she works harder at furthering her own ends than at anything else. She has secrets."

"As do we all, Glain." Alwen was reminded of Cerrigwen. Glain had deep insights that deserved to be examined, but Alwen wondered if her personal dislike of Nerys was influencing her perceptions. "Does she continue to defy you?"

"Not directly," Glain admitted. "But Ynyr informs me that she leads late-night rituals and clandestine meetings with some of the older acolytes. She claims they are advanced tutorials, gatherings of the more experienced of us for the purposes of training."

"You believe these activities to be something else?" Alwen asked.

"I believe they are training, sure enough," Glain struggled to hold a diplomatic tone. "For what, I cannot say."

"What about your dreams." Alwen had known for some time that Glain was a true oracle, born with the sight. Madoc had relied upon her skills. "What do your dreams tell you?"

"Nothing," Glain confessed, her sigh tinged with defeat. "Nothing beyond the Hellion's wrath, and Madoc's death."

One more blind spot, Alwen noted, masking her distress with a nod and a sympathetic smile. The loss of yet another of their meager defensive measures was a greater concern than she wanted to let on.

"I have no proof, no vision—only my instincts." Glain continued to plead her case. "But I tell you, Mistress, my instincts are screaming 'conspirator.'"

"I understand." Alwen laid a reassuring hand on Glain's shoulder. "Someone wise once reminded me to trust my instincts. It was good advice, and so I give it to you. Be wary, and watchful, and we'll soon see where those instincts lead you. The answers will come."

She felt Glain relax. "Thank you."

Alwen smiled and waved her away, giving serious thought on the aleberry pot warming in the coals. The spiced brew might help her find a deep enough sleep to dream. "It's late. I think you can put your worries to bed now."

Glain took her leave, more contented than when she'd come, but Alwen knew that she still struggled with self-doubt. Confidence would come, but Glain would be challenged, tested to the ends of her wits and her heartstrings. As would they all.

THIRTY-FOUR

Alwen glared at Madoc's scrying stone, wishing that the sheer force of her will could bring the visions that would not come on their own. She had spent nearly every hour in the days since Madoc had fallen in devotion to meditation and the incantations, and still the stubborn orb revealed nothing. It remained dark and clouded, as did her dreams, on the few nights she had actually fallen to sleep. The ancient voices and mystic guidance promised with the dream-speak had yet to visit her, and Alwen had begun to wonder if she possessed the power at all.

Had the gods abandoned her? She had lived in Madoc's rooms these past several days, enshrouding herself with all that was left of him in the vain hope of bringing herself closer to his wisdom. If anything, she found herself all the more adrift.

Alwen pushed the crystal away and rose from the seat at Madoc's hornbeam and hazelwood writing table to pace frustration away, again. Twenty steps across the thunderstones from desk to hearth and twenty more back again. She no longer paused at the window. Alwen could not stand the sight.

The devastation of the temple grounds was complete. What had not been razed by the Hellion had been destroyed by Madoc's last stand and the windstorm Alwen had summoned. And alas, sorcery was unable to undo what it had done. It was an ugly irony that, without Cerrigwen, an imbalance of power existed in the mystical realms and Alwen's magic was not enough. Eventually, time and careful tending would renew the grasses and gardens, but for now, the scarring of the land was too painful to behold. And then there were the funeral pyres.

Alwen sensed an unexpected presence outside her chamber door. "Come," she called.

The hinges groaned as the heavy door swung in, and Rhys stepped through. "You might at least allow me to knock. You nearly startled me out of my skin."

Odd, she thought, glancing at the curtained window. He was dripping wet. "It rains?"

The hint of a snicker barely flickered across Rhys's gloomy face. He looked as exhausted as she felt, and it seemed to her he'd aged years in the last few days. It showed in his eyes, and in his carriage. "I'm relieved to see you haven't lost your gift for sensing the obvious."

Her son was too much like his father, with his charm and practical logic. Alwen felt the pang of longing. Bledig had only been gone a few days, but already she missed him.

Glain appeared to deliver a fresh pot of aleberry and then excused herself, but Alwen noticed the subtle exchange of glances between her second and her son. She found it interesting that they worked so hard to hide what was obvious to everyone else.

"Your boots are wet. Get them off, before you sicken yourself." Alwen pulled a woolen blanket from the divan and held it out to him. "Take this and sit near the fire."

He began to take the blanket and then hesitated. "It's late. I can come again in the morning."

"Don't be daft." She let the wool drop, expecting him to catch it, and folded her arms. "Take it, and do as I say."

Rhys snagged the corner of the blanket as it fell, and his quizzical gaze met hers as Alwen's own words echoed in her ears. They were so foreign they sounded silly, and Alwen had to laugh. "Listen to me," she said, "chiding a grown man."

"Even a grown man can stand a bit of mothering now and then." Rhys wrapped the blanket around his shoulders and crossed in front of her to squat before the hearth. He reached for the aleberry pot and gestured for cups.

Alwen retrieved two cups from the sideboard near the window and then perched on the edge of the divan in front of the fire. Rhys handed over her drink and stretched his feet toward the blaze.

"I hadn't expected you so soon," she said. "But you have news."

"Hmm." Rhys nodded as he swallowed. "Yes. Hywel's whereabouts are unclear. I gather he prefers it that way, but it may be several days until he's found. Maybe even a week's time or more. I didn't think this should wait."

"Do tell, then." Alwen curled herself into the cushioned divan, nestling her cup in her lap. "Wait," she stopped, wondering. "How did you find your way back through the veil?"

"Strange thing," he said. "At first I thought it was that I remembered on my own, and then I realized I was guided." He shook himself, as if to toss off dark thoughts. "I don't mind saying, I am not at all fond of those woods."

"The unseen is unsettling." She smiled. "Now, tell me, what have you found out?"

"The village remains unaware of our existence," he reassured her. "As is the world at large, as far as I know."

"Did you find this man, Aldyn? The tavern keeper?"

"I did," Rhys said. "An interesting fellow, sly and calculating, but I have to say I like how he handles himself. While he may be a skeptic where magic is concerned, he is loyal to Hywel's cause."

"You trust him, then." Alwen was relieved that Rhys had confidence in their only connection to Hywel.

"I do, and he has Hywel's trust, which makes him a reliable go-between. While I was there, Hywel's messenger arrived. I sent word as you requested, and this man of Hywel's had word for you—well, Madoc, really—but now Hywel will know what has happened."

Alwen nodded for him to continue, eager to hear.

"It seems that Machreth has formed a new alliance, with another son of Cadell. The brothers have been at odds over Seissyllwg for years, and it seems Machreth has taken advantage of the rivalry, promising Clydog that he will be king, instead of Hywel."

"So first he turns them against each other, and then against us." Alwen's blood curdled. Soon they would be waging war on two fronts. "What of Cerrigwen? Any sign?"

Rhys shook his head and slurped the last of the brew from his cup. "Not Finn nor Pedr, neither. But then, I never ventured off the road." He grinned at her sheepishly. "I didn't quite dare."

"I don't suppose you would." Alwen smiled, remembering Rhys' last trip into the White Woods. "Cerrigwen will turn up eventually."

Rhys pulled the pot from the coals using the hem of the blanket and refilled his cup. "Things seem quiet now."

"Yes, well, this is only a momentary reprieve, you realize. Machreth will make his move soon enough."

"What about the tunnels? Can they be cleared?"

"I've thought long and hard on that," she said. "In the end I decided that it was best to leave the underground passages blocked. True, we won't have them as an escape route, but neither shall Machreth have them as access."

Rhys sighed. "We're long on enemies and short on allies, and stuck squarely in the path of a storm. I'll feel better when Bledig and Aslak return."

"As will I," Alwen admitted. "But for now, I believe Odwain has things as well in hand as can be expected."

"All from his sickbed?" Rhys shook his head in disbelief.

"His body is mending nicely," said Alwen. "But I'm not so sure about his heart."

Her comment caused Rhys's brow to furrow and his shoulders to sag. "Some things are hard to get used to."

Alwen's breath stalled in her breast, cut off by the cold clench of an invisible vise. She had succeeded in avoiding such a moment, until now. *Even a grown man can stand a bit of mothering.* Alwen winced as the echo of his words pierced her heart.

"Some things you never get used to," she advised. "You're not supposed to. That is how it is meant to be."

Rhys nodded and nearly smiled, as if her insight reassured him, or at least made him feel a little less alone with his loss. Alwen offered her silent thanks to the universe and a sigh of relief into her cup. She had not considered that giving comfort might actually be comfort, but she felt the tiniest bit better herself. "I am glad you're here, Rhys."

Rhys offered her the pot. "Have you found your answers yet?"

"Not all of them." Alwen declined the mulled ale, tempting as it was. "But I am beginning to master the workings of this place, thanks to Glain."

Glain's name brought color to her son's expression, and Alwen hid her bemusement. She approved, but would not embarrass Rhys by saying so. It was none of her business unless he cared to make it so, which he had not.

"These are traitorous times," he muttered. Alwen was amused at his play on the phrase. Traitorous or treacherous, it was all the same. Glain's appointment put her in a difficult, if not dangerous, position, which worried Rhys a great deal. "She is young, and unprepared."

"She is young, yes, but she is prepared, Rhys. She is also a wise little mouse, and smart enough to know how to keep you interested."

Rhys grinned at her. "Little gets past you, I see, even all the way up here in Madoc's throne room."

Alwen gave an all-knowing smile. "Very little."

Rhys's sly look quickly turned critical. "You aren't sleeping enough. It's not good for you."

Alwen snorted. "So now you're the sage."

"There are some things I can sense for myself."

Alwen searched her son's face for the source of the knowing she sensed behind his words, but found evidence only of his affection and empathy for her. "And what is it you sense?"

"You are suffering, just the same as the rest of us. Maybe even more." Rhys repositioned himself so he could look directly at her, allowing his gaze to acknowledge her disfigured fingers. "You're entitled to take the time to care for your own wounds."

"I'm fine," Alwen assured him, tucking her afflicted hand under the folds of her skirt. "But it does seem the harder I try to relax, the more awake I become. And I do need to rest."

"Of course you do," he said, lifting the aleberry pot. "Drink enough of this and you'll sleep."

"No doubt," Alwen laughed. "But too much drink will put me so out of my wits I might not remember my dreams when I wake."

"Ah." Rhys pulled to a stand, barefooted and blanket caped. "Then it's time for me to be on my way, and leave you to get a night full of rest or dreaming or whatever it is you need the most."

"I suppose that would be best," she conceded, reluctant to let him leave. "But my heart will rest easier, now, even if my mind will not."

With a wink and a grin, Rhys was gone, though she suspected he was not headed straight to the barracks just yet. Alwen did in fact feel more at peace than she had in days, despite the unhappy news Rhys had brought her. She did not need the scrying stone or the dream-speak to know that times would turn terribly worse before they turned the slightest bit better. Nor was there any more to be done than what had already been set in motion.

The Stewardry remained united, under Madoc's law, if not under his rule. She would see that his tenets were upheld, despite whatever unrest there may be. The Circle of Sages would be joined, somehow, though Cerrigwen had put that piece of the prophecy at risk. Though there were battles yet to be fought and betrayals to be overcome, Alwen believed that the prophecy would prevail. If she had learned nothing else from Madoc, it was that trust in the greater good was, at times, the only hope.

And so, Alwen decided, let the fates unfold. What was to come would come, and she had faith that the wisdom she needed would be given to her when the time was right. For the moment, maybe even what was left of the night, evil was at rest. So then, perhaps, could she be.

Alwen turned her gaze to the hearth, meditating on the golden glow emanating from the alder logs. She gave into the mind-numbing warmth of the flames, sinking deep within herself. Soon her thoughts wandered away, slipping into oblivion like mist escaping her grasp. Consciousness thinned until it was like the gossamer veil that separated one world from the next. All she needed do was let it unravel, and then there would be nothing left standing between Alwen and the dream fields.

* * *

Alwen stood upon an altar stone, robed in black velvet trimmed with gold. The gauzy haze that filled the chamber peeled away to reveal four indigo-cloaked-and-hooded devotees kneeling beneath her. Though the figures were faceless, they were known to her. Each had claimed a position in the circle in front of one of four rune marks on the marble sill surrounding the Well of Tears. Tallow-soaked torches illuminated the hollow, and a hawk perched on a rocky ledge in the shadows at the edge of the gathering, standing sentinel and bearing witness.

With her arms raised wide toward the sky, she called upon the ancient gods, invoking their presence in the cavern. "When one arc ends another begins, and thus, the Circle is forged."

The ritual was complete. Alwen stepped down from the altar stone and approached the frozen tarn. Kneeling with the others at the edge of the well, she drew a bone-handled dagger from the velvet pouch at her waist. She drew the blade across the palm of each hand in a single, sure swipe and waited for the blood to run. Alwen then placed her hands, palms down, upon the glossy black crust that capped the well.

Madoc, Alwen's mind whispered.

In answer to her summoning, the cavern trembled. The icy surface of the well wavered, and Madoc's visage appeared beside her reflection on the surface. Again, the cavern trembled. The stamped-earth floor of the chamber shuddered, and a thick, snowy vapor formed above the tarn. Frigid air turned humid, and with a hiss, the surface of the well dissolved and the waters were once again clear and lipid. Alwen reached into the well, and when she withdrew her hand, she was holding Madoc's staff.

Darkness closed in and then receded. Alwen next found herself adrift in a cloud of mist. No matter which direction she turned, a gray fog enfolded her. Suddenly, Madoc appeared at the edge of her vision, beckoning her toward a stand of witchen trees. The grove appeared both near and distant, within her reach and yet far beyond her grasp. In the next moment, she was bathed in moonlight, in a clearing at the heart of the stand. A hawk shrieked from above.

Before her stood an altar stone, dressed with indigo velvet trimmed in gold brocade. Upon the altar laid four gleaming silver-and-gemstone pendants, positioned flat in a circle, side by side.

The keys to the realms.

The jewel at the center of each pendant radiated with an inner light. The glow of each jewel swelled, growing stronger and brighter until they converged in a blinding flash of white.

When the flare subsided, Alwen saw a figure standing in the glow, behind the altar stone. A dark-haired man in a white cape waited. He held the bearing of a king. Alwen stepped forward and placed Madoc's staff in his outstretched hands.

The prophecy.

Alwen was overcome with joy. Peace spread over her, like the unfurling of a sheltering wing. Contented in the knowledge that the wisdom she needed awaited her, Alwen drifted beyond the dream fields into a healing sleep, where broken hearts were mended and wounded souls would be restored.

THIRTY-FIVE

"**S**overeign."

A whisper pierced the veil of sleep, pulling her back. "Sovereign!"

Alwen straightened with a start, struggling to focus her gaze. She felt as though she were half in the waking world and half still in the dream realm. It took a moment to be certain she had fully returned. Alwen began to sense the presence of someone new. "I have a visitor."

"Yes." Glain stood over her, looking horrified. "He and his men simply appeared at the gates."

Alwen pulled to a stand and stepped round the divan, waving Glain ahead. As sovereign, she would receive formal audience from the High Seat mounted on the rotunda in the central chamber of her suite. Her guest waited just inside the outer doors.

"I was not expecting a woman."

Before her stood Hywel, son of Cadell, ruler of Seissyllwg and soon to be high king of all of Cymru. Though his cape was brown, Alwen immediately recognized him as the man in her dream. "I was not expecting you at all," she smiled. "At least not yet."

Alwen crossed to the small rotunda in the center chamber and took her place in the sovereign's chair. She gestured toward the hornbeam and hazelwood desk beneath the double-transom window on the far wall and the more ordinary chair that stood behind it. "Sit, so we may speak plainly."

Hywel obliged without comment, pulling the plain slat-backed hornbeam chair so that it faced her throne. Even in routine movement, he had a stag-like grace that bespoke surety of purpose and physical confidence. He presented himself with unusual maturity, though he was barely older than Rhys. Alwen noticed his left hand gripped the tanned leather scabbard belt clasped at his waist. A habitual gesture, she deduced, a sign of stress.

"Tell me, Hywel, how it is you've crossed the veil." She watched him closely, assessing him. Coarse brown hair tousled around a dignified countenance, framing a barely bearded angular jaw and dark, deep-set eyes that darted from point to point, overlooking nothing. Alwen felt strength in him. "How did you find your way here?"

"Madoc showed me the way through the veil, though in the past I have entered through the cave, unnoticed." He glanced at Glain. "When we found the tunnels blocked, we came knocking at the gates instead."

Alwen nodded, careful not to show her surprise. Aslak was not the only soul Madoc had entrusted with the secret passage, after all. It made sense that Hywel of all people should have access to the Fane such as he needed.

Hywel folded his lithe frame to perch on the edge of the cushioned chair, hands on his knees, assessing Alwen in return. "Madoc has always afforded me refuge in the temple. My men and I are in need of its protection tonight."

"And you shall have it. Fane Gramarye will always be open to you." Alwen waved her hand at two silver cups warming on the hearth, awaiting their fill. "I keep ready a small supply of a particularly fine mulled ale. My own brew, in fact. Glain will pour for us."

Though everything about Hywel's outward appearance was common—from his plain riding clothes and wool cape to his well-worn boots—the man himself was anything but. His noble lineage and upbringing were evident in his posture, but Alwen sensed something darkly reckless barely restrained beneath the refined visage.

"So." Hywel politely accepted the cup Glain offered him, but he did not drink. He leaned back in the chair, giving the appearance of being at ease. "Madoc is dead, and you are now keeper of my fate."

"That I am." Alwen folded her hands around the bowl of her cup, brandishing Madoc's signet ring. "More importantly, Hywel, I am your ally."

"My only ally, it seems." Hywel's smile had a sardonic twist to it. "I have more enemies than friends. My father is dead and my own brother is in league against me, though that," he snorted, "was unavoidable."

"A heavy burden, to be predestined a man of greatness," Alwen acknowledged. "And the stuff of rivalries."

"Power is the stuff of rivalries, Sovereign," Hywel countered. "The having of it, and the keeping of it."

"So it is." Alwen took a sip of her aleberry. She sensed his thoughts to be organized, strategic, his emotions strictly controlled. Indications of a clever and highly disciplined mind, but what of his character? "However, you do not yet hold the power of which you speak."

"I will." He was quick to assert himself and fully convicted in his entitlement. "It is my birthright, my destiny."

"Yes," Alwen said, still observing him with care. She wondered if his pride and self-possession were founded on arrogance. To get a true sense of his nature, she would have to force her way deeper into his psyche, but Alwen decided to wait for Hywel to reveal himself to her. "And your privilege."

Her comment evoked a twinge of umbrage—evidenced by subtle symptoms that only she would notice, like the minute elevation of the pressure in his veins as his pulse quickened, and the tightening of the muscles of his throat.

Hywel raised his cup to his lips and swallowed its entire contents. "I am a man of honor, Sovereign, a king with a vision of greatness, not only for himself, but for his people. I am but humble means to a glorious end. I serve the prophecy with the same devotion I require of those who serve me."

Alwen nodded, reassured by his sense of duty. "I do not doubt your honor, Hywel. Nor do I dispute the nobility of your motives." Alwen took another sip from her cup, measuring him. "I wonder, though, if it is in your nature to accept any counsel other than your own."

Hywel grinned, finally revealing the self-awareness Alwen had been seeking. "Not that I have discovered, as yet."

Alwen smiled but did not soften the point of her words. "You must learn to rely on the experience and talents of others. You will never reach your throne without my wisdom, nor will you be able to hold onto it without the guidance of the council we have pledged to your reign."

"I know the prophecy, Sovereign." Hywel held out his cup, expecting it to be refilled. Glain complied and then returned to witness the exchange from her place near the hearth. "Perhaps even better than you. It is, after all, the missive that governs my entire existence. I accepted its promise and all that it requires long ago."

"But what about trust, Hywel." Alwen was ready now to speak of her truest concern. "Before you can accept someone's advice, you must first have faith in its merit."

Hywel frowned, sobered by a subject that obviously tormented him. "Trust is something I have learned not to give. It must be earned."

Alwen hadn't needed to reach very far into his mind to understand the price he had paid for his innocence. Hywel prized trust and loyalty, for their moral value as much as in self-preservation. Sadly, he had known them in such rare measure that now he questioned their very existence. "I suspect the earning of your confidence is very nearly impossible."

"There are a few souls who have succeeded," he allowed. "Though not quickly, or easily. It seems, however, that I have no choice but to hand my trust to you."

"Yes, well." Alwen felt empathy for him. "Circumstances being what they are. Still, I do respect your dilemma, having recently faced such a situation myself."

Hywel spat, "Machreth."

Alwen nodded, thinking also of Cerrigwen. "You see? Already we have a shared cause."

"Indeed." Hywel raised his cup to her. "The beginnings of our own alliance."

Alwen tipped her goblet in answer to his toast. "I would like that, Hywel, a bond between you and I that is founded on something more than the obligations of the prophecy."

"A mutual enemy is a start, I suppose." Hywel grinned again, this time giving a glimpse of genuine warmth, evidence to Alwen that he possessed the capacity for compassion and kindness. "I expect that, given time, you and I will come to closer terms."

"As do I," she agreed. "Time, however, is something upon which we may hope, but not rely. It may happen that you are called upon to lay your faith in me before you are ready. Will you be able to do this?"

Hywel paused a long while, weighing her logic against his reservations, and then decided to make a new stand. "I will."

"Well then"—Alwen beckoned to Glain for more wine—"we have what's left of this night to learn about one another, to find more common ground upon which we can stand, together. Where shall we begin?"

THIRTY-SIX

The unnatural stillness just before first light sent the skin of his forearms crawling. Finn MacDonagh rubbed at the gooseflesh and stamped his boots just to affirm his own presence with the crunch of the icy mulch underfoot. His nose twitched at the whiff of a rank scent, as though something had crawled under the brush somewhere close and died. A sinister spot, he thought.

Bitter winter air had laid a black frost during the night. The slick, spindly limbs of the naked oak hung low and heavy overhead. Daybreak forced the fog to retreat into the trees, but it lingered at the edge of the copse in defiance of the light. As though to shroud some horrible sight.

His woodsman's intuition hopped a-twitter, and Finn cast a furtive glance about in anticipation of some unseen threat. They had been following Cerrigwen's lead for days, wandering the magical maze that was the White Woods. He had begun to worry about what they had left behind. Did anyone know they had gone? He had also begun to worry she had lost her way. This far into the thick of it, nary a forest dweller could be seen or sensed, but the woods were far from silent. A fervent murmur from deep within a nearby witchen grove grazed his ears, and Finn felt his gut clench and chuck over in dread.

He glanced cautiously at his son. "What unholy fettle does she bring on us now?"

Pedr frowned. He reached out to pat his chestnut gelding, but the skittish animal would not be soothed. His horse snorted and shied sideways, and Finn's bay scuttled up against the trunk of an old tree. The silver mare, though, stood fast.

"We've been here too long," Pedr said. His voice was hoarse and tensed to a boyish pitch by anxiety. "It's time to move on."

"This is no place for dawdling, you're right about that. Stay with the horses. I'll go."

"Da," Pedr whispered.

Finn tethered the bay and turned back to look more closely at his son. He was bothered by the fear so plain in Pedr's bright blue eyes. "What is it, lad?"

"I don't like this. It doesn't feel right, none of it." Pedr swallowed hard and tried to hide his jitters. "Just be careful."

While he lacked his father's years of seasoning, Pedr had known his share of trials and trails. His gut was always dead-on. He possessed a strong intuition—like his mother, rest her soul—and it made him a more leery man than most. Though sometimes Pedr might be a bit too cautious, this was new ground for both of them. Finn had the same concerns.

He laid his hand on Pedr's shoulder and gave what he hoped was a reassuring wink. "I won't be a minute."

Finn picked his way through the mist and the moonwort, peering into the thicket. It was damned dark in the brush with naught but a mouse trail to chase. Still, Finn could follow his ears well enough.

In a small but well-hidden clearing at the heart of a hemlock stand, Finn spotted a dark huddle swaying to the cadence of an eerie chant. Sunlight pricked through the dense canopy and mingled with the shadows in a wraithlike dance. Finn's mouth went dry.

He pushed through the bracken into the open and approached warily. As he drew nearer, the mumbling grew strong enough for him to recognize as something vile and evil. His heart began to race.

In her left hand, Cerrigwen clutched a slender bone-handled blade. From the outstretched, downturned palm of her right, thick drops of her blood reddened the runes she'd carved onto a small square shard of oak bark. Sensing him, Cerrigwen turned slightly to snicker at Finn through wild, knotted tendrils of honey-brown hair, which he noticed for the first time were streaked white with age. *Or strain*, he thought.

"Always take time by the forelock, Finn," she rasped. "A moment's hesitation can cost a man more than his life."

Finn shook his head, bewildered by her words. Her tired, amber-colored eyes were darkened and crazed with some unspoken torment. He scarcely recognized the woman kneeling before him. In all their years together, he'd never professed to understand her, but now she frightened him.

Cerrigwen began to smear her blood over the bark, tracing the symbols with her fingertip and muttered something in a tongue he couldn't comprehend. Finn tamped the urge to yank her to her feet, surrendering his better judgment to his oath. It was not his place to interfere, no matter what evil she had conjured. He wondered with vague foreboding why the songbirds hadn't yet heralded the dawn. The sun was full up, but it still seemed dark.

With a banshee shriek that shook his bones, she smashed her hand onto the bloodied oaken shaving and crushed it into the earth. She threw her dagger to the ground, snatched up the bark, and held it to the sky. Cerrigwen pulled to a stand and turned sunwise, full circle, and then stopped to face him.

Finn gaped as she calmly reached down to pick up the blade and sheathed it, still crimson coated, at her waist. She looked at him then, as serene as ever he'd seen her. Cerrigwen slipped the bark into a cloth pouch tied to her belt, wiped her sticky, bloody palm on the front of her woolen cloak, and then held it out to him.

"Have you something to bind this?"

For a split second, he was dumbstruck. His instincts quickly snapped to, and he fumbled about himself for some sort of clean cloth. Hard pressed to find anything unsoiled after so many days on the road, Finn finally settled on his linen undershirt. With his own dagger, he hacked a strip from the hem.

"It's the best I can offer," he mumbled hoarsely. It was as hard to speak without spittle as it was to swallow.

Her lips curled in a cold and mirthless smile that unnerved him. "It will do."

Finn looked away, concentrating on bandaging her hand. The last thing he wanted was a conversation, despite the searing burn of morbid curiosity in the pit of his stomach. Some things were best not known where she was concerned, but this time, his hunch told him better. There was real trouble brewing, and he needed to be prepared.

"You should clean this up, once we find some water," he said, still fussing with the wrap. Finn split the last few inches of the rag with his teeth and tied the ends around her wrist to hold the cloth in place. "The last thing you want is a festering wound."

If Cerrigwen heard him, she ignored him. A quick glance at her face found her gazing blankly past him into the trees. Just as he screwed up the nerve to ask after her plans, she began to ramble in a furtive hush.

"Time is with us now, you'll see," she whispered.

"How do you mean?" he said gently.

"We've a clear path, before us and behind us."

"And you've made it so?" he prodded.

Cerrigwen nodded, but her eyes were absent of thought or recognition.

"I see. And what sort of bewitchment was that, just now?" Finn asked. Casually, he hoped.

"That was no bewitchment, Finn," she said wistfully to the trees. "It was a summoning."

"Of what, exactly."

"It was necessary."

The chill of panic rippled through him, and Finn squeezed her wrist roughly. "What is it you've called now?"

She stared at him wide-eyed and vacant, as though she still didn't see him. He gripped her arms and shook her until she blinked. "What, damn you!"

"Don't you look at me with such shock and disdain, Finn MacDonagh." Cerrigwen yanked herself free of him. "You of all people should know what I have lost, and what I must do to regain it." Her voice slid deep and malevolent. "In this more than any other cause, I will not be defeated. Not at any cost."

An aching shudder wracked his stolid frame and nearly threw him to his knees. His chest cinched so tightly around his lungs he couldn't breathe to speak. Finn feared for those they'd left behind, the Stewardry and his comrades, his brother, and especially his youngest boy. He had tried not to wonder what had befallen them.

"By everything holy, Cerrigwen!" he gasped. "What have you done?"

"Life demands sacrifices of us all, Finn. You'll make do, just as I have." She turned back toward the trail where Pedr waited with the horses. "Now come along," she ordered. "And be quick."

His hand reached instinctively for his dagger. For one fleeting instant, Finn considered ending her. The father, the brother, and the man in him screamed for it. Oh, he hated her enough. She was cold and mean and barren of grace or compassion. Finn had no doubt that Cerrigwen was beyond the reach of all reason. Someone must stop her, for the sake of every innocent life she might yet destroy.

But it was not to be him. Finn's grip on the hilt slackened. He fought to keep angry tears from blinding his reason and grappled his baser instincts against overruling a sacred edict. He could not forsake his duty, no matter what Cerrigwen had done. She was revered, a mortal vessel of unearthly wisdom, and Madoc himself had charged the MacDonagh clan with the sacred honor of serving her. Though Finn might not see the sense in it, powers far greater than he were at work here. Finn had to have faith in her righteousness. It was all he had left. For if ever his faith failed him, every decision he'd made in his life would be rendered nothing more than a miserable, unbearable mistake.

Finn begged for mercy under his breath as he followed Cerrigwen back to the horses, mercy for himself, his family, and the entire world. Bitter agony, this awful moment, and one Finn knew he would die regretting. For now, he could only hope to undo whatever harm Cerrigwen had wrought and keep her from wreaking more.

Lexicon of the Stewardry

Ard Druidh *(First Wizard)*
Sovereign of the Stewardry of Fane Gramarye

Cad Nawdd *(Army of Protectors)*
The castle guard at Fane Gramarye

Circle of Sages
Also known as the Stewards council, a circle of knowledge and
power forged by the joining of the four guardians of the realms

Coedwig Gwyn *(The White Woods)*
The magical forest near the ancient Welsh village of Pwll that
shelters Fane Gramarye

Crwn Cawr *(Circle of Champions)*
The protectorate created to accompany the guardians of the
realms in exile

Cymru
The lands known today as the Kingdom of Wales

Dream-Speak

The language of the dreamer, the timeless tongue with which the Ancients pass their wisdom to the Ard Druidh in the shroud of a dream, the power that can only be gained by drinking the waters of the Well of Tears

Fane Gramarye

The magic temple and last stronghold of the Stewards, hidden in the enchanted forest of Coedwig Gwyn near the village of Pwll, located in the province of Strand Tyrwi in the land of Cymru

Hywel ap Cadell, or Hywell dda (Hywel the Good)

Son of Cadell of Seisyllwg, heralded as the only ruler to unite all of Cymru under one hand and credited with the codification of the first written, binding law of the land

Keys to the Realms

Four talismans that channel and amplify the elemental forces of the universe:

> Lapis Lazuli—key to the Spiritual realm
> Moss Agate—key to the Natural realm
> Moonstone—key to the Celestial realm
> Bloodstone—key to the Physical realm

Mistress of the Realms

Each born only once in a generation, the four Mistresses of the Realms are descended of a magical bloodline that carries a unique affinity to one of the elemental dominions

Mystical Realms

The four dominions: Spiritual, Celestial, Natural, and Physical; their elemental forces: Water, Air, Earth, and Fire; and their corresponding magical arts: Empathy, Augury, Metamorphosis, and Alchemy

Norvik

A tiny fishing village located on the Frisian islets near the Danish borderlands, south of the river Eider; homeland of Aslak, great captain of the Cad Nawdd and leader of the Crwn Cawr

Obotrites

Nomadic Slavic tribes, also known as the Wend

Stewardry

A sorcerer's guild devoted to the stewardship and teaching of the old ways

Well of Tears

The enchanted pool whose waters hold the ancient secrets of the Stewards; by drinking of the sacred waters, the knowledge and experience of all who have come before is passed from one generation to the next

HIERARCHY OF THE STEWARDRY

The Principals of the Ninth Order

Madoc, Ard Druidh and Sovereign

Machreth, Proctor and Madoc's Chosen Successor

Alwen of Pwll, Mage and Mistress of the Spiritual Realm

Branwen of Pwll, Oracle and Mistress of the Celestial Realm

Cerrigwen of Pwll, Healer and Mistress of the Natural Realm

Tanwen of Pwll, Alchemist and Mistress of the Physical Realm

Glain, Leader of the Acolytes, Confidante to Madoc

The Levels of Mastery

Ard Druidh	Grand Wizard and Sovereign
Proctor	Second to the Grand Wizard and High Sorcerer, Heir Apparent
Docent	High Sorcerer or Sorceress, Master or Mistress
Acolyte	Accomplished Mage, Attendants to the Docents
Prefect	Second Rank
Apprentice	First Rank
Novice	The Beginner's Class

THE BLOODLINES

Clan MacDonagh
> Fergus, The Elder
> Finn, Brother of Fergus
> Pedr, First Son of Finn
> Odwain, Second Son of Finn

House Aslaksson
> Aslak, Chieftain of Norvik and Famed Captain of the Guard
> Goram, First Son of Aslak
> Thorvald, Second Son of Aslak

Tribe of the Wolf King
> Bledig Rhi, The Chieftain
> Alwen, His Life Mate
> Eirlys, Daughter of Bledig and Alwen
> Rhys, Son of Bledig and Alwen
> Domagoj, Blood Brother of Bledig

Acknowledgments

I am forever grateful to my loving husband Andre, children AJ and Morgan, and the rest of my family—who believed in me before I believed in myself, and kept the faith when I faltered.

My heartfelt appreciation to my dear friends Tammi Cole, Barbara Dahl, Beth Kelly, Gina Ford, and Sherri Williams—who bolstered my spirit and nourished my soul throughout my creative journey—and to author Carla Neggers, a gracious and giving person, whose generous support will never be forgotten. And, most especially, I acknowledge Jennifer McCord, without whose teaching, guidance, example, and friendship I could not have taken this journey.

Thanks to librarian extraordinaire Kristin Johnson, who shared her knowledge and resources so that I could write with authenticity; to the talented artist Sally J. Smith, whose artwork opened creative doorways; and to actors Rutger Hauer, for his unknowing support and encouragement of my writing, and Vladimir Kulich, whose gifted portrayal of a larger-than-life hero inspired an entire clan of noble warriors.

Special thanks to my agent Jennifer Schober, warrior goddess, wise woman, and kindred spirit, and the true champion of this work.

And last though certainly not least, I offer my undying gratitude to my editors Alex Carr and Betsy Mitchell, whose respectful guidance and enthusiastic support of this book have graced its pages in immeasurable ways.

AUTHOR'S NOTE

Historical fiction has fascinated me most of my life, especially those stories infused with myth and magic. When I was introduced to Mary Stewart's interpretations of the Arthurian legends in the late 1970s, I became truly obsessed with the chivalrous adventures and passionate heroes who so readily embraced honor, nobility, and sacrifice in defense of their people and their land. I felt personally connected to these tales, and for good reason.

The Welsh have a word for the call of one's homeland. *Hiraeth* has been described to me as a longing for the soil from which your lineage has sprung. It is a connection to the land of your forefathers that transcends time and distance and ever bids your return. Although I did not always understand it for what it was, I have always known that longing. I am, after all, a native daughter. As it happens, my great-great-grandfather and his brothers emigrated from the British Isles to North America around 1850, leaving behind nearly three hundred years of ancestry rooted in Cornwall and Wales.

While the story herein is nothing more than a grand tapestry woven from my own imaginings, it is important to note that some of the places and events which set the stage are real. For the sake of authenticity, I searched for unique historical events—events so unique that the suggestion that they might have been influenced by an unearthly power would be easy for most anyone to entertain.

Hywel ap Cadell, descended from a long line of kings, ruled in Wales from around 905 AD until his death in 950 AD. Hywel is credited by many historians with stabilizing the political and economic climate of the region by bringing all of the independent kingdoms under his sole control. It should be assumed that he accomplished this through no small measure of ruthlessness and brutality. However, Hywel understood that territorial disputes between clans and power struggles between kings led to the sort of unrest that threatened the unity of all nations and, in turn, made them vulnerable to outside influence and invasion. Through the codification of a body of laws that addressed issues of local governance, property rights and social conduct, and by adopting a policy of conciliation with England, Hywel maintained sovereignty and an era of prosperity and peace that was unprecedented in those times. The stuff, as they say, of legend.

Naturally, to someone so fixated on the mythology of my heritage, such a wondrous reign begged the question—*what if?* What if the old ways had a hand in the destiny of this man and magic truly had altered the fates of people by working through kings? And so were sewn the seeds of the Dream Stewards.

To tell such a mystical story with any sense of realism, I needed to find a place where the worlds of mortals and magicians might actually have met. Through an acquaintance, I discovered the centuries-old village of Pwll (which means "pool" or "well"). Pwll still stands at the bottom of an ages-old forest located between the towns of Llanelli, and Burry Port in Wales. Pwll is purported to have been built near and named for an ancient spring or well that was believed to contain waters with mystical powers. And so began this saga.

The Well of Tears is a tale that is part fact, part fable, and just a little bit fantastic. My intent was to take you beyond the historical record, into the mysterious realms that exist alongside what we know to be real. In this place, all things are possible.

Awen á bendithion...

(Inspiration and blessings)...

ABOUT THE AUTHOR

A lifelong writer, Roberta Trahan's first works of fiction draw upon generations of family history originating in Cornwall and Wales, as well as her love of the mythology and culture of her ancestral home.

After graduating from the University of Oregon with a journalism degree, Trahan pursued a twenty-five-year career in sales, marketing, and publicity. Eventually the lure of writing drew her back to her creative roots, and she is now a full-time novelist and core member of her local writing community—as a speaker, instructor, and member of several writing organizations.

The Well of Tears is her first book, but hardly her last. She is a Pacific Northwest native and currently lives with her family near Seattle, Washington.